THE STONE WARRIOR

BOOK ONE OF THE SACROSANCT RECORDS

M. N. JOLLEY

D1522749

To my dad, who taught me to love stories
And my mom, who taught me how to write them

CONTENTS

CHAPTER 1

"Sis, wake up. The field's on fire!"

Adelyn opened her eyes, vision bleary and dim in the low light. "Wh-what time is it?" She asked, rubbing one eye as she looked at her brother.

"Don't know. Get up, quick." John said, unusually terse, his huge silhouette towering over her bed. "Someone's lit the field ablaze."

Adelyn frowned, blinking a couple times as her sleepy brain pieced together what he was saying. Once it clicked into place, she sat up sharply, shock clearing away fatigue. "The horses—"

"Are fine," John finished. "Barn's safe, for now. Hurry."

Adelyn slipped off her bed, following just after her brother, scrambling to the ledge of the loft and sliding down the ladder without even touching the rungs.

She wore only a nightgown as they ran outside, but the harvest season had not yet set in, and the night air was still warm. Her bare feet crunched on sharp gravel, but she'd been playing in this yard for fifteen years, it couldn't hurt her any more than soft grass.

The field was doing an impression of an apocalypse. Smoke billowed up into the dark sky, black and choking, and the flames roared so hot and loud that Adelyn could feel and hear them all the way from the porch.

"Who did this?" Adelyn asked, looking out in horror.

"Don't know," John said, running his hands through his hair as he stared at the fire. "Gods be, we're going to lose half the crops."

"Abandon the crops," Adelyn said, already running as she spoke. "The horses. It's coming toward the barn, we have to get them out. Where's Papa?"

"Mom and Dad rode into town to get help," John said as he rushed to the barn behind her and helped to throw open the gates. Adelyn ran to the first stable door, mindful to keep her hands away from kicking hooves as she yanked it open and moved to the next, freeing one horse at a time. The great animals bolted for the exit as soon as they were free, and she didn't try to stop them—they were smart beasts with a strong sense of self-preservation. They'd not run far, but they would stay away from the flames.

That was one problem solved, but Adelyn didn't have time to celebrate. "Water!" she called, grabbing a bucket from where it hung on a post. "Start the pump!"

Her brother had already started the new machine, one that would bring up water so long as someone pumped the handle, and Adelyn thanked the Lords that they'd had it installed. If they'd had to draw water from a well the old fashioned way, they'd never stop the fire in time.

She waited, dancing on her toes in anxiety as she watched the pump shudder, then begin pouring out clean water into the bucket. It took an eternity to fill, then she sprinted out the barn doors, rounded a corner, and tossed the water against the red wall of the barn.

Saving the crops would be an impossibility. The fire was too great, spreading too fast. It would be all they could do to save the barn, which meant wetting it down and putting out any flames that got too close.

She passed John running by with a second bucket, working the pump herself to refill her own. As she ran outside, though, she saw it wouldn't be enough. The fire was too close already, and working bucket by bucket, the two of them would never be able to stop those flames.

Hoofbeats pounded up the lane and she stopped, running up to meet her parents as they reared up on their mounts.

Their father leaped down from his saddle. Adelyn expected him to help with the fire, but instead, he began walking toward the house.

"What's going on?" John called.

"Bandits," her father said, without looking over his shoulder. "Get a weapon."

John hesitated. "The fire!" he said, pointing back to the barn. "We have to put out—"

"Damn the fire!" their father shouted, slamming the door on his way inside.

Their mother explained, dismounting her own steed. "They took Molly and Brandon. We're going after them."

Adelyn blanched. Molly and Brandon were just babes— barely old enough to walk. Her father's anger made sense, and she felt her own rage build. "I'll get our horses."

Still, there was the barn. They couldn't just let it burn, could they?

Her step hitched as she ran, and she doubled back, calling to her brother. "John, you get the horses!"

"What are you doing?" Her brother asked.

"I can put out the fire," she said.

He seemed confused, then shook his head as he understood her meaning. "No, Adelyn. You can't—"

"I can!" Adelyn yelled back. "There's no time to argue! Get the horses."

Bounding inside the barn, she looked around for the tool she needed: a bucket of old paint, sealed with a tin lid.

Snatching up the bucket, she sprinted outside while cracking open the lid. Having forgotten a brush, she dipped her hand into the red paint, swirling it for a second. She then turned her attention to the barn, but hesitated.

Mama and Papa might have stopped her, but they were inside gathering arms, and John lacked the sand to stand up to his little sister. The three of them disapproved, but at the moment, she didn't care.

Slapping on the paint, she drew a simple shape, like a triangle. The fire was so close now, glowing against the wall of the barn. There was no other way. She did this, or the barn burned.

As she finished marking the triangle in paint, her father shouted behind her. "Adelyn! What in the blazes are you doing?"

Too late. The fire was too close. Any longer, and she'd have to back away or be trapped. Time to act.

Adelyn didn't know why she was a sorceress. She was a farmer, not a hero, and the needs of her home were more important than any magical heroics.

Still, she had been given this power, and abandon her if she wasn't going to use it.

Planting the palm of her hand against the wall of the barn, she poured energy into it, her strength sapping away as she readied the spell. She'd never done something so large, so grand, but the theory was the same. She remembered her practice in the wee hours of the night, where she wouldn't wake her brother or arouse the suspicion of her parents, and readied the spell.

Her father tried to approach, to intervene, but the fire had reached the barn and he couldn't get close. Flames were licking up a few paces away from Adelyn, and she was growing faint from the energy poured into the runes. She couldn't wait any longer.

"*Shtap!*" Adelyn cast the spell.

Force, raw and untempered, lashed out in all directions. The barn shook, her father was tossed away, and the flames were thrown back by the great wave of power. Like breath putting out a candle, the gale force winds whipped over the fire, sucking away air and tearing up chunks of burned crops from the ground.

The fire was not put out, not in the slightest, but it was rebuffed away from the barn, and having already consumed the crops nearest it, the fire could not spread back in.

Panting for breath, Adelyn took her hand away from the barn. She had paint on her nightgown, and blackness was edging into her vision, making her feel dizzy and faint.

She walked back toward her father and stumbled, slipping toward the ground. She felt arms catch her gently, and it took her a moment to realize that it was her father.

"That was foolish, Adelyn," he said, his tone reproachful.

"Sorry, Papa," she said, though she didn't mean it. The magic had been necessary. "I... A weapon. Where's Butler?"

Her father looked at her, then shook his head. "You stay."

Adelyn pulled away from him, anger rising. "I'm old enough! I can help!"

Her father shook his head, surveying the results of her spell "Maybe you could have helped, if you hadn't gone and spent your strength on this... magic. You're in no state to ride out and fight. Stay. Keep an eye on the barn. We'll talk about this when I return."

Adelyn swallowed, but couldn't argue further. When her father made up his mind, his word was final.

John called, from the front of the house. "Papa, your sword?"

He shook his head. "I'm taking a rifle. A cavalry saber won't do me much good here. We're aiming to put the bastards down and take the children back. Are you ready?"

John nodded, pulling up his horse. Their mother had her own rifle, and a revolver stuck in her belt.

Looking at his sister as he climbed into the saddle, John said, "Be safe, Sis. We'll be back soon."

Together, her family rode off to fight the bandits, their path lit by firelight and dim stars.

They never returned.

CHAPTER 2

Whether the magic makes the mischief, or the mischief brings the magic, the two go hand in hand. If you are given the powers Sacrosanct, do not thank the gods, but curse them instead, for in giving you that power they take away your life.

- Speaker unknown

SHARP STEEL BIT into the polished holly board, knife hesitating every few inches as Adelyn stopped to check her notes. She had been working on this particular etching for half the week, and after insomnia kept her from getting any real rest, she'd decided to spend the night finishing the piece.

It was a peaceful work, the only sound being the warm crackling of the fireplace and the whistling of the earliest birds as they began to stir. Adelyn sat cross-legged in the room's center, holding the two foot oval of wood carefully in her lap, whittling out small sections of the board and sanding down the edges, creating a smooth trench.

The design was of a map of the continent, though it was

not a map that a cartographer would have taken any pride in. The wide, flat desert across the top lacked any distinguishing marks, a large recess covering the southern border filled in for the oceans with none of the coastal islands in place, the mountainous terrain on the far western edge had only a few small dragons etched in permanent flight. Big cities had been given slight indentations to represent their presence and great rivers were marked with narrow grooves, but towns and creeks were nowhere to be seen.

The only part with detail was the Middle Western Plains, the region Adelyn called home. It still lacked labels or serious geographical notation, but there were dots representing smaller cities, a few major trade routes, and even a single tiny town of less than a hundred had its own slight divot carved into the wood. The only markings were in Sacrosanct, an old writing system composed of symbolic runes.

The map would never serve for navigation, but that wasn't the point.

Setting down her knife and reaching for a scrap of sandpaper, Adelyn spotted the rays of sunlight beginning to peek through faded curtains and sighed. She didn't have as much time as she wanted. She'd worked on the project for near the whole night, and would be too tired to use it come evening. Waiting to make the attempt would be a pointless waste of the day. Even still, she wished she could get a little rest before the day's chores began.

Satisfied that the final groove was properly smoothed and sanded, Adelyn yawned, blew away the sawdust, and inspected her handiwork. She first checked against a real map, ensuring every detail was in place, then checked her book to ensure that all the runes were correct.

Sighing, Adelyn glanced up at the ceiling and shut her

eyes in a brief prayer. There was nothing left to prepare, it was time to see if her plans would work this time.

Adelyn grimaced and retrieved her knife with her left hand, a sharp, heavy tool that'd been a gift from her father, wiping the blade off on a pant leg to clean off the dust. It was awkward to keep the tool in her off hand, but she needed her right hand free.

Thinking on the instructions written in her little book, she closed her eyes and focused hard on what she wanted, preparing her mind.

My family. I want to find my family. I want, to find, my family. I want...

The words echoed in her head, forming a sort of silent chant that she repeated until all the other distractions had been cleared from her mind. The long night spent carving had helped with this, ensuring that her thoughts were not clouded by a long day of work.

Grinding her teeth together, Adelyn tightened her left hand around the knife one more time, bracing herself. She hated this part. Raising it to her right hand, she put the knife blade against the palm where a thin scab was already present and pressed down, wincing as the steel cut into her skin and drew out a trickle of blood.

Before she could lose focus she turned her palm down and pressed it to the center of the map, willing the energy contained in her blood be transferred into the wood. Opening her eyes, she watched as the blood from her cut began leaking out, following the grooves carved into the wood, spreading to fill them in all directions. It wouldn't fill every groove, but that was fine, she only needed it to fill one.

Her thoughts ready, she whispered the words she had readied, speaking in broken Sacrosanct. *"Vota, iscov kin."*

For a second, nothing happened, and Adelyn worried

that the magic had failed. Before she could give up and pull her hand away, though, the blood seeping across the board began to glow. She smiled, but remained apprehensive. If all went according to plan, the blood would trickle across the map to a point, then burn a scorch mark where it ended. It would be a simple matter to check against an actual map, then, and she'd know where to go.

Rather than seeking out a single spot, the blood began spreading in every direction, moving faster, glowing hot and bright. Adelyn had to pull her hand away from the warmth. The acrid smell of rust and wood smoke began to fill the room as the blood became white hot. Bits of wood ignited where the glow had spread, as though it were lava.

Eyes widening, Adelyn dropped her knife and pushed the board off her lap, hopping to her feet and gingerly seizing the edges of the map. Hurrying to the fireplace, she tossed it in, so it could safely burn without harm to the rest of her home.

Taking a step backward, Adelyn squinted at the board for several moments longer, hoping that perhaps the spell would work anyhow and she could still catch a glimpse of a mark burned into the map, but there was no such luck. The whole board was spewing smoke up the chimney, and scorch marks covered most of the wood.

Sighing, Adelyn drew a white cloth from her pant pocket and wrapped it around her bloody palm as a bandage, looking up to the ceiling in frustration. She groaned, shaking her head and returning to where she had attempted the spell so that she could retrieve a scrap of notes and her book of magic.

That morning was her seventh attempt and her seventh failure in as many weeks at a spell that would locate her family. Each try had been by the book, following every rule and suggestion written in her magical manual, but it had all failed. The first two tries had not done a thing, and the third had only sparked before dying. Since then she had used blood rather than plain energy to cast, and since then she'd been getting a reaction, but those reactions had been the type that elicited only smoke and burned fingertips.

Adelyn scaled up to the loft that held her bed, ladder shaking as she climbed. Once up, she dropped her notes, flipped open the book, and started looking for what she'd done wrong.

Her patience wore thin after half a page. "Useless piece of—" Adelyn shouted and threw the book against the wall, watching it fall down the gap between the wall and the floor, to the room beneath her loft, out of her reach.

It's just as helpful there as it is in my hands, Adelyn glowered, deciding not to retrieve the little book from the bedroom below. She knew that the book wasn't a fraud, but that didn't keep her from growing bitter toward the author. Finding the book in a merchant's cart had been a small miracle, but a part of Adelyn wished she'd never read the damned thing. Ignorance might have been preferable to known impotence.

Defeated, she crumpled onto the straw mat that served as her bed, her head hitting a ratty old pillow. Frustration combined with exhaustion swept over Adelyn and hit her with the powerful desire to sleep for a month, which she pushed away. She'd had sleepless nights and worked through them before, she could do it again.

Coffee? No, that had run out a month ago, and there wasn't the money to buy more. Her mother had always kept well-stocked cupboards, but even those cupboards couldn't stay full for two months without replenishment.

Without coffee, an air of fatigue and misery will just have to do.

Clenching her fists, she winced at the pain in her right hand, reminded of the self-inflicted wound on her palm. She sat up and rotated her head to work out some of the stiffness that had built in her neck after hours of looking down at the project in her lap. The project that was now smoldering uselessly in the hearth.

"Damned useless book," she grumbled.

With a sigh, Adelyn got to her feet, stretched her arms one last time, and walked back to the ladder. She'd had her tantrum, she could suck it up for another day, get some rest that night, and start at it all again tomorrow.

After setting a little pot of water over the fire to boil, she took a wooden cup from by the mantle and stood to leave. Grabbing a slightly undersized coat off a hook by the door, she pulled it on and walked outside.

She had to brace herself against the windy morning. It was still only early into the harvest season, and the real bitter cold of winter was months away, but the windchill was miserable. Her brown hair flapped around with the wind in an unruly tangle, but she kept it out of her face by facing into the breeze.

"Lords, give us a short winter," she mumbled, nodding slightly to the sky as she trudged out to the stables. She doubted that the prayer would be heard, but if expressing her desire out loud made the planting season come even a day sooner, it'd be well worth it.

The stable was a sturdy old building, save for the wall on the northward side marred with scorch marks, one patch sanded smooth to conceal where she'd painted the runes. It had cost her father three silver swords to have it built, a price that seemed cheap at the time for all the use they got out of it.

Now, though, there were only three good horses in there sleeping under its roof, one for riding and two plow horses. Adelyn was expecting that come winter she'd need to sell one of the plow horses, she had neither the food nor the finances to keep them all.

Opening the door to the stable, she felt for a rope in the dark room until she found it, giving the sturdy cord a steady tug, pulleys and rope began pulling back several window covers built into the roof. It was no spirit powered lighting system, but it let in the sun's rays well enough. Besides, now that any hope of having a cable run to their estate for powered lighting was dashed, Adelyn supposed it was good fortune that the simpler pulley system was still in good repair. She didn't know how to fix the mechanism that operated the windows should it break, and she couldn't afford to hire someone to repair it. Any damage would mean her having to climb a ladder up to prop the windows open or shut every time it rained.

"Good morning," she said to the horses as she went about the morning's chores. The tasks weren't difficult, but Adelyn made sure to do everything carefully so as not to make a sleepy mistake.

It was a simple routine: She pulled off the horse's blankets, gave them a scoop of oats from the barrel by the door, turned them out to pasture. Even cleaning out the stalls, while demanding, didn't leave her with too much room for error.

When it came time to replace the horse's water, the pump took a little longer than normal to get going, coughing and spluttering. Adelyn pumped a couple times on the handle, working it for half a minute before the water started flowing smoothly. She frowned, but there nothing she could do about it besides make sure there were no obvious clogs. The water pump was another thing that Adelyn couldn't fix.

"Just a few more weeks?" She asked, without specifying whether she was talking to the Lords or the pump. "I'll have them back by then."

No answer came, of course, but the pump didn't give any more trouble, running as she filled the horses' troughs with hay. Setting her pitchfork in the corner, she wiped a little sweat off her forehead and smiled at a job well done.

Scooping her wooden cup into the barrel of oats, she pushed the door open and headed back to her house. She was glad to get back in the warmth, even if only for a little while to cook her breakfast. There was a wood burning stove in the corner, and a dining table in the center of the room, but she had no intention of using either.

Adelyn was anything but a cook, but she wouldn't be serving these oats to guests. There was neither honey nor fruit to serve as a sweetener, so it'd be unsuitable to serve anyways. As with her usual dining of late, she'd be cooking and eating from the same pot. She considered skipping the oatmeal entirely, not relishing the taste of plain oats, but doing the day's work without sleep or breakfast was out of the question.

Before tossing the oats into the pot, she dipped a rag in the boiling water, wiping her hands clean of dirt and sweat with the scalding cloth. The hot water stung on her cut palm, but she accepted that, dropping the rag and clasping her now-clean hands in a brief prayer.

Hoofsteps clopped outside. Adelyn cocked her head and stood up straight, cutting the reverie short, listening, her heart hammering for a second until she heard the two men talking and recognized their voices.

She dropped the oats in the pot, then walked to the door

and swung it open. "Jason, Roger, I'm just heating up a little breakfast. Are you hungry?" It was a false offer, she knew that nobody in their right mind would want to share in her meal, but Adelyn would be damned if she gave up common courtesy.

Jason and Roger were both in their mid-twenties, the former a little taller, the latter a little thinner. They had been out tracking a deer when the town was attacked, and as such were some of the only grown adults left for hire within a fifty mile radius. They'd agreed to come help on the farm twice a week for a price that was reasonable considering how overworked they had been around town. Even with how inexperienced they were with farm work, they had still been invaluable in preparing for what remained of the harvest.

Most of the crops were dead and burned, but there were still places where the fire hadn't spread, or where it simply hadn't caught, and it was vital that every bit of salvageable crops be harvested. She'd have preferred to hire just about anyone else, but there was no one else, and a fifteen year old girl could not handle the whole farm entirely on her own.

"What's cookin'?" Roger asked, dismounting his horse.

Adelyn smiled, stepping fully outside into the cold and pulling her coat a little closer. "Oatmeal," she supplied. "I'm afraid there's still no honey, but it's something to fill your belly."

The two men exchanged a glance, and then Jason shook his head. "We had a little something already, but thank you." Then, noticing Adelyn's hand, he added with a note of curiosity, "Did you hurt your hand?"

"Cut it on a loose nail," Adelyn said quickly. "Cleaned it with a little hot water and wrapped it up, should be fine."

Again, the two men exchanged a glance, and Roger

reached into a pocket to fish out a little chewing tobacco. "A lot of loose nails in your house. That's the fourth time, now? Might want to do somethin' about that. I didn't know better, I'd say you ticked off the god o' nails."

"It was a pitchfork before," Jason corrected. "And a couple slips of the knife while making supper, I think?" He looked to Adelyn with an eyebrow raised.

"Yes," Adelyn replied, glancing away, thinking on how to change the subject. "I've been clumsy lately. Any news from town?"

"Traders," Jason said, not pursuing the topic further. "Eight of 'em, carts, plenty of supplies. They're only passing through, said they'd be around until lunch to shop their wares if anyone cares to look before they move on."

"Yeah," Roger added, stuffing his wad of the tobacco into a cheek. "Apparently our town ain't got 'The kind o' clients they're lookin' for.'" He spat on the ground pointedly, but shrugged. "Not like anyone's got the money to buy what they're selling anyhow."

"Which is?" Adelyn said, chewing on her lip as she thought.

"What?" Roger asked.

"What're they selling? If it's something I might need, I'd like to ride in and take a look, see if maybe I can't haggle them down a bit."

"Oh," Roger said, spitting on the ground. "Fancy stuff. Jewelry, books, funny stuff in jars."

"Spices," Jason clarified, rolling his eyes. "They're bringing in rare valuables up from Westbrig. But they've also got a lot of books, stuff they're trying to get rid of since it's taking up space. Might be able to get a good deal."

Adelyn nodded, thinking a second longer. Books would be her secondary objective, but if she could find a manuscript detailing how to cast spells that was better than her terrible little manual, that would be fantastic.

Trying not to seem too eager, she said, "It might be worth looking into. I think I'll ride in and see if there isn't anything worth checking out." Nodding to herself a little longer, she looked at Jason. "That's the plan. I'll have breakfast and ride into town to speak about trade. Can you saddle up Butler for me?"

"Will do," Jason said, nodding and then turning to go do as asked.

"Much obliged. While I'm gone, see if you can get the grain cart fixed. The back wheel is still snapped off," Adelyn said, before adding to Roger, "When that's done, if you could get started splitting some firewood I'd appreciate it."

"Afraid you'll cut yer' hand if you take up'n ax?" Roger asked, receiving a harsh look from Jason for the quip. "Gotcha."

Adelyn frowned at the comment, but she had no rebuttal. She went with silence, turning to head inside and eat the hot oats that would qualify as breakfast, and then to gather up her money and her things.

The traders might have something useful, or they might not. Adelyn still had a few valuables that she hadn't yet stripped from her home and sold, she could ask and see if they'd fetch a fair price. Her real goal, though, was to find herself a bounty hunter. If she could do that, it'd make a hundred trips worth it.

Shutting the door behind herself, she yawned sleepily and muttered, "And, Lords betray me, while I'm there I'm getting some damned coffee."

CHAPTER 3

The "Legend of Marstone" is one of the most popular fairy tales in the canon of what I'm going to be generously calling 'Southeast Literature'. The tale—of a magic rock coming to earth from the heavens and inexplicably granting both power and rule to some random farm boy—was incredibly influential to the development of the provincial culture here. So influential, in fact, that no less than six towns are called 'Marstone', each more pathetic and empty than the last.

- Taken from an analysis of Southeast stories, culture, and folklore. It is valuable to note that the author had been forced to travel to the Southeast to write this report, under threat of losing tenure

AT TOP SPEED, it was a five minute ride into the little town of Marstone. Adelyn wasn't riding at top speed. It took half an hour at a reasonable pace, and in spite of the cold she still enjoyed the trip, appreciating the chance to ride Butler without the immediate pressure of her daily chores.

The traders were easy to spot. Big carts with jars, books,

and valuables stacked on display shelves were hard to miss. Even harder to miss were the people attending to the carts, with long brown robes that were of a foreign style, bearing arms that were as unfamiliar as the robes. The mere sight of three full grown people of working age in town square was enough to raise an eyebrow considering the circumstances.

Keeping an eye out for the five remaining traders, Adelyn slowed Butler to a trot and rode up to a hitching rail in front of the local tavern, hotel, and eatery: Maggie's. Maggie's was the hub for traders, who took advantage of the tavern's long hitching rail and the wide courtyard in front to park their horses. It was mutually beneficial; the traders had a convenient location to set up their wares, and Maggie's got some extra business both from the traders and the customers that they drew in.

Dismounting and tying Butler to the rail, Adelyn removed the long package she had strapped to his saddle and used the moment to size up the three traders by the carts. They hadn't yet acknowledged her, busy arguing with a local about prices, and as they haggled she finally noticed the armor they wore beneath their robes.

It was made of bronze, which wasn't all too unusual by itself. Copper and tin deposits in the mountains to the north made it much easier to produce bronze than to import iron all the way from the west, a slow and expensive shipment if there ever was one.

What was unusual was the shiny filigree worked into the plates. At first, Adelyn mistook the decoration for odd scratch marks, unable to get a clear view of the armor beneath the loose brown robes, but after a second look her eyes went wide and she realized it was hammered gold, arranged in Sacrosanct runes. They weren't wearing bronze out of thrift, they were wearing it because the armor could take spirit power.

Steel armor was great for turning away a blade or protecting from a physical blow, but it couldn't hold a charge of spirit for peanuts. The same was true of iron, for that matter. Bronze, on the other hand, was great at it. Gold and silver were perhaps better, and copper worked as well, but those alone made for a poor suit of armor.

With the golden runes and markings made in the armor, it would only take a little spirit to keep the traders well protected. A hundred years ago, they would have needed a sorcerer to keep the armor powered. Now, though, all they'd need was a few drops of blood and a spirit adapter.

Adelyn hesitated as she considered what the armor meant, suddenly uncertain about approaching the traders. That sort of armor wasn't cheap. The traders were either very wealthy, or working for someone who was. The bag of coins tucked away in her jacket suddenly seemed very small.

Their armament, at least, were less exquisite. They each had a matching weapon on their belt, resembling straight swords with a large hook on the end of each like you'd find on a shepherd's crook. Adelyn recognized them by description, if not by sight—a Watcher's Hook, a southwestern weapon used to disarm opponents. Beneath one of their robes, Adelyn also caught sight of a three-shot revolver tucked into a holster, the kind that would fire bullets as large as her thumb.

One of the traders caught her staring and was looking intently back at her, so she quickly busied herself with tying up Butler and generally looking preoccupied. The act came too late, and before she could think of an appropriate excuse for why she'd been quietly watching them for the better part of a minute, he had already crossed the ten feet between them and extended his hand in a greeting.

"Jeb," he said, his voice considerably deeper than Adelyn had expected, and with a subtle accent she couldn't place. His hair was dark, beard was short and wispy, and he could have been any age between thirty and fifty. "Are you looking to buy?"

"I—" Adelyn started, before realizing he hadn't asked why she'd been staring, or in fact even acknowledged it. She took his hand and shook it. "Yes, I heard you'd be in town for the morning. Are there only the three of you?"

"No," Jeb replied, pausing at the question. "The rest of our party is inside, getting a little food, but they aren't the ones to be conducting trade. What are you looking for?"

"Books," Adelyn said, dodging the question with a nonspecific answer. "But I had no breakfast before riding in, I think I'll go have a little food myself before we talk trade." It was only half a lie, the bland oatmeal she'd eaten was hardly befitting the title of 'Breakfast'.

Jeb put on a disapproving look and stood up straight, the motion making his robes bulge out a bit where his revolver was concealed. "Well, we'll be here most of the day. Take your time, but don't delay too much."

"I'll not be long," Adelyn said, putting a hand on the package she carried and sticking out her chin. "I'd simply rather not barter on an empty stomach."

Jeb frowned, but he didn't stop Adelyn as she took her bundle, stooped beneath the hitching rail where the horses were tied, and walked for the door of Maggie's Tavern.

The tavern was not owned by a woman named Maggie, despite its name. 'Maggie' was the name written on the painted sign hanging above the door, but for as long as Adelyn could remember, the tavern had been run by a man named Pete and his wife, Jenny. Now, it was just Jenny; Pete was in a cedar box buried behind the town hall.

Jenny was busy behind the tavern's bar, preparing something on the spirit stove while at the same time pouring drinks for two tables and boiling water for a fresh pot of coffee. She heard the bell above the door ring and looked over to see who had come in. The past two months had seen her blonde hair go almost entirely gray and made her look much older than her forty years, but she still had a warm smile to greet Adelyn.

Maggie's Tavern was the last thing that Jenny had left, and she would keep the old tables polished, the atmosphere inviting, and the stew appetizing until the day she died.

"Addy," Jenny said, her voice heard easily across the open room as she called out her pet name for Adelyn. "How have you been?"

"Keeping alive," Adelyn said, doing her best to return the smile but ending up with a vague, neutral expression.

Jenny nodded. "The farm?"

"Looks like we've lost about three quarters of the harvest," Adelyn said. "There'll be enough grain to get through the winter, but not to plant anew next year. We'll get by, though. Once I have my family back, we'll figure out something."

Pursing her lips, Jenny focused on the glass she was wiping clean for a moment before she responded. "Addy... I know you're attached to the farm, but have you thought what you'll do if you can't keep it?"

"I'll be able to keep it," Adelyn said stubbornly. "It's been in my family for generations, I'm not gonna be the one to lose it."

Jenny sighed. "It's been in your family for seven years,

Addy. Before the war, it belonged to a land baron, same as the rest of the farmland around here."

"But it's been our home," Adelyn argued. "Doesn't matter whose name was on the deed, we worked the land, we lived there, it was ours in the sight of the Lords. That's all that matters to me."

"Addy—" Jenny started to argue, then shook her head, smiling sadly. "I'm sorry, I don't mean to start a fight with you. I just want you to know, if you ever need a place, you can always come back and live here. I could use the help, and you're the closest thing to family I've got left."

For a moment, looking at Jenny's expression, Adelyn was taken back a decade, remembering the years she'd spent in this woman's care while her parents were off to war. Jenny was almost family, and Adelyn had to admit that there were worse fates than coming to work at Maggie's Tavern.

But she couldn't abandon her real family. "I appreciate it," Adelyn said. "But I'll be fine."

The tavern had five other people in it. One man, dressed the same as the three traders outside, was sitting at the bar and eating a bowl of the day's soup. Another sat in the corner, picking at a plate of food and seeming not to notice anyone else in the room.

Finally, two men and one woman were playing cards at a table, each holding a little pile of grubby cards and furiously tossing them onto the table one at a time. Occasionally, one of them would shout in joy or dismay as they took the pile of cards and shuffled them back into their hand. They were armed and armored, but in a mismatched variety of leather, steel, and bronze equipment. Adelyn assumed one of them was the owner of the long sharpshooter's rifle resting by the door. Their diverse equipment implied that they were soldiers for hire, working as escorts for the real traders. Just the kind of people Adelyn had been hoping for.

Approaching the table, Adelyn cleared her throat, just after a hand was finished, making a slight nod of her head to the open chair. "May I join?" she asked.

The three of them all stopped, looking up at Adelyn. Not a one of them was under thirty, and all of them had scars on their hands or faces which looked like they'd been earned in fights. Adelyn was briefly concerned, but she put her hands in her pockets and took a breath, waiting for a response.

Finally, the woman looked back to her own pile of cards, picked up the deck, and started dealing Adelyn in. "Two pins a point," she said. "If you don't have the coin, you can shove off. You know how to play?"

"I don't want to play," Adelyn said quickly, before she could have a full hand dealt. Pulling up a chair anyways, though, she set her bundle to the side and said, "I'm just looking to discuss business."

"If you're looking to trade, go talk outside," the woman said, rolling her eyes and scooping the cards back into the deck before dealing fresh hands to the other two players.

"I'm not looking to trade, I'm looking to hire," Adelyn said. "What's your name?"

Again, everyone at the table stopped and looked at her, until again the woman broke the silence. "I'm Rose. We're already hired," Rose said. "What's a kid like you need us for, anyways?"

Adelyn cleared her throat. She'd made this speech before. "I need someone to track down a band of outlaws who kidnapped my parents and brother and fifty other good people." That finally got everyone's attention, and Adelyn continued with a little more confidence.

"A little over two months ago, a group of raiders

attacked our town, killed seven of its citizens, grabbed two children, and burned several houses to the ground alongside most of our crops. When we got together a militia to ride after them and rescue the kids, our people were ambushed and taken captive." After a brief pause, she added, "They left the kids."

Rose frowned, then shook her head. "That's a matter for the authorities, not a couple bodyguards."

"We tried that," Adelyn said, "But the only military fort out here is a day's ride away, and by the time we got word to them, it was too late for their help. They said they're spread thin, and don't have the manpower to spare on a rescue mission when we don't even know where the victims were taken."

This time, the man to the left of Rose cut in, putting down his cards. "Right, 'cause the president's men can't be doin' their jobs, they have much more important things to be doing."

"Like tax collection!" the other man added.

Rose smirked, but stayed focused on Adelyn's story. "So, what do you want us to do? Spring a rescue? Fight an army? It'd take a lot more coin than you've got to convince me to fight a pack of armed bandits all on our lonesome."

Adelyn shook her head, smiling just a bit. "I just need you to find out where the victims were taken. That's what the army said they needed before they could help. Any locals who would have a chance of tracking our people down were already taken, and the bandits covered their tracks well. I just need someone who can find where they've gone, and then the proper authorities can deal with the rescue."

Tapping a finger on the table, Rose pursed her lips in thought for a second. "How much can you pay?"

Adelyn sat up, trying not to seem too eager. "I have thirty silver daggers," she said. "Once you have the location."

It worried her to bring up the money. She had the heavy coin purse tucked into an inside pocket of her jacket, and she could feel the weight hanging there. If these guards lacked scruples, they could take it from her in a heartbeat, and she could do little to defend herself.

It was the money her father had set aside to buy a new year's seed crop, if the farm ever fell prey to famine or disaster. Instead of using it to save the farm, though, she was risking it on a gamble to get her family back. Money for the farm had come from selling her things, hiring herself out for labor around the town until the harvest season's chores had grown too substantial, anywhere else she could get a bit of coin, but not a single tack had come from the money set aside. That money was for saving her family.

If anyone will agree to take it.

Sitting back, Rose shook her head, and Adelyn's heart sank. "Look, kid, I feel sorry for you, but chances are they were grabbed by slavers. Even if we could find out where they went, and even if we'd work for that little, by now they've probably been shipped off someplace across the map. You'd be better off keeping your money." Picking up the cards, she started to deal out fresh hands, losing interest fast.

"Wait, I also have this," Adelyn said quickly, grabbing the long bundle by her side and holding it up. Rose raised an eyebrow, pausing and waiting for Adelyn to continue. Adelyn did, pulling at the string keeping the bundle wrapped up to reveal the sword inside. "It's my father's cavalry saber. It's royal steel, worth at least another twenty daggers."

Rose sighed and kept dealing cards. "Hardly. Best of luck, but we're not going to help you."

Knuckles turning white as Adelyn clenched a fist, she felt hot words build in the back of her throat, ready to verbally abuse these bounty hunters. She was getting tired of the constant runarounds and refusal, and though these three were just one group in a long series of rejection, Adelyn was ready to blame them for every person who'd turned her money down.

Before she could ready her tirade, though, a voice piped up behind her that cut through the anger like a sharp knife. "I will do it!"

Adelyn had to turn her chair, scraping the legs against the floor so she could look over her shoulder and see the figure who'd spoken. Adelyn had initially dismissed him in favor of the three card players, but now that he was a more promising candidate, she gave him a once over. He was a man in his late twenties with dark skin and a short shock of black hair. He had a Watcher's Hook for a weapon, but bore no other similarity to the traders: He wore no armor, his clothes were a pair of loose fitting trousers held up by a belt with half a dozen pouches, his shirt was long sleeved and woolen, and he wore a pair of black gloves which matched his black leather boots.

"David?" Rose asked him. "Y'know we're on contract, right?"

"Do not worry, Rose, I will wait until our contract is complete." Turning his gaze to Adelyn, he asked, "May I hold the sword for a moment?"

Adelyn blinked once, surprised at the request, but she quickly pushed herself to her feet and crossed the two steps to his table, holding out the sword for him to look.

David took the blade carefully, holding it up to eye level

to look down the blade. "Well, that is certainly royal steel," he said, examining the rippled pattern in the metal. "Your father used it in the war?"

Nodding quickly, Adelyn supplied, "It saved his life more than once. It's a fine blade."

Setting it down on the table, David pulled the glove off his right hand and ran a finger across the steel blade, feeling the metal. With this test complete, he smiled and pulled the glove back on. "It is a fine blade. My name is David," he said, gesturing to the chair across from him. "You should sit down. I think I can find your people."

CHAPTER 4

Ansyr [Ahn-sir] Shield, Defense
  Atof [Ah-tohf] Water
  Bren [Brehn] Fire
  Byndyn [Bihn-dihn] Wrap, bind, detain
  Efrin [Eh-frihn] Cold
  Elben [Ehlbehn] Sword
  Gild [Gihld] Force
  Hash [Hah-sh] Sound/Noise
  Heyl [Heh-ihl] Heal
  Iscov [Ihs-cohv] Find, look for
  Kin [Kihn] Family
  Nert [Nehrt] Door
  Rahk [Rahk] Break, smash
  Shane [Shahn-eh] Light
  Shtap [Sh-tahp] Throw, push
  Vend [Vehnd] Wound
  Vota [Voh-tah] Blood

- List of commonly used words in Sacrosanct. Note the high concentration of words to be used for combat (Ansyr, Bren, Elben, Rahk, etc.) due to the frequency in which

Sacrosanct is used for battle magic. Also note, Sacrosanct uses only four vowel sounds—Ah, Eh, Oh, and Ih

ADELYN SIPPED COFFEE, slurping a bit to keep the near-boiling liquid from scalding her tongue. It was piping hot, sweet, rich, and vastly better than the boiled bean water that Adelyn always ended up with when she prepared it at home.

Five minutes had gone by, and during them David said very little, though he insisted on buying her breakfast while they discussed details of business. Adelyn wasn't about to say no to a free meal, but in the intervening minutes between his walking to the counter to order and his returning with a plate of bacon and fresh biscuits, he'd been quietly "hmm"-ing and examining her father's sword. When Adelyn began to ask a question, he just shook his head without offering an answer, adding that Adelyn should finish her meal before they talked.

"The food here is good," Adelyn observed, gnawing on a slice of bacon.

David nodded absently, but Adelyn noted his bowl of soup that'd been there since she arrived, still sitting half full off in the corner of the table.

He set down the sword, drumming his fingers on the polished wooden table before finally looking up at Adelyn. "I have thought things over. As a freelance, I am currently working on another contract. It will be closed very soon, then I will be free to accept your offer. I will take this sword as an upfront payment, along with a payment of twenty five silver daggers once the task is done. I will also keep track of my expenses so that I can present you with an itemized receipt upon the completion of the job. If I am unable to complete the task, I will return the sword to you, and you will be under no obligation to give me any further compensation. Does this seem reasonable to you?"

Adelyn started to nod in agreement, but caught herself and frowned. She sipped the coffee to give herself a second to think it over. "What guarantee do I have that you won't simply ride off with the sword and never return?"

"You have my word," David offered confidently. "Those who know me know that I keep my word."

Adelyn shrugged, setting down the mug. "But I don't know you, and I don't intend to be taken in by a drifter keen on robbing me. I'm not paying for promises, no matter how trustworthy you may be. I will pay you in full once you have the location of my parents, not before."

David shook his head. "I do not work for free, and you could just as easily be trying to trick me into working without payment. What is to stop you from selling the sword or refusing payment once I return?"

"We will write up a contract, and both sign it," Adelyn offered. "You'd have a guaranteed payment that way, enforced by a court of law."

"A court of law? There is no court of law near here," David countered, shaking his head. "The nearest town with any government officials is a day's ride away, the nearest town with a judge is nearer to a week. It would cost me more in travel and time than for the job itself before I got any payment from you, if we had to rely on the court to settle things. Besides, I want the sword before I go after them, I am shy a weapon and it is good steel."

Adelyn raised an eyebrow at the excuse. "Your Watcher's Hook isn't weapon enough?"

David sighed, rubbing his forehead with his gloved right hand. "It is just called a 'Hook'," he said, sounding used to offering the correction. "The Watchers do not carry weapons. If you must call it by a title, it's a 'dueling hook' when less than two feet in length and a 'long hook' if it is any longer."

"Apologies," Adelyn said, fighting the urge to roll her eyes or make a snide comment. "But is your..." She glanced at the weapon on his belt, guessing at its length, "Dueling hook... not a good enough weapon?"

"I like to have options," David explained, nodding slightly. "A single blade can be lost rather easily, and there are times when a second weapon can be extremely helpful."

Adelyn hesitated, then took a bite of the food, chewing as she talked. "Then we're stuck. I can't trust you to keep your bargain if you're paid upfront, and you can't trust me to pay you fully once you have the information I need."

A second went by, and David rattled his fingers on the table as he thought. "If you would like, you can accompany me on my search, so long as you can ride a horse and pledge to follow my instruction should there be any kind of conflict. It will not be easy, but it would give you a sure way of tracking my progress."

Adelyn smiled, realizing his trick. If she said no, then it'd be her fault for not accepting his reasonable solution to the problem. If she said yes, then she'd have to accompany him on what could be a weeks- or even months-long journey, something she couldn't possibly afford to do. The farm needed her.

Either way, though, David was clearly bluffing. He wanted her to turn down the offer, so that he'd be negotiating from a position of strength.

"Fine," she said, nodding. "I'll go with you."

"Excellent." David beamed. "As I said before, it will not

be long before I am free of my current contract. It will be a week's time or less before I am ready."

Adelyn blinked. She had expected some form of protest or resistance from the freelancer, but he hadn't even blinked when she agreed to his terms. Thinking quickly, she offered, "Now, wait, I do have one other thing to add, if I'm going to accompany you. I cannot afford to pay both your expenses and mine on a long trip, and pay your whole fee as well. If I ride with you, I will only cover your expenses and fifteen daggers, not the full twenty five." It was a ludicrous offer— Ten daggers was vastly more than her expenses would total, but if they haggled they would come to a fair middle ground.

David thought for a second, and then nodded in response. "That sounds fair. I assume you have affairs you need to put in order?"

Adelyn nodded without thinking, only realizing after a second what she was agreeing to. She needed his help. She was incapable of finding her family on her own, as she'd demonstrated for the seventh time that morning by the fireplace. Even with that in mind, though, going along with him was insane. She wasn't a bounty hunter or a tracker, she was a farmer, and the only farmer who'd be there to take care of her family home.

She had to confess that it would be immensely satisfying to be there in person when peace officers rounded up the bandits and paid them back in full for their crimes. Still, that was not something she could let play into her decision; no matter how much she wanted to deliver justice person- ally, personal satisfaction did not trump the needs of the farm.

Setting down the sword, David said, "I should be back in three days. One day of travel, a day to handle my affairs, and a day to return. Four days at the most, should I be held up. You can deal with whatever you must during this period, be prepared to leave as soon as I return."

"These traders only have you under contract for another day?" Adelyn asked, surprised. Getting started as quickly as possible was always good news, but that was remarkably coincidental timing.

"Not exactly," David said, leaning in a bit and lowering his voice. "I had intended to wait until we had all made it to Drushlak, but I can simply handle my affairs now instead. It will cost me a portion of my reward to have everything handled early, but I can abide by that. Here, keep your sword until I return," he added, sliding over the cavalry saber and getting to his feet.

"Reward? Where are you going?" Adelyn asked, confused.

"Where am I going? Enjoy your breakfast," David replied, offering no explanation. After a moment of thought, though, he said, "Here, hold onto these for me as well." Digging in a pocket, he passed her a small silver disk and a wrinkled piece of folded paper. Aside from that, he gave no reason for why he had gotten out of his seat and was walking toward the bar.

Adelyn would have looked at the paper, but David kept her attention focused away from the objects in her hand.

The dueling hook on his belt was not held in place by a traditional scabbard, as the curved end to the blade would made that impractical if not impossible to draw. Instead, it was held in place by a small leather strap around the hilt, which could be unclasped by popping a button. David did so, drawing his hook and raising it in one swift motion as he walked straight toward the trader sitting at the bar.

With a quick forward-back tug, David pulled the dull

inside edge of the hook around the neck of the trader and jerked down with sudden force, pulling the well armored man off of his stool and sending him flying backward onto the ground. With incredible speed, David's free hand shot forward and withdrew the gun from inside the trader's robe while he was still falling backward.

By the time the trader landed with a heavy 'thud' and the rattle of his armor, his own revolver was pressed firmly into his cheek. David was kneeling over him with a calm expression, one hand on the gun, the other hand on the trader's throat.

"Simon Maher, you are hereby bound by law and ordered to surrender," David instructed, coolly, speaking as though from a script. "If you struggle, I will not hesitate to shoot you. Do not—" He paused at the click of a hammer being pulled back, followed by the fluttering of cards and the scraping of three chairs on the stone floor.

David looked up, but he kept the revolver firmly in place, and kept the downed trader in his eyeline no matter where he looked. Jenny had drawn a double barreled shotgun from underneath the bar and had it pointed at him, and the three mercenaries who Adelyn had been speaking to a moment ago were now drawing their own weapons and stepping forward.

Glancing between the two new threats, David said, "Stay back for a moment, I am working as an official agent of the law. I would rather you did not shoot, if we make too much commotion it will spook the other three."

Rose, apparently not hearing or not caring about David's request, raised her sword and approached within striking distance. "David, you'll drop that gun right this second. We were hired to defend these men, not kill 'em."

"I am not going to kill him," David said, his tone nonchalant. "If I did, I would get barely a third of the bounty. He is a felon smuggling stolen property to Drushlak." The trader started to try and wriggle free, and David pushed the gun harder against his cheek.

Rose hesitated, but didn't lower her sword. "That don't mean anything, and you've got nothing to prove it."

David paused, and then glanced over at Jenny. "You own this establishment?" he asked. Jenny nodded curtly, but didn't otherwise move. "I am operating fully within the confines of the law. If she stabs me," he nodded toward Rose, "She will be committing the crime of assault, against a federal employee in the course of his duty. If she kills me, then it would be murder." He tapped a finger against the side of the gun, then added, "The part about the federal employee will stay the same."

Jenny frowned, lowering her shotgun just a little. "Do you have a badge?" She asked.

"A badge? I do!" David confirmed. "Rose, you can lower that sword, I already said that I will not be shooting this man unless he struggles. Adelyn?"

Adelyn jolted, surprised to hear her name being called in the midst of all the confusion. "What?" she asked, realizing that she had already gotten to her feet.

David didn't look up at Adelyn, his attention focused on the man he had hostage, but he addressed her with a request. "Can you come over here? Bring those papers I handed you."

Hesitating, Adelyn looked at Rose who was looking confused and angry, then to Jenny who just looked confused. She approached and knelt by David, holding out the papers. "This?" she asked, holding up the wrinkled square of blue paper, which was stuck to a silver badge labeled 'Officer of Maintaining the President's Peace'.

David nodded. "Read it aloud, please."

Adelyn unfolded the paper, scanning it once before repeating the warrant out loud. "'Wanted, dead or alive: Simon Maher, Alyx Maher, Jebediah Naiman, and Rebecca Crowell, for the theft of government property and the grievous injury of two federal employees. Return of their cargo subject to additional reward.'"

Glancing between Rose and Jenny again, Adelyn shrugged. "It seems like he's telling the truth."

From the ground, the trader—Simon Maher, apparently —glared up at all of them. "You let me go or I'll—"

David punched him, pulling the gun away for just a second before returning the barrel back to Simon's face. "Is that enough for you, Jennifer?" he asked, not looking up at the diner's matron as he asked it.

Lowering the shotgun entirely, Jenny said, "That's fine, but get out of my tavern. I won't abide any violence in my property."

"As soon as I can," David agreed. "Rose, how about you?" It was clear that however Rose went, the other two men would follow.

Rose hesitated for a second, but kept her sword up. "Papers aside, we're still paid to protect these men, and I'll honor that."

David nodded. "I have to return their carts and cargo when I take them in, so that the property which is stolen can be returned to its rightful owners, and the property which is not stolen can be sold at auction to pay for their legal defense. Their armor, however, is not something I want or need, and not something that they will be allowed to keep."

Rose sheathed her sword. "Do you want me to keep this one restrained while you deal with the other three?"

Smiling, David said, "So that, if it looks like I am going to be killed, you can set him free and stab me in the back?" He pulled away the gun and got to his feet, nodding. "That sounds fair."

Rose blinked, then shrugged. "Sure. Good luck."

"I will not need it," David replied, checking the revolver to make sure it was loaded with all three rounds.

Adelyn wasn't about to miss what would happen next, so she hurried to follow behind as he walked to the exit. She waited until he had crossed into the brisk harvest air, then sticking her foot in the door to leave a small gap so she could watch.

David, pistol in one hand and dueling hook in the other, pointed the revolver loosely toward one of the traders and pulled the trigger.

The traders, who had not yet seen him, jumped at the sudden bark of gunfire, and one of them fell to the ground and screamed in pain, clutching his leg where a huge iron ball had just been buried. Adelyn watched him for a moment, but her attention was quickly diverted to the other two.

Before either of the standing traders could draw their own pistols, David sent his second shot into the closer one's arm, making her drop her gun just as she started to pull it from its holster. With only Jeb left, David leveled the pistol at his head just as Jeb finally managed to draw his own gun and aim it toward David.

"Drop your gun or I will shoot you down," David said, keeping his own revolver raised, with just one shot still loaded in it. "My aim is better than yours, and that armor will not stop an iron bullet from taking off your head."

He hesitated, but didn't drop his gun. David fired. Jeb clenched and his own gun went off, but his shot went wild and the ball tossed up dirt many feet away. David's shot struck home just to the left of Jeb's collarbone, punching through armor and bone alike.

Stepping forward, David dropped his empty gun and kicked the off-balance trader squarely in the chest, knocking him to the ground and sending his own revolver flying from his hand. David caught the new gun by the barrel, spun it around in his hand like a trick shooter, and then pointed it back to his side at the first trader he'd shot, whose leg now had a bloody, ragged hole in it. The trader had gathered enough of his senses to draw his own gun, but had not had a chance to aim it before David drew a bead on him.

David didn't have to say a word, he just held his new revolver steady and the trader dropped his gun. "Surrender! I surrender!" he said, throwing up his hands.

"Throw away your hooks," David said, taking a step back and gesturing with the pistol between the three traders, all of whom were bleeding on the ground. They all obeyed, none wanting to get shot again. Staying cautious, David kicked the weapons away, along with the two loaded pistols that were still lying on the ground.

Once the three traders were all properly disarmed, David stood up straight, stuck the revolver in the waistband of his pants, and glanced over at Adelyn. "I will see you in three days. Be ready for me."

CHAPTER 5

The Lords have no beginning, no end. They did not come from anywhere, they always were, and they always will be. The same is true of their mount, the great dragon, who will live so long as the Lords watch over it. We as peoples living off of the dragon's back must, then, take care to preserve our domain and keep our realm pure, for if the Lords look down upon us and observe sin and corruption, they may see fit to purge us and let others care for the realm, others who are not so sinful.

- Tarraganian doctrine, from a sermon delivered in the High Church in Triom

DAVID DID NOT WASTE any time getting ready to leave, and did not bother to make conversation with anyone as he did so. Disarming the criminal traders took only a little time, and once that was done—and their arms and armor given to Rose—their hands were bound with rope. He had to tend to the gunshot wounds of his prisoners before leaving, cleaning and bandaging the injuries, but that also took a mere couple of minutes. They'd need a real doctor eventually, but that could wait until evening.

Adelyn watched him ride away, wounded prisoners in tow, and then, with a shiver, turned to head back inside so she could think. She could always simply give David the sword and tell him that she'd changed her mind and he should go it alone, but then she was back to the original problem of trust.

Then again, while she didn't relish the idea of going out with David to track down the kidnappers, it would at least give her control of the situation. She could be there to make sure things went smoothly.

Pulling a chair up at the table where David had been seated, she pulled back her sleeves and finished breakfast, eating quickly now that she was no longer distracted by a strange tablemate. Thinking the situation over as she chewed the last bit of bacon, she finally arrived at a workable idea that would make her journey possible.

Swallowing the last dregs of coffee, she picked up her empty plate and walked over to the counter, hopping into a stool and holding out the mug. "Can I get a refill?"

Jenny smiled, taking the mug and pouring it full. "That was some fight," she commented, rinsing the crumbs off the plate and wiping it down with a clean cloth.

"You should have seen it outside," Adelyn replied, "He took the three of them on and won without taking a scratch."

Jenny whistled, setting the plate in a drying rack and tossing the cloth back into the sink. "So they were criminals? The traders, I mean?"

"I guess they were taking stolen goods up someplace," Adelyn confirmed, nodding and taking a drink of the coffee.

A second went by, as she worked up the courage to say, "Jenny, I need a favor."

Jenny stopped, turning her full attention to Adelyn with a slight frown. "What's wrong?"

"Nothing's wrong," Adelyn said, shaking her head. "But I may be away for a few weeks, and I need you to care for my horses. Not Butler—he'll be with me, but the others."

Jenny sighed, shaking her own head steadily. "I can't do that, Adelyn, winter's coming on and I can't afford—"

"I can pay you," Adelyn interjected quickly. "I have a few silver daggers now, and if I can't get the rest of it by the time I return..." She glanced at the bar, then at her coffee, clenching a fist and bracing herself to finish that sentence. "You can sell one of them to cover the cost. Not Jack, we still need at least one plow horse for next planting season and he's the strongest, but Trigger should fetch a fair price."

Jenny blinked, eyes widening a bit as she recognized the significance of the offer. Rather than saying yes or no, she asked, "Where are you going?"

"You saw that man who captured the traders?" Adelyn asked, and Jenny nodded. "I hired him to track down the bandits who attacked us. I'm riding with him to lend a hand and to ensure he won't simply ride off with his down payment and never return."

"You finally got someone to agree?" Jenny asked, surprised, almost impressed. Mulling it over, the tavern owner finally gave a short nod of her head. "I can keep them for the winter, at least until you get back," she finally decided. "But if you find those gods-forsaken bastards and set the army on them, you won't need to come up with any money."

Adelyn immediately brightened at that. She had doubted that Jenny would flatly refuse her offer, but she was also unsure where she would get the money to pay for several months' worth of care for two horses even if she succeeded. Jenny had just given her a free pass... As long as David was on the level, and as long as they were able to track down the bandits.

"Thank you," Adelyn said, as soon as she remembered to speak. "Thank you, so much."

Jenny shook her head. "Just find them. You can't bring my husband back to life, but you can bring justice to the people who killed him."

Adelyn nodded, sipping her coffee for a moment. The clock on the wall chimed once, and she looked up sharply. "Is it one already?" she asked, shocked that the time had slipped away so quickly.

Jenny looked up at the clock and nodded. "Unless the clock was broken in the past hour, yes."

"I need to get home!" Adelyn announced, her mind racing with all the untended work that needed to be done. This was supposed to be a short errand, maybe an hour and twenty minutes round trip, but she'd been gone for well over two hours and still had to ride home.

Throwing back the coffee to down what was left and burning her throat in the process, she tried to ignore the wave of panic and anxiety that she was feeling. She set down the cup, gave Jenny thanks one last time, and turned. She only kept from sprinting to the exit because Jenny didn't allow running in her tavern. Stopping to grab her father's sword and the cloth bundle she had wrapped it in, she scurried out the door.

Once outside Maggie's, with no rule to keep her from doing so, she sprinted the last ten paces to Butler's side, strapped the bundled sword onto his side, untied him from the hitching post, and hopped into the saddle. It was an exercise in self-control not to ride him back at a full gallop.

As she rode, Adelyn took deep breaths and tried to calm down, reminding herself that the farm wouldn't fall apart if she was gone for a day. Jason and Roger weren't dullards, they would get work done without her to supervise. If she was going to be leaving for weeks or months to find her family and her neighbors, she'd have to come to terms with the fact that she wouldn't also be able to care for the farm.

"It's fine," she reminded herself, pulling her coat a little closer as a gust of wind caught it. "Things will survive a day without you. They *have* to survive a day without you."

Adelyn made it back to the farm in good time, looking back and forth to see if she could spot either Jason or Roger out in the field, or perhaps in the pasture. No sign of them, which meant they were probably inside, having a little lunch of their own. It was past one, after all, she couldn't expect them to work constantly.

Hitching Butler in front of the house, Adelyn removed the parcel from his saddle, then turned toward the house to go warm up a bit and see if she could find her farmhands.

"Then you're an idiot!"

The shout came from inside, just before Adelyn could open the door. It sounded like Jason, but she couldn't be sure, and even if it was him she wanted to know what they were shouting about before bursting in on the conversation.

The next voice sounded like Roger. "I'm just sayin', we don't know for sure that's what's meant, all we know is that Adelyn—"

"Of course we can be sure! Just think about it—the injuries on her hand, the bad luck this town's had, and now this! It's the last bit of proof that I need."

"'Is jus' a book, though. Maybe she jus' found it interestin' or somethin'."

Adelyn's eyes widened as she processed what Roger had just said. Somehow they'd found her little magic book. She hadn't left it sitting out, had she?

No. It would have been in her parent's bedroom after she'd thrown it, and that room was kept locked. They'd managed to stumble upon it anyways.

"Clearly not. If she was just casually interested, that wouldn't explain everything else. We already knew before we found this book, it's just the final nail in the coffin. Face it —" Tugging the handle, Adelyn threw the door open to confront the two men, just in time for Jason to finish shouting, "Adelyn's a witch!"

Adelyn slammed the door behind her, getting the attention of both of them as they turned. Roger wore the expression of a child caught with his hand in the cookie jar, but Jason maintained a level expression. Her book of magic was in his hand, held out like he'd been waving it for emphasis.

The house had been ransacked, though it took Adelyn a minute to notice. So much of her furniture and possessions had been sold already, there wasn't much to search, but it seemed that Jason had certainly tried. The charred bits of wood in the fireplace had been scraped out, remains from her failed magical experiment drug out onto the floor in a heaping mess of black ash. The pantry had been emptied, the stove was open, the pots were all on the ground, and the door to her parent's bedroom looked as though it had been broken open by an ax.

Jason was the first to collect himself, licking his lips and raising the book he'd been emphatically gesturing with a moment ago. "Adelyn," he said, his voice an odd mixture of surprise and feigned confidence. "Care to explain this?"

Adelyn deflected the question, asking, "Care to explain how *you* found it? I don't recall leaving the master bedroom open for visitors." It was a stupid question—they'd obviously been looking, but Adelyn didn't know how else to respond except with passive aggression.

Jason scowled, lowering the book. "Well, you must have," he said, blatantly lying. The broken door was only a few feet behind him, plain evidence that someone had smashed it open. He didn't seem to care. "So, do you admit it?"

"Admit what?" Adelyn asked, putting a hand on the bundle tucked under her arm and feeling the hard wooden hilt beneath the canvas wrap. "It's just a book. I found it interesting."

It was a pathetic lie. Books on magic were never a common commodity, and after the war, after the Thirteen, they'd become even more rare. Adelyn had only found the little manuscript through luck and shrewd haggling with a trader. It was common knowledge that Adelyn wasn't rolling in silver swords, if she was still holding onto a book about magic, there was a reason for it.

"You're a witch," Jason said, elbowing Roger in the ribs to snap him out of his surprise.

Roger nodded once, backing Jason up. "It's kinda obvious. You'd gotta be an idiot not to tell."

Adelyn shook her head. "I'm no witch. I'm a sorceress."

"Is there a difference?" Roger asked, confused.

"Yeah," Adelyn said, relaxing a bit. "'witch' and 'wizard' are names associated with the *Thirteen Wizards*. I don't hurt people with my power."

Jason frowned, waving away the discussion. "How long have you been keeping your powers a secret?" he asked, warily.

"A few months," Adelyn admitted, her grip returning to the concealed hilt of the cavalry saber.

"A few months?" Jason asked, narrowing his eyes. "So that would have been, what, just before we were attacked?"

Adelyn clenched her free fist, feeling a sudden jolt of anger at his insinuation. "I lost my family in the attack. If you're saying that—"

"I'm not saying you did it on purpose," Jason interjected, his tone skeptical. "But everyone knows that you people bring bad luck, if your father didn't bring that down on you to begin with."

"My father?" Adelyn asked, warily. They could insult her —she could tolerate that—but implying that this was all her father's fault was not something that Adelyn would abide.

"Everyone knows he's a traitor," Jason said. "Gave up his men to the president in exchange for a plot of land. Gods don't like it when a man betrays his own."

Rage built a little more in Adelyn, and she started, "My dad is no—"

"Doesn't matter," Jason said, passively shutting her down. "It's your fault, either way, for not saying anything when you first found out about the magic. You kept it a secret, lied to us and you've been working on some hidden project ever since that's bound to bring us more misfortune."

Adelyn was surprised that Jason knew, but she tried to pretend she didn't know what he was talking about at all. "A hidden project? What—"

"Don't play dumb," Jason cut in. "We both know you didn't cut your hand four times in the same spot while making breakfast, or chopping firewood, or whatever other excuses you can come up with."

Swallowing, Adelyn gave up pretending. "I've been

trying to locate my family, but I haven't been able to get the spell right."

Roger snorted, but Jason just shook his head. "Is that the best excuse you could invent?"

"It's the truth," Adelyn insisted.

"Really? Where's your, eh…" Jason glanced down at the book, squinting a moment to read the words. "'Something to Hold'?"

Swallowing, Adelyn realized how pathetic the truth was going to sound. "It caught fire." Roger snorted again, and Adelyn shot him a glare. Turning to Jason, she changed her tack. "Give me the book."

Jason shook his head. "I'm taking this book into town. Then, I'll tell everyone that you're a *witch,* and that you've been doing things with your magic behind closed doors. Once that's done I'm going to burn it. It's for your own good. Maybe, if the gods are just, some good fortune will return once you stop using your 'power'."

Adelyn chewed her lip, trying to think up what else she could say. If they told the town, it would make things very difficult for her. It wasn't illegal to be a sorceress, but she could still end up in a lot of trouble if they blamed her for bringing the attack.

Glancing to her side as she thought, Adelyn finally said, "Give me the book, or I'll take it from you."

Roger hesitated and looked to Jason, concerned, but Jason only smirked and said, "I doubt you could."

"What makes you think that?" Adelyn asked, moving one hand to emphasize the large knife on her belt. "I'm armed."

"With a knife?" Roger spat. "I got me one of those too. You're not scary."

"Not just with a knife," Adelyn said. Despite being younger than both of the men, she was glad that she was taller—it allowed her to loom a little bit, and it made it harder for them to intimidate her, and hopefully would let her scare them a little in return. "I'm a sorceress. I don't need a knife."

Smirk widening, Jason raised the book and read aloud. "To cast a spell, a witch or wizard—" He paused, glancing at Adelyn. "Huh, this *does* call for a witch, not a sorceress. Interesting."

"Your point?" Adelyn asked, though she felt a sinking feeling as she realized where he was going.

Jason continued reading. "A *witch* must have three things. Something for Power, a source of spirit to fuel their spell. Something to Imagine, an idea to form the spell into what they wish. And—and pay attention here, Adelyn, you may have missed this part—Something to Hold, to make their magic manifest." He lowered the book, looking her up and down in an exaggerated fashion. "I'm not seeing a staff anywhere. Roger, you see a staff anywhere?"

"No," Roger said, shrugging. "No wand, neither."

"You don't have any magic," Jason finished, closing the book. "So how exactly do you plan on threatening us?"

Adelyn didn't feel particularly confident, but she smirked back anyways, pulling the string on the bundle she carried. "Who said anything about magic?" She asked, as the canvas slipped away from the sword and fell to the ground.

Adelyn had to adjust her grip to take the handle of the saber in her right hand, holding it out in her best impression of a fencer's stance. She didn't know how to use the weapon—her experience had been play-fighting with sticks against her older brother—but she was strong enough and was approaching six feet tall, and neither Jason nor Roger had any combat experience either.

Holding up the sword and trying to keep the point from wobbling in the air, she made her voice sound as calm as possible and slowly commanded, "Give. Me. The. Book."

It was Jason's turn to hesitate, taking a step back and leaning toward Roger to whisper something in confidence. Roger nodded, frowned, shook his head, then smiled and nodded again.

"Stop!" Adelyn ordered, not wanting the two of them planning anything. "Just give me the book, and you can leave."

Jason nodded, holding out his free hand in a placating gesture. "Fine," he said. "Lower the sword, I'll toss you the book."

Nodding, Adelyn lowered the sword a bit, though she kept it at the ready. It wasn't like she could or would use it, she didn't want anyone to get hurt, but the idea was that they wouldn't know she was bluffing.

Jason tossed the book in a high arc. Adelyn had to take her eyes off of them and reach up to snatch it out of the air with her free hand, still just barely grabbing it.

Roger tackled her at the waist and sent both of them backward, slamming into the door. Adelyn heard wood splinter and the door opened, both of them tumbling into the dirt outside. She dropped the sword, though she kept her hand on the book, open to a random page with detailed sketches of various runes.

As Jason stepped forward to grab the sword from where it had hit the ground, Adelyn shoved Roger away, scooting back on the dirt to get a little distance between her and the farmhands. Jason raised her father's sword in an offhand way, pointing it loosely toward Adelyn.

"I'd like that back," Jason said, nodding toward the book as Roger got to his feet.

Adelyn looked up at Roger, then at the book in her hand. The page it was open to was a little wrinkled from being thrown and caught, but was mostly legible, with a long, thin rune drawn to demonstrate a basic symbol for force or energy.

Eyes widening, Adelyn held up the book, focusing hard and pushing what energy she had into the book. Paper wasn't great at storing spirit, but Adelyn didn't need a battery, she just needed something to hold for a few seconds, and the runes she needed were all right there in front of her.

Her spell wasn't complicated. She first imagined a wall of force slamming into Jason and Roger, but thinking better of it she instead pictured a single blow slamming into Jason. If she spread it out too thin, it might not work.

Pushing the book forward in a shoving gesture, Adelyn shouted, "*Shtap!*" at the top of her lungs, and the little pool of energy she'd stored in the book rushed out of the pages like a thunderclap, forming an intangible ball of power that slammed into Jason's chest with the strength of a bucking horse. The sword fell from his hand and he was launched headlong back inside, landing on the floor with a resounding 'thud'.

Pushing herself to her feet, Adelyn held up the book and tried to conceal the sudden wave of exhaustion that came over her. She was already exhausted from her lack of sleep, and with that sudden exertion it was a chore just to keep standing, but she carried herself forward on tired feet, kicking Jason in the chest once, then twice. First, to keep him down, but second for insulting her father.

"So," She asked Roger, who was looking wide eyed

between her and a groaning Jason, hanging back from the combat, too much a coward to try and help his friend. "Do you still want the book?"

Shaking his head quickly, Roger said, "J-just take it!" he flinched away when Adelyn stepped forward and snatched the sword off the ground. She considered going for the bundle to wrap it up again, but that would be too much of a risk, and she just wanted to get out of there. Keeping her eyes on the door in case Jason came rushing out, she backed up until she nearly felt her back bump into Butler.

It was a trick keeping a hand on both her weapons while untying her horse, but once Butler was free of the hitching post Adelyn allowed herself to look away for a moment so she could climb into the saddle. There was no good place to holster the sword, but Adelyn slipped it through a belt loop, making sure that it wouldn't cut her or Butler while she rode, then pulled the reins and turned to flee from the farm.

She just had to make it to town before Jason or Roger, then she could explain herself, give her side of the story. If Adelyn was the one to tell them about her power, then she might have a chance to get everyone on her side before they heard about her scuffle with the farmhands. She had to get there, or—

Or...

Adelyn remembered her little pouch of coins in her coat, where the total sum of her wealth was jingling. She remembered her father's sword on her belt, the knife she always kept on her belt, the little book of magic still in her hand. She couldn't have forgotten Butler if she tried. Her greatest assets, and all four of them were already on her person.

Even at a full gallop, Adelyn had a few minutes to collect her thoughts. She was glad that she'd slowed her pace coming back to the farm, because it meant she could put on the speed for the trip back to town. Without slowing Butler's pace, she steadied her breathing and tried to think.

Getting some rest was near the top of her priority list. The sleepless night and her sudden exertion moments earlier were catching up to her. If it wasn't for the caffeine and the calories she'd taken in at Maggie's, she wasn't sure if she would still be in the saddle.

The cold was actually proving to be helpful here. On a warm, comfortable, spring day the weather would have made her even more drowsy.

David had already left, but she knew where he was heading. It wouldn't be too hard to head the same way he'd gone. If she couldn't find him and they passed in the night, though, she'd be left a city over and lose her chance to find her parents. In two months, nobody else had looked twice at her payment, and that was before two months of expenses made her offer dwindle to a pittance.

Adelyn knew if she left, nobody would stick around to mind the farm. The harvest that year was going to be minimal anyways, few crops had survived the fire, but even that little bit was important. With nobody to take charge, they would go untended.

Well, that wasn't true—if she vanished without making arrangements, Jason or Roger or someone else would probably complete the harvest anyways, but Adelyn would never see a penny of profit when they sold the crops, which was the same thing as far as Adelyn was concerned.

Drawing within sight of town, Adelyn returned her focus to a short term plan. Jenny was the person to talk to. She knew everyone in town, she could smooth things over most easily, and if Adelyn did skip town she'd need to tell her so she could collect the horses.

Once Adelyn passed the first house on the edge of town,

it was only a minute to reach Jenny's. It was a small town and roads were all clear. Adelyn jumped down and tied Butler to the post before hopping over the rail and running to the door, ducking back into Maggie's for the second time in as many hours.

"Jenny!" Adelyn called, as she walked in, eyes adjusting from the slight gray overcast weather outside to the brightly lit dining area. She had to take a second to actually find Jenny after she called out her name, the tavern's owner was delivering food to a table off to the side.

Looking up, Jenny put on an expression of surprise as she set down a plate, wiping her hands on her apron as she walked to Adelyn. "You're back quickly," she said. "Was there a problem on the road? You look exhausted."

Adelyn shook her head. "We need to talk. In private."

Jenny frowned, raising an eyebrow. "Is this about your horses? I'm a little busy right now, I need to start on making supper, but we can talk in a little while."

"No," Adelyn said, stepping to the side to keep Jenny from walking back to the bar. "We need to talk now. It's urgent."

Her frown growing more pronounced, Jenny stepped further to the side to get around Adelyn. "Give me a little time, Adelyn. Go wait upstairs, I'll be up soon."

Adelyn wanted to protest further, but a voice of reason in her head pointed out that she needed Jenny's help, it would be prudent to stay on her good side. "Hurry," she implored before turning and walking around to a door on the back wall that led to a flight of stairs.

Going up two steps at a time, Adelyn crossed into the first open room. It was just one of the guest rooms that Jenny would sometimes rent out to travelers, but it was comfortable, clean, and had comfortable chairs. Sinking into one of them, Adelyn tapped a few fingers on the arm rest and waited, thinking up what she was going to say.

"Adelyn?" Jenny asked, shaking Adelyn's arm.

Adelyn blinked and sat up, surprised to see Jenny in the room. "What?" She asked, blearily.

"You fell asleep," Jenny explained. "What did you want to talk about?"

Adelyn knew she couldn't have been asleep for that long, but it still worried her that she'd lost time when she was in such a rush. "I've... got something I need to tell you," she said, glancing at the door to her left. It was closed, giving them a modicum of privacy.

"I got that," Jenny said, nodding. "What's up?"

Adelyn hesitated, but the clock was ticking and she didn't know how soon Jason or Roger might show up. "I'm a sorceress."

A second went by and Jenny nodded, processing the information. "Okay," she said, after another moment went by. "That's... news, but why the rush to tell me?"

"Jason found out," Adelyn said, studying Jenny's face to get a sense of her reaction, deciding not to go into the details about how. "He said he was going to tell everyone. I wanted it to come from me, first." Jenny nodded again, and Adelyn continued. "He and Roger think I've been using my magic to do something bad. I tried explaining to them that it was a tracking spell to find my family, but they didn't believe me."

Jenny didn't speak for a few seconds, but when she did, she said, "Adelyn... I... believe you."

Adelyn raised an eyebrow, a little worried. "Then why do you sound so unconvinced?"

Breathing slowly, Jenny took a few more seconds before she said, "This isn't public knowledge. I only know because word gets around, and I hear a lot of rumors I shouldn't's."

"What?" Adelyn asked, trying to hurry things along.

Jenny sighed, looking at her hands as she spoke. "When our people were ambushed riding after the bandits, just after the raid. They didn't just get taken by surprise. Our people outnumbered the bandits, we wouldn't have gone quietly. They were captured because the bandits had a wizard with them."

"A sorcerer," Adelyn said without thinking. She immediately regretted the correction, but it was too late to take it back.

Frowning, Jenny looked Adelyn right in the eye. "Whoever it was, they and their friends killed seven people, my husband included, and took another fifty prisoner."

"Sorry," Adelyn apologized. "But that wasn't me."

"Do we know that?" Jenny asked, though she didn't sound like she was accusing Adelyn. "You weren't in town when our people rode away, you could have been anywhere."

Adelyn swallowed, feeling a cold chill run through her. "I was at the farm! The fire had almost spread to the stable once already, I had to stay to keep our horses safe, and—"

Jenny shook her head. "Whether that's true or not, do you think you can make everyone believe you?"

Adelyn didn't need much time to think about the question, then she shook her head. "I should go," she said, pushing herself up from the chair and reaching into her coat for the little bag of coins she kept there. "Will you still watch my horses?"

Jenny stood up as well, reluctantly nodding. "I can't promise anything, if people start causing trouble on account of them—"

"That's fine," Adelyn said, digging five silver daggers from her bag. They were tiny little coins, no wider than her little finger, though long and slender to match their name. Five daggers was more than a most people made in a month, and it pained Adelyn to hand them over when she had so many expenses still to pay and so little hope of any new income, but there wasn't a choice. She was in a hurry, there wasn't time to invent a new solution to her problems. "How long was I asleep?"

"Fifteen minutes, maybe," Jenny said, accepting the money without comment. "Twenty at the most."

Adelyn was glad for the sleep, but she still wished she could have that time back. She didn't know if Jason or Roger had made it back to town yet, or who they had spoken to if they were back, but fifteen or twenty minutes was more than enough time for them to have caused a lot of trouble.

Tucking her remaining money away, Adelyn said, "I'm afraid you'll need to retrieve the horses yourself. I'm short on time as it is."

Jenny nodded. "Just do me one favor."

"What's that?" Adelyn asked, as she moved toward the door.

"Swear on the gods that you're being honest with me."

Adelyn hesitated, her fingers tightening on the door's handle. "Jenny, you know I don't believe in—"

"Yes, I know, you're Tarraganian," Jenny said, brushing it off. "I don't care. You can make promises on your dragon for a week, but it doesn't mean anything to me. Swear on what *I* believe in."

Adelyn loosened her grip on the handle a bit, unsure of what to say. "I—" She started, glancing up at the ceiling and then back at Jenny. "I can't. I don't mean to slight your religion, but I won't speak apostasy and abandon my own beliefs for yours. I'm sorry."

Jenny sighed, shaking her head. "Go," she said. "I'll keep

our bargain. But don't come back until my husband's death has been paid back in full."

A second went by. Adelyn considered offering another word of promise or assurance, but there was nothing else she could think of to say. Turning the handle, she slipped out of the room and left.

CHAPTER 6

Recently, a group of engineers have managed to develop a simple mechanical engine which turns a flour mill, powered by magical energy (also called 'spirit'), extracted from blood. The extraction process, done by placing the blood in a gold or silver bowl and leaching the spirit from the blood, is inefficient, but the developers hope to improve on the process as time goes on.

Of course, for a talented witch or wizard, there are several other options for extracting magical energy. The most common, the use of which is explained in further detail in the next chapter, is using the wizard's own physical energy. While not a powerful source of energy, it is not harmful to the user in any way, making it a popular choice for most basic magical applications.

The next most popular choice is, of course, blood. The blood must be human, though it can be taken from someone other than the wizard using it, and it must either be specially preserved or else used immediately after being drawn. The advantage to this is that blood, when properly used, is a far more potent source of energy than physical energy, with even a few drops being able to power most basic applications. In fact, you will rarely encounter any spells which require more than what you can extract from a large cut, and no spells explained in this book will require more than a prick of your finger.

The third source of spirit is rarely used, and for very good reason. In extremely dire circumstances, a witch or wizard may use their own memory as a power source. While extremely potent, it is an incredibly difficult source of power to harness, and accidents can be incredibly damaging to the mental health of the wizard. There are techniques to mitigate the risk (See Chapter Seventeen), but it is not something which should be used lightly.

Lastly, the most powerful source of spirit is the life force of another human, or the witch or wizard themself, the energy given up upon their death. For obvious reasons, the use and application of this source of power will not be discussed further in this book.

As can plainly be observed, all of these power sources share one thing in common: They draw from the energy created by human life. This had led many researchers to conclude that humans must have some level of distinction from animals. However, after a study made by Claud Baudelaire (at great risk to his person), he discovered that, in fact, the blood of dragons can also be used as a source of spirit, and in fact it is, if anything, more effective than human blood.

This, of course, is...

- Excerpt from "Magic, a Wizard's Companion and History", by Joab Michelson

ADELYN SLIPPED into the brisk wind outside and glanced around, pulling her coat tight. Nobody was out in the courtyard, waiting to pounce, so she took a breath and kept going, running down a mental checklist of things that she would need. She had no food, but she had eaten a good meal an hour earlier. If she had to, food could wait until the next morning. A change of clothes could wait too. David would hopefully have travel supplies, so nothing was needed there, just so long as she could find David.

He hadn't said the name of the town he was going to, but he had ridden out to the north, and there was only one real town within a day's ride of her hometown: Maise.

Maise was the next best thing to a city that you could find within a hundred miles. Adelyn wasn't there often, but it was always bustling with people, coming and going with business, buying and selling goods, delivering mail and news to one another. Almost eight hundred people lived there, six or seven times the usual size of Adelyn's hometown and a dozen times larger now that half her neighbors were lost.

It was also the only place you could find any governmental authority within a few day's ride. It wasn't a massive military occupation; less than half a dozen soldiers were stationed in the city at any given time, usually, but it was still more than you could find anywhere else. David had to be there if he was anywhere.

It was strange to Adelyn to be heading back so quickly. She'd visited only a month prior to speak to peace officers and beg them for help, and again a month before that for the same reason, when she normally rode up to Maise once in a year after harvest. It was late in the day to start the trip, even at a clipped pace she wouldn't be arriving until nearly dusk, but she couldn't exactly just delay her trip until morning.

Mounting Butler, she turned to start the ride, trotting out of the courtyard without any resistance. Once she was out of town, Adelyn knew she would be fine—There weren't many men or women left in town who could ride after her, and there were even fewer horses. There would be little or no pursuit, and even the smallest head start would be plenty to get away. She just had to get out onto the road.

Her town wasn't large. It was less an escape and more of a brief jaunt past a dozen houses and a barn. Still, riding slowly down the dirt road, Adelyn's imagination ran wild, and she knew an ambush was around the side of every home and behind every wall, with a dozen soldiers mounted to chase her hiding in the barn. She told herself that these thoughts weren't even remotely plausible, but had trouble believing it until she made it onto the dirt trail that signaled the edge of town.

Once she was on the trail, Adelyn sped up her pace quite a bit, moving at a quick trot. There wouldn't be anyone riding after her, but she didn't want to come into Maise well past dark if she could help it. She kept an eye on the sun, wishing she hadn't sold her father's pocket watch, trying to estimate when she'd ridden an hour. Once she guessed that enough time had passed, she slowed and stopped, taking a second for her and Butler to rest.

Adelyn was beginning to regret not bringing along any water. She had been in a hurry to leave, sure, but with hindsight, a minute or two to fill a bottle with water to bring along wouldn't have hurt too much. There were a few little creeks running not too far off the trail, but she didn't have time to detour toward them and still make it to her destination before nightfall. Swallowing on a dry throat, she spurred Butler on, moving at a less anxious pace.

The ride to Maise was longer than Adelyn was accustomed to. The sun was just about to slip behind the horizon and give way to night when she came into view of the town, and by the time she was passing the first couple of houses, the sun was totally out of view. Adelyn paused for a moment at that, nodding to the sky once in appreciation before returning her eyes to the road and yawning.

The city had apparently installed spirit lights in the month since last she visited, as every twenty feet or so there was a metal pole with a brightly shining glass orb on top, thin copper wire running between each pole and occasionally shooting off to a house, delivering modern power to the people of Maise.

Finding David was imperative, but not immediately urgent, and she had a theory as to where she could find him in the morning. He had to go to the military depot if he wanted his bounty, and that would have been closed by the time David arrived. Until then, she could sleep.

The inn was right next to the combination general store and mail depot, and together they were the two largest buildings in town. Both were three stories tall, monsters of buildings as far as Adelyn was concerned, looming over the town like giants.

It cost two bronze swords and six pins for a meal and lodging, which included a space in their stables for Butler. Adelyn had to make change from a silver dagger, an exchange that the innkeeper begrudgingly agreed to, swapping out one large silver coin for many more in bronze. Adelyn was certain that upon counting the large handful of disparately shaped coins she'd find that she had been shorted a few pins, but she wasn't in the right state to argue over pocket change. She wanted to eat, get up to bed, and get herself in between a real mattress and some warm covers.

She practically inhaled the soup along with four glasses

of water to ease her dry throat, then took herself and her few possessions up two flights of stairs to her room. It was a strange thing, to come to the top of the staircase only to find another staircase, but Adelyn was too sleepy to have more than a passing interest in the oddity.

Yawning as she reached the top of the *second* set of stairs, Adelyn looked from door to door, trying to remember what room was hers.

"There we go," she mumbled tiredly, seeing a pair of numbers painted on a door at the end of the hall. She had no key, the doors locked from the inside. She walked to her room, old floors creaking beneath her feet and beneath someone else's as well.

A hand grabbed the back of Adelyn's collar and yanked her down, nearly sending her into a backward tumble. She flailed her arms in a wild attempt to maintain her footing, but only kept from falling because an arm slipped under her arm and tugged her back upright. Even as she realized what was happening, a gloved hand slipped over her mouth to muffle any screams.

She screamed anyways, but the attempt made little noise and she just got a taste of dusty leather for her trouble. Before she could struggle any further, the figure who had grabbed her took a couple steps backward and kicked shut the door to one of the rooms, leaving them in a dark space lit only by dull lamplight shining in from outside.

Adelyn was tall, especially for her age, and strong to boot. When she struggled, though, her captor only adjusted their grip and moved their body in a subtle way, effortlessly neutralizing her attempts to pull away. She then tried a more direct approach, jamming an elbow toward her captor's belly, but that attack was robbed of strength by the lock she was held in.

Feeling something sharp press against her back, Adelyn stopped struggling.

Her captor finally spoke. "I am going to take my hand away from your mouth," he said—it was a clearly male voice, and it seemed familiar. "If you scream or call for help, I will cut your throat. Do not speak at all, unless answering my questions. If you understand, nod once."

Adelyn nodded once, and the leather glove slipped away from her mouth. Her mind raced as she tried to figure out an escape plan. If he meant to rob her, she couldn't let him know about the thirty daggers in her pocket—it'd be better to get stabbed in the back and escape with her money than to let him take it.

"Good," he said, though his hold didn't loosen. "Does anyone else know that you are here?"

Adelyn almost told him that she'd gone to the military, or that she was a presidential employee. That was a bad lie and she didn't think she could keep it straight if she tried, so she chose honesty instead. "The—the innkeeper knows I've got a room, but no one else."

"Good," he said again. "Where are your weapons?"

"I have the sword, on my belt," Adelyn said. "You can take it."

The man hesitated, but his grip still didn't loosen. Adelyn was starting to get uncomfortable; being held with a knife to her back was less than a pleasant experience. After several seconds, her captor said, "You... intended to kill me with a cavalry saber? On your own?"

Adelyn blinked, confused. She'd not threatened him. This was just a robbery, wasn't it? Her captor would have to be insane to think that a random passerby was an assassin, unless that passerby already knew her, which meant...

Eyes widening, she asked, "David?"

His grip wavered for a moment, finally loosening, though only by a fraction. "Yes, of course it is me. You followed me here."

Adelyn was at a loss for words, a flurry of questions running through her mind. One particularly pressing question rose to the top, though, and she asked, "Can you let me go?"

A hesitant second went by, then David said, "If I let you go, do not try to run away or call for help. You should know, I do not need a knife to your back to kill you."

Adelyn shuddered but said, "Okay." The arm around her slipped away and the pressure of the knife disappeared. Before she could step away, David jerked the sword from her belt, tossing it onto the bed where it would be out of easy reach. Adelyn hesitated, asking, "Should... should I turn on the light?"

A second went by, and David said, "Do it." Adelyn felt the wall, finding the switch after a second. She wasn't used to powered lighting indoors, but it was a quaint convenience to have the room lit at the flick of a finger.

Turning to face David, she saw that he was dressed similarly to how he'd been that morning, though he had on no belt and as a result, his dueling hook was absent from his waist.

"I am going to check the hall," David said, drumming his fingers against the side of his leg and watching Adelyn carefully. "Sit down, and do not try to leave."

Adelyn swallowed, spotting a chair and taking a seat. David stepped outside for a moment, and she reached into her jacket pocket, finding the little book of magic and hurriedly pulling it from her pocket, flipping it halfway open. It had worked once, it could work again. Finding the pages of runes, she flipped pages until she got to the page listed with runes of fire, which seemed an appropriate and —hopefully—more effective a weapon than pure force.

As David came back inside, Adelyn stuck a finger on the page and slipped the book, and her hand, into a coat pocket.

"Explain to me your plan," David said, sitting down on the edge of the rumpled bed. There was only the one chair in the room, and it was occupied by Adelyn, so his only other choice would have been sitting on the floor.

"My plan?" Adelyn asked, still confused. She still wanted to talk her way out of things if possible. A fight might have been satisfying, but as tired as Adelyn was, she couldn't go throwing around magic for long. The book would be a backup plan, nothing more.

David nodded. "An ambush in the night, I understand that. But you would have been in a position to ambush me when I came back to Marstone, and in any case your sword would be a poor choice of weapon for a surprise attack. It is too unwieldy in close quarters. To take me in the night, a dagger would be far better. Did you plan on using your knife?"

Adelyn shook her head. "I wasn't coming to kill you. People found out—eh, I had personal issues come up and was compelled to get out of town for a couple days. I had been hoping to leave with you straight from Maise."

David raised an eyebrow, looked at the sword, then looked back to Adelyn. "Straight from Maise..." he said idly, mulling over her words. "In that case, I must request your forgiveness for my misunderstanding of the situation. I took you for an assassin, come to kill me."

"Why would an assassin come to kill you?" Adelyn asked, a little startled by the idea. She wanted no part of working with a criminal, no matter how affordable his rates.

Shrugging, David offered, "Bounty hunters do not make easy friends, but we make quick enemies."

Adelyn frowned, but the explanation made sense. After seeing him go to work that morning, she wasn't surprised to hear that he had a few enemies. Paranoia, it seemed, would be a regular part of life for someone in his line of work. "I see," she said, nodding her head.

"I see..." David repeated, tapping his fingers against the side of the bed, drumming them in a rhythm for several seconds before he said, "I understand if you do not wish to take me on for the job you require, all things considered."

Adelyn chewed her lip, thinking it over. As off-putting as the whole experience had been, she needed his help, now more than ever. "Can we leave tomorrow?"

"Tomorrow," David said reflexively, before deciding. "I believe I can finish arrangements with the local authorities in the morning. We should be ready to leave by noon, if all goes well."

Standing, Adelyn removed her hand from her pocket, leaving the book, and brushed her fingers where the knife had pressed against her back. There was a small cut in the fabric where the blade had been, though it felt like her shirt beneath was undamaged. "Buy me a new coat," she said, adrenaline wearing off and exhaustion setting back in. "And you're still hired."

"That is completely fair," David agreed. "I will purchase one tomorrow."

"Good," Adelyn said, still nervous, but deciding that she could plan better on a full night's sleep. She didn't need the new coat because of the cut—it would have been easy to patch—but her old coat was getting small on her, and was worn and ragged, and soon wouldn't be worth patching. She extended her hand to shake. "'Till morning, then."

David looked at her hand, then tentatively reached out and accepted it, shaking quickly and pulling away. "Untill morning, then."

Adelyn backed out of the room, stepping a few feet down the hall to reach her own. She locked the door.

CHAPTER 7

Each coin is worth fivefold of the previous type, and is weighted properly to the value of the metal it's cast from. Bronze coins weigh slightly more than silver, then, despite having the same denominations—pins, daggers, and swords.

To avoid price confusion, silver pins are sometimes called tacks in common parlance, but silver daggers and swords are exchanged infrequently and thus have no such slang associated with them. If someone refers to a dagger or sword, it's understood that they mean bronze unless they call for silver specifically.

The only coin which is an outlier is the gold piece, which is singular in that it does not then get split into the above denominations. The gold piece, being worth one hundred twenty five tacks or over fifteen thousand bronze pins, is of such value that anything larger would be used only by banks, and even then only rarely.

- Taken from notes about the costs and exchange rate in the nation Triom, written before the coinage was made into a national currency.

. . .

ADELYN WOKE up sluggishly to a wooden rapping sound at her door, rubbing her eyes blearily as she tried to remember where she was. She'd not had an easy time getting to sleep —first worrying about being one room over from a man who'd nearly killed her, then worrying about going on a weeks-long journey with him—but once she had quit tossing and turning and finally turned in, her sleep had been deep and untroubled. Exhaustion proved to be an excellent anesthetic for her troubles.

She had no clock, but the sun was well up and the birds had stopped singing when she awoke. Startled by how late it was, Adelyn nearly fell out of bed as she hurried to her feet, thinking of all the chores she'd left untended. The horses would be half starved by now, and—

Looking around the room, she saw her slashed coat, sword, and shoes in a pile by the inn's bed, and remembered where she was. "Lords betray me," she muttered, putting a hand to her head and taking a deep breath in relief. Just for that morning, she had no responsibilities except to be ready when David finished his business.

She was feeling particularly good. A full night's sleep had put a positive spin on her problems, and she was finally on a solid path to finding her family and her neighbors. A good meal for breakfast would make things even better, and if the weather was as good as it looked through the window, the day was going to go very well.

Three sharp knocks came on the door again, followed by a now familiar voice. "Adelyn?"

"Just a minute," she called back, grabbing her boots from the floor and tugging them on from a standing position, hopping on one foot a bit as she pulled on the second one. Running a hand through her short hair to smooth out some of the tangles, she pulled on her jacket and put on a big smile, trying to look like she hadn't just woken up.

Opening the door, she saw David holding up a new woolen coat in one arm, reaching out to rap on the door again with the other. He was fully dressed, with a satchel under one arm and his dueling hook on his belt. "Good morning," he said, pleasantly. "I have settled my contract, those traders are now the responsibility of the military. I am ready to leave as soon as you are."

Adelyn glanced back at her room, then at herself. She had nothing to pack. She didn't even have a change of clothes, excepting the new coat. "Just give me a few minutes to pack up my things, it might take a while," she said, smirking as she accepted the new coat.

Not so much as blinking at the joke, David just nodded, though his tone betrayed a hint of confusion. "Fair enough. Take your time," he said. "I will wait for you downstairs."

Shaking her head, Adelyn said, "No, I—there's nothing to pack up. I was joking."

David glanced inside her room, then back at Adelyn. "Joking... Oh, I apologize. I am not good with jokes."

"Got it," Adelyn said, pulling on the new coat and retrieving her scant possessions from the pockets of the old one, quietly palming her book so that David wouldn't get a good look at it. "So, the one about the dragon in the clouds would be over your head?"

"Yes," David said, nodding his head in agreement.

Adelyn blinked a couple times, then shook her head as she bundled up her old coat under an arm, grabbing the sword off of the floor. "This is yours," she said. "Please, take good care of it."

"Of course I will," David said, holding it up in the light.

Satisfied, he straightened and looked back to Adelyn. "Do you need to eat before we leave?"

Adelyn nodded, then realized a question she should have asked a while ago. "Wait, where are we going?"

"I will explain that while you eat," David said, turning toward the stairs.

Adelyn unloaded some of the large handful of pins she'd gotten as change to pay for a light lunch of meat, bread, and coffee. It was by no means as good as Jenny's cooking, but it was filling. Taking a first sip of the coffee, Adelyn waited for David to explain his plan.

"The way that I see it," David started, tapping his fingers on the table in an idle pattern. "There are really only two ways this could have happened: Either the bandits who attacked your town went south, down to the coast, and sold off your family and neighbors as slaves to an unscrupulous captain. If that happened, then your family is on the opposite side of the continent, and your slavers are vanished in the wind. That would be hopeless, of course, it would take years to track them down. Even if we did, recovering your family or friends would be impossible."

Adelyn was partway through a bite of food as David told her that the recovery might be hopeless. Her expression froze, and she tried to keep from letting that completely erode her confidence. She'd known that was a possibility, and David had said there was another option. Swallowing on a suddenly dry throat, she gestured with her fork and tried to keep her sudden anxiety from showing as she asked, "What's the other way?"

David answered the question by reaching into a pocket on his satchel and producing a map. Compared to Adelyn's loose, magical rendition of the continent from the morning prior, David's more localized map was still a work of art. Instead of conveying artistry by taking license with appearance and shapes, though, his map was art in its precision and detail. It only showed the Middle Western Plains and surrounding areas, but what it covered was rendered more accurately than any map Adelyn had ever seen.

"They may have gone north," David said. "Not all the way to the desert, of course, but a hundred or two hundred miles. There are several trade routes up there, and the inhospitable terrain past Petra makes it an area not often patrolled by the military. Slavery may still be in a very gray legal area while the new laws are sorted out, but kidnapping is still very illegal, and they would want to be as far away from a military presence as possible.

"This is us," David said nonchalantly, pointing to a small dot labeled 'Maise' on the map. Drawing his index finger upward, tracing a roadway, he said, "And here is Drushlak. It is six days away, probably seven for us since we're leaving in the afternoon. If your bandits sold slaves anywhere within a hundred miles, someone in Drushlak will know."

"How will we know if it's the right slavers?" Adelyn asked, pushing away her empty plate.

"If it is the right slavers?" David replied, folding up the map. "I do not imagine that there are an overabundance of large bandit groups kidnapping whole towns in the area. Even if we cannot find them, we will find someone who knows them. It is a place to start. Are you ready to leave?"

Adelyn grabbed her coffee, throwing back the last sip and setting it down before nodding. She was hesitant to ride off to an unknown city with David, but she had her book as an ace in the hole. If the situation got out of hand, she could blast him a mile away with magic. Her misgivings could be ignored, there was work to be done.

"Let's go," Adelyn agreed, buttoning up her new coat as she got to her feet.

It was noontime before they were both saddled up and on the road. Adelyn on Butler, David on a big brown stallion called Ace.

They rode for ten minutes in silence, passing out of town and onto the empty dirt road. The terrain past Maise was pretty similar to that of her home, as far as Adelyn could tell: Fields, wheat, open patches of grass, small patches of trees near ponds or rivers. Even so, it all seemed just barely wrong, a twin to the land around her home, but subtly different in a thousand ways that she couldn't put her finger on. She'd never gone past Maise before, so everything they passed was a totally new sight to her eyes.

"Do you fight?" David asked, breaking the silence.

Adelyn raised her eyebrows, surprised by the question. "What?"

"Do you fight?" David asked again, simply but insistently.

"No," Adelyn said, shaking her head. "I mean, not really. I can fire a rifle a little, but I don't have one to use. Dad took his rifle with him when they were bushwhacked."

"Hmm," David thought, frowning. "How much experience do you have on long trips?"

"Some, not much." Adelyn considered it. "I've never gone past Maise, but I've plenty of experience riding, and I've slept under the stars more than a couple times."

"A couple times..." David mused. "That is good. You do not have a sleeping bag, though."

Adelyn shook her head again. "I didn't have time to pack properly before I left."

David thought for a minute, twiddling the leather reins between his fingers. "We would be better off if you could defend yourself. I do not expect a conflict, but should there be one, it would be helpful to have you at my back, and to not have to watch out for you."

"Sorry to disappoint," Adelyn replied, shrugging. She expected David to reply but he only fell silent, turning his eyes back to the road and letting the subtle noise of wind become the only sound between them.

A minute went by, and then Adelyn decided to bring some life back to the conversation. "So where did you learn how to fight like that?"

"How to fight like that?" David asked, glancing over his shoulder at her. "Like what?"

"With those traders," Adelyn clarified. "Eh, the criminals. They were no bunch of shrinking violets, but you beat all of them without taking a scratch."

"That was not a true fight," David said, shrugging. "I caught them all by surprise, we never had a chance to come to blows. In my experience, if it comes to real fighting, I have already made an egregious mistake."

"Egregious?"

"Very bad," David clarified. "I could have fought them directly and won, but that is a pointless risk to take. A real fight can be fun, but it is also stupid."

Adelyn mulled on that for a second. "Still, where did you learn? Maybe that wasn't a fight, but you still know how, right?"

"I fought in the war," David supplied, twisting the leather rein in his fingers again. "People did not survive long in war if they did not know how."

A few seconds went by while Adelyn chewed on her next question before working up the courage to ask. "Which side?"

David didn't respond for a while, and at first Adelyn

thought he just wasn't going to reply. Just as she was about to move on, though, he said, "I fought with the Stone Warriors."

"You're serious?" Adelyn asked, eyes widening. "*The* Stone Warriors? The mountain-side, killed-a-dozen-soldiers-each Sovereignty Fighters?"

"The Stone Warriors did not fight for the Sovereignty," David said, shaking his head. "We—the Stone Warriors, that is, fought for territory and for a small king. If the 'president' had offered autonomy in exchange for neutrality, the mountain's Chieftain would have abandoned the fighting. The president did not make an offer, so the president's soldiers were slaughtered when they tried to come through Stone Warrior territory."

Adelyn would have called him a liar if she hadn't seen him fight. She had seen him take on those traders, though, and his skill was a testament to his story. "Still, you kept our northern border safe for more than a year. Nearly won us the war."

"Us?" David asked. "So you supported the Sovereignty?"

"I was seven when the war ended," Adelyn said. "I supported who my parents supported. They both fought to stop the president's army, for all the good it did."

"For all the good it did... So you are neutral, then."

Adelyn shook her head. "Not really. It doesn't matter much what I think, but it's been almost eight years and I still don't support the president. Maybe if he got around to establishing some law and order out here, that could change, but we've been on our own out here paying taxes and getting dragon spit in return since the war ended and that's not changing fast."

David nodded, but didn't say anything in response. Adelyn, taking that as a signal to keep talking, continued.

"He can call it a 'New Rule' all he wants, but as far as I can see he's just a king going by another label." When David didn't respond to that, Adelyn cleared her throat and changed the subject. "Anyways, you're with the Stone Warriors, there are a lot of people who'd call you a hero."

"And a lot of people who would go out of their way to kill me in my sleep," David pointed out. "Not everyone is forgiving, and when you take no prisoners you leave many people upset."

Adelyn fell silent for several long moments, looking off to her side at the familiar-yet-alien countryside view.

A thought occurred, and she asked, "Didn't most of you get killed by the Thirteen?"

David didn't respond for a minute, and when he did, his voice dropped to something much harder to hear. "Have you ever seen a sorcerer fight?"

"No," Adelyn said.

"There was one sorcerer with the Stone Warriors. He did not go into battle often, since it was decided he was worth keeping hidden, but when he fought he was an unwatched terror. A sorcerer, trained, who really knows what he is doing, is worth fifty men on the battlefield. Two of them working together, they can cover their weaknesses and guard one another's backs, combine their skill and power with magic."

He sighed, running a glove through his stiff black hair. Thinking for a moment on his next words, he finally said, "There were maybe six hundred Stone Warriors in total. Some General under the president had decided it was a good idea to keep throwing men into the mountain pass where those six hundred siblings in arms were deployed, to try and break through. Seven thousand, eight thousand of the president's soldiers, maybe more, and they were all killed. No prisoners, almost no survivors to tell their tale.

"Someone higher up the chain of command than me, one of the Stone Warrior's generals, I suppose, got word that there was an armored company moving toward that mountain pass. It was supposed to be an easy target. They set up at Rocksfield, an open pass between two mountains. When the fighting started, though..."

Adelyn didn't need him to finish. She'd heard more than a couple horror stories about what the Thirteen had done on the battlefield. "You were massacred."

David cleared his throat, drumming his fingers on his leg repeatedly as he recounted the story. "I do not know if the president's soldiers lost a man. Certainly the wizards never took a scratch. Five hundred good men, well trained, all dead the same as if they had not fought back at all. I have heard people say you could hear the screams from ten miles away."

"How did you escape?" Adelyn asked. For a second she had wanted to correct his use of 'wizard' out of habit, until she remembered who he was talking about. 'The Thirteen Wizards' had been the ones to give the word a bad name, of *course* he called them wizards.

David's voice brightened a little, though not quite to his normal tone. "I did not escape," he said, shrugging. "I was not among the soldiers who were at the massacre. Another fifty or so had been held back as a reserve. After that battle, though, resistance crumbled and the president's army came through without any more trouble."

"That's lucky," Adelyn said, as they passed under a few trees, crossing through a small wooded grove.

"Lucky," David agreed, slowing his horse, first to a trot,

eventually coming to a stop. Starting to dismount, he instructed, "Get off your horse."

"Why?" Adelyn asked, obeying nonetheless.

Untying the bundle holding the cavalry saber, David said, "I am going to teach you to survive in a fight."

CHAPTER 8

It's the common flu that truly shows the limitations of sorcery when it comes to medicine.

A sorceress may alleviate pain, they may clean the sinuses and throat of phlegm, they may lower the temperature of the patient to assuage their fever. They might return appetite, or give strength to those weakened by such sickness. However, in doing all these things, the sorcerer will kill their patient.

Without pain and weakness, the patient will overwork themselves and leave their body too weak to fight the disease. Without phlegm to be expelled, the body cannot remove foreign viruses. Without fever, they cannot kill those pathogens residing inside with heat.

A sorcerer, left alone with a fever patient and no understanding of the disease, will kill their patient eight times in ten.

- Taken from a larger essay on the limitations of magic in medicine, found on the second floor of the Presidential Archives in Triom

.   .   .

ADELYN NEARLY TRIPPED BACKWARD as she dismounted
Butler, barking out a laugh. "You must be joking," she said,
as David finished unwrapping the sword.

"I do not joke well," David reminded her, walking over
and turning the sword in his hand so he was holding the hilt
out to Adelyn. "You cannot learn to use a sword in six days,
but a little experience is better than nothing."

Adelyn would have laughed again, but David seemed
serious. Raising an eyebrow, she asked, "What if I stab you
on accident?"

"You will not," David replied, casually. "I will be showing
you defensive techniques." He kept the sword held out with
quiet insistence, waiting for Adelyn to take it.

Adelyn frowned, leaving the sword in his hand for a
moment. She wanted the strength he offered, but she was
still uncertain. "Are you sure? Time is of the essence, and—"

"We will only practice when we stop to rest the horses,"
David said, alleviating the worry. "And it could save your life
if we get into trouble."

"Do you expect trouble?" Adelyn said, taking the sword
by the handle and gripping it tightly in her fist. She had to
admit, it felt good to have a weapon at hand, and learning
how to use it would come in handy.

"I do not expect anything," David replied. "But that does
not mean we will not come across something troublesome
and unexpected. If you do not want to learn, I will not bring
it up again, but it is a useful skill to possess."

"No, I'll learn," Adelyn decided, nodding her head a
couple times. She saw no reason not to, as long as it didn't
slow them down.

"Good," David agreed, tapping a couple fingers on the
handle of his dueling hook. "You are holding it wrong."

Adelyn blinked, looking at the sword in her hand. "Huh?"

"Here," David said, reaching forward, then hesitating. "May I?"

Pausing, Adelyn had to figure out what he was asking. "Oh, right, yes," she said.

Once she had assented, David put a hand on Adelyn's, moving her fingers around. "Your grip is too tight. You are not holding a club. Keep it loose and flaccid, to give you better handling."

Adelyn smirked, but went along with his adjustment. "Don't I lose power if I do that?"

"You do not need power unless you are chopping firewood," David replied, shifting his body to the side. He hesitated, then asked, "Can you make a fist?"

"Yeah," Adelyn said, holding up her left hand, fingers balled like she was going to punch someone. "My brother showed me how."

David considered for a moment, then said, "Your brother does not know how to make a fist."

Adelyn blinked, looking at her hand. "What's wrong?"

"You have got your fingers wrapped around your thumb," David said, again moving her fingers around. "Punch someone with that, and you will break your own finger."

Flexing her hand a bit once her fingers were rearranged, Adelyn nodded. "This is better?

David smiled, stepping away. "Much. If you do well with the sword, I may teach you some hand-to-hand techniques as well. Hold out the sword and turn your body like this."

Adelyn nearly got whiplash from the change in subject, but obeyed, looking at David's stance and copying it. He held out an invisible sword off to his right side, feet positioned at a ninety degree angle spaced a little ways apart. Adelyn mirrored his pose as best she could, holding out the sword in her hand and copying his footwork.

"Good," David encouraged. "If you keep your body turned, you present a smaller target to any opponent trying to land a blow. But you need to hold the sword with the blade perpendicular to the ground. Here, like this…"

And so the lesson went. David made no mention of how to move or attack, focusing entirely on stance and grip, showing several different defense positions, but offering no movement and no mention of how to attack.

Around fifteen minutes went by like that, and by the time David was wrapping up the sword and they were returning to the saddle, Adelyn's arm was starting to feel tired. It wasn't that six pounds of sword was much weight, but holding it out at arm's reach for an extended period was more taxing than she'd expected.

They rode for another hour before stopping again in a similar grove of trees, giving the horses a brief respite and returning to their training. David used his dueling hook to demonstrate a few basic sword motions, and then he set Adelyn to repeating them ad nauseum while he sat against a tree and made notes in a small journal, glancing up occasionally and commenting on her form, giving critique or compliment. Then it was back on the road, another hour of riding, another ten minutes of practice, and again, and again, as the sun slid across the sky.

This pattern repeated three more times before they arrived at a small town. Adelyn didn't know its name, and David had to retrieve his map to find the town there before he could properly name it as 'Sothsai'. The layout was similar to Adelyn's hometown, with a handful of scattered homes built by the road and the handful of important buildings near the middle.

"We'll stay here," Adelyn said aloud as they approached the town's inn and saloon, a squat two-story affair. "I'm going to see if the general store's open so I can buy some supplies, if you'd get us each a room."

"Get us each a room?" David asked, as he stopped his horse and dismounted. "It would be cheaper to rent a single room and share."

"Forgive me for being cautious," Adelyn replied, tying Butler to the hitching post and stretching her arms. "Get two rooms."

David considered it for a moment, then nodded. "Will you want me to wake you in the morning?"

Adelyn blushed, shaking her head. "This morning was a rare case, I'm normally up well before sunrise," she assured him. "Are you going to eat the dinner here?"

"The dinner here?" David stopped for a moment with his hand on the door, then nodded a couple times after considering the question.

"I'll get my room number from you when I get back, then. See you soon," Adelyn said, turning toward the small general store.

The storefront was clean and well-lit. There was a spirit light inside which bathed the whole room in a cool blue glow. Bags of grain and beans were stacked against a wall, and shelves lined neatly with jars and boxes of supplies of all kinds were stacked behind the counter. There was no clerk to be seen, but a bell jingled above the door when Adelyn walked inside, and within a few moments an older man in brown pants and a white apron came bustling out from a back room.

"Can I help you?" He asked, his voice a little rough.

"Just looking to stock up on supplies," Adelyn said. "Are you open? I can return in the morning, if you'd rather."

"No, nonsense, we're always open," the old man said, waving his hands to dismiss the notion. "Edward, is my name, a pleasure to meet you. What can I do you for?"

"Adelyn," Adelyn told him, shaking his hand. "And quite a lot. Do you have a pen?" He did, and pulled over a small pad of paper to join it so he could make notes. "Okay, well, I'll need food for a two week trip, a sleeping bag, two sets of traveling clothes, a spool of string, three yards of linen cloth, and a few blocks of wood. Holly, if you've got it."

Edward took several more seconds jotting down everything, then read his notes back to Adelyn to make sure he hadn't missed anything. "I'm afraid I may not have much in the way of clothes your size," he commented. "But I can get you the other things. Is pine okay, for the wood?"

Adelyn wanted to check her book for reference, to ensure that pine could work as a base for a magical tool, but she just nodded to avoid looking odd. "Sure, that'll be fine."

"You need the food right away? I have some dry goods, 'course, but I could bake some biscuits tonight and have them packed for you come morning."

"Sure," Adelyn agreed. "The food and sleeping pack I'll pick up in the morning, can I get the other things now?"

"Of course, of course," Edward mumbled, shuffling to a shelf to retrieve the string, then heading to his back room for everything else.

...

Five minutes later, Adelyn was leaving the store a little lighter of coin but carrying a bundle of clothes stuffed in a bag under one arm and pockets bulging from the other supplies.

She found David for her room number, then found her room to unload the various purchases, and finally changed into a set of clean clothes before heading down to dinner. As she had been warned, the clothes were not a perfect fit, but with the liberal use of a couple drawstrings and aggressive tucking of her shirt into the trouser waist, she was able to achieve a passable fit.

David was gone when she returned downstairs to eat, so she avoided conversation and took down two bowls of soup before heading back upstairs to get to work.

Adelyn was relieved to check her book and find that pine was, if not ideal, at least a serviceable base for a magical tool. With her new knife in hand, she set to whittling, taking her time at the task. She didn't want to be caught unarmed again, not after the fight with Jason and Roger, and especially not after the encounter with David.

It took a couple hours, but she eventually got the three blocks of wood carved down into the shapes of crude but passable runes: A wide ring with an inset circle, a similar rune composed a narrow triangular point, and a more chaotic design resembling a spreading bolt of lightning, with jagged corners and no obvious pattern. A defensive rune, a rune of power, and a rune of fire. The best arsenal she could make in an evening.

She wanted to refine the three little weapons more when she got the time, but it seemed wise to sleep. The sun had been down for quite a while, and tomorrow would be a long day. Running the string through openings in the three wooden runes, she fashioned a simple necklace and set it by the bed before climbing under the covers to rest, falling asleep with fits and starts.

Smoke was pouring in from under the door, filling the

air with a choking smog that made it hard to see and harder to breathe. She blinked, groggy and confused, feeling someone shaking her arm. Turning to look, she saw her brother John, urgently trying to wake her.

"It's a fire, someone's set fire to the field. Wake up, it's a fire, someone's—"

Adelyn shot awake, sitting up in a cold sweat and looking around the room, checking in a panic for any smoke. There was none, she was alone in a dark room with no smoke and definitely no fire. She didn't know how long she'd slept, but it couldn't have been long.

"Lords give me peace," she muttered to the ceiling, more out of frustration than as any real prayer. She tried closing her eyes again, but after the nightmare, her body had decided that it needed no further rest. All she managed to do was toss and turn, twisting around under the covers as she tried to sleep.

Giving up, she kicked off the blankets and pulled on her boots, creeping toward the door and peeking out, trying not to wake anyone else in the building. The downstairs was all but abandoned in the night, nobody around except a small rat chewing on crumbs. The rat, too, scurried away when it saw Adelyn, leaving her alone. There were still gently glowing embers under the mantle, crackling as they kept the building warm, casting the whole room in a cozy light.

Approaching the fire, Adelyn stooped to its side, digging a heavy iron poker out of its holder. Rather than prodding the fire, though, she gripped it loosely in her right hand and took a couple steps back, positioning her feet at a right angle to each other and spacing them a little ways apart.

Holding up the poker to her right side, she thought about the forms that she knew and moved the poker slowly through the air before returning to the defensive stance.

Lacking an edge, she kept the poker's fork pointed to the ground. Her grasp on the 'weapon' stayed slack as she moved through another form, blocking a slow and imaginary attack that came in from above, and then from the side, and then back to her resting position.

Next time she was in a fight, she intended to win.

CHAPTER 9

And the gods did fill the universe with life, each continent to itself being given its own creature, and its own god to tend to it. And the god of the earth did say, I will watch over your creations, and the goddess of the water did say, I will watch over your creations, and they did war. The god of the earth came at her with the might of the mountains and the plains and the desert, but the goddess had only water, and though she strove with all of her might, the god of the earth bore down upon her and she could not win. And so it was decided that the god of the earth would watch him and his portion thrice over, and the goddess of the water would watch only her and her one portion, and so the dispute was settled.

- The Tome of the Gods, Volume 4

"AGAIN," Adelyn said, raising her father's sword to a ready position.

"The horses are well rested, and we are nearing the city," David reminded, keeping his weapon lowered. "It is late enough in the afternoon already. We should be back on the road if we want to get any questioning done tonight."

Adelyn shook her head, staying stock still otherwise. "One more time," she said. "I've almost got it. One more time, then we'll leave."

"As you wish," David said, his expression never changing as he raised his dueling hook and swung it in a sudden overhand attack.

Moving with all the practiced grace she'd managed to learn in two days, Adelyn took a step forward and threw up her saber to meet the weapon in the air, turning the flat and pushing to the side so that David's hook slid away from Adelyn. That was the easy part. As David pulled his hook toward himself, Adelyn flicked her blade out and away.

It was by a hair's breadth, but she kept her weapon steady, narrowly avoiding the clank of metal on metal that always came just before the sword was wrenched from her grip by the curved end of David's hook. She was almost surprised to have finally executed the maneuver, and that surprise was followed by giddy excitement as she saw the blade still clutched in her hand as David stepped away.

Stepping back, she raised the tip of her sword toward David, held it steady, and beamed. "I got it," she exclaimed, feeling a rush of pride. "The attack failed, and I've still got my weapon. I *got* it."

David spun his hook in one hand, snapping it onto his belt, returning Adelyn's smile with a nod. "You are improving."

Walking over to Butler, Adelyn wrapped the sword back up in its cloth bundle before remounting so they could ride back to the main road. "So how much longer 'till I'd qualify to join the Stone Warriors?" She asked, grinning.

David hesitated halfway through mounting his horse,

then seemed to realize she wasn't serious. "Not for a while," he responded, hauling himself into the saddle. "Unless they have been refounded while nobody was paying attention, you may have trouble getting on the waiting list."

Adelyn's grin stayed firmly in place as she turned Butler, steering toward the road. In the six day's ride to the city, traffic had been growing more and more regular, and as such, they had started moving a little ways off the main path before swordplay lessons. Not so far that they'd have trouble finding their way back, just enough to get out of view from questioning eyes who might ask what they were up to.

As they returned to the road, David cleared his throat, checking to ensure nobody was within earshot.

"What's up?" Adelyn asked, curious.

"I should fill you in on my plan," David explained. "The city we are going to, Drushlak, is not a friendly place to outsiders. We have business there, so I do not expect outright hostility, but they generally take poorly to people coming around and asking a lot of questions."

"I'll keep my head down," Adelyn said. "But I don't see how we're going to find out what we want to know without asking at least a couple questions."

David nodded, expecting her to say that. "I am going to frame myself as a buyer, asking for especially cheap slaves— illegal merchandise will be less expensive than legitimate. The city is a trading hub, so even if your townsfolk did not get taken through here, it is likely that someone heard something about a large volume of new, discount slaves in the area."

"Makes sense," Adelyn agreed. "I'll be... What, your daughter?"

"My apprentice," David said. "Since I am teaching you

the sword, it is not untrue. I will not lie to them, only tell the truth in a way that makes our real goal unclear."

"I... Why?" Adelyn asked.

"Because I do not lie," David said. "Do not mention my combat history, by the way."

"Okay," Adelyn chewed her lip, considering. "When will—"

She stopped at the sound of a horn blaring out in front of them, followed by the distant sound of hoofbeats.

"What's that?" Adelyn asked, looking around sharply.

Tense, David whipped his head around, hand on his hook. Adelyn thought the urgency around him was almost palpable, his caution practically making the air buzz.

"Be ready, but I think that..." A dog barked, and he nodded. "That is the sound of a party chasing after a runaway slave."

Adelyn began scanning the tree line, as though she expected to see someone covertly running through the bushes. "Should we do something?"

David shook his head, drumming his fingers on his knee and frowning, the tension in his stance slowly fading. "We cannot do anything to help without making a scene and ending the possibility of finding answers here."

Frowning, Adelyn said, "Could we—"

"No," David interrupted. "Whatever you were about to suggest, no. Pray, if you want."

Adelyn sighed. "Is that really all I can do to help?"

"It is all you can do to help," David replied. "Unless you want to abandon the search for your family and friends."

Distantly on the road, two figures were approaching, armed riders kicking up clouds of dust as they galloped. They rode on massive black mounts, two hands taller than any horse Adelyn had seen before, and carried rifles and swords that looked ready for any battlefield.

David pulled his horse to the side of the road and Adelyn followed suit, leaving the way open. The riders passed without giving them a second look, and they carried on toward the town.

Adelyn clenched her fists and almost called after the riders, thinking she could delay them or hinder their progress. Still, David was right, she couldn't risk making a scene.

Twenty steps later, David stopped in place, and Adelyn's horse nearly bumped into his. "Hold it," he said, raising a couple fingers.

Adelyn furrowed her brow, then followed his gesture. Looking up, she had to squint for a moment before seeing someone crouched in the tree above them clad in a sopping wet shirt, stained old pants, and bare feet.

Realizing he'd been spotted, the man put a hand to his lips in a frantic plea for them to stay quiet.

David shook his head, calling up to him. "Your hiding place will not work. They have dogs, they will find you."

Looking around urgently and then back to David with a panicked grin, the man hissed down in a stage whisper, "I swam through the river! They can't smell me after that!"

Shaking his head again, David said, "That is not how it works. They can just pick up your scent on the other side of the river. You are as good as caught."

The runaway swallowed, rubbing his face with a muddy hand. "I—No! I can still—" A dog howled, much louder than before. He began pleading with David, hoping for a miracle. "Please, you have to help me. I'm not a slave!"

Adelyn frowned. "Then why—"

"Are you a criminal, then?" David asked.

"No!" the man said, looking around nervously as the sounds of men and dogs grew even closer. "I just—"

"What's going on over there?" Someone called from the woods, having spotted David and Adelyn in the road. "You two! Have you seen something?"

David swallowed, tapping his fingers out on his leg in a rhythm. "I am sorry," he said quietly, before calling out. "Yes!"

Adelyn bit her tongue, anger boiling up at the situation. "David, we could—"

"Let me handle this," David said.

A figure emerged from the woods, tall and brusque, a six-shooter revolver on his belt and a short weapon in his hand covered in grass stains from where he'd been hacking at bushes and trees in the way. He glanced up at the tree that David was parked in front of, saw the man hiding there, and carelessly raised his gun.

"Come on down there, Willy," the man said. "We've got you clean."

"Please!" the runaway said again. "I just need a little more time—"

"You've had your time, Will," the man insisted, spitting on the ground. "Dobson wants his money back, and you don't got it. Are you gonna come down, or do I gotta shoot you out of that tree?"

Someone else approached from the wood, led by a dog on the end of a taut leash, and Will deflated as he saw his chance of escape shrink from miniscule to nonexistent.

"What's going on here?" David asked, glancing to the man with the gun.

The man gestured with the barrel of his weapon. "Willy here tried to skip out of his debt, couldn't pay his dues. We gotta do something about that, or others might get it in their heads that they can just leave whenever they like without paying what's owed."

"How great were his debts?" David asked, looking up at the man who was now climbing down from the tree. "Perhaps I could help."

"Suppose you're welcome to pay what's owed, if you're feelin' charitable," the man said, "But it ain't gonna do Willy too much good. Runnin' away like this, that's ten years or so of good labor whether he pays it back or not."

David frowned, but nodded. Willy had a desperate, wild look as he got to the ground, but could see no escape as his eyes flitted back and forth.

"Who do you work for?" David asked, looking down on the man with the gun.

"Fella called Dobson," the man responded. "Or whoever. Lotsa slaves means lotsa runaways, always good money in getting 'em back. I—"

Willy hit the man over the head with a tree branch, then threw the wood at the leashed dog and took off, sprinting down the dirt road in a mad dash. Adelyn felt panic and hope as Will ran, and for a moment she thought he might even get away.

The armed man swore, raising his revolver and aiming for half a second before pulling the trigger.

His gun jammed, clicking on a chamber but failing to fire. "Damn!" he exclaimed, gesturing with an arm to the person beside him so that they could continue pursuit.

Adelyn tried to think of a spell she could cast that would delay the bounty hunters, but nothing sprung to mind. She couldn't just throw up a wall of magic to block their path, that would be too obvious, and—

One of the giant horses came crashing out of the trees, directly in front of the runaway. Will didn't even have time to yelp in surprise before a club came down on him, hitting the back of his head hard enough that Adelyn heard the impact from fifty feet away. Will fell forward and hit the dirt in a slump, arms splayed out.

"Gods damn it all," the bounty hunter muttered, spitting on the ground. "Hope that didn't kill 'im, I wanted that bounty for tonight."

Adelyn was frozen in shock, watching as the rider dismounted and crouched, checking on Will, then throwing the runaway over their horse like a sack of grain and climbing back into the saddle.

"Adelyn," David said sharply. She didn't immediately respond, unable to look away, but David repeated her name and she looked over at him, catching his eyes for just a second before he averted his gaze. His expression was blank and distant, but his posture made it look as though he was ready to throw someone across the road.

"Let's go," Adelyn said, turning her horse. David nodded once, knuckles white as he clenched the reins of his own mount.

"Thanks for the help, stranger," the bounty hunter commented, as they turned to leave. "If you come by the fights later, I'll buy you a drink after I win."

"Sure," Adelyn said absently.

Neither of them wanted to talk, so the only sound as they traveled was the toot of a horn and a few dogs barking behind them. Eventually, that faded as well, and then all that could be heard was the sound of hooves on dirt.

They reached the river twenty minutes later, where a ferry was set up to let horses and men across, and where a few of the slave catchers had a small shack for lounging when they were not pursuing a target.

Adelyn barely paid attention to the ferry's fee, or even

the grandeur of the wide river, and ten minutes later they were on the other side, slowly walking their horses into the city.

Distracted as she was, Adelyn made it another minute before she finally looked up to take in the city they were in, and when she did, she was shocked almost as much as she'd been when Will made his escape.

The city was *huge*. Long wooden buildings were built on both sides of the street, and that street just... kept going. She could see it off in the distant horizon, more than a mile down, where houses continued flanking both sides of the road. As they passed an intersection, she saw that the structures ran off in both directions as well, and all seemed to be populated. There was not a lot of traffic on the road, allowing them to walk along unimpeded into the city, and letting her see far down the street where it hit a T intersection, more buildings blocking her view beyond that.

"What are all these buildings *for?*" Adelyn asked, looking around.

"Storage and labor," David responded curtly. "Lodging is mostly further to the west, there is a small market in the direction we are headed now."

Adelyn felt dizzy for a moment. "And how many people live here?"

"Live here? Ten thousand, if I were to make an estimate," David said. "It is small for a city, but a busy trade hub due to its being situated on the river."

"Small," Adelyn repeated, glancing around. "Okay, if you say so, but—" A whistle blew somewhere, loud and shrill, cutting off Adelyn's words. "Another runaway?" She asked, looking around.

David raised an eyebrow but shook his head, spinning his horse so he could look around. "I do not know..."

People swarmed from the buildings, pouring out onto the streets in a rush. The roads, previously empty, were crowded within moments, as men and women rushed to and fro, pushing roughly past anyone who got in their way.

"End of the work day," David said, though it wasn't clear if he was saying it as explanation to Adelyn, or if he'd just realized it himself. He began tapping his fingers on his leg, looking up and down for somewhere less crowded. "I—we should get off the road."

Adelyn nodded, feeling overwhelmed herself. This place was ten times bigger than the largest town she'd ever been in, and it seemed as though the whole population were gathered around on the streets. "Where?"

David pointed, and Adelyn followed the line to a smallish building nestled between the larger structures. It had no sign, but looked to be the only place that people weren't flooding out of, so it was as good a choice as any.

It took them a full minute to cross the sixty feet to the building, having to skirt around pedestrians and push through people. There was a hitching post out front, and though Adelyn was skeptical of leaving their horses outside in the chaos, she didn't see much of an alternative. She had her money on her person, the other valuables in her saddle-bags would have to be safe on their own for a couple minutes.

Tying Butler in place, she first ensured that her silver was still in its pocket, safely tucked away, then she resolved to stay by the window and simply keep an eye on her horse.

Pushing inside, Adelyn found it mercifully absent of crowds, and David breathed a sigh of genuine relief. There were a few people milling about, but the little room had nowhere to sit, so it was not a good place to spend leisure time.

A young woman was going over ledgers from behind a window. There was a big grated iron door next to her, and beyond that were fenced off shelves with provisions by her side so that showed off her wares while keeping them safe from thieves. She glanced up as the door opened, eying Adelyn and David.

"Can I help you two?" The shopkeeper asked.

"Lodging," David said. "Trying to find some."

"Well we don't have a proper inn here, but there's some rooms in the back you're welcome to," she said. "It's a tack for the night."

Adelyn balked at the price. "A silver pin for two rooms?"

"That's for one room," the shopkeeper corrected, her tone derisive. "You don't like the price, you can take it or leave it. Do you have horses? We can put those up in the livery for three swords apiece."

Gaping, Adelyn forgot to haggle for a moment. "That's robbery!"

"It's how much it costs, girl," the woman replied, shrugging.

Adelyn was going to try and argue it down, but David put up a hand, fishing in one of the pouches on his belt and retrieving a small silver coin and a few larger bronze disks. Glancing at Adelyn, he asked, "Did you want a room to yourself?"

Chewing her lip, Adelyn decided against it. The cost was too high for what she'd be getting. "No," she said.

"Okay," David said, turning back to the shopkeeper. "How do I pay you?"

She pushed something on her side of the window, and a drawer opened out for David to drop the coins into. "Your horses out front?"

Glancing out the window to confirm that Butler was still

there, Adelyn nodded. "Mine's the black horse with the white mark on the front that looks like he's wearing a suit, he's got the brown stallion."

Frowning, David asked, "Is that why you named him Butler? The fur pattern?"

Adelyn grinned back at him. "Seemed a fitting title."

"I'll have someone see to 'em," the woman said, nodding and pulling the drawer back. A second later, she pushed out a small key. "That'll get you through the back door. If you want hot water, that's an extra charge. I can leave some food for you, that's—"

"An extra charge?" Adelyn finished. "We have provisions."

She shrugged. "Suit yourself."

David took the key from the drawer. "Where are 'the fights'?" He asked.

"Hmm?" The shopkeeper asked.

"A bounty hunter mentioned something about there being fights," David explained. "I want to go see them."

"Ah," she said, frowning to one side. "Those are going to be west of town, but I wouldn't go. They're crass displays of—"

"Thank you," David said, cutting her off and turning to Adelyn. "We should rest a moment and have something to eat, then head to those fights. People who we want to speak to may be there, and it will be quicker than trying to track them down individually."

Adelyn chewed her lip in thought, then nodded in agreement.

CHAPTER 10

Thulcut meat is very difficult to prepare, due to the highly acidic nature of the flesh. However, when properly treated, it is quite tender and has a subtle and excellent flavor, and it has a remarkably long shelf life until prepared. Here is a particular favorite recipe of mine. You'll need a cut of meat, preferably taken from near the fin joint, where the meat has the most flavor. Submerge the meat in water and add two tablespoons of baking soda for each pound of meat, then let sit for forty eight hours.

Once treated, mix together two parts egg, three parts flour, a few pinches of salt and pepper, and seasoning to taste. (I use my fish and seafood rub, page 147.) Coat the meat in the mixture and let sit for four more hours, then cook over a low flame for thirty minutes, turning occasionally. Cut into strips, serve with fresh vegetables, and enjoy!

- "Seven Hundred Recipes Everyone Should Know"

THE SUN WAS STARTING to set as they picked their way through town, navigating the throngs of people awkwardly. It was slowly thinning out as workers went to their homes or settled in saloons for a drink, but a great number seemed to be heading in the same direction as Adelyn and David, toward the fights.

They passed a power station, and Adelyn briefly stopped to marvel. She'd seen generators and power converters before—Maise had a fairly impressive one, even. This one blew them all away. It covered the area of a house, with brass teardrops taller than Adelyn hanging from pylons that were ten feet tall at the very least. Short, thick cables ran in from the pylons to blood collection reservoirs and generators, and narrower lines were strung out, spreading in a spiderweb toward the rest of the city.

"What are those?" Adelyn asked, pointing at one of the teardrops.

"What are those?" David asked, turning to look and parse what she was asking about. "Oh. Batteries. They store spirit, so that it doesn't need to be generated constantly. Brass has a lengthy half-life for spirit, and at that size, they could probably store a reasonable charge for most of a day."

Adelyn faltered on a word. "Half-life?"

"Spirit never really runs out naturally once it is stored in an object, it just drains to near nothingness," David explained, apparently ready to give the clarification. "The more full an object is charged, the faster it gives off power— the 'half-life' refers to how long it will take to lose half the energy stored in the object."

Adelyn nodded, chewing on her lip. "How long—"

"We should keep moving," David said, shaking his head. "I want to arrive before it is too crowded."

They resumed walking, and Adelyn noted the buildings flanking the power station. Raising an eyebrow at the symbols painted on the side, she asked, "Hospitals?"

"When people get injured, they bleed," David explained,

nodding. "Might as well build the power station close to a supply of free blood."

"These buildings look new," Adelyn pointed out. "I think they built the hospitals around the power station, not the other way around."

David shrugged, skirting around a few pedestrians who had stopped to talk. Adelyn followed, passing the hospital buildings, and walking into view of the arena.

The fighting pit was not elaborate, a six foot deep hole in the ground maybe fifty feet across, a wooden fence assembled around it to keep people from falling in. A ramp was on each far end of the pit, just a simple pile of dirt packed into a wedge shape. Light sconces were spaced every six feet or so along the inside of the fence, copper wire strung to provide them all with power.

People were already gathering, and though the pit wasn't totally thronged yet, the edge of the fence was crowded. The way the pit was designed, you could only see the action clearly if you were within a few feet of the edge, and though the edge was wide and long, it was obvious that latecomers would not be able to watch the fight well.

"So, who are we looking for?" Adelyn asked, walking up to the fence and leaning against it.

"Anyone who looks important," David said, standing by the fence next to her and looking around. "Look for someone wealthy, or in fancy clothes. People who seem to have authority. I do not have any contacts here, but it should be easy in this city to find someone who works in the slave trade."

"Like him?" Adelyn asked, pointing at a man in a fine black suit across the pit. The suited man was talking privately to someone holding a sword and dressed in old, ragged work clothes, who seemed to be listening in rapt attention.

"We can ask," David said, stretching a bit as he stepped away from the fence. "He certainly matches the description."

Adelyn waited for David to move, but he in turn waited for her. She finally got the hint and moved to lead the way, breaking a path through the growing crowd of people to make it to the other side of the fighting pit.

As they walked, Adelyn asked, "So these fights, what are the rules?"

"There are not many, unless it has changed since last time I was here," David said, running his fingers along the fence rail as they walked past. "Both fighters are allowed any weapons they want, unless it is an unarmed bout. Whoever submits first is the loser. If they are knocked unconscious, they are the loser. If they are killed, they are the loser."

"People die?" Adelyn asked, almost walking into a drunk man who stepped up to the fence without checking his surroundings.

David followed her new route around the drunkard, shaking his head. "Not often. If anyone gets a reputation as a killer in the ring, it makes them into a target for the other fighters. It is not against the rules, technically, but in a blood sport like this you are better off making friends than enemies."

"And you can use any weapon?" Adelyn asked, keeping the conversation going.

"Any weapon, excepting those that use gunpowder. They have to own the weapon and have it in their possession. Generally, fights are by people of equal skill and armament, though—opponents have to agree to what they will face. The winner gets a percent of the money gambled against them, too, so if they far outclass their opponent, they will not make much of a profit." He shrugged, glancing around at the slowly thickening crowd. "You can watch in a little while, they usually shout the rules before every fight."

Finally reaching the man in the suit, Adelyn tapped on his shoulder to interrupt the conversation with the fighter.

The suited man made a small gesture to his conversation partner, then turned to Adelyn. He looked her up and down, then turned instead to David. "Can I help you?"

"We need to ask you a couple questions," David explained. "Do you have a moment?"

He looked between David and Adelyn, then shrugged. "Yes, they're good fighters. I won't say more than that, insider information and all. Good luck on your wagers." He started to turn back to the ragged fighter, but David stopped him.

"Our wagers... we are not here for details about the fight. We want someone with information about the region's slave trade." That got the man's full attention, and he put on a charismatic smile.

"Are you looking to buy?" He asked, again putting his other conversation on hold. Slapping a hand on David's shoulder in a familial gesture, he said, "Dobson's my name, it's a pleasure to meet you!"

David tensed slightly and pulled away from Dobson's hand, but got back on track. "We are looking for a very particular set of slaves."

Dobson nodded, thinking it over for a moment. "Well, I need to finish up some business here, but if you don't mind waiting a little while, I can get to you soon. The first fight should start in ten minutes, it will give you some entertainment while you wait."

"That will be fine," David said.

"Oh," Dobson added. "And, if you're going to bet on the

first match," he leaned in, almost whispering to David. "Wilkes is a choice pick."

"A choice pick... Thank you," David said, turning back toward the fighting pit.

Adelyn leaned back against the fence in frustration, kicking at the dusty ground. They were a pace or two away from someone who might know where her parents were, and they were watching an empty pit of dirt to kill time.

A noise came from across the pit, and she turned to watch the crowd thicken and buzz with excitement. Squinting, she needed a moment to spot what they were reacting to.

A woman dressed in light leather armor pushed her way through the crowd, nodding graciously to the clamoring mob, but otherwise seeming not to notice the noise as she descended the ramp. Adelyn could see she was carrying a short spear, but more surprising was the leather whip on her belt.

Reaching the end of the ramp, the woman spun around and raised a fist in a simple salute to the crowd, eliciting a cheer from the people.

"She's going to use a whip?" Adelyn asked, surprised. "Is that really an effective choice for a fight like this? I know that the White Death had one, but I had assumed they mostly had it to look intimidating."

"The White Death used their whip," David corrected darkly, lowering his eyes and speaking in a low tone. "None of the Thirteen really needed magic to kill you. A lot of the Stone Warriors used whips, too. A whip is a fine weapon, and nearly as good at disarming an opponent as a hook. But what this woman has is not a whip."

"What?" Adelyn asked, looking back at the fighter, who was now entering the fighting pit. The weapon was far away, but it was clearly a coil of leather with a flared bit of wire at the end. "I'm not an expert, but that's clearly a whip."

"Just watch," David said, not offering any further explanation.

The next bit of commotion came from behind them, and Adelyn turned from the fence to see a burly man carrying a short sword and matching buckler, though he wore no armor. He was holding his weapons in the air, pumping them up and down to work up the crowd.

Adelyn recognized him. He was the bounty hunter from that morning, who'd tried to shoot the runaway. He didn't notice Adelyn staring daggers at him, too focused on pumping up the crowd.

Nearby, a bookie with a canvas bag and paper tickets was shouting, "Place your bets! Place your bets! Fight in three minutes!"

"Are you going to bet?" David asked, with mild interest.

"No," Adelyn said. "I don't gamble, and I don't know who's going to win anyways."

"She is," David said, pointing at the woman in leather, who was now stretching out her arms and jogging in place while her opponent entered the pit at the other end.

"Good," Adelyn said, hoping to see the bounty hunter get his teeth knocked in. "Are you sure?"

David said again, confidently. "Trust me, she will win."

"Which one is 'Wilkes'?"

"I have no idea."

Adelyn didn't know one way or the other, so she didn't argue, watching as both fighters set their weapons on the ground, crossed to the center of the pit, and shook hands.

Returning to her weapons, the woman didn't rearm herself right away. Instead, she knelt in the dirt, taking a pen knife from a pocket in her armor and pricking her thumb, holding it up to the sky so that a thin trail of blood ran down her finger. With her other hand she pushed the pen knife into the dirt, snapping the blade in half, and then she held the broken handle of the knife next to her bleeding thumb, muttering something that Adelyn couldn't possibly hear over the crowd.

Adelyn grimaced slightly, annoyed by the public display of spirituality. To David, she asked, "Does she really think her 'gods' will help her win a blood sport like this?"

"I do not see why not," David said back. "I believe there is a god for combat. It only follows, since there seems to be one for everything else. I assume that is why she broke the knife."

"Sacrifices," Adelyn said, spitting out the word like an oath. The woman seemed to be done praying, at least, and she dropped the handle of the knife and took up her weapons, the not-whip going in her bloodied hand.

A horn blew. The fight began. Both fighters circled, warily, some forty feet away from each other and slowly closing. By the time they were anywhere near striking distance, the woman had crossed to the other side of the pit and her back was to Adelyn and David, and the bounty hunter could be clearly seen snarling as he watched for an opening.

The woman struck first, cracking her whip tentatively forward. In response, the bounty hunter raised his shield to block the attack and it struck off, harmlessly, but she jerked her arm around and struck again. The shield went up once more, but this time his block was a little off, and the end of the whip was able to wrap around the top of the shield. Adelyn thought nothing of it, until the woman threw her arm back, putting a lot of weight into the motion, and the buckler was wrenched from his grip.

Adelyn sat up at that, surprised. "What was that?" She asked, her voice drowned out by similar exclamations of excitement or disappointment from the crowd.

"I told you, it is not a whip!" David said casually, though at volume that Adelyn could hear over the clamor. Pointing, he told her, "Watch the handle!"

Adelyn watched, and though she had to squint, she saw the woman subtly adjusting her thumb away from what Adelyn had mistaken for a bit of decoration on the handle. There was a little marked piece of silver smeared in blood. A trigger.

"The weapon is powered?" Adelyn asked, the realization striking her. The blood from her prayer would provide plenty of spirit for the weapon.

"Yes!" David exclaimed. "It was too stiff to be a whip!"

Adelyn looked back at the fight, asking, "What else can it do?"

David shrugged. "I have no idea!"

Adelyn turned back to the fight, seeing that the hunter had retreated several paces as his opponent advanced, cutting off any chance of retrieving his shield.

The woman cracked her whip in the air, a loud distraction, then lunged forward with her spear, stabbing it in a powerful thrust. He dodged to the side, striking with his blade, but the attack was wide and only scraped her leather armor. The woman spun, yanking her whip around. There was no crack of leather, but the weapon wrapped around him like a coiling snake.

In horror, the bounty hunter looked down at the whip as the leather went rigid, locked around him like a belt. Before he could jerk away, the woman adjusted her grip on the handle of the whip slightly, and without warning he began convulsing in pain, sword falling to the ground.

"It can do *that*!" David added cheerfully, as the woman held up her short spear to her opponent's throat, letting the whip continue to shock him with bursts of pain.

"YIELD!" she roared, loud enough that Adelyn could hear over the clamoring crowd. The whip finally went slack around his waist, out of spirit and unable to keep up the attack.

Glowering from where he knelt, the man stayed silent, breathing heavily.

"She's good!" Adelyn shouted, feeling guilty at being entertained by the blood sport.

"I have seen better," David replied, shrugging.

A few more seconds went by as the man panted, leaning slightly away from the spear at his neck. The woman mouthed the word 'yield' again, quietly.

Rather than yield, though, he threw his arm up to push the spear away and rolled, pulling the whip from the woman's grip as he reached his shield, seizing it and getting to his feet. Adelyn expected him to use it for defense, but instead he threw the shield like a discus before his opponent could react, clipping her side. While she was off guard from this attack, the bounty hunter lunged, unarmed but with significant momentum.

The woman's reaction was as quick as his surprise escape had been, whipping the butt of her spear around and holding it out, striking her opponent in the chest like a battering ram. The back end of the spear didn't even budge as the full weight of the man crashed into it, throwing him to the ground, again panting for breath. Spinning the spear around, the woman held the pointy end of the spear against his neck, again shouting for him to yield.

There was no delay this time before the hunter rolled, barely avoiding the tip of the spear as the woman stabbed at him. He didn't even get to his feet, instead producing a knife from within his sleeve and jamming it into the woman's calf. She screamed in pain and staggered back, but was quick with her spear in spite of the pain, swinging it around and slapping away the knife in his hand.

She didn't go for submission this time. Her attack was fast and vicious, stabbing repeatedly before the bounty hunter could get out of her reach. He rolled out of the way of one attack, going for his sword, but her second thrust struck home. The tip of the spear sunk deep into the joint of his shoulder, making him cry out in pain. She moved in and struck with the butt of the spear, hitting him in the gut. Sure that he was downed for a moment, she limped over to his sword, trailing blood from the wound on her calf, the crowd almost silent as they watched everything play out.

Picking up the sword, she turned back to her downed opponent and jabbed down with the blade, putting his own sword through his good shoulder. He coughed something out, to which the woman responded quietly, and then he shouted it louder.

"I yield!" he screamed, and as soon as the words were spoken a horn blared.

Before the horn's call could stop echoing two people in white and red pushed through the crowd, running a stretcher down the dirt ramp, followed by a third figure in the same uniform. They dropped the stretcher by the bounty hunter, lifting him together. Two of them picked up the stretcher and ran off, carrying him away in the direction of the hospital. The third medic said something to the woman, and she shook her head.

They argued for a moment, then she accepted a roll of bandages and allowed the medic to assist her in limping out of the arena, in the opposite direction that the other medics had gone.

"That is why you try not to make yourself a target," David said. "It was unwise of him to keep fighting."

"You don't say?" Adelyn asked. David nodded. Staying silent for a moment, Adelyn decided to change the topic. "Should we go talk to Dobson?"

"Yes," David said, pushing away from the fence and turning to try and find him.

Dobson was a few yards away, speaking quietly to another man in black who was holding a short sword in one hand. Adelyn pushed through the crowd, letting David follow in the trail she blazed, reaching Dobson without jostling more than a couple people.

"And just remember, you're better off losing than being killed. Don't be an idiot," Dobson was saying.

"Okay, yes sir, got it," The man was saying, nodding repeatedly at everything Dobson said. "I'll do you proud."

"Excellent!" Dobson declared, smacking the man on the back genially. "Good luck out there!" then, he noticed David and turned to them, his smile broadening. "Didn't I say Wilkes was the pick? Didn't expect she'd have to get so brutal, but that's just the way, sometimes."

"You know how to pick them," David agreed. "I am surprised you are not upset that one of your bounty hunters was hurt, though."

Dobson shrugged, smiling. "My man, if I lost my temper whenever someone in my employ got hurt, I'd hardly have a handle to fly off of! Wilkes works for me too, y'see."

"That man," Adelyn asked, gesturing to the person Dobson had been advising. "Are you a trainer?"

"No, no," Dobson said, shaking his head. "Malcom's mine. I let them fight, to save up if they'd like to buy their freedom. I make money, they get good exercise, and if they get hurt too badly, well... the city needs power, eh?"

Adelyn tightened a fist slightly, and she noticed that David mimicked the motion. Dobson didn't seem to notice, showing no sign that he saw or cared.

"Right, that is fair," David said, nodding. "Is this a good time?"

"An excellent time," Dobson said. "Just a second. Sir!" Raising a finger, he called over one of the men collecting bets. "Twenty swords on Peters." The man scratched out some notes on a paper and handed it over, taking in exchange a jingling bag of bronze.

David cocked his head. "I thought Malcom was yours?"

"He is. He's terrible," Dobson explained. "And if he somehow wins, I get some of my money back from Malcom's winnings anyways. Now, you said you're looking for a particular type of worker? What do you need, then, special skills? Education? I'm sure I know someone who can help you, if I don't have what you need myself."

"Not exactly," David said. "There would have been a group of new slaves about two months ago, some forty or fifty people. We are trying to track them down."

"Oh," Dobson said, his bright demeanor fading. "I can't help you with that."

"You cannot help me with that? Why not?" David asked.

"'Cause I don't know where they went," Dobson explained. "I barely heard they existed. They weren't for sale. Besides, even if I knew who ended up acquiring them, you'd just go off and cause trouble with the people I do business with."

"We are not trying to cause trouble," David promised, as a horn blared in the background to signal the start of the next fight. "Just finding some missing people."

"Nothing I can do. It's just business, but I won't be sending you to stir up problems with my clientele." Dobson turned himself a bit so he could see the fighting pit, keeping an eye on the battle.

"We can pay you," David promised, having to talk over the crowd and the clang of swords in the background. "You are interested in business. This is business."

Dobson shook his head, keeping his eyes on the fight. "I don't think so. I'm not so easily bought." Then, shouting toward the pit, he called, "His left side is weaker!"

David considered it. "How about a wager? I will fight anyone you pick, and if I win you tell us. I am assuming you can pull some strings with the organizer to make that happen."

That caught his attention. "I'm friends with the man in charge. What do I get if you lose?"

"If I lose? Fifteen silver daggers," David promised. "That is three silver swords."

Adelyn blinked, looking at him in surprise. "David—"

"It is my fee," David whispered back. "If I lose, you will not owe a tack more."

Staring at him wide-eyed, Adelyn realized he was serious. It was a shot, however risky, at finding her parents, and it risked nothing for her unless David gave up the search once he lost.

Dobson looked David up and down, then frowned and looked back toward the fighting pit. "You look like a killer, and no man in his right mind would make that bet unless they were pretty damned sure they could win. No deal."

Feeling the opportunity slipping away, Adelyn jumped in before David could make a counter offer. "What if I did it? Same deal. I'll fight anyone."

"Adelyn?" David asked, startled. "What are you—"

"You've been training me," Adelyn cut him off. "I've got a shot at it, at least. Maybe not a good one, but we've got to try. If you're willing, that is," she added to Dobson.

Dobson took another second looking Adelyn up and down. "Do you really have the money?"

"It's in my pocket right now," Adelyn said. "We can get one of those men with the bags to write up a receipt and hold the money for us and everything. I'll need a sword."

"You can use Malcom's, assuming he doesn't break it in the next couple moments. Keep out of his reach!" he shouted, over toward the fighting pit. "Go get one of the bookies, I'll take that bet."

"Adelyn!" David said, urgently, not bothering to keep his voice low. "You cannot do this!"

"Yes, I can," Adelyn said, feeling the weight of the wooden runes hanging around her neck. "Trust me. I can do this."

"And if you cannot? This will not come from my fee—I will wager my money on myself, but I am not going to throw it away on a fool's errand."

"You'll be paid," Adelyn said, though she didn't know how she'd cover his fee and his expenses. David would have to be fine with her coming up just shy of what he was owed, it was all she had.

"You are going to lose this fight," David said, his words harsh. "You have hardly got six days of experience. There is no way you can win this under your own power."

"Then we are out of options." Adelyn looked David in the eye, hoping he would understand that she wasn't being immensely stupid with the bet. "I am doing this fight. You can't stop me."

"Then good luck," David said, not seeming to get it. "You *will* need it."

CHAPTER 11

The president's Law, being unset and unclear in many regards, must therefore come down to the judicial discretion of whatever law enforcement runs the land. It might be legal, for instance, to buy for yourself a slave in one city, then unlawful to use that slave in the next. Until official laws are announced by an agent of government, local rule must be obeyed in whatever way local men enforce it.

Because of this, ladies and gentlemen of the jury, I argue that you must acquit. Whatever acts my client may have committed, it was done in a land with no true law, and thus any enforcement of that law would be done as an act of vigilante justice, which is, of course, illegal.

- Transcript from the trial of Quincy Aaron, who murdered four people after losing a game of chance

DOBSON HAD to pull a couple of strings with the event organizer to slide her wager into the schedule, but with a little haggling and argument, he managed to get Adelyn on the roster between two larger bouts, explaining that the fight would be over quick and wouldn't interrupt the rest of the evening's schedule.

"Just remember, you will need to stay calm," David reminded Adelyn, waiting by the gate with her, drumming his fingers against the fence.

"I know," Adelyn said, moving through the forms he had shown her, to be as practiced as possible.

"And you know that you will not be as trained as they are. You cannot possibly beat them on raw skill," David continued. "I only showed you defensive stances, not how to fight back."

"I know," Adelyn repeated, nodding her head a bit as she raised the sword back to the basic defensive posture, looking down to check that her feet were properly positioned.

"And do not move so stiffly, you need to be quick on your feet," David told her.

"I know, David," Adelyn said, lowering the sword. "Don't worry so much. What will be, will be. My cause is the righteous one, and I'm sure the Lords will grant me luck."

David frowned. "You were mocking a fighter for their religion a moment earlier."

"They were fighting for money, and praying to a false god. I make no prayers, I just know that my cause is one which the Lords will smile upon." Adelyn raised her sword again, looking away from David as she returned to her warmup practice. "Have faith. I can do this."

"No, you cannot," David said, frowning. "This is not suicide, but it is damned close. You are throwing away your money and risking your life on a fool's errand."

Adelyn wanted to tell him she had a trick up her sleeve, that she had her magic to win the fight, but she was worried that someone might overhear and that the bet would be called off. "You have the ticket, right?" She asked, referring to the little receipt they'd had a bookie prepare, listing the terms of the bet in a curt shorthand.

"I have the ticket. In my pocket," David said. "But you might as well have given him your money now. You *cannot* win."

"Can't," Adelyn said, rolling her eyes as she moved the sword through the practiced block maneuver.

David frowned. "What?"

"Say 'can't'," Adelyn said.

"Can't," David said, puzzled.

"Okay, now say it without me telling you to," Adelyn said. "You never say 'can't,' you always say 'cannot'."

"I do not," David protested.

"You *don't,*" Adelyn smirked as she returned to her basic position.

David didn't respond for a few seconds, and when he did he said, "Your forms look good. Do your best. Do not let your defensive position waver, and keep the blade straight and steady."

"Thank you," Adelyn said.

She didn't want to use her magic. It was possible there would be backlash, maybe even serious trouble if she used it so publicly. David might get scared off, quit and run, but unless she got very lucky in the first few moments, Adelyn couldn't think of another alternative.

Dobson took that moment to walk over, looking smug. "This fight's almost over, and then you're up. Sure you don't want to back out, girl?"

"Call me Adelyn," Adelyn said, shaking her head as she continued her practice. "We've made our bets, we will keep to them."

"Of course, Adelyn," Dobson said. "Good luck in the pit, try not to get hurt too badly. This is Gabe's first real fight in a while, he's been trying to get back on the ticket for a month now, but nobody'd agreed to fight him."

"Why's that?" Adelyn asked.

"Last woman he fought, ended up in a shallow grave," Dobson said. "It was an accident, but still. I'm sure he'll go easier on you."

Adelyn swallowed on a suddenly dry throat. "I can do anything I want to win, right?" She asked, wanting to double check.

"Your weapons and armor have to be approved, but otherwise yes," Dobson said.

"And everything I'm wearing and using is fine, right?" Adelyn asked, lowering her sword.

Dobson nodded, chuckling. "I might recommend taking off your coat, but yes."

Adelyn considered, then shrugged off her coat, balling it up and handing the bundle to David, making sure that her little book of magic was thoroughly concealed. "Thanks," she said, feeling notably more limber.

"Don't mention it. You're wearing a necklace?" Dobson asked, nodding his head toward the twine around Adelyn's neck that held her little magic weapons. Their outlines were clearly visible underneath her cotton shirt, and it was clear they'd get in the way.

"Good luck charm," Adelyn lied. "I'm keeping it."

"If you insist."

A trumpet blared, signaling that the last fight was over and done with. Adelyn looked and saw that both fighters, while a little battered, were able to walk out without the aid of a medic. There was no reason to delay the next fight.

"Do your best," David said, reassuringly.

"Try not to die," Dobson added, less reassuringly.

Adelyn nodded, gripping her sword tightly as she

pushed open the gate and walked down the ramp into the pit. She could hear a couple bookies shouting out, "Special fight! Place your bets now!" She shut them out, focused on what was in front of her.

The sun had dipped almost below the horizon, casting long shadows across the spectators and leaving the fighting pit covered in shadow, only lit by the soft spirit lights ringing the arena.

The crowd's buzz dimmed as they saw her, wearing traveling clothes and holding a borrowed sword, tall for her age but clearly not fully matured. Looking around at the crowd, Adelyn felt her claustrophobia more intensely than ever, able to see people all around her, all watching, all staring. The abnormal lighting gave her a strange view. She knew she was being watched and could see many figures, but they were cast in darkness and she couldn't distinguish any individual in the throng.

From across the arena, her opponent entered. She'd caught a glimpse of him earlier, but this was her first chance to really see him. He wore white clothes and no armor, except a few pads on his shoulders and knees, and for weapons he carried a dueling hook in his left hand and a long hook in the right. Adelyn swallowed, her mouth feeling dry, unable to fake confidence.

Remembering the show she'd seen the other fighters put on, Adelyn turned to the crowd, raising up her sword and giving a cheer. It came out quieter and more feebly than she'd meant, a tentative, "Hey!" to the crowd, and it got none of the cheers she'd hoped for.

Setting down her sword, Adelyn walked to the center of the pit, watching her opponent to the same.

"I'm Adelyn," she said, shaking hands with the man. "Good fight?"

"Gabe," he said, "I'll try not to hurt you too bad. Shouldn't be difficult."

Adelyn pulled her hand away, walking back to her borrowed sword and picking it up from the dirt. Before she could even properly turn around, she heard the horn blare, and she had to scramble to spin, planting her feet and raising her sword in her basic defensive stance so she wouldn't be taken from behind.

Gabe didn't bother with subtlety, apparently not wanting to tire himself out with a long fight. He ran with both swords gripped tight and raised in the air, preparing for a wide attack that would come from both sides. Adelyn didn't know how to defend from that, she'd only practiced against David using one sword, never two. Fighting off the attack was inevitably going to fail, so she made a new plan.

She could duck, let him take the sword out of her grip, and hit him with all the magic she could muster. The runes didn't have to be in her hand, she could use them while they hung around her neck, so she kept the sword out, waiting until the last minute to duck away.

Gabe was twenty feet away, then fifteen feet, then ten, covering the distance in the time it took her to blink. Adelyn waited, hoping to catch him completely off guard when she struck back. Ten feet away. Six feet. Four feet. Adelyn got ready to duck away.

He tripped.

It wasn't a minor slip. His foot landed wrong, either too late or too soon and he totally lost his balance, eyes going wide in shock and arms going out to flail as he suddenly found himself falling forward with no control over his trajectory. He had the presence of mind not to drop his hooks, but they did him little good to regain his balance as both his feet came off the ground.

Adelyn didn't have any more chance to react than he did. She barely realized what was happening, and then her arm took a sudden jarring shock. Her practice paid off: She didn't drop her sword, keeping it raised and held still throughout the impact as Gabe, unable to help himself, fell on her sword.

The blade went clean through, entering somewhere below the ribcage and coming through just off the small of his back. He made a choking sound, dropping the hooks from his hand and looking down at the sword that was almost hilt-deep in his diaphragm. Adelyn looked at him in shock for several seconds, then let go of the sword and staggered back, screaming.

Gabe slumped to the ground, his expression not pained so much as confused, trying to figure out how the sword had ended up inside him. He looked up at Adelyn, then back down at the hilt of the sword, then slid onto his side, no longer looking at anything.

"Medic!" Adelyn shouted, looking around, trying to get someone's attention. The crowd had gone silent, confused and unsure how to react. "MEDIC!" Adelyn screamed again, trying to get someone to move.

A horn blared, finally, and the three people in white medic uniforms all but flew into the pit. One rushed to Gabe's side and kneeled next to him, the other two towing a clean stretcher. They carefully removed the sword and pressed some kind of white packing into the injury to slow the bleeding, carrying him carefully up on the stretcher and moving at the highest speed they safely could toward the far ramp.

The silence broke, finally, as a handful of men and women started to cheer. They weren't cheering for Adelyn, they were cheering that they had won. No doubt the odds against her were extravagant, and they'd just made bank. Judging by the rest of the crowd's murmurs of frustration and disgust, most of them hadn't gone with the long odds.

Adelyn staggered back, only then realizing that her clothes were covered in blood that was dripping down from her hands. Turning toward the gate, she walked in a daze toward the exit.

David reached Adelyn halfway down the ramp, taking her shoulder and speaking to her urgently. "Your sword," he said. "I was not paying attention. Was it bronze or steel?"

"I—" Adelyn had to think, startled by the question. She couldn't remember, her thoughts were shooting off in a thousand directions. "I don't know. I don't remember."

"Where is it?" David asked.

Again, Adelyn could barely focus on the question. The blood felt thick and syrupy on her hands, and the smell of iron was overwhelming her senses. "I—I think the medics took it with them."

"The medics took it with them. Are you sure?" David asked.

Adelyn paused, then nodded, confused. "Yeah. What—"

David didn't stick around for the rest of the question, sprinting past Adelyn and across the fighting pit, after the medics. Adelyn looked after him for a moment, then turned her back to the pit and continued her shuffle up the ramp, blood dripping down from her fingers as she pushed open the gate and walked out, looking around for any familiar face in the sea of people.

"You've either got the gods on your side, or the luck of a dozen seasiders," Dobson said from Adelyn's side, making her jump and spin to see him. He was annoyed, but didn't seem mad at her specifically. "But you won, gods damn it all, I can't deny that. I need to oversee some fights now and see to my men. Come and talk to me tomorrow, I'll give you what you deserve."

Adelyn frowned, briefly lost. A second passed before she even remembered what he was talking about. "Uh, yes, that sounds okay."

Dobson nodded, starting to give her a little rectangle of rigid paper, only then seeming to note the blood on her hands. "Oh, for the gods," he muttered, turning and shouting. "Can someone get this girl a towel?"

"Th-thank you," Adelyn said, looking around. "Is there somewhere I can sit and wait?"

"Over there, that bench should do," Dobson said, pointing. "Oh, and before I forget, your friend—David, was it? He gave me your things. You, eh, probably don't want them now, I'll send one of my people over with it once you're cleaned up. They'll give you my card, too," he added, holding up the paper rectangle.

Adelyn mumbled a thank you to that, then turned to walk to the bench.

Someone brought her a towel and a bucket of water, and she made a minor effort to wash off her arms. There was still blood splattered all across her clothes and even some on her face, but with her hands clean she felt a little better.

The crowd cheered, apparently enjoying another fight, one less unexpected and disappointing.

A man dressed in black brought over Adelyn's bundled up coat and handed it to her. She pulled it on, feeling immediately warmer and glad to have the familiar and comfortable weight of the coat around her.

Trumpets blew and people cheered at irregular intervals as the sun dipped lower and lower, the dusk sky growing gradually darker as it transitioned into a starry night.

Adelyn stayed on her bench, half hearing the clamor of

the crowd, staring at the dirt, focusing on nothing in particular.

The courtyard around the fighting pit was colder than it had been, but fires and torches and the warmth of the crowd kept the temperature from becoming frigid.

Sometime long after the sky had slipped solidly into night, the last of the fights ended with raucous cheering and excessive fanfare. The crowd, which had been growing thicker and thicker as the night went on, finally started to disperse, all but evaporating once people collected their money.

One of the bookies came by, holding a bag of jingling coins. "Your winnings," she said, giving her the bag.

The bag was surprisingly heavy, though Adelyn couldn't have guessed how much money was in there. "What?" she asked, unsure why she had it.

"Not many people thought you'd win. That's your cut of their bets," the bookie provided.

"O-oh," Adelyn said, tucking the bag into her coat. Her pockets felt awkwardly full, too many bags and books stuffed into too little space.

The bookie wandered away to handle other business, leaving her alone.

"He is going to live," a voice said, coming from Adelyn's right. She looked up to see David, looking tired.

"Hmm?" Adelyn asked, blinking once.

"The man. Gabriel. Doctors were able to stitch him up," David said. His voice sounded ragged and weak, like he'd done too much cheering in the crowd without giving his throat a rest. "If all goes well, he will recover without complications."

"I..." Adelyn didn't know what to say to that, but she felt

a sudden weight vanish from her shoulders that she hadn't noticed before. "Thank the Lords."

"Thank the surgeon," David said, sounding worn. "You must be tired."

Adelyn hadn't noticed until he said it, but she felt surprisingly weary once he asked. "I am."

"We should get to our room." David reached out his hand to help Adelyn up. He seemed to wobble a bit when she took it, somehow looking more tired than she felt, but Adelyn brushed it off.

They walked in silence, traversing the road far more quickly than they had when it was thick with people. The dirt roads felt strangely eerie in the night, barely lit, the buildings all hulking silhouettes that lacked distinction. A few people were out strolling drunkenly home, but even as they walked, more lights were extinguished and fewer people could be seen, until there was not a soul but them outside, walking wearily to their room.

Once to the back of the shop, David fumbled with the key, hands shaking as he tried to unlock the door. It took him three tries, eventually pushing it open, revealing a small room with two cots and a miniscule bathroom.

Adelyn immediately shrugged out of her jacket, using the sink to wash her face, her heels bumping against the toilet where she stood. Not caring about the extra cost, she said, "I'm taking a hot shower."

"Enjoy it," David said, locking the door to their room. "I am going to sleep, I will wash up in the morning." He collapsed onto the bed, and Adelyn heard him lightly snoring a second later.

The shower felt incredible, stripping away layers of blood and sweat, the heat suffusing her body with warmth, dissolving tension and stress and leaving her feeling clean and relaxed after the pressures of the day.

Dressing in clean clothes she'd bought the few days prior, she went to her bed, curled up beneath the covers, and slept.

CHAPTER 12

There are those who would say that what we do is futile, but to them I say,

I come with the might of righteous intent at my back, with all the fury of a man fighting for a better world.

This world has been broken by endless centuries of war and strife, but I know we can end it forever, uniting us all under one kingdom and ending the plague of conflict.

There lays a great struggle ahead of us all, but if we keep courage and strength, and do not falter on our mission, we can end the countless years of suffering.

We fight for humanity.

We fight for peace.

We fight for the sake of the continent.

And I know we can win.

- Excerpt from "To Prepare for War", Speeches and Quotations of President Lancaster

ADELYN AWOKE to the sound of running water and lifted her head, blinking a couple times as she looked around the room. The other cot was rumpled, with covers bunched and one pillow fallen to the ground. The bathroom door was shut, so Adelyn guessed that David was washing up.

Stretching and yawning as she sat up in bed and swung her legs over the side, Adelyn saw her coat bundled up on the ground and paused, glancing between the door and the bundle. Her little book of magic was in there, she didn't want David to see that. It looked like the bundle was where she left it, but a paranoid part of her started worrying that he'd go through her things the moment she let her guard down.

Tugging on her boots and lacing them up, Adelyn heard the water shut off in the bathroom and the subtle creaking of floorboards as David got out of the shower. She grabbed her coat off the ground, pulling her arms through the sleeves, making sure that the book was stuffed deep into a pocket before taking out the rectangular card she'd been given the night before.

Before she read the details written on the card, the door to the bathroom swung open and David walked out, wearing pants and a white, sleeveless undershirt, a silver chain around his neck. He was in the process of pulling on his left glove, and looked up in surprise to see that Adelyn was awake.

"Oh, you are up," David commented, standing awkwardly in the doorframe.

With a bit of surprise, Adelyn realized she'd never seen David's arms before, as they were always covered by long sleeves and gloves. Normally she'd not have noticed, but she was certain she would have remembered the tattoo on his left arm.

At first, Adelyn mistook the tattoo for an old burn scar. The points of ink were in such a tight pattern around his arm that it was hard to distinguish them as unique markings, and against his dark skin they were difficult to define. After a second of squinting Adelyn recognized the tattoo for what it was: Thousands of black dots, each no larger than a period, set in in rings running all the way up his arm from his wrist.

"Good morning," Adelyn smiled, getting to her feet.

"Good morning. How did you sleep?" David asked, hesitantly moving from the doorway and walking over to his bed, pulling on his right glove before retrieving the cotton shirt he usually wore from where it hung on the doorknob.

Adelyn considered the question, fiddling with the card in her hand. "I slept well enough," she said, shrugging.

"A long day often leads to good sleep," David commented, buttoning his shirt and stuffing the waist into his pants. "So did Dobson tell you anything last night?"

"We're supposed to go talk to him today," Adelyn said, holding out the business card with the address noted down on it. "I would have been too tired to remember anything last night."

David took the business card, scanning it briefly. "There is our morning plan, then," he said, tightening his belt with a dozen pouches into place. "Watchers be with us, he will have useful information and we can ride out by the afternoon and be back on the road."

"What's your tattoo mean?" Adelyn asked, curiosity getting the better of her.

David hesitated as he reached for a boot, deciding what to say. "I had it done during the war."

Adelyn tilted her head. "Was it a regimental thing? I know some soldiers got tattoos for the squad or regiment they were with, but yours seems way too large for that."

Rubbing his temple with middle and index fingers,

David closed his eyes and sighed. "Do not ask about my time in the war," he said, in a flat tone. "I have done all I can to put that time behind me."

Adelyn frowned, but didn't press the issue further. "So where did you go last night?" She asked, changing the subject. "Checking on Gabe couldn't have taken that long."

"I was busy," David said, leaning to resume pulling on his boots.

Her frown deepening, Adelyn said, "Busy with what? You were gone almost the whole evening."

David shook his head, leaving one boot unlaced as he sat up to make eye contact. "Do not press the issue, Adelyn."

Annoyance bubbled up, and Adelyn crossed her arms stubbornly. "I am paying you—"

"To help you find your family," David cut her off, standing suddenly. "Not for every second of my time. There was nothing I could have done to help track down any slavers last night, and unlike your family, I am not a slave. I do not have to wait on you every second of the day."

Adelyn clenched a fist, feeling an urge to knock him flat. "If you—

Again, David didn't let her finish. "Why are you doing this?"

"I just wanted to know where you disappeared to last night," Adelyn said. "But you're—"

"Not that," David said. "This whole affair. Hiring me. Crossing the length of the country and abandoning your farm."

Blinking, Adelyn had to think for a second to shift gears in her head. "To save my family," she said. "To bring them home."

"To bring them home? There were fifty or sixty people left in that little town you live in," David said, shaking his head. "Most of them probably lost people they cared for, and I am sure that some had more money than you, but you were the only one hiring mercenaries two months after the fact. You were the only one leaving home on a half-day's notice to chase after rumors with a man you do not know. Why?"

"I care about my family!" Adelyn said, almost shouting. "Is that so strange to you?"

"Yes!" David shot back with equal volume. He hesitated for a second, seeking for words in the middle of his retort, then stammered out, "Adelyn, you—we—*you* almost killed a man last night. He did not kidnap your family. He was guiltless, and last night he nearly died."

"I didn't mean for that to happen," Adelyn said, shaking her head.

"You did not mean for that to happen, so... what?" David asked. "You were going to skillfully disarm him with your expertise at swordplay?"

"No," Adelyn admitted, shaking her head. "But—"

"Or maybe you thought he would realize that you were fighting for a good cause, then he would just throw down his sword and let you win?"

"No!" Adelyn yelled.

David threw his hands out to his side, palms raised. "No? Then what? You've been throwing yourself into sword practice with a vengeance, Adelyn, but the only way you were winning the fight is if you got lucky or if you fought dirty. None of those options end without someone needing a medic."

Adelyn felt the weight of runes around her neck, and her fists tightened. "I could have done it," she said, almost under her breath.

"*NO!*" David shouted, taking a step forward toward

Adelyn. He couldn't exactly loom over her, they were of an equal height with each other, but he gave his best glare. "You could not have won without nearly killing him. You are kidding yourself if you think you stood a chance in that ring. No matter what you say, you are too weak to do this on your—"

Adelyn gave into temptation, throwing her fist forward to meet David's chin. It was a clumsy blow, and he slapped it away easily, blocking her attack almost out of reflex. He stepped back and raised his arms into a defensive pose, but Adelyn had no intention of even trying to follow up the attack.

David breathed heavily for a second before he lowered his arms, fingers drumming rapidly against the side of his leg. "You are going down a road that leads to the destruction of you and everyone you meet."

"Because I got in one fight?" Adelyn asked, throwing up her own arms in mock defeat. "Because I'm learning to defend myself? Because I want to see my parents and brother again?"

David didn't respond, watching Adelyn with an expression that she couldn't read. Frustration and...disappointment?

Adelyn took a deep breath, then said, "So that's it? You're done? I'll pay your expenses from the trip so far, but I want my sword back." She didn't want to go it alone, but if David was leaving, she would make the best of it. She had a solid lead, a sword and a little knowledge how to use it, she could make it alone from there.

"I will honor our agreement," David said, shaking his head as he pulled his legs close and began tying his bootlaces. "I am going to cease training you in the sword, as I fear what you might try and do if I were to continue. Do not ever try to strike me in earnest again."

Adelyn felt relief at that, but also apprehension. "If I do?" She asked, though she already knew the answer.

"If you do, I will assume you are trying to kill me, and I will respond appropriately," David said, his tone flat.

Swallowing, Adelyn nodded. "I am going to go check on the horses, then we can see about Dobson," she said, mostly as an excuse to leave the room.

"I will follow in a moment," David said, running a couple fingers through his shock of dark hair.

Adelyn retreated from the room, heart pounding. What had been a vague fear in the back of her mind was forcing its way forward, reminding her how foolish it was to go off on an adventure with a strange man she barely knew. She would be safe from David, as long as she was able to get in the first hit with a spell, but that only helped so much.

Breakfast was eaten from her bag of provisions. The biscuits were starting to get a little dry, but went down easily with water, and the jerky was jerky—it wouldn't be spoiling anytime soon.

Adelyn tipped the stable hand again when she retrieved her horses, on top of paying the rather generous sum for keeping the horses for one night. She hadn't lost all sense of her finances, but she'd looked through the bag of winnings from the night before, and the totality of the coins added up to almost an entire silver dagger's worth—a tidy sum. With that in mind, she felt okay with giving a little extra to the man, after she'd checked to make sure the things in her saddlebags were still as she'd left them.

Once David joined her, they rode out, passing rows of squat wooden buildings. David navigated by street signs, checking the card occasionally to confirm that they were headed in the right direction.

Before Adelyn could ask if they were lost, David reigned in his horse, stopping in front of one of the nigh identical buildings. Squat, wooden, built like a massive tinderbox, with nothing to distinguish it from dozens of identical buildings save for the numbers painted on the door. There was a doorman sitting on a heavy wooden box and with a heavy looking maul sitting next to him, apparently to keep out undesirables, though his beer belly and receding hairline made him less than an intimidating figure. A hitching post was by the door, so they left their horses tied up, tipped the doorman a few pins to watch them.

"Y'll have'ta leave your swords out here," the doorman said, nodding to the hook and saber, now a matched set hanging from David's belt.

David sighed but didn't argue, undoing his belt and sliding off the scabbard, leaving both in the doorman's guard and giving him an extra pin, as well as a stern look. The doorman moved the weapons into the box he sat on, locking it up, and smiled.

"All safe 'n sound," he said, patting the box as he sat back down atop it. "Welcome in."

The door led them into a small room with white walls, chairs against the wall, and a single woman sitting behind a desk, filling out some kind of paperwork that Adelyn didn't recognize. She looked up at the sound of the door, seeing the two of them walk in, and then lifted up another sheet of paper to check some notes.

"Adelyn and David, I assume?" She asked, looking from the paper to the two of them.

"That's us," Adelyn said, closing the door behind her.

The secretary nodded, gesturing to a couple chairs. "Wait a moment, if you will."

David sat down at one end, so Adelyn pointedly moved to the chair furthest from him, watching the secretary with some curiosity. There was some kind of metal box on her desk with four switches, and a pair of lights above each switch.

She flipped the switch from its middle setting up, then down, then down again, and so forth in a complicated pattern, moving the switch so quickly that Adelyn couldn't keep track of them or even begin to guess at what she was doing. Glancing sidelong at David, she realized he was subtly moving his lips and tapping out his middle and index fingers in time with the clicks, apparently counting the switches.

A moment later a response came, with the two lights above the switch flashing back and forth, and Adelyn finally realized she was watching a conversation, using the up-down switches as a code. She couldn't guess what they were saying, but apparently David knew, so she grudgingly got up from her seat and moved the four chairs down so she was next to him again.

"What are they saying?" She whispered, leaning in so that she wouldn't have to talk at volume.

David shook his head, focused on watching the switches and flashes, tracking the conversation. Adelyn pursed her lips, sitting back in her chair and waiting for the secretary to finish her communication.

A minute or so went by, and then the secretary pushed herself to her feet, stepping to open the door just behind her desk. She opened it, and Dobson stepped through, bearing a wide grin and open arms.

"Adelyn, David!" he said, extending both hands to shake.

Adelyn stood and accepted the greeting, but David refused, shaking his head and raising a palm to stop Dobson.

"What do you know?" David asked, standing.

"To the point, eh?" Dobson asked, his grin never faltering. "Well, well, I'll tell you once we're back in my office. If you'll follow me, this way!"

David nodded and Adelyn followed behind him, going in after Dobson, who led them into the factory proper. Yellow lines were painted on the wooden floor to denote where they were supposed to walk, an open pathway that cut straight through the factory floor.

Dozens if not hundreds of people were at work, hunched over tables or standing in front of large, whirring machinery. The gleam of brass and bronze twinkled throughout the building, accompanied by clinking metal and an oily, smoky odor.

"What do you make here?" Adelyn asked Dobson, glancing between the workers.

"Machine parts," Dobson explained, reciting the beginning of a speech that he seemed accustomed to giving, his voice loud and boisterous. "Most older factories don't have the tools or capacity to build the rune boards and other spirit technologies for modern equipment. We make the parts to order, ship them to factories around the city, and it goes into everything from farm equipment to communication lines. I have programmers and engravers working around the clock to keep up with demand."

"You have them," David said, his voice low. "You employ them?"

"I own them," Dobson corrected. "Some, 'till their sentence expires. I give them training to learn a trade, and once they're free, I often end up hiring them back on as paid workers. Best thing for everyone!"

As he said that, Adelyn finally took notice of the people stalking the factory floor, not working, simply watching the laborers. She hadn't noticed before, but they carried whips and cudgels on their belts, and seemed to be watching for even the tiniest hint of idleness among the slaves. David had his head low and eyes forward, apparently not interested in looking around the factory.

They passed by a row of processed silver ingots, stacked neatly on a low shelf. They were the size of coins, little square rectangles the size of her thumb stamped to look like the parapet of a castle. There were hundreds of them, a true fortune of metal. She'd known Dobson was wealthy, but here she was walking past what to her was an enormous fortune, set out on a shelf like scrap wood or old tools.

"Be on your guard," David whispered, leaning in close to Adelyn and jolting her away from the idle thoughts. "Earlier, he made sure to confirm that we had no weapons. We may need to run."

Adelyn looked to him, startled, but didn't respond. She was afraid she'd blurt out something rash and tip off Dobson, so she held her tongue, staying within the painted yellow line as they walked through the factory. She could see some things in a finished state as they reached the end of the floor—lamps, metallic panels that were used in generators, large brass orbs that most likely served as batteries.

Dobson's office was near the back of the factory, and as large as the facility was, that walk took most of ten minutes at a casual pace. Dobson tried to cajole conversation out of them, but David's responses remained terse and Adelyn was only slightly more forthcoming in responses. When they finally reached a wooden door with the name "Jacott Dobson" written on an engraved silver plate. Dobson swung open the door and walked inside, gesturing for them to follow.

"Let me do the negotiations," David whispered, before they went inside. "He may not take you seriously."

The office was a stark contrast from the cluttered and busy factory floor. A heavy oak desk sat in the middle of the room, Dobson moving to sit behind it. Behind him, a window with thin curtains let in some natural light, which was complemented by a glowing spirit lamp on his desk, and on the two side walls were a matched set of landscape paintings, one showing icy mountains and the other depicting a calm ocean vista.

Adelyn almost didn't notice the two guards flanking the doorway as she walked in, silently looming behind her and David. One closed the door behind them with a solid click-clack of the handle, leaving David and Adelyn alone with Dobson and his guards.

"Sit down," Dobson said, taking a stack of papers from his desk and tapping them so they formed a neat pile before sliding that pile into a drawer.

Adelyn waited for David to sit, then followed suit, setting her arms on the wooden rests and waiting.

"Now," Dobson said, asking a pointless question. "How can I help you?"

"We are here to retrieve the information you promised us," David said, pulling from his pocket a leather-bound notebook. "Tell me everything you know about the slaves you sold two months ago, and whom you sold them to."

Dobson hesitated, tapping a finger on his desktop. "What was your name again?"

"David Undertow," David said, frowning at the non sequitur.

"And yours?" Dobson asked, looking to Adelyn.

"How's this important?" Adelyn asked.

Dobson shrugged. "Humor me."

"Adelyn," She said. "Adelyn Mayweather."

Dobson grinned, turning back to David. "Well then, you see, Dave—do you mind if I call you Dave?"

"Call me David," David said, drumming his fingers on the armrest. "That is what I told you my name was."

"David, then," Dobson corrected. "There's a bit of a problem here, one that I'm sure any gentleman of business will understand, and—"

The creases grew deeper on David's forehead as he frowned, annoyed. "A problem here? Tell us what that problem is," he said, fingers drumming faster, forming a rhythm that beat out like a tiny set of drums.

Dobson shrugged, sitting back in his chair. "Well, if we're both being honest, I think you know what the problem is. Adelyn did not win that fight last night."

"What?" Adelyn demanded, cutting in before David could speak.

"It's true!" Dobson declared. "Nobody in their right mind would call that 'winning'. You got lucky, girl. There's no shame in that, but it's not like you fought off Gabe in earnest!"

Adelyn clenched her jaw, tightening her fist around the armrest of her chair to fight the growing desire to hit Dobson across the face, but David cut in before she could come up with a hot retort.

"If you do not tell us what we want, we will go to the proper authorities," David said, his voice remaining level, though he glanced his head from side to side, as though checking his surroundings for threats. Pulling his silver badge from a pocket, he raised it for Dobson to see. "I am a peace officer. I will turn you in as a criminal, and explain that you are breaking a contract. Whether she won through skill or luck, that does not matter."

Dobson laughed, leaning back further in his chair with a broad smirk. "And, what? You think the local constable will throw me in prison? Make me sweat in a cell 'till I talk? Please." Sitting forward and resting his elbows on his desk, he said, "At worst, I'd give them a few bronze swords as a 'fine' and get the whole thing dismissed."

David frowned, and Adelyn started worrying that he didn't know what to say. He did manage to come up with another retort, but even as he spoke it, Adelyn already knew it wouldn't work. "I will tell them you are an accomplice to the slavers we are tracking."

Dobson tapped his finger on the desk. "Slavery is legal," he said, shaking his head. "If these supposed slavers did anything criminal, I don't know about it. I do have a counter offer for you, though."

David stopped his hand on his armrest, tensing his body as though preparing for a fight. When he responded, his voice was flat, and the words came out one at a time in a slow rhythm. "What is your counter offer, Dobson?"

"I'll pay the value of the wager," Dobson said. "What was it, three silver swords? I'll count out that value and we can call it square. I don't care about your pocket change if it's going to cause me this much of a headache."

"That is not what we agreed on," David said. "Tell me what we need to know, now. You do not want to test me."

Dobson cleared his throat, and the two guards behind them shuffled forward from the shadows, looming more closely behind David and Adelyn's seats. "Please," Dobson said. "Let's not let this devolve into empty threats."

David looked like he was about to throw himself to his feet, glaring across the desk, but he restrained himself, grasping for words that would coerce Dobson into holding up his end of the bargain.

"David," Adelyn said, quickly, trying to establish an air of calm authority. She had an idea, but it was one that she needed his help for unless she got very lucky.

David hesitated, turning to her. "I have things under control," he said, resting back in his seat for the moment.

"We do not want this devolving to bloodshed," Adelyn said. "If things go wrong because of this negotiation, you'll still be paid." She would be able to afford it, if Dobson did pay the extra silver, but she didn't want silver. She wanted her family back, and her home restored.

David waited a second longer, then sank back into his seat fully, fingers resuming the rapid beat on his armrest.

Adelyn took a couple deep breaths, counting off, wanting to sound as confident as she possibly could. Pushing to her feet, she said, "May I have a moment to think about it?"

Dobson raised an eyebrow. "It's take it or leave it, girl. I'm sympathetic for you, but this is the only deal I'll offer."

Taking a step back, Adelyn glanced between the two guards, planning out her next move. Both were armed with cudgels and revolvers, and they had on leather work clothes that would help against most blows. She'd have to move quickly, take the gun from one and shoot the other, striking before they could respond.

"Fine," Adelyn said, not hiding her grin as she shot out her hand at the nearest guard's revolver, "I'm going to leave i—"

The guard grabbed her wrist easily, ready for the move, and twisted backward. Adelyn cried out in pain, and the guard drew his cudgel, ready to knock her down her should she get away.

David spun in his chair, but he couldn't twist fast enough to avoid the gun leveled at his head by the second guard. Fast as he might have been, he wouldn't be able to dodge a bullet at point blank range while in a sitting position.

"Ow!" Adelyn shouted, wincing as the guard twisted her wrist further back, eliciting shooting pains and twisting her body toward the ground. "Lords—Ow! Let me go!"

"She tried to shoot you, sir," the guard with a cudgel said, easily holding Adelyn down despite her straining efforts to get free. "What do we do?"

"Lock her up. The peace officer, too," Dobson said, his grin audible. "Let them stew a few days while we work out the sentence with a judge." He tutted, and Adelyn could see through watering eyes that he was shaking his head. "You should have taken my offer, girl."

Adelyn swallowed. She was done in a physical contest, but that's not the only tool she had at her disposal. This could still work.

Blinking back tears of pain, Adelyn began trying to think through what she'd have to do to cast a spell to escape this predicament.

David beat her to it.

CHAPTER 13

ROBERT: Simply put, ma'am, we can't beat them.

IRA: Can't, Robert? The scouts say that they barely have thirty-score men.

ROBERT: That may be true, but the Stone Warriors are brutal warriors, and they know their land. Our numbers can't be brought to bear in those mountains, and without that advantage, we are slaughtered every time we try and pass through. Without some way to predict where they'll be, it's simply not tenable to continue sending men into that pass. Maybe if we drew them out into a more open conflict—

IRA: They'd never fall for something like that. They are savages, not fools. How many troops have we lost thus far?

ROBERT: Fifteen thousand casualties, half of those dead. Another four thousand have fled or abandoned their posts. It may be time to consider abandoning the mountains for now. We can circumvent them, it'll take time, but we can do it if—

IRA: That's out of the question. Morale is already becoming an issue. If we have to retreat from the mountains and go on a thirty-day march just to get back to the front lines, we'll lose half our soldiers to desertion alone. We've got only one choice.

ROBERT: Ma'am?

IRA: We'll call in the Thirteen.

ROBERT: I'm not sure if that's wise.

IRA: The Thirteen are undefeated in battle. At a full ride, they can be here in a week. Our forces in the north can defend until their return.

ROBERT: That's not what I mean. The Stone Warriors have a wizard of their own. He's said to be unmatched. He's killed two other wizards that we know of—well, a witch and a wizard, rather—and he's been confirmed to have fought and killed a full squad of fifty men singlehandedly.

IRA: They're all said to be 'Unmatched' until someone else comes along and beats them. Even if he was a match for one of the Thirteen, which I doubt, he'll be fighting them as a group. Nobody would survive that fight, regardless of who they are.

ROBERT: Still, we all know how [Redacted] will—

IRA: The Blue Flame. Obey protocol, use their code titles.

ROBERT: The Blue Flame, then. You know how he will seek out challenges. If he tries to fight the Stone Warrior's man in single combat, he could die.

IRA: Very well. Send him and two others... Say, the Clear Cloak and Redshot, to clear out Beor Keep. It should be undefended, an easy fight for them. That'll keep him away from reckless challenges, and secure us a fortress as well. I don't care how good this Stone Warrior wizard is, he won't be walking away from this fight.

ROBERT: Yes, ma'am. I'll draft up the orders and send them.

- Classified transcript of a conversation between Commanding General Ira Johnson and General Adjutant Robert Carson, discussing the issue of the Stone Warriors

BEFORE ADELYN COULD EVEN CHANNEL power into the runes around her neck, David exploded from his chair, planting both his feet against the desk and kicking hard. He fell backward in his chair, rolling onto the ground in a perfect somersault.

As he landed and came to his feet, David waved his arms out frenetically, slapping against his chest and then bouncing up with palms raised as he shouted a word that Adelyn did not recognize.

Power thrummed out from him, so vibrant and alive that Adelyn could feel it from several steps away. Bolts of spirit, thrown like daggers.

The guard pulled the trigger on his gun, but it only clicked impotently. The spell struck him then, throwing out his feet from under him.

The standing guard abandoned holding Adelyn, trying to swing at David with his cudgel, but David deftly rolled to the side, then hit the guard with an open palm strike. The strike hit home in the guard's chest, and rather than merely staggering him, the guard went still as a statue and fell backward onto the ground.

The first guard tried to get up, but his heels seemed glued to the floor, and he couldn't sit up. Adelyn came to her senses and snatched the revolver away before he could grab it, but it seemed a token gesture now that both men were disabled.

"So," Adelyn said, looking around. "You're a sorcerer."

What else was he lying about? Her mind raced, trying to fit pieces together.

"Yes," David said, placing a hand on the conscious guard and whispering a word. The guard's eyes rolled back in his head, and he fell to the ground.

Something clicked in Adelyn's head. "You said there was a sorcerer who fought with the Stone Warriors... Lords, I'm stupid." *He's not just any bounty hunter, he's a killer. An enormous one, at that.* She felt hypocritical for judging him—wasn't she doing the same thing, hiding her power? Still... she'd had her reservations before, and now she trusted David even less.

Sighing and drumming his fingers, David said, "We can talk about this later. You are not stupid."

"Thanks," Adelyn said.

David shook his head. "But *this* was stupid."

Adelyn threw up her hands. "Didn't have much of a choice, he wasn't going to talk to us. Do you think more guards are coming?"

David shook his head. "We did not make a lot of noise, so it is unlikely anyone heard and called for a guard."

Dobson spluttered, finally catching up to the situation. "You killed my guards!"

"Not dead," David corrected. "Unconscious."

Adelyn pursed her lips. "When were you planning on telling me about your power?"

David shrugged, chest heaving as he caught his breath from the sudden exertion. "About my power? Never, if I could help it."

Something clicked into place, and Adelyn asked, "Gabe didn't just trip, did he?"

David shook his head.

Dobson sat up in his chair then, exclaiming, "Ha! You *did* cheat!"

Shrugging, David turned to face the slave owner. "Yes. Tell me what I want to know."

"Not gonna happen," Dobson said, leaning to the back of his seat as though he were trying to press away from the violence.

Adelyn raised the gun she'd confiscated, thinking she could threaten him. "I'll shoot you if you—"

"Adelyn, no," David said. Pausing, he added, "I jammed that gun, anyways."

Adelyn furrowed her brow. "If he doesn't want to tell us, we have to make him."

David exhaled, though he seemed to be showing the barest hint of a smile. "Information under duress is likely to be a lie. If he will not talk, he will not talk."

Dobson nodded emphatically, but Adelyn said, "What if we threaten to kill him?"

David was going to respond, but was cut off by the slaver. "That's not as scary as you might think. You're not the only wizard in this game."

David froze. "You have got a wizard in your retinue?"

Shaking his head, Dobson said, "The man you want. With the slaves. If I talk to you, he'll find out and I'm as good as dead anyhow."

"You are lying," David said.

Adelyn swallowed and chewed on her lip, but said, "He's not."

David spun to look at Adelyn. "Did you know this?"

Adelyn chewed her lip, deciding not to lie. "Yeah, I did. It didn't seem relevant."

Looking back to Dobson, David clenched a fist. "Who?"

Shaking his head, the slaver said, "Keep asking me questions, my answer isn't going to change."

"You're awfully cocky for someone we've got at the end of a knife," Adelyn commented.

Dobson shrugged. "He already said you're not gonna hurt me. Far as I'm concerned, situation hasn't changed."

Adelyn chewed her lip, thinking about the situation. Dobson really didn't seem as concerned as he should have. He was just patiently sitting, waiting, as though—

"Lords take me for a fool," she muttered. "David, he called for help."

David raised an eyebrow, then had the same realization Adelyn had just felt. "He called for help... the wire. He sent a message to his secretary." He thought about that for a moment, then added, "We should run."

Adelyn nodded, walking to the door. "I assume you don't mind fighting our way out?"

David hesitated, then reached out a hand. "Give me that gun."

Complying, Adelyn handed it over.

Hands moving smoothly, David popped out the cylinder, removing it from the revolver's housing completely and letting it fall to the floor. "I do not want you to shoot anyone," he said, tossing down the rest of the useless weapon.

"I'm supposed to be unarmed?" Adelyn asked.

David tapped his fingers against his leg, then crouched and picked up one of the cudgels from the ground, passing it to her.

"Thanks," Adelyn said, holding the club out.

"You are welcome," David replied. "Follow my lead. Stay low. I can shield us from bullets, but try not to make it too easy for them to hit you. Are you ready to run?"

She nodded, and he threw open the door. They ran.

Their boots pounded on the wooden floor as they ran down the painted yellow path. Adelyn took deep, quick breaths, the oily smell of the factory permeating her lungs as she worked to bring in air so she could keep running. The workers—The *slaves*—all around them barely reacted, a few looked up to see what was going on, but most kept their heads down, not willing to get involved.

The same could not be said for the foremen. One particularly brave soul—or, perhaps, one who hadn't been told of David's magic—stepped into their path, bracing himself like a wrestler ready to take a hit. His stance sank low, he raised his arms to the side, holding his cudgel in one hand, and waited.

David slammed into him like a charging bull, hitting with many times more force than should have been possible. The foreman pinwheeled as he was tossed to the side, slamming into a wide brass plate mounted to the factory floor.

They kept running. Adelyn didn't even have to slow her pace. Two of the foremen were more courageous than she had originally taken them for, though, because even after seeing David brush off the first man, they still seemed determined to try and stop the mad dash to the exit.

David didn't even bother striking them directly; he just waved his hand, barking a few words that Adelyn recognized as Sacrosanct, though she couldn't place their meaning. The foremen yelped in surprise, clutching at their face as they staggered back. One bumped into Adelyn as she continued running past, but they made no move to stop her.

Apparently, that was enough to put off anyone else who might try and stop them. Adelyn never even had to use her cudgel.

They made it across the factory in a couple minutes, unimpeded after the three foremen. David threw open the door into the small foyer, but as Adelyn skidded to a stop next to him, she put a hand on his.

David twisted his hand away sharply, almost barking out a spell on reflex—Adelyn could even feel the spirit in his glove.

So that's how he's doing it, she thought. He didn't have any visible tools of magic, but apparently his gloves were doing the trick.

"What?" He said, after calming himself.

"Only three people tried to stop us," Adelyn said. "They couldn't possibly take you on one at a time, so it follows…"

"So it follows," David said, nodding. "There is an ambush outside. I know."

"And you were just going to charge into that?" Adelyn asked.

David shrugged. "Sure."

Blinking, Adelyn said, "Uh…okay, then. Go ahead."

Throwing open the door into the foyer, David walked inside confidently. Nobody tried to stop him, and Adelyn followed behind, holding her cudgel warily. "What's the plan?"

"I go out there and disable anyone who tries to stop us," David said. "We take our weapons from the door guard. We leave. If we are lucky, nobody will follow us. If we are unlucky, we will have to evade pursuers."

Again, Adelyn couldn't really argue. He strolled to the door, firmly grasped the handle, and swung it open.

He slammed it shut immediately as gunfire roared outside like thunder. A few bits of wood splintered out from the far wall as shots made it past him, then bullets began hailing against the wooden door, creating popping sounds like hailstones against the wood. David's lips moved as he worked out a spell to keep the door from being blown into splinters, taking a deep breath as he did so.

Exhaling with a grin, David said, "There are a *lot* of them out there." Shutting his eyes, he counted in his head, then said, "Twenty-two of them."

"Do you need help?" Adelyn asked. "Or..."

David shook his head, reaching around his neck and pulling out the silver chain he wore there, revealing an interlocking set of silver rings hanging from the end. Letting the rings dangle from his hand, he said, "I have this under control. I cannot jam that many guns, but I can shield from the bullets. It will be fine. Once the gunfire stops, break open the box with our weapons, and get the horses ready."

"What if someone attacks me?" Adelyn asked.

Shrugging with a smile, David began spinning his hand, inscribing a silver circle in the air with the rings. "They will not have the opportunity."

The gunfire stopped, and David threw open the door.

Only one gunshot rang out, unsupported by the volley of fire that had rung out before.

The gunners were arranged in neat, practiced firing lines, though their armaments and clothes were not so organized as their stances. All were hastily reloading their weapons, but even the fastest hand wouldn't have been able to get a repeating rifle loaded fast enough, never mind a revolver. David leaped out the door, lips moving in a near-silent chant as he dove at the nearest opponent, feet barely touching the ground as he dove in for the attack.

The gunner dropped her rifle, going for the sword on her belt, but David was quicker. One hand kept the silver rings spinning in the air, but his other shot out, grabbing her wrist and twisting away.

Hand gliding, he pulled her sword away, holding it backward and slashing in time to block an attack from the side, twisting his new sword so that the blade went to the ground. A third attacker came from the side, but their feet were kicked out from beneath them as they approached, buying David time to parry the second assailant and then drive an elbow into the first.

Bullets started to fire out as guns were loaded, but they hit a spell and were diverted, kicking up clouds of dust and angry red flashes of light as the projectiles got near David. After a few moments, he was walled off by the guards or bounty hunters, whatever their title was.

A few noticed her standing in the doorway, but she made no move to attack, and so they paid her no mind. David was dodging and weaving like a hare between wolves, at least if the hare had a sword and the powers of the divine backing it up. One big man, wielding a short blade, managed to get behind him and swing, but David easily ducked the attack without looking, kicking his leg back and hitting the big man right on the knee, which bent that leg backward in a way it was never designed to go.

There was a clang of metal against metal a second later as David met swords with a duo of new opponents, parrying between the two of them and backing away. One managed to get their sword past his own, but when they did, the blade was diverted by the same angry red light that had blocked bullets. The sword's blade seemed to fare better than a bullet, and the attack almost struck home, but after having to push through the magical defense to get to David's exposed flesh, it was moving slowly enough that he could slap it away with his silver chain.

He stabbed with his sword, driving it into the thigh of

the attacker who'd almost hit him, then released his weapon and rolled to grab a new one from off the ground.

Invisible force struck both of his dueling partners and they staggered back, giving David the chance to scurry away yet again before he could be surrounded.

The brawl continued like a game of keep-away, David constantly backing away and dodging from the group, letting their bodies act as a shield to ensure that the band of attackers could never bring their force to bear against him, dodging those who did get close with unnerving reflexes. He'd lose one weapon in blocking an attack and not bother trying to retrieve it, going for a new one from one of the many people bleeding or unconscious on the ground.

He rarely struck back, but when he did, the blows were decisive. A younger lad, thinking he could get past the shield, rammed a loaded revolver a foot away from David's face and actually managed to pull the trigger before the weapon was slapped away. Like all the other shots, this one was diverted into the dirt, and David further twisted the gun back with the lad's finger still inside the trigger guard.

Outside of the defensive shield, and David's alarming ability to dodge attacks before they struck, there seemed to be little magic in use. Adelyn could feel the spirit buzzing in the air, but she only had the faintest idea what David was actually doing, and his chanting Sacrosanct words were so low and quick that she couldn't have made them out even if he hadn't been surrounded by a dozen active combatants.

Remembering she had a job to do, Adelyn glanced around for their horses. Thankfully, they hadn't been stolen; simply moved to a hitching post a few paces away, to be out of the firing line.

Crouching by the strongbox that their weapons had been stored in, she examined the lock. It was a heavy deadbolt, not something she could just kick open. Turning to look around for something to use, she saw that, to her alarm, the area had been picked clean of weapons.

A few stragglers in the fight had apparently seen fit to take up the swords and clubs that had been dropped and toss them as far away from the fight as they could manage, so that David couldn't keep picking up new weapons. Two combatants had pulled back, and were guarding the hoard of lost swords, holding rifles and watching. They didn't fire —they were as liable to hit a friend as a foe—but they were content to wait for an opportunity to shoot.

Looking back at the fight, she tried to take stock of the situation. Only six combatants were still left standing, but they'd finally managed to surround David. None attacked, and all stayed a few paces away, content to watch and wait for an opening, having learned their lesson about attacking recklessly.

David had stopped twirling his silver rings, holding his sword two-handed with the chain dangling around his wrist in case he needed it. He'd stopped chanting, and his chest was heaving up and down in heavy breaths as he watched the other fighters warily, though his mouth was still twisted in a toothy grin.

Adelyn puzzled at this for a moment. David was out of breath, clearly. Tired, even. Meanwhile, they seemed, well... perhaps not fresh, but at least energetic. Why weren't they attacking? The longer they waited, the longer he could catch his breath.

The realization came to Adelyn all at once, as she looked around to all the people he'd left on the ground. He had fought them all off, taken them out of the fight, but there was remarkably little blood, and many were starting to move. If any had been killed, they were in the minority.

Those with lighter injuries, or disabled by magic, were already starting to come around and collect their wits.

David didn't have time to collect his.

Adelyn felt the string around her neck, the crude runes she'd whittled hanging there. She couldn't use magic without tipping her hand, though. She'd have to help David another way, unless there was really no other option.

David seemed to hesitate as he came to the same realization she had, glancing at one of the people who had managed to sit up. His opponents took this as an opening, and a woman in black dove in for the attack. David ducked beneath her sword, spinning and retaliating with an elbow, sending the slaver staggering backward, and raised his blade up to ward off any further attacks.

His strike was solid, but not enhanced in any way by magic. The woman in black was thrown backward and sent tumbling to the ground, but it was only a second before she came into a defensive crouch and was back to her feet, scraped by the tumble but still in fighting condition.

David took advantage of the opening, lashing out and the next-most right warrior, striking hard, but he'd failed to take into account their weapon—the fighter was armed with a hook.

The man with the hook blocked and twisted their weapon in a disarming move, and while David could have normally pulled out without issue, he had to contend with five more assailants pressing their opportunity. They charged in, forcing David to release his blade so he could dodge backward, leaving him unarmed save for his chain.

Glancing around for a weapon and seeing nothing, David shouted, "Adelyn! I could use a weapon!"

Adelyn looked at the cudgel in her hand, deciding it couldn't hurt. "Here, use—"

Bullets rang out, and Adelyn felt fire explode in her arm. The two people guarding the cache of weapons had apparently decided she was a threat, and turned the guns on Adelyn. She dropped the cudgel, staggering back into the foyer and out of their line of fire.

Putting a hand to the upper part of her left arm, Adelyn felt her fingers come away wet with sticky blood. She could still move the limb, that was a good sign, but the pulses of agony and hot blood soaking her sleeve were nonetheless alarming.

Her vision turned red as she looked outside to see that someone new had joined the fray against David, taking the total number of active enemies up to seven—or nine, if the two with rifles were to be included.

Hissing at the pain in her arm, Adelyn stuck her head out the door, trying to glance at the enemies around the corner. Two more shots rang out, chipping the door frame inches above her head.

Ears ringing, Adelyn yelped and pulled her head back. "David!" she shouted back. "I can't help you!"

Unless...

She put a hand to the runes around her neck, realizing what she had to do. Heck, she even had plenty of spirit, she could do this.

Sitting down, Adelyn scooted on her butt toward the door, with her back toward the weapon box. Her head was low enough that she'd be behind cover, as long as she didn't sit up too much.

She hesitated. What was she going to do? Make a shield that would block bullets? Even if she had the power for that, she had never done something so strong and tangible, and if she screwed up, she'd get a couple more bullets right through her chest.

Could she hit them with force from that far away? She glanced again, receiving a loose shot in response. The bullet went wide, but reminded her what would happen if she stuck her head out for long.

Too far.

"Adelyn?" David called. She looked over at the melee, and noticed that he was looking at her, confusion visible in his expression. He didn't know she'd been shot. Furthermore, he needed her help.

What she needed was David's skill, so she could block the bullets and charge them.

One of his opponents charged, and David slapped away their attack with his silver chain, a flash of light indicating that he wasn't completely out of magic. His shirt was soaked with sweat and he was panting, though, and Adelyn didn't think she had long to help him.

In that case...

She scooted back inside, then got to her feet. Backing up a few paces, feeling more lightheaded than she expected, Adelyn built up a head of steam and started running.

"This is stupid, this is stupid," she mumbled to herself as she ran through the doorframe. Bullets fired the moment she was clear into the road, but it was clear that they hadn't expected her to come out at speed. If she ran straight toward them, she'd be an easy target that even the realm's worst marksman could hit, so she didn't run toward them.

Bending low to scoop up the cudgel off the ground with her good arm, Adelyn sprinted to the melee, where David was completely surrounded. She couldn't fight against a trained warrior, she probably couldn't even defend herself for more than a moment. She was losing strength fast, and could feel the blood dripping down her arm.

None of that mattered. Even the most incompetent fighter could still swing a club at an unaware target.

Her cudgel swung, held in a one-handed grip, and hit the nearest of the combatants with a satisfying CRACK. They fell forward, and before the group had time to react, she swung again, striking someone else on the side of their knee.

The joint bent sideways, and Adelyn almost felt sick as they went down, screaming. The rifles had stopped firing on her; she was clear of their line of fire for now, but there was a new problem: five remaining enemies, all of whom had better weapons than mere cudgels.

Or perhaps, she realized, those enemies weren't a problem. She'd created the opening that David needed, and he leaped forward, whipping the chain around the neck of one enemy, gripping both ends of the chain tight in one hand and twisting, digging the silver into his victim's neck.

The chain had did its work, and David dropped an unconscious opponent to the ground, twirling to Adelyn's side and blocking attacks from two of the three standing enemies.

"I need your blood," David said, as the two of them faced off the three enemies. "May I?"

Adelyn frowned at the comment. "What? Use it!"

David put a hand to her arm, and she winced in pain from the bloody wound there. There was a little tingle of spirit as David pulled it from her blood, converting life force to energy. That tingling faded and moved as he pulled the energy away, coalescing into a ball of force that he held in his left hand, which he jabbed forth, roaring out a pair of words that, for once, Adelyn recognized.

"Gild Shtap!"

The spell rushed out in force, but had Adelyn not been

able to feel the magic coalesce and take form, she'd have assumed that nothing happened.

David had made... a shield, but a perfectly form-fitting one that surrounded each of the three targets with a magical barrier that blocked all movement. They had enough room to twist their faces into expressions of shock and horror, but that was all.

Adelyn could tell it wouldn't last long; she could feel the spirit draining away into the surrounding air, and knew it wouldn't last more than a few moments.

Aware of this, David moved quickly, putting a hand to each trapped opponent, one by one, forcing his hand through the barrier and whispering a spell. As he touched each, their eyes rolled back in their head, and they seemed to slump against the magic forcing them to remain upright. All the while, David kept his victims between himself and the gunners, waiting until all three were out for the count before he started spinning his chain once again, giving it just enough speed to form a circle in the air while he walked out into the open.

Both gunners fired once, earning red flashes of spirit for their trouble, then hesitated.

"Drop your weapons!" David shouted, walking toward them.

They obeyed, and then took it upon themselves to turn and run as fast and far from him as they could.

Adelyn looked around, surveying the scene. David was the last man standing, and he hadn't taken a scratch. He looked exhausted, yes, but his sweat-soaked shirt hadn't even been torn in the melee. She realized that—since taking down the two fighters with her reckless charge—she'd just been standing there, slack jawed, thoughts a little hazy.

"Adelyn!" David shouted, spinning once he was certain

that the two former gunners weren't going to turn around and try to rejoin the battle. "Are you all right?"

Adelyn tried to wave in a casual way, to show that she could shrug off her injuries like any battle-hardened soldier would be able to. "I—*ow*," She hissed, feeling the stabbing pain in her arm resurge in time with her pulse. She was surprised that she wasn't blushing as she admitted defeat and called, "No!"

David picked up his pace, crossing to her side and taking a closer look at the injury. "Abandon me, Adelyn, I am sorry, this is my fault."

"You didn' shoot me," Adelyn pointed out. *Am I slurring? "Am I slurrin'?"* She asked, listening to her own voice. She felt dizzy.

"Damn," David said, looking at all the blood. *"Damn. I...hold still."*

Getting to his feet, David ran to their horses, some thirty feet away, digging furiously through the saddlebags until he found the linen cloth Adelyn had packed, the thread, and his knife.

Running back, he slid on his knees to a stop by her, hastily cutting a bandage. His hands hesitated before he took her arm, and he asked, "Can I remove your coat?"

Adelyn frowned, gritting her teeth. "Are you being *modest?"*

"Sorry," David said, hesitating briefly before he pulled away the coat and simply cutting off Adelyn's sleeve.

Upon seeing the injury, Adelyn nearly fainted. The bullet hadn't gone through the bone, but it had ripped out a chunk of flesh the size of a dagger coin from the side of her arm. David hissed as he saw it, ripping away a cut of the cloth and bundling it up. "Apply pressure," he said, placing the bandage over her injury.

Adelyn was having trouble thinking clearly. "Can't you, jus'... magic?"

"I am terrible with healing," David said. "The answer is yes, but not quickly, and only to the point of stabilizing the wound. We need to get out of town. Wait here."

He ran back to the horses, stopping to kick someone who was starting to sit up, then quickly led both Butler and Ace back to Adelyn.

"Try not to black out," David said, pulling Adelyn to her feet.

Adelyn nodded, her vision blurring as she got to her feet. David had to all but lift her into Butler's saddle, tightening a few straps so that she wouldn't have to do much to stay in place once she was seated. She just kept the bandage in place, letting David do this.

After stopping to break open the weapon locker and retrieve his hook and her father's cavalry saber, David leaped into his saddle, took Adelyn's reins and rode away.

CHAPTER 14

"We cannot stand for this injustice. Whatever the results, the actions taken by the so-called 'Thirteen' are unconscionable. Anyone, man or woman, who kills so indiscriminately, with such fervor, deserves punishment to the fullest extent of the law. But, in spite of this, our new president comes in, claiming to be a deliverer of peace and freedom for the world, yet he pardons these criminals and sends them on their way to continue their rampage without even the confines or excuses of a war to give their evil a purpose. If we allow them to roam free, mark my words, people will die."

- Quote taken from protest speech after President Lancaster's pardon of the Thirteen Wizards. Speaker unknown

ADELYN FOUND that the fight to stay conscious in the face of blood loss was less thrilling than the fight to defeat the army of corrupt slavers had been. She kept the bandage pressed against her arm as David led Butler, feeling blackness close in around her vision.

Thinking clearly was hard, but David had insisted that she stay awake. He seemed to know what he was doing, so she didn't argue, but...sleep sounded *really* nice. What was the problem again?

"David," she said, feeling lightheaded and dizzy from the constant motion of her horse. "I need to talk or something."

"Or something..." David mumbled, looking around. "We have still not even passed the edge of town. If we speak, we may not hear an ambush."

Adelyn wanted to rub at her eyes, but one hand wasn't responding well, and the other was busy holding a bandage in place. "It's that, or I think I'm gonna pass out, I'm having a hard time concentrating right now."

David swallowed, then nodded. "Okay, fine. What did you want to talk about?"

Shrugging her good shoulder, Adelyn said, "I dunno. Anything. Something. Why didn't you tell me you were a sorcerer?"

"It was not relevant," David said. "And people tend to be...shall we say, jumpy around those who have magic."

"Right, yeah," Adelyn said. "Why's the air flash like that when you block bullets?"

"Like what?" David asked, glancing side to side at the buildings flanking the road. Nobody else had come after them, yet, but that couldn't last forever.

"Flashy, red," Adelyn said. "Bullets don't do that when they hit stuff, so it's the magic, right?"

"Oh," David said. "Intimidation, mostly. I want people to know that I am deflecting their bullets. If I just reflected the projectiles into the ground without the flash, it would not look nearly so impressive."

Adelyn giggled. "You're showing off?"

"I am weakening the morale of my opponents," David said, glancing away from her so that she couldn't read his expression.

"Why not just bounce the bullets back at 'em?" Adelyn asked.

David paused, twiddling the reins between his fingers. "If I did that, then I may as well just carry a gun and shoot them myself. I do not kill, Adelyn."

"You *did*," Adelyn pointed out, frowning.

"I left everyone there alive," David said, "Assuming they get remotely adequate medical attention. Some were bleeding, but none had fatal injuries unless their doctor is a complete fool."

"No," Adelyn smirked as she thought of a joke. "I mean... in the war. You were a stone... *war*rior, right?"

David frowned at her, a mix of concern and frustration. "Yes, I killed people in the war, and then I swore never to do it again, along with swearing never to tell a lie or break a promise. I take those vows seriously. Adelyn, we need to stop."

"Why?" Adelyn asked, looking around. They were still in the city. That was bad, right?

"Why? Your face is as pale as a..." He grimaced, trying to think of a good metaphor. "A very, very pale thing. You are in no fit state to keep riding."

Adelyn shook her head in protest, and nearly fell off her horse as the dizziness caught up to her. Her vision darkened for a moment, and when it cleared, David was pulling them into an alleyway.

Hopping down from Butler, landing more heavily than Adelyn would have expected, David held up his arms. "Let me help you down."

Annoyed at the treatment, Adelyn started to climb

down, saying, "I'm not some kid for you to mollycoddle, I can—"

She slipped to the side, falling into David's waiting arms. Scowling, she stood and backed away.

"Drink something," David said, pulling her canteen away from Butler's saddle and passing it to her. "A lot of something." Taking his own canteen, he did the same, chugging half the supply before lowering the drink. Seeing that Adelyn still hadn't taken hers, he said, "Adelyn, you are dehydrated. Drink, please."

Begrudgingly, Adelyn obeyed, bending her injured arm so that she could drink without removing pressure from her wound.

"Let me take a look at that," David said, once she'd had a long drink of her own. She pulled away the bandage, and he inspected the bloody hole in her arm, careful not to touch or agitate the bullet hole. "I don't suppose you have the ball you were shot with?"

Adelyn shook her head. "Why's it matter?"

"If it was a solid lead ball, it is easier to heal than something with a steel jacket. If any flecks or shards of metal get left behind, it mucks with my magic." Frowning at the injury for a moment longer, he added, "Hold on a little longer. I think I have a spell that will help either way."

Returning to his horse for a moment, he dug through his saddlebags, retrieving a leather-bound journal. Flipping through the pages quickly, he landed on a set of pages decorated with intricate Sacrosanct patterns. Adelyn couldn't even begin to read it. She knew single runes, but this was a page of Sacrosanct written out with full syntax and grammar. A complicated spell if she'd ever seen one.

"That heals arms?" She asked, looking at it.

"It stops bleeding and heals surface tissue," David said.

"It will not undo your injury, but it will take away the immediate danger of blood loss. Hold still while I do this, I do not want to slip or make a mistake."

Adelyn made the connection a second later. "Did you heal Gabe?"

"Yes," David confirmed, nodding. "Hold still. I have to focus."

He performed the spell quickly, muttering words in a chant. Over half a minute, the stinging pain in her arm subsided to a dull ache, and she could feel the blood actively stop flowing from the wound.

"That's...wow," she said. The dizziness hadn't subsided, but she didn't feel as though she was being actively drained of strength, either.

David stared at her for half a minute, catching his breath. Finally, digging in the saddlebag, he pulled out a piece of dried beef and handed it to her. "Eat something. It will help recover your strength."

Adelyn accepted the food, but hesitated. "I'm sorry," she said. "I screwed up back there. If I hadn't been an idiot, I wouldn't have gotten shot."

David looked at her as though she'd sprouted a second head. "Adelyn, no. It was my fault, I was overconfident and did not plan for how they outmaneuvered me."

"I barely helped with two of 'em, and I got shot!" Adelyn said. "You fought the whole group without taking a scratch!"

"Yes," David sighed, "But I am a wizard. I did not expect the same from you."

Adelyn chewed her lip, wondering if he could have known that his words carried insult where comfort was intended. "David, I—"

Horns interrupted her, the same hunting call that they'd heard the day before.

"Damn," David said. "We have to go. If they come again, they will have steel armor."

Adelyn nodded, climbing back onto Butler, making sure she did it without assistance. She was still dizzy, but had a bit more strength after the spell and the food.

David led again, pulling her reins as they poked out of the alleyway, checking to ensure that there were no waiting enemies to ambush them before he took off at a gallop out of town.

Hands free from the task of steering, Adelyn held onto Butler's saddle, going along for the ride. She wasn't sure if she heard the howl of dogs yet, but the horn certainly sounded again, a clear reminder that they were being pursued.

They rode out past the last few buildings at speed, hoof-beats pounding out a beat on the ground.

"Can you cast a spell to throw them off our trail?" Adelyn asked. David shook his head, focused on the road. "Then what?"

"We have to stay ahead of them!" David shouted back.

Adelyn had guessed that, but it didn't seem the time for a smart comment. She wished she had a weapon—she could have grabbed one from the pile, but it was too late for that now.

The next time that the horns rang out, Adelyn realized they were coming from both sides of the road—the bounty hunters were flanking them. She held tighter to Butler.

"David!" she called, as they rode. "I need a weapon!"

David looked over his shoulder, then shook his head. Adelyn scowled, but there wasn't room for argument.

Sure, I only just saved your life in that fight, that's no reason to make sure I can defend myself.

She remembered the huge black mount that the bounty

hunter had used the day before, then looked at her own steed, trying to do the math. How far behind were the hunters? Would Butler be able to outrun those huge horses for long enough to escape?

Somewhere in the distance, a dog barked. Adelyn felt her heart sink—it wouldn't be the horses that did the trick, the dogs would catch them first.

David stayed focused on riding straight, and she tried to at least get her bearings. Maybe they were far enough ahead that they would lose the hunters. Based on the sun, they were riding west, parallel to the river, which meant that whoever was to their left couldn't get out to the side very far. If someone managed to beat their pace with them and ended up riding past to circle around for an ambush, she or David would at least notice.

If they came around from her right side, though, they could force her and David toward the river, where they'd be stuck. They'd have to fight their way out, against Lords know how many enemies.

If David had realized this, though, he showed no sign. In fact, he turned them toward the left, veering in the direction of the river.

"What are you doing?" Adelyn shouted. Was he planning to cross? That would just soak their saddlebags. River crossings were slow work, and by the time they crossed, the bounty hunters would be on their heels, and they could just do the same. Besides, Butler was hardly the most courageous of steeds—she could barely coax him to hop a two post fence. If there was gunfire and dogs, he might panic and drown before they made it across.

David again didn't answer, his head low, focused on navigation. He had to slow as they entered the woods, though the trees were spaced wide enough that they could keep up a clipped pace.

Another horn bellowed, this time a quick rally with three short staccato notes. There came another dog's howl, and she could swear that the sound had to be right behind them. It was only a matter of time until they were caught.

They came out into a clearing facing the river, and David didn't slow.

Again, Adelyn asked, "What's your plan? We're going to be caught, if—"

Throwing out his hand, David shouted out a chant of words, twisting his fingers in elaborate patterns to match. He kept his course straight, leading them directly toward the river.

Instead of sinking into the river, though, his horse just kept on riding straight. Hooves struck down over the water, but just before they would have kicked up a splash onto the riverbank, the hoof hit down onto air in a splash of red energy.

As she came in behind him, Adelyn felt the enormous well of spirit stretching out over the river, and realized what David had done.

"A bridge!" she shouted, pumping a fist in the air as she figured it out.

Butler did not understand, and reared up in shock and fear before the water. His reins slipped out of David's fingers, and Adelyn was nearly tossed from his back, having to grab at the saddle horn and hold tight.

"Adelyn?" David yelled. "I cannot hold this for long!"

Adelyn grabbed Butler's reins, trying to steer the stubborn horse forward. "Butler doesn't like the water!"

"Well *make* him like the water!" David shouted. "This—

is really—hard!" He grunted in exertion, forcing power into the bridge.

Again, she tried to coax Butler forward, but her horse couldn't understand that the water was safe. Without being able to see—

"Paint it!" Adelyn shouted.

Beads of sweat forming on his head, David asked, "Paint it—*what*?"

"He can't see!" Adelyn explained. "Tint the magic, so—"

David hissed a word and twisted his wrist before she could finish the explanation, turning his magic black. Adelyn could see the barrier now, stretching halfway across the river. The edges weren't sharp or crisp like she'd imagined, but instead seemed to fade and be wicked away wherever water splashed against it.

The outline of the bridge pulsed every couple seconds as David reinforced it with spirit, growing out a bit and solidifying against the water trying to pull away at it and dissolve the bridge, and Adelyn saw with every pulse that David seemed to wince away at the effort.

"Come on!" David shouted, turning to lead his horse across, no longer waiting for Adelyn.

Another horn rang out, this time with four sharp notes, and she complied. Butler seemed hesitant, but at least was willing to entertain the idea of placing a hoof on the black barrier. Once convinced that it wouldn't break under his step, Butler finally edged forward, trotting onto the magical bridge.

They made it across, and David released the magic, letting it fade out naturally. Turning, Adelyn watched in fascination as it dissolved into the water, like a long strip of sugar dissolved in hot water, eaten away in less time than it had taken to cross.

"That was amazing!" Adelyn said, grinning ear-to-ear as she turned back to him. "How did you do that?"

"Magic," David said.

"Well, yeah," Adelyn conceded, "But I thought that once you cast a spell, you couldn't keep it powered like that without casting it again. And that was some bully spell, it held up—what, that'd have to be three thousand pounds? I—"

"Are you a witch?" David's words were ragged and tired, but his voice cut through her exuberance like a knife.

Adelyn froze, looking at him. "What? Why—"

"You have runes around your neck," David continued. "Sacrosanct runes, for channeling power. I felt them when I was healing you."

"Those are just good luck charms," Adelyn said automatically. "I—How?"

"I am a wizard," David said, simply. "Are you a witch?"

Adelyn swallowed, turning to face David and stare him in the eye. He looked away, staring instead at the river. "I am not a witch," She said.

David drummed his fingers on his leg for a moment, considering. "Fine. I trust you. We should—" A twig snapped behind them and he spun in the saddle, hand raised in an immediate defensive posture. "Who is out there?"

A voice in the trees said several improper words, then shouted back. "We got you surrounded, wizard! Don't try and run!"

Adelyn frowned. The voice was vaguely familiar, though she couldn't place it. It was feminine, but had a rough quality to it.

"We should talk!" David shouted. "Come out, so I can see you."

"And kill me? Not likely!"

Arm lowering, David called, "Not likely... I did not kill a one of those bounty hunters outside Dobson's factory. I will not kill you either, nor do you any harm unless you bear arms against me first!"

There was a second's pause, and Adelyn whispered, "David, we don't have time for this. You bought us a little time, but not enough to—"

"Fine! Don't do anything quick!"

The bounty hunters came forward, slow and cautious. There were four of them in total, and none had the huge black mounts of the other bounty hunters.

One woman spoke, the one apparently in charge. "You two's under arrest."

"Under arrest..." David mused, reaching for a pocket. The bounty hunters all jumped, hands twitching over weapons, but David held up his free hand and moved slowly, pulling out a silver badge. "I am a peace officer. This girl and I are tracking down a group of bandits who attacked a town in the west."

"Sorry," The woman said, looking between the two of them. "But that's your problem. We're takin' y'all in."

Adelyn spotted heavy bandages wrapped over the woman's ankle and heel, and finally she remembered why she recognized the bounty hunter. "It's...Wilkes, right?" She asked, remembering the night before in the fighting pit.

The bounty hunter grinned, inadvertently showing off a gap in her teeth. "Lydia Wilkes. You saw me last night?"

Adelyn nodded. "How did you find us?"

"Figured y'all would have a trick up your sleeve," Lydia explained. "River crossin' seemed like just the thing."

David glanced between them. "Will you be willing to accept a bribe to let us go?"

Lydia shook her head. "Got a reputation to uphold. If'n it comes out I caught you and let you run off, I'll be out of a job."

Sighing, David said, "You have integrity. In that case, you should let us go, because we did nothing wrong."

Lydia just curled up her lip in an unimpressed expression, but one of the other bounty hunters seemed to hesitate at that.

David turned on her, sensing the opening. "What is your name?"

The woman paused, then said, "Riley. Mabel Riley."

"This is pointless," Lydia said. "We got you square. You're played out."

"Riley," David said, ignoring Lydia. "Look at the girl I am with. She is a year from even turning fourteen. She was upset, so she yelled at Dobson, and made up an idle threat to scare him. Do you really need to drag her to jail for that?"

"She don't look thirteen," The third person in their group, a man on Lydia's right, spat.

"She is big for her age, but she is still just a kid," David pleaded. "A kid who made a stupid decision. From one peace officer to another, please, let her go."

Lydia was about to object, but Riley cut him off. "I didn't come down here to hunt down kids," she said, directing her words toward the other three bounty hunters. "Did you?"

Pursing his lips, Lydia sighed. "Gods, I—Jake, you have that blindfold?"

Adelyn raised an eyebrow, watching from her spot several paces away. The man to the side of Lydia, apparently Jake, dug in a pocket and passed it over. Lydia took the strip of cloth and drew a knife from her belt, slicing the blindfold in half. Realizing it was a prayer, Adelyn rolled her eyes, but it seemed like the motion helped Lydia make up her mind.

"How much is the bribe?" She said to David, huffing and looking put out.

"Can I trust you not to turn on me the moment you have been paid?" David asked.

Lydia rolled her eyes. "I'm honest, don't you worry."

David nodded, opening one of the pouches on his belt. "Tell them," he said, "That we overpowered you, then rode south. If not..." He touched the coin he'd produced, intoning several words that Adelyn didn't recognize. Opening one eye again, he added, "You will regret it for the rest of your natural life."

He pulled his hand away, revealing a gold piece.

Adelyn stared, almost uncomprehending. David was carrying a gold piece. That was twenty five silver daggers, as much money as she'd ever seen in her life in one place, and he just had it in his pocket. She'd heard traders joke that the only use they had for gold pieces was as paperweights, since nobody could make change for that amount of money. It was enough money to buy a new year's seed crop, as much as Adelyn's whole savings, And David had it, *in his pocket.*

The bounty hunters apparently had a similar reaction. "I —" Lydia stammered.

"Gods be," Mabel whispered.

David looked at Lydia sternly. "Tell them."

"Uh-huh," Lydia nodded, not taking her eyes off the gold piece.

David dropped the coin in the dirt, then turned his horse. "Adelyn, let's go," he said, turning to ride. She followed, galloping until they were far enough past the bounty hunters to be out of sight, then slowing to a more sustainable pace.

"I'm fifteen, you know," Adelyn said, once they were slowed.

"I know. I said you were a year from turning fourteen," David pointed out. "Not which way. I was honest."

"You have a strange way of being honest."

David sighed, his voice sleepy. "But I am indeed honest, so it does not break my vows to never lie. Can you sleep in the saddle?"

"I...don't think so?" Adelyn said. "I've never tried."

"Shut your eyes and try to rest," David said. "Even if you do not sleep, it will help you keep your strength. We have to keep traveling through the night."

"Why?" Adelyn asked. "They sent everyone in the wrong direction, we're safe."

"Yes, for a moment," David looked over his shoulder, checking to ensure that the bounty hunters had kept their word. "But they'll eventually realize that they have been had, or at least think we have slipped their pursuit, and then they will come looking. We have to get far enough away that they will not catch up."

"Oh," Adelyn said. "Shouldn't you be the one to rest, then? You've got to be as tired as me."

David shook his head. "I am fine. I will lead your horse. Try and rest."

CHAPTER 15

(Author's Note) For Beginners:

This chapter is for the Witches and wizards reading this who are just beginning to develop their talent, and lack proper tutelage. If you are an experienced magi, looking to expand your knowledge, or if you are reading this book for academic reasons, you may skip past this footnote with no fear of missing anything of relevance.

For those of you still reading, I understand that many of you will want to use your powers as quickly as possible. For reasons which will become apparent as you grow in wisdom and experience, I cannot stress enough that this is a very bad idea. Without proper understanding of what you are doing, and the practice to execute it properly, you will almost inevitably end up causing harm to yourself and those around you.

However. I also understand that a good many of you wizards are eager to try things as soon as possible, and are thus going to ignore my warnings here. Therefore, I have provided a list of simple instructions and basic spells for you to use and follow so that your experimentations will not kill you.

Firstly, under no circumstances should you use anything

except your raw spirit to power your spells. Blood, while power-ful, is extremely temperamental. Even if you can control it, it can easily overfill your runes with power, causing damage and poten-tially starting fires. As for your other methods of power, under-stand that they are not only capable of causing permanent damage, but in fact will inevitably cause it.

Secondly, do not attempt to cast complicated spells. Stick to direct physical manipulation. Attempts at illusions, psychic communication, or whatever else you may want to try will result in failure, no matter what you think you can accomplish.

- Foreword, "Magic, a Wizard's Companion and History", by Joab Michelson

"WE NEED TO GET DOWN THERE," Adelyn found herself saying, urgently looking out the window, but she knew it was too late. The fire had already gotten too close, and when she turned around, she realized it had gotten inside.

Her brother? Where was—she blinked, realizing that she hadn't been in her house at all. She was at the bottom of a pit, surrounded by high walls on all sides, and the fire was approaching from there, growing closer by the second. She tried to find something to put it out with, but all she had with her was blood, leaking out from the dead man lying on the ground, a sword through his chest. The world was rocking under her, moving up and down in a rhythm, like the motion she felt riding Butler—

Adelyn started awake, opening her eyes to find herself in Butler's saddle. "How long was I asleep?"

"A couple minutes, at the most," David said. "Perhaps one."

"At least I managed to fall asleep at all," She noted.

Blinking sleepily, Adelyn looked around. The sun had

set an hour prior, something she remembered clearly. It was dark out, but the full moon and the thin clouds ensured that it was not impossible to see.

"How soon will we stop?" Adelyn asked. She could still hear the river running to their side, they'd been following it all day.

"Tomorrow evening," David said. He had deep bags under his eyes and seemed barely aware, but spoke with certainty. "Adelyn, I...I need to talk with you."

"What?" Adelyn asked, surprised. *What's wrong?* "What about?"

"Anything," David's expression was concealed by darkness, but he sounded sheepish. "Like earlier. To keep awake."

"Oh," Adelyn said, "Right. Eh...do you know what Azahim said when all of his waters dried up?"

David frowned, raising an eyebrow and glancing toward Adelyn. "I thought you looked down on those beliefs. Azahim is one of the Divinities, right?"

"The 'god of the oceans and seas'," Adelyn confirmed. "But it's a joke. I didn't convert in the past day."

Frown deepening, David said, "I have told you, I am bad with jokes."

"Sure, if you say so," Adelyn said. "Doesn't mean you can't enjoy them. So, what did Azahim say when his waters dried up?"

"When his waters dried up? I do not know," David said, looking back toward their course.

"I haven't a notion," Adelyn smirked. When David didn't laugh, she added, "An ocean. I haven't an ocean."

David nodded, and Adelyn thought she saw the hint of a smile. "I get it," he confirmed. "But if you plan on telling jokes all night, just know that you will have to explain them to me. Most people find that tedious."

"Sure," Adelyn said. "Maybe I'll steer away from the jokes, then." Staring up at the sky, Adelyn watched the stars as thin clouds passed under them, creating a twinkling pattern that flickered like points of light reflecting from smooth water or polished scales.

Without thinking about it, a question popped into her head and she spoke it aloud. "David, do you keep any faith?"

David froze, taking a second to collect himself. He apparently hadn't been expecting that topic change. "Why are you bringing this up now?"

"Curiosity," Adelyn said, still watching the stars, letting Butler do the steering. "I don't think you follow the "Divinities", but it never occurred to me to ask."

"No," David said, steering to the side of a fallen tree. "I do not believe in the Divinities."

Adelyn smiled. "So, what do you believe in? That doesn't answer my question."

David eyed her, then shrugged. "If you must know, I have faith in the Watchers."

Stifling a giggle and hoping that David couldn't see her smirk, Adelyn asked, "Really? I haven't seen you do any spooky soothsaying. And aren't you supposed to eat fish every day?"

David twisted the reins in his gloved fingers. "I did not bring up the discussion. If you are going to mock me, I—"

"No, I'm sorry," Adelyn said, catching herself. "I just haven't really heard anything, eh...reasonable, I guess, about you people."

Avoiding her gaze and drumming his fingers against his horse's neck David put together some words and spoke. "Us people? I take a less mystical approach than some other practitioners," he admitted, hesitantly continuing. "The thing about the fish is just a bit of slander. It is a common religion among sailors and coastal towns."

Raising an eyebrow, Adelyn asked, "So, if there's no candles and weird prayers, what *do* you...believe? Do?"

David sighed. "It is a way of life more than anything. The Watchers are stewards of this world, it is their job to shepherd us and keep life flowing. I try and live to a set of standards, so that I can...keep faith, I suppose."

"What, do you think they'll take away your powers if you're not all faithful?" Adelyn asked, trying to keep the question from sounding insulting.

Shaking his head, David said, "I doubt it."

"Why not? Don't you think—"

David cut her off before she could finish the question. "Yes, the Watchers choose certain individuals and grant them an implement of their power so that we mortals can use magic. However, if they were to take away my magic for any sins, they'd have done so already." They were both silent for a moment, and he asked, "So, how about you?"

"Hmm?" Adelyn asked, her mind still on the trail of magic and sorcery.

"Do you keep any religion?" David asked. "You definitely do not pray to the Divinities, I have seen you scowl when you see people make their sacrifices. I heard you mention your 'Lords', but that could refer to many things."

Adelyn hesitated, then decided it was only fair. "I'm Tarraganian," she explained.

David laughed, making no attempt to hide his mirth. "You believe we're all riding on the back of a giant dragon? And you were going to mock me for *my* faith?"

Scowling, Adelyn said, "It's not meant to be taken literally," she explained, reciting something she'd said a dozen times before. "The Dragon is symbolic, to represent the greatness of the planet. Besides, there's plenty of scientific evidence backing up much of the Twin Books of the Lords."

"The Twin Book of the Lords...the Lords being the brothers in charge of everything?" David asked, amusement clear in his tone. Adelyn nodded, and he shrugged. "Okay, you heard me out, so I will ask. To what evidence do you refer?"

Adelyn had to take a second to recall some of what she'd read. "Well, biological scientists—not even Tarraganian scientists, mind, so they weren't biased—have discovered tiny organisms living on the skin or scales of animals, so it's entirely logical to assume that we could be the tiny organisms living on the scales of some even greater organism. And geographers have determined that the entire planet is broken up into biomes like our own, each an approximately oval shape, like scales."

David shrugged, folding out his own bedroll. "Biomes like scales? Because they are...roundish? If you say so, but that argument seems a bit flimsy to me."

"It makes more sense than a bunch of inconsistent sadists in charge of keeping an eye on things," Adelyn shot, adjusting her position in the saddle.

"Sadists?" David asked, sounding less offended than curious.

"You said they pick who becomes a sorcerer or sorceress, right?" Adelyn asked.

"Yes, that is correct," David agreed.

"Then explain why they decided to back up the Thirteen," Adelyn said, trying not to sound as bitter as she felt. She knew David's beliefs had to be wrong, and he didn't know about her own magic, but it was still insulting to hear him imply that she'd been granted power by the same selection committee that had chosen a band of mass murderers.

David didn't respond for a while, staring up at the sky and twisting the reins between his fingers as he thought. "Would you kill someone to save your family?"

Adelyn thought about the question, gazing up at the stars before she answered. "It depends," she said. "Who?"

"Just some stranger. Someone with a weapon, who is trying to stop you from rescuing them." Adelyn couldn't see his face, but his voice sounded low and more tired than it had been a moment before.

"Yes," Adelyn decided, seeing where David was going. "But it's not the same. I wouldn't slaughter people like animals, I wouldn't—"

"How about to rescue everyone kidnapped?" David asked. "The whole town, your parents, your brother. You said it was fifty people or so, right? How many lives would you take?"

"I guess, less than fifty," Adelyn said. "But anyone trying to stop me would be bad people, it would be their own fault for getting in my way."

"Bad people. Okay. So, you kill forty people. Does forty sound reasonable?" Adelyn shrugged, and David continued. "Thirty, just to be totally fair. You kill them all, but it is all right, because you are saving more lives than you took, and the people you are fighting are evil for stopping you."

Adelyn frowned, unsure what to say to that. "Okay, sure. But the Thirteen didn't try to save lives, they just fought so that the 'president' could have more power over everyone."

"It is a metaphor," David interjected. "And every soldier, no matter who, thinks they are fighting for a just cause." He was briefly silent, then continued. "So you kill them. But, rather than the bad people breaking and running away, they come at you again, in greater numbers than before. This time it is forty people, forty people you did not know about before. Do you kill them?"

Adelyn didn't respond, not wanting to be trapped by her words.

"Let us say you do," David said, his back to Adelyn, tapping his fingers out against his leg as he spoke. "And, instead of finding your way clear, you find that you have rallied more enemies than ever to come and stop you. So you kill fifty people, and then you are too invested to back out, so you kill sixty more. But they are your enemies, and you are fighting to save lives, so it is alright."

"It isn't the same," Adelyn said, feeling exasperated. "How can you be defending them? The Thirteen were monsters, they—"

"I am not talking about the Thirteen, I'm talking about myself," David said. Adelyn could hear his breathing, heavier than it had been a moment earlier. "When the president's troops first marched through the mountains, the Stone Warriors...well, it was thought that, if the bloodshed was brutal and quick enough, the mountain pass would be left alone. But that never happened. Instead of scaring enemies away, more and more came. Soldiers would say, 'Mom, I'm off to slay the monsters in the mountains'. The bloodshed never ended, not until the Thirteen came and ended the fighting in the mountains for good."

He fell silent, and Adelyn tried to think of a response. "You did what you thought was best," she said. David didn't respond. "If the Thirteen hadn't come, you could have saved the Sovereignty and won the war."

"The fighting in the mountain pass was not for some greater cause," David said, his voice quiet, his body tense, almost frozen save for his hand, which was almost blurring as he drummed his fingers to a rapid beat. "No matter what we were told, no matter what you heard, it was so that the local king would not have to give up his land." Then, his voice nearly inaudible, he asked, "Do you know how many people I have killed?"

Adelyn shook her head subtly, but realized quickly that David probably couldn't see the gesture in the darkness. "No," she said.

"If I told you I had killed as many as any of the Thirteen, would you think me a monster?"

Adelyn had no response for a moment. "No."

David's body seemed to relax, but his voice remained quiet. "How can you condemn them without also condemning me?"

Adelyn had no words for him, so she stayed quiet, looking up at the stars and trying to ignore the nagging doubt in the back of her mind.

"David," She said, after a long silence. "What are we going to do? We didn't find what we needed."

He didn't respond. She knew he hadn't fallen asleep—he was still staring at the stars and tapping his fingers against his leg fast enough to sound like faint applause.

"David?" She asked again. He didn't react. "I'm sorry, I didn't mean to upset you."

He kept silent, and she gave up trying to coax a response from him. So long as he stayed awake, it was fine.

The night passed slowly, but the chill of the wind kept her alert through most of it. The weather had been a little warmer as they went north, but with the sun down and a cold river running not twenty paces away, that did little to help. Worse, her shirtsleeve was gone, and while the blood on her coat had at least dried, it was only a single layer to keep her warm.

"I do not know how to find your family," David said, after they'd ridden for an eternity in silence. "We can try again at another city, but I doubt that will succeed. Even if we find another slaver who worked with the people you want to find, they are likely to be sworn to just as much secrecy."

"Then what c-can we do?" Adelyn asked, teeth chattering as she responded.

David hesitated, glancing back at her. After several seconds, he asked, "Are you... all right?"

"C-cold," Adelyn said, shaking her head. "But I'm fine."

Slowing his horse, David said, "We should start a fire."

Adelyn shook her head again, more emphatically. "I'm f-fine."

"We are far ahead," David insisted, though his words came slowly, like he was having to focus on each one. "We can stop, start a fire, and...they would not follow us into the night, they would be just as tired as us."

Adelyn chewed her lip. "But are you sure?"

David nodded. "It is fine."

Adelyn nodded. She was intensely tired, and David seemed more weary than even she felt. Maybe he could rest a bit, while she warmed up.

Looking back toward her, David almost drove his horse straight into a tree—it was the mount, not the rider, that steered out of the way.

"The horses need to rest, right?" She asked, blinking. Why hadn't she thought of that before?

"... Right," David said, stopping.

Smirking, Adelyn asked, "How were you planning on staying awake until the evening?"

David watched ahead of him. There were a few sparse

trees, but they were few enough that he could see to the horizon. "I can... push through. I am fine."

Adelyn laughed. "And I'm not c-cold."

David stopped. "Fine. We are stopping."

Adelyn nodded, slowing Butler to a standstill.

David slipped down from his mount, looking around the area. "Gather some wood, and I will start the fire."

Chewing her lip, Adelyn looked around, trying to determine where she was supposed to gather the firewood from. There weren't enough trees around that she could just pick up fallen branches. The woods were thicker across the river, but that wasn't a help to her at the moment.

She walked back to the tree David had almost walked into, looking around for anything she could scavenge. There were a few twigs, which she gathered, trying to guess if they'd burn for thirty seconds, or if they'd last a full minute before being consumed in flame.

Walking back, she found David asleep on the ground, lying on his side. He hadn't even taken off his boots.

Adelyn pursed her lips, then dropped the sticks, walking to her saddlebag so she could find a clean shirt.

She braced against the cold as she removed her jacket, but pulled the second shirt over the first rather than replacing it. She was glad for once that the fit was loose and baggy, it slid over her old shirt nicely.

Yawning, she took a biscuit from the bag of provisions, chewing on it lethargically. David probably had the right idea, but she wanted to stay awake in case their pursuers had actually stayed on their heels through the night. It wasn't her first sleepless night.

Her paranoia payed off not ten minutes later. She had been watching the way they came, but seeing nothing, gave up and decided to look for more firewood.

As she turned and looked around, she spotted a point of light on the horizon. It moved and flickered, the light resembling a tiny flickering candle...

Or a torch.

"Dammit," Adelyn said, running back to where David slept. She didn't bother with subtle methods, grabbing his arm and tugging to wake him.

David's eyes flew open, and she saw panic in his eyes for a moment before he recognized her and the shock passed back into exhaustion. "Adelyn," he mumbled, sleepily. "Did I fall asleep?"

"Someone's coming," Adelyn said. "They found us."

David furrowed his brow, sitting up and looking around. He saw the torchlight and squinted at it, trying to make out the definition. Once he came to the same conclusion she had, he sat up, anxious and alert.

"I..." He said, mouth opening and closing as he looked for words. "I cannot fight them."

"So we run," Adelyn said. "Can you make a bridge again?"

David shook his head.

"Then—" Adelyn said.

"You have to run," David said. "Let them take me. I will be fine."

Adelyn shook her head. "I need you."

"You need me," David repeated. "I will be no good to you if we are both in a cell. Better you stay free."

"But—"

"No."

Adelyn looked back up at the torchlight. It was getting closer.

"Where?"

"Across the river." David sat up. "You will have to

swim it."

Adelyn blanched. "It's freezing, I can't—"

David shook his head. "No choice. That or you will be caught."

Adelyn sucked in a breath, looking back at the river.

David ran to his horse, yanking off one of the saddlebags and carrying it to her. "Take this. Keep it dry. *Do not* let anyone get it. Burn it before you let anyone read it."

Looking at the bag with a twinge of apprehension, Adelyn accepted it.

"Get dry as soon as you are safe," David responded, helping her load the bag onto Butler's saddle.

She climbed onto the saddle next, looking down at him. "David—"

"Wait," David cut her off. He put his hand around his neck, retrieving the silver chain that he wore. "Keep this safe as well. Go. They are getting closer."

Adelyn took the chain, holding it over his saddlebag and letting the links of silver slip through her fingers. "Good luck," She said, turning toward the river. It was moving fast, and Butler nickered as she steered him toward it.

David watched her go for a second, before turning away to get ready for...something. Adelyn couldn't watch what he was doing, busy with coaxing Butler into the water.

"Come on," she whispered to her horse, rubbing his neck. "It's not far, we just need to cross."

Butler refused, stopping at the riverbank and refusing to go forward. She spurred him onward with her heel, but lacking actual spurs, the gesture was not as effective as she'd have liked.

She hopped down from the saddle, taking the lead and trying to pull Butler forward, but he still refused. The water lapped at her heels in the attempt, soaking her socks with frigid water. "Come... on!" she grunted, tugging fruitlessly at the animal's reins.

Swearing, she let go, letting Butler take a few steps backward from the water. Running to her side, she pulled at the straps, taking down David's bag. She couldn't swim, but the water didn't look that deep, she could just make it across, right?

Pulling the bag's strap over her shoulder, she sucked in a breath and jumped into the water.

It was *cold*. So cold that the breath was sapped from her lungs in a second, and she had to gasp, getting a mouthful of water for her trouble. The river was deeper than it looked. She felt her feet touch dirt, but only after her head was underwater.

Kicking, she pushed her head above the water, trying to breathe, but she only got a tiny bit of air before she was pulled under again.

The bag filled with water, pulling her downstream and forcing her deeper under the surface. She flailed her arms, but that provided no force.

Magic?

It was her only hope. She was tired and weak, but forced energy into the runes around her neck, thinking of a spell that would throw her forward in the water.

Two problems presented themselves. First, the spirit in the runes vanished almost as quickly as she could fill them, yanked away by the water rushing past.

Second...she couldn't speak. Her mouth was full of water, and she couldn't keep her head above the river long enough to choke out any words of power. No spells would be coming to her aid.

Her vision showed only darkness, with the tiniest highlights of white flicking in and out from the foam from atop the river. The moonlight did nothing to help her navigate by. She kicked her legs and flailed, feeling her thoughts cloud and grow fuzzy.

Hitting the riverbank, Adelyn grabbed at dirt, fingers clawing frantically to try and pull herself to safety. Finally able to suck in a long breath of air, she began coughing, lungs trying to force out the water she'd inhaled.

Feet looking for purchase, she found a rock beneath the water and used it to push herself up, crawling onto the river-bank. She wasn't totally certain which side of the river she'd ended up on, but at the moment, she was just happy to be back on land.

David's saddlebag was still over her shoulder, and though her clothes felt like ice, she wasn't dead. She wanted to shut her eyes and sleep, but part of her realized that was a bad idea.

Still...maybe just for a moment.

She shut her eyes, taking a deep breath, Adelyn gave herself a moment to sleep.

CHAPTER 16

A Captain and a Clergyman were arguing at the top of a hill, overlooking a great battle. They had found a spy from the enemy army while the battle raged and were trying to decide who deserved to take the captive spy as a slave.

The Captain said, "I serve and fight for a noble leader, and will work this slave for all of his days to build great machines of war, so that we may slay our enemies in battle."

But, the Clergyman said, "I serve and fight for the gods themselves. I will work this slave both night and day in service of holy works."

And, as the battle raged on, neither could come to an agreement. Finally, the spy spoke.

"Why not a contest?" he asked. "You both seem to have a just claim. So, why don't you go into battle, and whoever kills more soldiers will have the more noble claim?"

Both the Captain and the Clergyman found this agreeable.

So, the Captain raised his sword, charging down the hill toward the enemy masses, cheering, "FOR THE KINGDOM!"

The Clergyman, not to be outdone, raised his own sword and charged after him, cheering, "FOR THE GODS!"

The two men both slew a great number of foes, and by the end of the day, the battle was won. They found one another after the battle and both began to brag, proclaiming their exploits and victories. They could not agree on who had the greater claim, though, and so the Clergyman suggested that they again ask for the spy's opinion.

When they returned to the top of the hill to ask, though, they found that the spy had taken their horses and gone home.

- Taken from a collection of jokes written in a private collection

"ADELYN. *Get up. The barn's on fire, you have to—*"

Her eyes shot open and Adelyn sat up in alarm, looking around, the brief nightmare making her momentarily forget where she was.

A gentle breeze made her shiver, and now that she'd started to move the desire to sleep was light enough that she could shake it off. She had to get dry, and warm, or the cold would kill her more surely than any bullet.

Looking around, she was glad to see that she'd made it across the river after all. The trees were thicker here, and she'd made it away from whomever was riding toward them.

Standing, she felt the bag around her waist start to grow lighter as water trickled out. Looking around, she couldn't tell how far downstream she'd been washed, but she knew it couldn't be more than twenty or thirty paces—the river wasn't flowing fast enough to have carried her further.

The torch flickering in the distance was much closer, almost to the point where she could make out the people carrying it. She stepped away from the riverbank then crept upstream, trying to watch and see what David was doing.

Wrapping her arms around her body to try and keep warm, Adelyn had to remind herself that she couldn't start a fire without giving away her position. She didn't want to flee into the woods until she was sure that David had been captured. It was still possible, he could be preparing an ambush, planning on fighting off whomever it was with the torch, even—

David was asleep. She spotted his body slumped on the ground in the fetal position, snoring slightly. Adelyn bit her lip, disappointment overwhelming her hope.

It could still be a trick? Luring them into a false sense of security?

She doubted that. Backing a few steps further into the trees to stay out of sight, she watched the torch get closer, and soon was able to spot the half dozen riders following the firelight.

"Hold up!" one of them shouted, and by squinting Adelyn was able to make out that he was pointing. "Over there!"

They circled around, spreading out in case their quarry made a break for it. Moving in in a half circle, they pulled around David.

"Is that him?" Another of the riders asked, the one holding the torch. He was the only one Adelyn could make out distinctly, with a cleanly trimmed beard and an ugly old scar on his forehead that was easy to spot even from so far away.

"Fits the description," the first said. "Where's the girl?"

A third rider piped up, voice sneering. "Who cares? The reward is for the wizard."

The first rider responded, a sneer in his tone. "We could be sure he's the right man."

"Why's he still sleeping?" A fourth rider asked.

"Must be tired. Let's hope he stays that way, it's a long way back to Petra and I don't want him struggling."

Petra, Adelyn thought, watching. *They're going to Petra.*

A pair of riders hopped down, their forms little more than silhouettes in the night as they approached David. One held a length of rope, the other a waterskin.

"How're you gonna spend your cut?" The one with the rope asked, as they looked down on David.

"Shut up and get him tied!" The rider with the scar called. "We don't get paid until the wizard picks him up."

Adelyn gasped, clasping a hand over her mouth a second later.

One of the riders looked her way, facing the tree line. "Did y'all hear that?"

Another shrugged. "Just the river."

"Give me that torch," The rider said, still looking at the tree line.

Adelyn scrambled backward, heading further into the woods.

The wizard.

Either it was a lordly coincidence, or they knew who had attacked her city.

Someone held up the torch in the direction of the tree line and Adelyn froze, holding her breath and hoping she'd not be seen. She couldn't see their eyes, only their forms, so if they spotted her—

"You're paranoid. Nobody's out here but us."

"What if it's the girl?"

"Abandon the damned girl. What's she going to do, throw rocks at us?"

They pulled the torch away, and Adelyn turned, hurrying into the woods. At first, she tried to creep slowly, but then started running, stumbling occasionally as she hurried deeper into the trees. She tripped and fell once, but caught herself, scrambling back up and running.

Despite the windchill, the running felt good. The ache from her wound was numbed by the cold, and the motion brought life back to her legs and her pounding heart warmed her a little.

It was unclear how long she ran for before her adrenaline finally gave out. Stumbling against a tree and panting, she looked around.

She couldn't see the torchlight, nor anything else. That had to mean she was safe, right?

Gathering firewood took only a moment, but that moment of calm gave her time to think.

She had left behind all of her supplies. Her saddlebags, and with them, her provisions, her saber, her books.

More than any of that, though, she had lost Butler. The horse had been a gift from her father, and she'd raised him from a foal. It felt like a piece of herself had gone missing, and she had to take a couple deep breaths as she worked to keep tears from welling in her eyes. Now, more than ever, she was truly on her own.

Trying to calm herself, she considered that the bounty hunters—or whoever they had been—would probably take Butler with them. If she rescued David, she would rescue Butler as well. It was just further incentive to find them.

Once she had enough firewood, she used a spell to light it. It caught right away, and she sat dangerously close to the flames, letting them warm her wet clothes. Her frozen fingers felt like they began to thaw, and she finally took the time to process her situation.

They knew a wizard. Hope wasn't gone. She just had to make it to Petra, rescue David, and find out from those riders where her parents were. It wouldn't be hard to find someone with that forehead scar, right?

Opening David's bag, she sorted through the contents, cringing as she looked through. There was a change of clothes, a knife made of royal steel that rippled in the firelight, a bag of coins, and...

"Damn," Adelyn said. The rest of the bag was full of books, with not a scrap of food to be seen.

Pulling them out, she flipped through each. Two were paperback novels, printed on cheap, pulpy material. The writing on the covers was still legible, but the words inside had bled to the point of unreadability.

Looking at the cover, Adelyn read, "The Adventures of Billy Ross?" It was an adventure serial—the cover helpfully had 'Book 6' written on the bottom—about a boy with a magic sword. It wasn't exactly high literature, to say the least. Setting the novel aside, she looked at the other paperback, which was another novel—some kind of pulp mystery that she didn't recognize. Neither were too valuable, and would be easy to replace.

The other two books were more interesting. They were journals, but much better assembled than the flimsy paperbacks. The first Adelyn opened had words inked by a pen, and they'd survived the river well enough to be read, though the wet pages stuck together and one ripped as she turned it a bit too forcefully.

Reading the first page, Adelyn frowned in confusion. It was a neat, easily legible cursive scrawl, and above many letters and words there were specific pronunciation guides written in the margins. The words themselves were not confusing, but the content itself was.

She read the passage twice before speaking aloud. "A joke?" She asked to nobody. Glancing at it again, she added,

"A *bad* joke." It was a short bit about a Captain and a Clergyman arguing over a slave.

She flipped the page, and saw another joke, and then another. Rather than reading the whole text, she held it up, flipped through the pages gingerly, and counted—thirty jokes in total, most of them taking up a whole page to themselves.

After the jokes, she found detailed charcoal sketches in far worse condition. Hand-drawn lines done in ink were still in place, but the actual charcoal had bled badly, leaving only the vaguest impressions of faces, with equally blurry writing below that presumably gave the names or descriptions of the portraits.

She flipped through the rest of the book, to see what else was in it. It was about a hundred pages in total, half of which she'd already looked through. The rest was mostly text, some of it filling whole pages, some of it in much shorter segments, mostly looking like notes and copied messages. As curious as she was, Adelyn didn't have the time to read through it all, and she felt like it would have been an invasion of privacy to do so anyways, so she set it down by the fire to dry and started looking through the second book.

Flipping to the first page, she noted that the writing had survived the river, and then her heart almost stopped as she saw what was written there.

Runes. Pages upon pages of runes, each drawn on the page with a careful hand, labeled thoroughly with the magic words that each rune corresponded to, and marked down with meanings and definitions. She flipped the pages, reading through it, elation growing as she saw what was all in the book. Forty pages were dedicated to runes, and then another ten had notes on grammatical usage and assembling runes together in order to cast larger spells.

The remaining half of the book had very specifically designed runic patterns, each with an incantation written at the bottom, and a name. She glanced at a few of the names; "For healing broken bones", "Large-scale protection against magic", and "Communication at long distances" were among them, alongside dozens of others.

There were no instructions on the use of any spells or magic, which meant that Adelyn wasn't going to be able to use many of them, but it was still a massive treasure trove of knowledge. Even without knowing much beyond the basics of spellcasting, she could use the runes listed in the first half of the book for countless purposes, and that was going to be a huge help.

A thought struck her and she closed the book for a moment, looking over at David's bundle of sopping wet clothes. Reaching over to the shirt's sleeve she turned it inside out, then grinned. There was red thread stitched into the cuffs, forming intricate runes. She had no idea what they meant, but that didn't matter—she could look it up in the book. The clothes were tools of power.

She set the rune book by the fire as well, on its side and partly open so that the pages would dry. Hanging David's clothes and silver necklace from a tree branch, she smiled at her work and returned to the fire.

Her own clothes would take longer to dry, but she wasn't about to take them off and be exposed to the cold with naked skin.

Turning her hands over to warm the backs of her fingers, Adelyn took in a deep breath. She was alone, but she could do this. She had all the tools David could provide, and she knew where she had to go.

First, though, she needed to get dry, and she needed to sleep.

...

Adelyn searched in despair through the contents of David's bag, looking for something she knew didn't exist. It was the third time she'd done so, and for the third time, she failed to find even the tiniest scrap of something edible.

Her stomach grumbled, annoyed at her for skipping breakfast, and for skipping lunch, and for preparing to skip dinner. Her legs were sore from walking all day, aching almost as much as her arm, and while she had plenty of water to drink from the river that had nearly killed her, the lack of food was getting to her.

She kept moving. She'd woken up early, and been walking since then. Without knowing where Petra truly was, she just had to keep following the water upstream and hope that it led to the city. She couldn't get lost, which was the one boon that her plan really had.

Adelyn was beginning to feel like a regular adventurer. Armed with magic, dealing with the hazards of the wilderness, sleeping under the stars at night and overcoming challenges as they arose. Her trail barely required any navigation skills whatsoever, and she'd mostly run from her hardships, but even so she still felt a certain kinship to the rugged heroes of storybooks.

Admittedly, I'd trade some of the ruggedness for an inn and a hot meal, but nonetheless.

It couldn't be more than a day's walk, right? The riders had shown up quick enough, which meant the city had to be less than a night's ride away...assuming that the riders came from the city.

The sun had forced away the cold, to Adelyn's gratitude. The weather was getting warmer the further she went, and she barely needed her jacket once the sun was up. In an attempt at staying clean and proper, she had taken off the sleeveless shirt and washed it in the river as best she could, and was letting it dry over the top of the bag.

She was beginning to worry that she'd have to wait another night before finding the city. The sun was starting to set, and she'd seen neither traveler nor trail.

As the sun dipped lower, though, a few buildings came into view, then a few more. It wasn't the organized, industrial city that Maise had been, instead looking more like her hometown had been blown up to a hundred times its original size.

Not wanting to look as though she'd wandered in from the woods, Adelyn walked at an off angle until she came to a road, then followed it in toward the buildings. The cobblestone road quickly gave way to brick, creating real paved streets that turned off at acute angles and bent into dirt alleys at random moments. If someone had planned the city, they'd done so while drunk and half asleep.

She wandered in no particular direction, looking around at the wooden buildings built with no regard for creating an environment that was easy to navigate. A few pedestrians were walking along, but they gave her a wide berth.

Most of half an hour went by before she looked up to find herself a few paces away from a boarding house, the smell of stew and grits drifting out of the open door. Her stomach growled again, and she decided that this was the place for her to stop. Walking through the doorway she looked around, seeing a dining table set up to the right and a desk to her left. A few women and a pair of clean shaven men sat at the table, silverware clinking as they ate a healthy dinner from a stewpot resting on a wooden trivet at the center of the table.

One of the women looked up at Adelyn and frowned, waving a hand at her in a dismissive gesture. "No, go away," she said, her tone curt and dismissive. "We don't offer charity here. Paying customers only."

Adelyn raised her eyebrows hesitantly. "I..."

Looking down at herself, she realized why she'd gotten the reaction. She was filthy, wearing clothes caked in dirt and residue from the river. Her hair was a tangle, and though she'd gotten used to it, she had to admit that she stank.

The woman sighed and got to her feet, walking over to the desk in six long strides. Though she was slightly shorter than Adelyn, the woman still managed to convey that she looked down on the girl, and she pointed at the door with an expression that was obscured by layers of makeup. "If you need something to eat, one of the taverns in the southern district might give you something, but this is an upright establishment, not an orphanage."

"I have money," Adelyn started, trying to explain. "I just wanted to get a little food and a place to sleep."

"Come now, Bridgette," one of the men said from the table, smirking. "If she has money, let the girl have something to eat."

The woman, Bridgette, sighed deeply as she looked Adelyn up and down. "All right, girl, how much do you have?"

"How much is it for dinner?" Adelyn said, collecting herself a little.

"It's eight pins for dinner," Bridgette said. "If you want the room, it's four daggers, and that gets you breakfast tomorrow as well."

Adelyn did a bit of mental math, and then asked, "So,

three swords and a dagger for three nights? I'll probably be in the city for a few more days."

Someone at the table laughed, but Bridgette only clicked her tongue. "If you have the money, yes," she said. "But if you want me to believe that you—"

Adelyn reached into her pocket, searching out a silver dagger by feel and drawing it from the coin pouch. She could have used a smaller coin, but she wanted to make an impression. Tapping the coin on the desk as loudly as she could manage, she asked, "Can you make change?"

Bridgette blinked twice, looking down at the coin, then up at Adelyn. "Where did you get that, child?"

"It's mine," Adelyn said, simply. "Pardon me if I don't explain further."

"You stole it," Bridgette said, raising a perfectly made eyebrow. "Didn't you?"

Adelyn glared. "I'm no thief, I've simply had a little trouble on the road. Can I buy dinner or not?"

Bridgette hesitated, startled but trying to keep her composure. "I—please, have a seat, I'll need a moment to get your change from the back room."

Adelyn nodded, walking over to the table and sitting down next to the two men. She helped herself to a bowl, ladling stew from the pot.

The stew was, perhaps, the best thing she'd ever eaten. It wasn't the seasoning, or the meat, or the texture, but the hunger that made it so satisfying. She took down two bowls with cornbread and plenty of salt, and was working on her third when Bridgette returned with change and a small, shiny key.

"Your room is up the stairs, last door on the left," Bridgette explained. "There's hot water, just give it a moment for the pipes to carry it up."

"How much?" Adelyn asked, calculating if the hot water was worth it.

Bridgette raised an eyebrow. "Four daggers a night, like I said."

"But, for the water," Adelyn added.

Several people at the table laughed, and Bridgette smiled. "Water is included," she said. "Where have you been staying that charges for water?"

"I—" Adelyn blushed, wiping her mouth with a napkin. It came away with the grime from two days without a shower, as well as the food residue on her lips. "Never mind."

She accepted the key, and got up to walk to the desk so that they could handle finances.

"Four nights, was it?" Bridgette asked, as she got out a pen and started making up a receipt.

"Three," Adelyn corrected, getting out her silver dagger and setting in on the desk. "If I think I'll need a fourth night, I'll let you know."

"We may end up fully booked if you don't reserve the room now," Bridgette pointed out, making notes in flowing cursive.

"Three nights," Adelyn repeated. "If you're full, I can find someplace else to sleep."

"If you insist," Bridgette said, making a note of it on her paper. "That'll be three bronze swords, one bronze dagger, and eight pins for the dinner."

"I thought that was included in the price of the room?" Adelyn asked, frowning at the extra fee.

"If you had a problem with the price, you should have brought that up before you helped yourself to my food," Bridgette replied calmly, her pen moving smoothly across the paper, then spinning it to face Adelyn. "I have a receipt here, if you'd just like to sign."

Adelyn chewed on her lip for a moment, but finally decided not to argue. It would take time to go find another boarding house, and she'd still have to pay for the stew either way, there was no getting around that. Taking the pen, she briefly scanned the document to make sure there were no other sneaky fees, then hesitated over the line.

She'd given her name to Dobson. Her full name, too, so there could be no confusion. If someone started putting up wanted posters or asking around for someone by her name, Bridgette might hear word, and Adelyn had no doubts that Bridgette would turn her in in a heartbeat.

Realizing that she was taking too long, Adelyn signed the first name that came to mind, then gave the paper back to Bridgette. The boarding house's matron read the paper, took the coin from the desk, and opened her coin purse to make change. "It's nice to have you staying here, Jenny Anderson," she said.

Adelyn felt guilty for using Jenny's name, but it was just an internal concern. There was no chance that word of this would make its way all the way back to her hometown, and the owner of a random bar in a little town wasn't exactly a family name—Jenny would never know that she had been used as an alias.

Adelyn watched carefully as Bridgette counted out change, and then counted it herself to make sure. It was all correct, of course, but she wanted to make the gesture anyways.

Nodding to those at the table, Adelyn commented, "Gentlemen, ladies." She walked over, took two more pieces of cornbread from the tray—she'd paid for it, after all—then turned and walked up the stairs to her room. She had to awkwardly hold the food in one hand to fish the key from her pocket, but after fiddling with the lock for a moment she got the room open and, once inside, finally started to relax.

Finding a table to set down the cornbread, she walked to the bathroom and turned on the shower. Cold water sprayed from the showerhead, gradually growing warmer as she undressed, setting aside her dirty clothes and waiting a second longer for the shower to get completely hot before she stepped in, keeping her injured arm raised out of the stream.

The hot water felt incredible. At home, they'd used an old-style tub for bathing, and since even with a pump it was inefficient and wasteful to fill it with hot water four separate times for the whole family to get clean, so by the time she got to it, the bath was always tepid and had a film of soap and dirt floating on top. A warm shower was a luxury on any day, and as cold and grimy as she felt, it was a small slice of the Lords' Grace.

She didn't even start to clean herself for some time, and when she began, she took her time, wanting to stay in the shower as long as possible. Whatever water heater was kept at the boarding house apparently had a strong supply of spirit, because the warm water never faltered or began to chill. Only when her fingers were starting to wrinkle did she turn off the water, retrieve a towel from under the sink, and begin to dry herself off, finding a brush behind the mirror and using it to pull the knots and tangles from her hair, finally starting to feel like a person again now that she was properly clean.

She opened the bag and sorted her possessions with her good arm, munching on the the cornbread with her other. While heavy lifting or deft motion was difficult with her injury, holding a piece of cornbread was simply enough.

The day was catching up to her quickly, weariness from the walk making her long for sleep. As much as she wanted to go out and find David, she wanted rest more. She could find him tomorrow.

Settling on that plan, she collapsed into bed. Sleep was only seconds behind her.

CHAPTER 17

Sabbatar:
Bequeath, m'Lady, and Ia'll be t'noblest of Kingdoms.
Victoriana:
But, m'Lord, for whence shalt you acquire your lands?
Sabbatar:
Through folly, dame.
Victoriana:
And whence shall approach this folly?
Sabbatar:
Why, I shall approach it, o'course!

- Excerpt from 'A Comedy of Kingdoms', classical translation.

(NOTE: Piece is not significant for its quality, but rather for its age. Currently, it stands as the third oldest record of a stage play, and is the oldest of a comedy format. In its original language, it seems to be written in a form of rhyming poetry. Due to deterioration of many pages, segments have been patched together from separate translations, and much of the remaining script lacks the original cadence of the poem.)

Adelyn was experienced at waking up tired. She'd done it often enough at home. Chores had to be done in the morning, regardless of how little sleep she'd gotten the night before, and so she'd learned to force herself awake and put off rest until she had the time.

Even with fifteen years of practice, though, there was only so much that her body could put up with before deciding it was time to shut down and recover, and Adelyn had reached her limit. When she woke up, sunlight was streaming through her window, and the birds had already stopped singing for the morning.

"Buh?" she muttered, raising her head from the pillow and looking around, hair hanging in a frizzy mess.

Three more knocks came on her door, and she blinked a few times, looking at it.

"Hello?" Came Bridgette's voice, and then the handle started to wiggle, a key ring jingling from the other side of the door. "Are you in there, girl?"

Adelyn sat up sharply, finding a few words. "I'm here!" She said. "What do you need?"

The handle stopped moving, and a half second went by before Bridgette responded. "It's washing day," she said. "I change the sheets and towels once a week. I didn't see you at breakfast, so I assumed you'd woken up early and already left for the day."

"Sorry, I overslept," Adelyn said, pushing herself out of bed and rubbing her eyes to try and work some of the sleepiness out of them.

"I see," Bridgette said, a note of disapproval carrying through the door. "I will return in a little while, then."

"Thanks." Adelyn stretched, moving to the bathroom and running the water, cupping her hands so she could splash some into her mouth. She had another long day ahead of her, and she'd slept through too much of it already.

She took a brief shower, resisting the temptation to savor the hot water for longer than necessary, then dried off, combed the knots from her hair with the brush she'd found, and dressed in David's pants and shirt. They weren't a perfect fit; she had to roll up the sleeves and cinch the belt particularly tight, and she was still lacking in clean underclothes, but it was a start, and they were the least dirty thing she had to wear. She hid most of David's things under the bed, but kept his bag, his money, his knife, and his book of runes.

Bridgette wasn't in the main room downstairs, so Adelyn glanced in the back and found her washing dishes from breakfast. She cleared her throat, and the matron turned, raising an eyebrow at Adelyn's attire.

"Can I ask a favor of you?" Adelyn asked.

Bridgette clicked her tongue for a moment, thinking. "What do you want, girl?"

"I was hoping that you could put my clothes in with the other washing," Adelyn explained. "I left them on the bed in my room."

"Of course," Bridgette said. "It's four pins for washing service, mind."

"That's fine, thanks," Adelyn said. She turned to leave the boarding house, before pausing for one more question. "Where's a general store?"

"Head north one block, it's on the corner," Bridgette supplied, returning to her washing.

"Thanks," Adelyn said again, heading out toward the street.

At the general store, she bought a notebook, two pencils, a new coat to replace her torn, bloodied one, two sets of underclothes, four pairs of socks, and—after a moment of consideration—a hat with a wide brim. The lot cost her most of a bronze sword, but she paid with little hesitation.

Using their washroom to change, she put her old garments in the bag along with the new purchases. She thanked the general store's manager, then went to find a peace officer's station.

She had to ask directions three times, getting lost in the maze of streets and alleyways, but strangers seemed far more friendly now that she wasn't coated in enough dust and dirt to grow crops in. She wanted to start by checking with law enforcement, to see if they knew of any bounty hunters in the area, anyone who might be working with criminal bandits.

Lords, if she was lucky, they'd just be able to point her straight to David, and would volunteer to help her spring the rescue. Then she'd just need to find out where the bandits were, and the peace officers could mount their rescue.

The station was a big building with a steel door, painted red and white so that it'd be visible and unmistakable from a great distance. She walked up to it confidently, strolling toward the building with a spring in her step. So far, so good. Even if they couldn't identify the man with the scar who she'd seen apprehending David, she could come back here once David was free and get their help springing the rescue of her parents.

Trying the handle on the steel door, she found that it swung open freely. The lobby had a bench to the right of the door, a few chairs on the far wall, a desk to her left with a door behind it, and a larger, iron-bound door to her right.

One woman stood by the desk, chatting to a man working some kind of brass device and making notes.

They both looked up at Adelyn's entrance.

"Can we help you?" The woman asked. She had on a white uniform with a gold star sewn onto the lapel, signifying that she was a local sheriff. Whoever sat at the desk wore the same, except that he wore the silver star of a deputy.

"Yeah," Adelyn said with a smile, facing the pair. "I'm trying to find some people, and—"

The iron door swung open behind her, and she looked to see who it was.

Her heart stopped, then kicked into high gear as it came back to life, sputtering and pounding so fast she felt it was going to rip its way out of her chest.

Standing in front of her, wearing the same deputy's uniform, was the man with the scar.

"I'm sorry, what was that?" The sheriff asked again, her tone a little confused. "Who're you looking for?"

"I—" She stammered. The scarred man looked at her with a hard gaze, chewing on his cheek as he thought. He was unmistakably the same man she'd seen before, even his expression was almost identical.

He's a peace officer. They—they're all peace officers.

"I should go," Adelyn finished. "Sorry."

The three peace officers seemed confused, but didn't stop her as she stumbled out the door, walking away in a straight line across the street.

She entered a building at random, realizing only after she'd walked in that it was some kind of saloon.

The setup was different than what she was used to, only vaguely resembling the dining rooms or boarding houses or taverns that Adelyn usually patronized. The arrangement of tables was like that of a Maggie's, but there was no bar to pick up your food, and nobody was drinking anything harder than soda.

A hostess met Adelyn at the door, beaming at her. "Good morning!" she said. "Can I help you?"

"I, eh—" Adelyn paused. She'd just walked in here to get off the street and away from the peace officer's station, she didn't have a plan. They seemed to serve food, though, so she said, "I wanted to get something to eat?"

The hostess's face flickered for a moment with confusion, but her smile quickly returned. "Is it just yourself?"

"Yes," Adelyn said, glancing around. Her heart was pounding in her chest, but she took a breath and did her best not to show it. "If I could sit away from the window, I'd appreciate it."

"Of course," the hostess nodded, waving an arm and gesturing Adelyn back to a table near the middle of the cafe. She would still be visible from the window, but she would not be plainly obvious to anyone looking in. She set down a thick piece of paper on the table, then said, "One of the servers will be with you in just a moment."

Adelyn nodded, though she wasn't really listening. The peace officers were working with—No, working *for* the same people who'd taken her family. She was lucky that none of them recognized her by description.

"Would you like anything to drink?"

Adelyn started, looking back quickly to see a young man setting a glass of water on her table. He wore black clothes and a white apron, a notepad tucked into his pocket. "Uh, coffee," she said, after processing what he'd asked.

He grinned, and the cheerful expression went all the way up to his eyes. "Sorry, did I startle you?"

"I wasn't paying attention," Adelyn said, blushing. "It wasn't your fault."

"I'll wear a bell next time," he replied, his grin staying firm as he pulled the notepad from his apron. "I'm Stephen, by the way, I'm your server. Cream or sugar with that coffee?"

She thought about the question for a moment, trying to force away the panic. "Is the coffee any good?"

Stephen was caught off guard by the question, then said, "I drink it every day. It's good."

"I'll take it black, then," she said, shaking her head. "In a really big mug."

Stephen laughed, nodding and making a show of noting that down on his pad. "Really... Big... Mug. Got it," he said, "I'll be back with that in a moment."

Adelyn smiled, then darkened again as her thoughts turned back to the situation at hand. There was one bit of good news: she'd found her quarry, which meant she'd found David. It was almost certain that they had him locked up in their office.

A thought struck her, that made her shiver, despite the cozy warmth of the cafe. It seemed unlikely that David had escaped. From what examples she'd seen, he was more than a competent sorcerer, and yet they were keeping him restrained. The security they had on him was almost certainly overwhelming, if it was able to keep him in custody.

Or, then again... maybe it wasn't. Adelyn remembered her flight across the river. The water had choked her, making it impossible to speak, keeping her from any magic. Unless David knew a trick to cast spells without speaking Sacrosanct, all they could do was gag him and keep a guard on watch so he couldn't remove it. That would still be hard for her to get around. Adelyn had no clue how to handle a hostage situation, and she didn't want to make a move to free David only to end up with a bullet in his head.

But it wasn't impossible.

The solid sound of a mug being placed on wood made her jump in alarm, and she turned to see Stephen setting down her coffee.

"Sorry," Stephen said. "Didn't mean to startle you... again. Are you all right? You look pale."

Adelyn shrugged. "Sorry. Long morning. Lots going on."

"Sure," the waiter said, though he glanced in the direction she'd been staring as he pulled out his notepad. "You know what you want to eat?"

"Huh?" Adelyn asked, before noticing his gesture to the paper on the table. Glancing at it, she saw different foods listed, with prices and descriptions. "Oh, right. The soup."

"Which one?" He asked, pointing more precisely at the menu to highlight two options. "There's a beef stew, or tomato soup."

Adelyn looked back at the menu. "Right," she said. "The stew, I guess."

"Got it," he said, tapping his notepad and picking up the coffee pot. "I'll go put this in."

Adelyn nodded, taking a moment to sip her coffee, then looking back to the sheriff's office. Nobody was coming and going at the moment, but that could change. She didn't know how far away "The wizard" was, or if they had a way to contact him directly. He could have shown up yesterday, for all she knew.

Thinking on it for a while, she watched someone approach the station, then continue past and walk toward the stables next to it. This turned her attention, and she started to wonder about the stables. It didn't look like the building was directly connected to the station, but that didn't mean it couldn't be useful. In fact, it was possible—

Something jingled behind her and she raised an eyebrow, looking over her shoulder. Stephen was standing there, holding a bowl of soup in one hand, gripping the coffee pot in the other, a ring of keys dangling from his thumb.

"Didn't want to startle you again. I couldn't find a bell, but this worked," Stephen explained, wiggling his thumb to make the keys jingle, then setting the bowl of stew on her table. "More coffee?"

Adelyn looked down at her mug, noticing that it was almost empty. "Uh, yes please," she said, holding it out to be refilled.

"If you stare out that window any harder I'm going to start worrying that you are planning a jailbreak," he mentioned, pouring the coffee.

"What?" Adelyn asked, heart skipping a beat, a denial automatically springing to her lips. "No, I—"

He laughed, shaking his head. "I'm kidding," he said, after a moment. "Though, now I'm not so certain."

Adelyn took a moment to feel foolish, then rolled her eyes. "Are you going to call the peace officers over here to arrest me?"

He pondered the question for a moment. "I don't think so. People have this weird habit of not paying when I have them arrested, and I get stuck with the check."

"How many peace officers are there, anyways? That's a pretty big stable."

Stephen set down his coffee pot, counting on his fingers and looking up as he thought it out. "Well, there's the Sheriff, Patience... Clayton, Virgil, Tristan, Louise... Duncan, can't miss him with that mark on his face. I think one of them's named Dustin, maybe? A few others I don't know. So maybe ten or twelve? But they don't all keep their horses in the stable, it's mostly there for impound."

"Impound?" Adelyn asked, before slurping on the coffee. It was good to know the man with the scar's name, Duncan, but the information about the stable was more pressing.

"Stolen stuff," he explained, shrugging. "And property of the people they arrest. They have to put it somewhere, right?"

She shrugged. "I guess. Couldn't they just give it back to the people it was stolen from?"

"Not if they don't know whose it is, or if the thief, y'know," he put a finger to his throat and made a cutting motion, then stuck out his tongue and lolled back his eyes with an accompanying choking sound.

"Right, I should have thought of that," Adelyn said. "So —" The line of thought hit her like a train. They would have taken her and David's horses, and that meant that Butler was in that stable. She grinned, suddenly feeling more cheerful. She didn't have her horse back, but she at least knew where he was, and that was the first good news she'd had all day.

"So...?" Stephen asked, confused. "Did I miss something?"

"Sorry," Adelyn said. "Lost in thought."

Stephen nodded. "Sure," he said. "You let me know if you need anything else, all right?"

"Sure," Adelyn said. As he walked away, she idly put the soup to her mouth and tried it, but her attention was elsewhere.

A plan was what she needed, above all else. A way to break David out, without getting him or herself killed in the process.

Motion at the peace officer's station across the street caught her eye and she looked up, watching out the window for a moment and feeling her heart start to pound in her chest. The man with the scar was crossing the street, heading right toward the cafe door.

Adelyn threw herself to her feet, thinking she'd make a break for the door. She quickly realized that it was a stupid plan, though. It'd be impossible for Duncan to miss her if she came tearing through the exit like a hawk fleeing a dragon, and if he hadn't recognized her before, he certainly would wonder why she was running then.

Instead of running, Adelyn turned and walked smoothly toward the back of the cafe, keeping her hands tight on the strap of her bag and trying not to look too stiff.

Stephen was reading from his notepad to someone through an open space in the back wall, but he hesitated when he noticed her, lowering the pad and crossing to her, asking, "Is something wrong?"

Adelyn swallowed, glanced over her shoulder for a second, then stammered, "B-bathroom."

Steven glanced past Adelyn in confusion, then nodded at the question and pointed around the corner. "Oh, of course. Over there, first door on the right."

"Thanks," Adelyn said, hurrying to follow his directions and get into the bathroom. She'd been hoping for a back door leading to an outhouse, but no such luck—the bathroom was attached. The door was unlocked, so she stepped in, slamming it behind her and looking for a lock. She found it, a flimsy bolt screwed into the door, and latched it —it wouldn't stop someone from kicking in the door, but it might keep the peace officer from walking in on accident.

Alone, she finally took a moment to breathe, taking in big gulps of air and leaning against the wall. Her heart refused to stop pounding for almost a minute, and until she calmed down she had trouble arranging her thoughts into anything coherent.

Once the adrenaline burst wore off she sank to the floor, feeling stupid. Of *course* someone from the peace officer's station was going to show up at the cafe. It was just about lunchtime. It was right across the street. Thinking about it, Adelyn realized how lucky she was that it hadn't happened with a peace officer that she didn't recognize.

She rubbed her eyes, trying to think of how she was going to get out. She couldn't just loiter in the bathroom forever, and she couldn't wait until Duncan left. Without leaving the bathroom, she had no way of knowing if he was still there.

Looking inside the sleeve of David's shirt, Adelyn examined the runes stitched into the cuff. She recognized the circular patterns right away, and though many of the other runes were alien to her, it was clear that the runes were set up for defensive magic. She could probably channel a decent shield if she had to, but that wasn't going to make a useful weapon. If she had to blast her way out, she was going to be lacking for good tools unless she used David's actual book of runes. Using the book seemed to much a risk, and so she had no weapons.

Standing up straight, Adelyn glanced around the bathroom for a moment. There was a toilet in the corner, its lid open. A trash can sat next to it, with a wadded up scrap of paper next to it. The sink had a single handle for water, a small flat shelf for a bar of soap, and a washrag was draped haphazardly over the edge of the sink's basin.

Crouching, Adelyn picked up the paper, putting it in the trash can. She closed the toilet lid, then crossed one step over to the sink, turning on the water and washing her hands. They weren't dirty to begin with, but she took her time anyways, eventually drying her hands on the washrag before folding it and hanging it neatly on the shelf by the sink.

The bathroom was hardly a clean sanctum, but it was the best that she could manage under the circumstances. Sitting down cross-legged on the floor, Adelyn removed her hat, put her hands together, looked up at the ceiling, and began to pray.

"Lords, I need your help." She hesitated a moment, then continued. "I know I have been absent in my prayers of late, and for that I apologize. I have been in great distress recently, and while this does not excuse my absence, I hope it will at least explain it.

"I am trapped. I can't go home without my family, and I can't move forward without David. I can't rescue him on my own. Even with my power, I don't have the tools or the talent, and even if I had, I'm about to be found out by that peace officer. I need to get by him and, more than that, I need a way to get into the station and rescue David from the prison. I know he is recusant, but he's a good man, and he's committed no wrongs."

She paused, then added, "And, even if he has committed any wrongs, I need his strength to rescue my family and friends.

"You ride on the back of the world, and I am merely a tiny fraction of what you oversee, but I pray, give me your help so that I can make your world a better place." She dropped her hands, feeling unsure. No special insight struck her, and no noise outside implied that something miraculous had happened to drive Duncan out of the cafe.

Pushing up to her feet, Adelyn brushed off her knees,

retrieved her hat, and inspected herself in the mirror for a moment.

Delaying more wouldn't help. She couldn't wait forever. If the Lords were going to assist her, then they would have done so already. There was no point in waiting any longer. They would come through, and she would be able to sneak past the peace officer, or they wouldn't. Tucking her hair into her hat, she briefly wished for a better disguise, and for an arm that didn't ache when she raised it.

She set aside those wishes, took a breath, and left the bathroom.

The scarred officer didn't spot her right away. Adelyn saw him speaking with the hostess, giving her a moment to act. Stephen was talking to a cook through a window, and rather than heading to the door, she approached him instead, digging in a pocket for money.

"I have to go," she said without preamble, passing him a bronze dagger. "This should cover the food."

Stephen had to take a moment to turn and register what she'd said before looking at the coin. "This is a bit much. Did you even eat that soup?"

Adelyn looked over her shoulder, seeing that the officer was being led to a table. She turned back to Stephen, shrugging. "I still ordered it."

"Right, uh...do you need change?" Stephen said, before adding in a more hushed tone, "Is everything okay?"

"No, thank you," Adelyn said, "I'm fine. I just need to leave."

"Sure," Stephen said, stepping closer to her. "But if you need anything, feel free—"

"I'm fine," Adelyn said again, more force in her tone. "Goodbye. Thank you." Spinning in place, she strode to the door, not daring to look around for the officer with the scar, in case he would notice her looking.

When she was only a few paces from the door, a loud voice shouted in her direction, cutting across the dining floor. "Hey! Girl!"

She ran, not waiting to see if he had anything else to say

CHAPTER 18

It has been suggested that those who live on the borders of our continent grow up to be 'better' men and women than those in the open plains and forests, and there is some level of reason to this statement. The harsh mountains to the west, for example, require a very harsh type of person to match, one who can live in the bitter cold and scale rough terrain as part of day-to-day life, and who must deal with living under the shadow of the dragons who live deeper west. The same could be said of the people living in the barren deserts in the northeast, or even of the coast covering our southern border (Though the coast is so heavily populated that a softer individual could make their way without having to battle the hardships, relying on others to fight the thulcuts and build shelters to ward off storms).

While this is true, though, and while it's reasonable to say that those who live on our borders are tougher or stronger, to say that they are 'better' is rather a stretch. Busy with the difficulties of survival, few border societies have produced many poets or great works of art. What nomad cultures live in the desert have barely even adopted the written word, and the stories that come from coastal cities are vulgar and common at their best. No, I

think it is far better to say that while you can create stronger
people on the borders, the truly best of us come from within the
heart of the gods' great continent.

- Excerpt from Constantine's Musings on the Nature of
Men, written from his home near the center of the Middle
Western Plains

BREAKING INTO A FULL SPRINT, Adelyn slammed open the
door and then caught herself, spinning back to face it. She
couldn't hit him with magic, but that didn't mean her magic
was useless. Raising her arms, she tried to focus on a simple
spell and called, *"Ansyr!"*

Energy coursed through her, creating a vague shimmer
in the air as a magical shield formed in front of the door.
The scarred officer was only a few paces behind her, but he
hit the magical wall like a bull into a fence—it wouldn't last
long, but the barrier would slow him down.

Not waiting to see how effective her spell was, Adelyn
turned and ran across the street, skidding around a horse-
drawn cart and then turning to run down the side of the
road at full tilt. There was only one place she could think to
hide, and if he saw her go in, it would be as good as useless.
She had to get to the boarding house, and she had to do it
quick. She just hoped she could find her way without
getting lost.

A whistle rang out somewhere well behind her. She
looked over her shoulder, but with her field of view shaking
unsteadily while she ran, there wasn't much that she could
see clearly beyond the confused looks of passersby watching
her flight.

Nobody tried to stop her. A few people looked as though

they considered it, but before they could make up their minds, Adelyn had scrambled around them.

Within two blocks, she was panting for breath. The spell had taken a lot out of her to begin with, and she was running full tilt without any warmup. She kept going, pushing her legs to keep moving. If another whistle blew, she didn't hear it, but she heard the commotion behind her and simply assumed that it was coming from the noise of a dozen peace officers hot on her tail.

Only once she was in sight of the boarding house did she allow herself to slow down, glancing over her shoulder. If he could see her now, she couldn't go in, she'd just be trapping herself. She saw no sign of him, though, or any other peace officer—only confused pedestrians. Taking a breath, she opened the door of the boarding house, resisting the urge to throw it open and sprint inside.

Even while trying to show some restraint, she still opened the door with a heave, and Bridgette—busy folding bath towels on the table—leaped up from her chair in surprise.

"Jenny!" she exclaimed, looking between the slammed door and Adelyn's face. Her expression of shock was almost comical under the heavy makeup she wore. "What's possessed you, child?"

Adelyn panted for a moment, then said, "Sorry," too out of breath to offer a further excuse.

"You look like you've been chased by the Pariah himself!" Bridgette took a few steps toward Adelyn, looking back at the door, though this time she seemed more curious about what could be on the other side of it. "Are you all right?"

"I just need to go to my room for a bit," Adelyn said, after she took a couple breaths. "I'm fine."

"Nonsense," Bridgette said. "Sit down, I'll get you some water, and you can tell me what happened. It's fine, Jenny, nobody is going to hurt you."

Adelyn almost resisted the urge to scream, but her frustration quickly overcame her. "No!" Shoving with her good arm, she pushed Bridgette to the side, striding purposefully to the stairs.

There was a second of sputtering confusion, and then Bridgette caught up to Adelyn and grabbed her by the arm. "Jennifer Anderson, either you explain to me what you are doing, or pack up your things and leave my boarding house. I won't have you dragging trouble into this establishment, do you—"

A knock came at the door, making her falter in her speech. Before she could continue, Adelyn pulled away and ran to the stairs, scrambling up them as fast as she could. Bridgette apparently decided to handle the knocker first; she didn't try to follow.

Hands shaking, Adelyn unlocked her door, slammed it behind her, and quickly locked it again. It wouldn't protect her for long, but it might delay Bridgette, or Duncan—whoever came after her first.

Hearing voices, Adelyn sank to the floor and pressed her ear to the boards, trying to listen in. The voice was familiar, and her heart sank as she heard it—the scarred officer had found her.

"... Can call me Duncan, if you please. No, thank you, I'll only be a moment. I'm looking for someone, I was hoping you could help me find her."

"Of course, Duncan. Can you tell me who it is you're looking for?"

"A young girl, by the name of Adelyn Mayweather. Looks to be fifteen or sixteen years old, little shy of six feet tall, brown hair, green eyes. She was shot in the arm a couple days ago, so it's likely she has on a cast or a sling."

Adelyn held her breath, looking up at the window. It was shut, but the curtains were open, and it probably wouldn't take much effort to get the pane open as well. She was only on the second story, that was a survivable jump. If she waited until Duncan was at her door, then—

"I've not seen anyone like that, officer."

"Are you certain? Witnesses say they saw a girl matching that description run in here not five minutes ago. She may have slipped past you, she's quick."

"I don't believe so."

"And you've seen no other girls come in here?"

"Well, there's Jenny."

"Jenny?"

"She checked in a week ago, but she's been down with the ague since then. I think I'd have noticed if she was running about."

"Do you mind if I see her?"

"Not at all, though you'll want to keep your distance. She's probably asleep in her room. Let me find my key, I'll be just a moment."

"Take your time."

Adelyn blinked, then realized what Bridgette was saying. Getting to her feet as quietly as she could, she turned off the light switch, threw off her hat, and then looked across the room for anything that would throw off the story.

The curtain had to be shut. A sick girl wouldn't sleep with the curtains open. She took a step forward, then winced as the floorboard creaked below her.

Footsteps clattered on the stairs behind her, and Bridgette projected her voice as they walked. "Jenny? Are you awake, child?"

Using their noise as a mask, Adelyn hurried across the floor, trying to slide across the floorboards without making a sound. Grabbing the curtains, she pulled them closed, casting the room in shadow.

A knock came at the door, and Adelyn threw her hat on the floor behind the bed, hoping that Duncan wouldn't come inside. Diving onto the bed, Adelyn spun, struggling to pull off her shoes without taking the time to unlace them.

A key jingled and she abandoned the task, grabbing a cover and pulling them over herself, turning so that her back was to the door, her left arm beneath her body and buried by covers—it hurt to lie on her wounded arm, but she didn't want to be facing the door. Pulling her knees up so she was in a fetal position, she closed her eyes, pushed her head into the pillow, and tried to keep her chest from heaving with exertion as Bridgette opened the door.

"See?" Bridgette said, her voice hushed but still audible. "She's been like this for most of a week. I was going to call the doctor, but she came downstairs for breakfast this morning, so I know she's getting better. Poor thing, she can barely keep down soup."

"I see," Duncan said. The floorboards creaked as he took a step forward, but that was as close as he came. "And you're sure you didn't see anyone come in?"

"Not a soul," Bridgette confirmed. "Now, let's leave the girl to her rest, I'd hate for you to catch what she's got."

The door shut, and while Adelyn heard them speaking as they went downstairs, she couldn't make out any specifics. Thirty seconds went by, and then a minute, and then the front door shut and a single set of footsteps began approaching her room. The door opened with a creak, and Adelyn couldn't resist the temptation to look over her shoulder to see who it was.

"He's gone, Adelyn," Bridgette said. "Now why don't you come downstairs and tell me what's really going on?"

...

Adelyn reluctantly filled in Bridgette over twenty minutes and a glass of milk, courtesy of Bridgette. Adelyn would have preferred coffee, but the beverage wasn't so much offered as simply given, and she wasn't about to start complaining to the woman who'd just lied to a peace officer for her.

Adelyn had given some thought to concocting a suitable lie for Bridgette to explain why Duncan had been following her, but by the time she sat down at the dining room table to tell her story, she found that there was nothing she could think of that would sound plausible without being equally incriminating.

She wanted to know why Bridgette hadn't just handed her over to Duncan, but when she tried to ask, Bridgette refused to answer.

She left out any mention of David's history with the Stone Warriors or anything related to her magic or David's, and she kept the travel between her hometown and Petra light to keep the story short, but aside from those details she kept things as accurate as she could: the bandits attacking her home, the wizard who kidnapped her family and neighbors, the fight at the factory. When the fight came up, Adelyn left off mentioning how many people were involved, only saying that David won against several slavers with her help.

"So, after I got a room here, I went to check in at the peace officer's station, and found that they were the same people who'd taken David," she finished. "Duncan saw me, I think, so he followed me back here. You know the rest."

Bridgette took a drink from her mug—she had poured

herself a coffee, Adelyn noted—and she took a moment to savor the drink before setting the mug down on a saucer and responding. "The president's men couldn't find a drink of water in a new well," she said, shaking her head disapprovingly. "Miscreants and layabouts, the lot of them. The government gives out badges to any veteran desperate enough to ask for one."

"So you're not going to turn me in?" Adelyn asked, biting her lip.

Bridgette smiled, and for a moment Adelyn thought she was going to laugh. "Lords no, child! I'd no sooner turn you over to those brigands than I'd throw you into a pit of snakes. If I thought you were dangerous, I'd not have let you stay in my home."

"Right, of course," Adelyn said. She stared at the table for a few seconds, and then added, "Sorry for lying."

Bridgette did laugh, then, though only for a moment. "You do not need to apologize for that. As bad as things are these days, I understand why you'd not be willing to trust strangers. To lie is only a sin if done to harm those under the Lords' protection. You meant no ill will."

Recognizing the doctrine immediately, Adelyn said, "I didn't realize you kept the faith."

"Too few do, these days," Bridgette said, looking into her coffee. "I am surprised that you are a believer, though, from our first meeting I'd have assumed you worshiped those 'Divinities'."

Adelyn blushed. "I was not in the best of sorts then. If I'm being honest, I haven't been steadfast these past months."

"You are working to restore balance to the world," Bridgette said, her tone that of a teacher explaining something simple. "This shows your faith more truly than any prayer. Stay true to your task and the Lords will protect you."

"A sword would come in better for protection," Adelyn commented, frowning. "I don't know how I will be able to rescue David without a weapon."

Bridgette thought about it for a moment, taking a drink of her coffee. "I don't have a sword to lend you," she said. "But if there is anything I can do to help, I will do so."

Adelyn considered for half a minute, and an idea thought struck her. "Can I borrow your makeup? I think I have an idea."

...

Crouching at the end of the street, Adelyn peered around the corner, keeping her frame low and the cloak pulled close to her form. The sun had set many hours prior as Adelyn gathered and prepared what she would need, and the sky was cloudy, so what light there was on the street came from the distantly spaced lampposts, which only covered some of the streets and none of the alleyways. There was plenty of shadow for her to hide in, which helped avoid any second looks from what few pedestrians were still out well past dusk.

She held her hastily made staff close to her chest, hoping it wouldn't be too conspicuous until she needed it. The homemade wand in her bad arm was easier to conceal, and she held it against the inside of her forearm to keep it hidden.

Her face felt dirty, like she'd gone too long without washing, and she had to resist the urge to wipe at her eyes— it would only smudge the makeup, which had taken a lot of time and effort to put on how she wanted.

The street was clear, but Adelyn hesitated to move. She tried to think of anything she'd forgotten, any way that her plan could fall through—nothing came to her. Either her plan would work or it wouldn't, there was nothing remaining to change or prepare.

Pulling the hat down over her face, she straightened and took a step forward, then back, checking that the coast was clear one last time before moving. Before she made her way, she also tried again to think of whatever else she could have forgotten.

"Oh, Lords abandon me," she finally muttered, and without delaying for anything else, she pushed forward, walking down the street toward the peace officers' station.

The street was empty. As she passed under the glow of the various lamps she looked around furtively, but there was no one to see her. She almost stopped before passing in front of the station itself, feeling the urge to turn and run, but that wasn't going to help. She had to keep walking. Gripping the staff even tighter in her right hand, she walked past the door, heading to the front entrance of the stable instead.

Checking the door, she saw a flicker of light come from the gap between the frame, and before she could have any second thoughts, she passed the staff to her left hand and took the wand instead, readying the spell.

It was a fairly simple bit of magic, according to David's book. She'd had little opportunity to practice it, though, so if it didn't work—

Adelyn pushed those thoughts away, trying to concentrate. The spell had to work. It was going to. She put her belief into that idea, focusing on what she wanted to happen, filtering energy through the wand and pressing it against the left side of the door frame as she whispered, *"Rahk absen torvurn gild."*

The words were clunky and imprecise, but they did what she needed them to do. There was a quiet popping noise, and the door broke free of one hinge, sagging in its frame. As quickly as she could manage, Adelyn repeated the spell on the lower hinge, popping it with a quick burst of energy.

There was a voice inside, calling out in confusion. "Is someone there?"

Adelyn grinned, readying her next few bits of magic— these were simple. Easy enough that even she couldn't possibly screw it up. She channeled energy into her staff, and then into the makeup caking her face. That ready, in the most booming voice she could project, she shouted, "*Shane!*" as she kicked in the door.

Bright light erupted from the tip of the staff and from her face, runes blazing where they were marked in black makeup on her cheeks. The door flew in several feet before crashing to the ground, and Adelyn pointed the staff forward and stormed inside.

Only one peace officer was inside, a young man she hadn't seen before. As the light from the tip of her staff subtly waned, he blinked his eyes a few times to clear his vision and then looked up at Adelyn in shock.

She was dressed all in blacks and whites, a cloak caped over her left arm, a loop of rope strapped to her belt, a band of wooden sticks strapped visibly in a bandolier over David's shirt. Her wide-brimmed hat would have cast her face in shadow had her eyes not been glowing. If she'd known how, she would have made wind whip up around her to make the cloak blow around, but that was beyond her at the moment, so she settled for walking quickly and letting it flow from the movement. She hadn't bought a new pair of boots, either, but had at least invested in a pair of sharp spurs to give her step a distinctive clink as she strode into the stable, glowing staff trained on the peace officer who staggered back in fear.

The makeup tingled against her skin as she kept up the energy flowing into it so that it would continue to glow, and already she knew she wouldn't be able to maintain this magic forever, but she only needed it for a minute or two.

"Don't call out," She demanded, a line she'd practiced a couple times to get it as intimidating as possible. "Cry for help, and it'll be the last act you ever make before I tear your lungs from your body!"

The peace officer had a pistol strapped to his hip, but he didn't try to go for it, instead throwing his hands in the air and stumbling backward, only saved from tripping onto the ground because he walked into the desk at the back of the aisle. "I surrender!" he said, his voice cracking.

"Throw your pistol to the ground," Adelyn demanded. "Slowly."

The officer obeyed, hand moving cautiously to the holster on his waist, drawing out the gun with two fingers so it wouldn't look like he was trying to draw. Once he turned around, Adelyn moved her staff—still glowing with blinding energy—to her left hand, kneeling to take the pistol from the ground.

Training the pistol on him, Adelyn let the glow go out of her staff and face. "Do you have a pair of handcuffs?"

"I-In the drawer," the officer said, his hands back in the air. He frowned as he saw the makeup, white foundation caked on her face that lost its menace without the magical glow, but with the gun functioning as a new threat, he didn't act to try and stop her.

"Get them," Adelyn said, "And then cuff your hands to one of the stables."

The officer continued to obey, wrapping the cuffs

around a support beam, then cuffing both hands in place. "Please," he said, "Don't hurt me."

"I don't want to," Adelyn said, waiting until both his hands were secure before stuffing his pistol into her belt. "Don't make any sudden noises, and I won't have to."

Keeping one eye on the officer, she stepped back to the collapsed door, picking it up and propping it into place in the frame. It wouldn't stand up to close inspection, but at least it would be less obvious to passersby at a distance.

"You know the sorcerer who was locked up a couple days ago?" She asked, returning her full attention to the officer.

"Yeah. David Undertow, says he fought with the Stone Warriors," the young officer said, his eyes widening a bit as he put two and two together. "You're the girl he was—you're a witch?"

"Yes," Adelyn said, biting back a scathing comment. Explaining that she wasn't a witch, because she wouldn't kill people with her magic, wasn't exactly going to be productive when she was trying to look threatening. She had a question ready, but before she could ask it, she heard a nicker and turned.

Her intimidating demeanor notwithstanding, she couldn't help but grin as she found her horse in a stable a few paces away. Butler seemed scared—and with good reason—but Adelyn showed her teeth in a smile to see her favorite stallion.

Still, she could rescue him in a moment. David had to come first. Turning back to the officer, she asked, "Where are David's weapons?"

A moment passed, and the officer glanced down at his hands for a moment. Before he could contemplate an escape, Adelyn withdrew the pistol, holding it slack in her hand. He got the message, and gestured with his head. "Cabinet over on the far wall. It's locked."

"Do you have the key?" Adelyn asked, glancing at the cabinet.

"No," the officer said. "They keep it in the main office, you'll have to get it from—"

Adelyn retrieved her wand, took a couple steps toward the cabinet, and poured some energy into a quick spell. *"Rahk absen torvurn gild."*

The magic wasn't as pretty as it could have been, but the small hinges on the cabinet door snapped—the iron in them shielded from the spell somewhat, but a concentrated burst of energy was still enough to pop the hinges from the wooden frame.

"All right," Adelyn said, grinning as she opened the cabinet and surveyed its contents. "This is exactly what I need."

...

Adelyn popped the hinges confidently on the door to the peace officer's station, but rather than simply kicking it in this time, she backed up and got a little magic ready. First, she charged up the runes on her face, turning the white makeup into a glowing visage with a few seconds of effort. Then, she held up her right hand, forced energy into David's glove, and with as intimidating a voice as she could muster shouted, *"GILD SHTAP!"*

The thick wooden door flew inward as though hit with a battering ram, crossing half the room before crashing to the ground and skidding into the far wall.

Using the confusion generated by the door's sudden flight, Adelyn took in her surroundings and stepped into the peace officers' station. The layout was much the same as it had been, though it was lit by a lamp now that the sun was set, and the two chatting peace officers had been replaced with one, reclining with a hat over her eyes.

The officer started and sat up as Adelyn strode inside. Seeing Adelyn's glowing visage kept her off guard long enough for Adelyn to prepare an attack, wheeling to face her and raising a hand clad in one of David's rune-stitched gloves. She channeled energy into the magical tool, but didn't cast the spell she had ready.

"Surrender, and I won't hurt—" She started, but before she could finish the sentence the door behind the desk was slammed open and Duncan came out holding his shotgun, ready to fire.

Adelyn's words were faster than his aim, and she beat him to the draw, twitching her hand sideways and calling, *"Shtap!"*

The blast was unfocused, and a wave of invisible force slammed into Duncan's whole body. Though his finger twitched on the shotgun's trigger, both barrels firing, the shot was massively wide of Adelyn. Pellets buried themselves in the floor, and Duncan went spinning, releasing one hand from his shotgun and grabbing the doorframe to keep from being tossed to the ground.

Before he could regain his senses, Adelyn forced more energy into the glove, feeling her strength drain as she did so. "Give up!" she demanded. "I don't want to hurt you!"

A second went by with nobody moving, and then Duncan spoke. "I knew that was you earlier," he said.

"You're an idiot for falling for my illusions," Adelyn retorted. "I never left the cafe." She had prepared the lie in hopes that Bridgette wouldn't get in trouble. It was by no means certain, but it was the best protection she could offer.

"You're here for the Stone Warrior, right?" Duncan asked.

"Just give me the key to his cell so I don't have to blow down the doors," Adelyn replied. "I don't want anyone to be hurt, I just want to get David and leave."

Duncan looked at the peace officer at the desk, then back at Adelyn. "You didn't do any fightin' back at Maise. Your spell earlier didn't seem like much, neither. I'm not so certain you *can* hurt me."

Adelyn hesitated for a second, then pulled the revolver from her belt and held it pointed at the ceiling in a gesture. "I don't need magic to hurt you."

There was a pause, and then the peace officer at the desk shifted back, banging her fist against the back wall. "Virgil, can you hear us?"

A second went by, and then a voice carried back. "Yes ma'am, Louise."

Louise kept eye contact with Adelyn as she spoke, calling back, "You got your rifle trained on the prisoner?"

"Yes ma'am," Virgil called back.

"Great. If you hear any fightin', put him down. Not worth the risk."

Adelyn hesitated, looked between Louise and Duncan, then lowered the revolver. Duncan hadn't made a move to retrieve or reload his shotgun, and Louise didn't look to be armed, so she wasn't worried about them attacking her. They watched each other, nobody willing to make the first sudden move. The light had all but drained from Adelyn's painted face, leaving the room lit by only the dim lamp.

A thought occurred, and Adelyn shouted toward the wall, "David, can you hear me?"

"I can!" David called back, his voice slightly muffled. "You should leave!"

"I'm gonna get you out!" Adelyn called back, keeping her watch on Duncan and Louise.

David's tone grew more exasperated, and he shouted back, "I appreciate the effort, but I will be fine! Get out of here!"

Relaxing a bit, Adelyn shouted, "Whatever you say, I still need your help. I can't rescue my family without you."

Duncan moved a half step toward Louise, and Adelyn twitched, almost drawing the revolver on him. He stopped, putting his hands in front of him in a placating gesture, then pulled a chair from against the wall and sat down.

With no response from David, Adelyn called, "You still hearing me?"

"Yes," David called.

Adelyn explained, as quickly as she could. "They're working for the wizard who took my family. They're not just gonna take you to court, they're going to sell you to him."

Duncan swore, glancing to his two allies. "Gods be—how did she know that?"

"I *said* there was someone in the woods!" Virgil called, from across the wall.

"I am serious, Adelyn, you should leave. I cannot come with you."

"Why not? I—" Adelyn stopped, shoulders slumping, and she lowered her voice and herself toward Duncan. "He promised not to try and escape, didn't he?"

Duncan raised an eyebrow. "Yeah, he did. How'd you know?"

"Lords damn it all," Adelyn muttered, raising her voice to shout again. "You're not trying to escape, David, I'm rescuing you. Totally different!"

David didn't respond for a moment, and Adelyn was about to follow up with another shout when he said, "Well, okay, but even so—"

"All this is very nice," Virgil shouted, cutting off David,

"But you're forgetting that I have a very fine piece aimed at this wizard's head, and if you so much as make a move to break him out, I'll pull the trigger."

Adelyn chewed her lip, glancing at Louise. "Tell him to lower the gun."

Louise shook her head. "If I do that, there's nothing to stop you from shooting us."

"How about I toss the revolver on the ground."

"You're still loaded for bird and beast with all that gear you're wearing," Duncan pointed out. "Even if your magic is weak, you've got us over the barrel."

"What if—"

David interrupted, shouting, "Adelyn, are you using my tools?"

"Yeah," Adelyn called back. "I figured you wouldn't mind, given the circumstances."

"You've got my belt?"

"Yes," Adelyn shouted, resting her hand over the belt buckle. "Why?"

Duncan pushed himself to his feet, taking a step forward. "Hold on now, don't—"

"Rahk Shane!" David called. "Kill the lights!"

A bullet rang out, the gunshot almost deafening even from a room over. In the same moment, Duncan leaped forward, grabbing at Adelyn.

Amidst all the chaos, she almost didn't process what David had said, and she lost her train of thought as the peace officer tackled her, sending both of them to the ground.

Her head slammed into the floor, and her vision went blurry. The revolver had fallen out of her hand at some point, and there was something heavy on top of her—no, someone. Duncan, and he had a hand on Adelyn's arm, pinning her to the ground.

"Adelyn!" David shouted. "The spell!"

She tried to blink away the fuzz on her vision, focusing on magic. Pouring energy into the belt buckle was harder than it should have been, but by shutting her eyes she could easily conjure up thoughts of the lights going dead, shrouding the room in darkness. *"Rahk shane!"*

Energy ripped out of the belt buckle, casting out in random directions. The spell was unfocused and vague, but still strong enough to break filaments and disrupt the spirit flowing into the station's lights.

The whole room went black.

CHAPTER 19

Equipment and Gear recovered from the battlefield at the Rocks-field Battle Site:

138 Steel Swords, var. Quality.

104 Bronze Swords, var. Quality

137 Steel Short Spears, Combat Ready

86 Steel Spearheads, var. Quality

12 Short Bows, Combat Ready (Note—we lack any troops trained with this type of weapon)

231 Leather Jerkins, lined w/ steel plates, Combat Ready

250 Lbs. Misc. Armor, Combat Ready

Due to the intervention of the Thirteen Wizards, this gear was taken almost exclusively from the deceased enemy soldiers, the "Stone Warriors", with none being retrieved from our own men and women. It is difficult to tally the lives saved by their arrival, but the amount of equipment made available by the actions of the Thirteen speaks for itself.

In truth, it was the intervention of only ten of the Thirteen. The Blue Flame, the Red Shot, and the Clear Cloak were on a separate mission infiltrating a secondary base of the "Stone Warriors". This base, a gold mine set into a nearby mountain,

proved to be mostly abandoned, guarded only by a small reserve.
It appears that the gold reserves in the mine were completely used
up, and though we will send an inspector to confirm this claim at
some point in the eventual future, this secondary mission appears
to have been a failure.

(Cont. on page 4.)

- Financial notes related to the Rocksfield Massacre,
found on the third floor of the Presidential Archives
in Triom

ADELYN TRIED to ready another spell, something to throw
Duncan off of her. The light in the room had gone out
completely, and though she felt the weight of the large
peace officer pinning her, she couldn't see him.

Channeling energy into the glove on her right hand, she
put some thought into throwing him backward with a
magical battering ram. Then, she felt a fist smash into her
face, completely derailing any concentration she may have
had. The energy was still in the glove, but as Adelyn tried to
collect her thoughts to try again, another blow crashed into
her face, and she felt something crunch in her nose.

Blood ran from her nostrils, and she felt the spirit in it
tingling as it ran down her cheeks. No time for an attack, she
couldn't even—another blow made her cry out in pain, and
in desperation she tried at the only spell she could think of,
shouting, *"Shane!"* and harnessing the blood on her face to
fuel the spell.

Light burst from the runes on her cheeks, blood fueling
it to glow brighter than anything she'd tried before, and the
darkness of the room trebling the effect. Adelyn was nearly
blinded by the sudden onrush of light even with her eyes
shut, and Duncan, his face only a few feet away from hers

and totally unprepared for the spell, swore and fell backward, throwing his hands in front of his eyes to ward off the light.

Now with a second to think, Adelyn pulled her concentration away from the light, thinking again on the spirit stored in her glove. She shouted, *"Shtap!"* letting the spirit go in as tight a blow as she could manage. It hit Duncan hard and he rolled off of her, thrown to the ground.

Adelyn's face felt like it was on fire, the spell burning against her cheeks even as the light steadily dwindled. She opened her eyes and was assaulted by the brightness emanating from her face, but by squinting she found that the light was no longer so overwhelming, and scanning the ground around her she saw the revolver. Snatching it, she scrambled backward on the ground and then to her feet, pointing it at where Duncan lay groaning on the ground.

"Drop it!" Louise shouted, and Adelyn looked up to see the other peace officer, Duncan's shotgun held in a steady grip.

Adelyn hesitated, but held onto the gun. "If you shoot me, then I'll shoot Duncan."

"David is probably dead," Louise said. "You heard that gunshot, same as me. There's no point to any of this anymore. Drop the gun, witch, and I won't have to put you in a box next to him."

Her fingers shook, and Adelyn almost lowered it. The light was still strong enough to see by, but shadows were darkening by the second, and the burning in her skin wasn't abating. "You think you can shoot me?" She asked, praying that her voice didn't quaver.

"Duncan hit you well enough," Louise pointed out, eyes flickering to the peace officer on the floor, who had rolled onto his back but made no further move to stand. "This shotgun here will put you in a lot of hurt at such a short range."

"Duncan got in a sucker shot," Adelyn countered, trying to sneer and finding that she couldn't feel her cheeks well enough to be sure of the gesture. "I'm ready for the shot. You pull that trigger, the pellets are just going to smack into a spell and hit the ground."

"Are you sure about that?" Louise asked. "I'm loaded with steel pellets, special for hitting witches. Your magic won't work so well against these."

Adelyn swallowed on a dry throat. "Well—It's—" Her vision started to go red as she spluttered, the burning sensation creeping up her face and down her neck. She didn't know the words to stop the spell, and even if she did, she needed the light to see, but it was getting hard to think. Gritting her teeth, she managed to finish, "It's Duncan's life you're gambling."

Louise was about to retort, when the sound of an explosion rang out from the other side of the wall. By instinct, Adelyn snapped her head to the right to see what had caused the noise, making shadows ripple throughout the room as the only light source turned.

The shotgun roared, the pellets shooting out with a gout of sparks and flame. The fire in Adelyn's face turned to red hot pain, and she felt something rip at her cheek as steel pellets tore through her flesh. The shot didn't take off her head, but only by virtue of her movement a second before, throwing her face just outside the line of fire.

A hand snatched at her face from the darkness, but she didn't have time to jerk away before the fingers pressed against her cheek, the touch cold against her burning, wet skin. Another hand grabbed her by the arm, but the grip was loose and free, not aggressive, holding her only with four fingers.

The room went suddenly dark as the runes on her cheeks lost all power. The shotgun roared again, and there was a fleeting flash of light. Steel pellets pattered against her with no more force than if they'd been flung by hand.

Adelyn's ears were ringing, so she couldn't make out the exact words, but the figure next to her clearly chanted out in a string of Sacrosanct, and she recognized David's voice.

Now that the peace officer was out of ammo, David's chant shifted, holding Adelyn's hand in his own and using the glove she wore to channel a spell. Light returned, a glowing ball that cast the room in blue, and showed that the female peace officer was pinned against the wall by invisible force.

"Keep the gun on him," David said, pointing to Duncan.

"What are you going to do?" Adelyn asked. They'd won the fight, but now they had to escape before more peace officers showed up or it'd be a repeat of last time.

"What you paid me for," David said. He crossed to the desk, throwing open drawers and sorting through them. He found stacks of papers and letters, and rather than going through them, tossed them all into a heap on the desk.

The bottom drawer was locked, so he bashed it open with the butt of the peace officer's shotgun, reaching in and pulling out a bag of coins. He poured those onto the desk as well, sifting through them, then froze.

"What?" Adelyn asked.

The peace officer pinned to the wall groaned before David could respond, trying to move her arms.

David looked around the room urgently, thoughts flickering across his expression. "We—we should go. More peace officers will be arriving soon."

"The horses are outside," Adelyn said. She'd tied both Butler and Ace to a hitching post, loaded up with all their saddlebags in case they had to make a quick getaway. She poked her head out the broken doorframe, to make sure nobody was waiting to ambush them.

Looking up and down the street, Adelyn realized that the spirit lights within half a block of the peace officer's station were all dead, and for a moment she felt a twinge of guilt at the destruction, but she didn't have much time to linger on the thought.

"It's clear," she said, pointing to turn David's view to the hitching post a few feet away, where she'd left Butler saddled next to David's brown horse.

David caught on immediately, running to the post to throw the ropes off—Adelyn hadn't bothered tying a knot, knowing they'd need to make a quick getaway.

Instead of getting mounted right away, though, David said in a low tone, "I know where your family is."

Adelyn frowned. "You got that from a bag of coins?"

"I'll explain later," David said. Then, raising his voice, he said, "Once we get out of the city, it would be a good idea to double back and ride south, to shake any pursuers."

He stayed by Butler for a moment to give Adelyn a hand up, then jumped on the back of his own horse in half the time it would have taken Adelyn had she both her arms and a stepping stool.

Together, they turned and rode into the night.

...

They fled without stopping, navigating the city's twisting roads without much care for stealth. Outside the city, they had to slow their pace to avoid obstacles without the street-lights to guide them, but they kept a clipped pace until the city had been out of sight for an hour, and then steered off of the roads and traveled in a northwest direction for another hour after that.

They didn't turn south. David explained that he'd only said that in case someone was listening—he didn't expect a tail, and he expected that he could fight off the dozen or so peace officers if they did catch up, but the precaution would help.

Adelyn gave in first, waiting until they were in a wooded bit of countryside before slowing Butler to a trot and calling to David. "I'm played out," she said, rubbing at her eyes with a hand and wincing as the pressure stung her flayed skin where the shotgun had struck. "I need to stop. They can't still be after us."

David stopped, looking around. "If you would sleep in the saddle, I can lead Butler," he offered. "I would rather—"

"I can't sleep in the saddle," Adelyn said. "And we'll both be useless if they catch us while we're too tired to stand. We proved that once already. If they're coming after us, they'll catch us one way or the other."

David considered it, drumming his fingers against the side of his leg for a second as he thought it over. "Fine. Here is as good a place as any to stop. I will start a fire."

"Won't that call attention?" Adelyn asked, dismounting from Butler and carefully climbing to the ground.

"A small one," David clarified, hopping down from his own horse and looking through the saddlebags. "The light will not carry through the woods, and I will mask the smoke with a spell."

"I'm not hungry, and even if I were, there's nothing to cook," Adelyn pointed out. "It's all jerky and old biscuits."

David paused, then continued looking. "You have salt, correct?"

"A little," Adelyn said. "But—"

"The fire is so that I can boil salt water to clean your face," David said. "How badly does it hurt?"

Adelyn hitched Butler to a strong branch, then pulled a handful of oats from the saddlebag and held it for him to eat. "It stings," she said. "I was only grazed by a couple pellets, though, so it's not awful."

"What about where the pellets didn't hit?" David asked. "Did the magic burn?"

"Oh," Adelyn said. She put a finger to her face and winced, commenting, "Not too badly. It only stings when I touch it."

"That was a foolhardy idea," David said. "That much spirit so close to your skin is liable to cause permanent damage."

"It worked, didn't it?" Adelyn pointed out. "I got you out of there."

David was silent for a few moments as he scanned the ground for sticks and branches, picking up a few and carrying them to a bit of open ground. "Fair enough, I suppose that you did." Pausing, he added, "I like the cloak, by the way. You should keep it."

"Oh," Adelyn said, having almost forgotten about the black cloak she wore. "Thanks. Do you think it was intimidating?"

David pursed his lips, then hedged, "I think it looks good on you. Can you bring me my pot?"

"Huh?" Adelyn asked, caught off guard by the non-sequitur.

"To boil the salt water," David explained, stacking the wood into a pile of tinder.

"Right," Adelyn said, looking through his bags and retrieving a little pot. "Why salt water?"

"Salt grounds out magical energy," David explained,

taking the pot and pouring water into it from his canteen. "Just like iron or lead or anything else, but it also dissolves easily and is not toxic if you swallow it."

"There's no energy left," Adelyn said, walking back to Butler to get the pouch of salt. "The spell died out in the fight, and I haven't charged up the runes since then."

"It did not die out, I killed it," David said, kindling the fire. "But there is always a little ambient static that is difficult to remove, and it will function as an irritant if I do not clear it away. It is worth mentioning, you should clean your magical tools with saltwater or mineral spirits after using them to reduce wear. It will not matter for most metals, but cloth and wood will require maintenance if you want them to last."

Adelyn sat next to David, watching the fire slowly flicker to life. A gentle breeze made the flame crackle and waver, but with a bit of coaxing it caught and stayed.

"I will need my glove back," David said, gesturing to the black leather gloves on Adelyn's right hand

Tugging off the glove, Adelyn handed it over, not bothering to take off the other since David hadn't asked. "Of course," She said. Leaning in to pass over the glove, she caught the scent of something pungent and wrinkled her nose. "What's that smell?"

"My clothing," David explained sheepishly, pulling on the right glove. "They soaked the clothes they gave me in saltwater and garlic before letting me wear them, so I could not turn them into a weapon."

"So what'd you use?" Adelyn asked, watching David sort through the bandolier, pulling out a wand.

"Hmm?"

"You used something," Adelyn said. "To get out of your cell."

"Ah, yes," David said, gesturing with the wand and muttering a few words. As soon as he did, the smoke from the fire condensed, then dissipated into the air without a visual trace. "Yesterday morning, when they were changing shifts on who was guarding me, I ripped a scrap of fabric from my pant leg and put it in my mouth. I was able to suck out the salt, leaving me with a bit of fabric that was usable as a magical implement.

Adelyn walked back to her saddlebags to retrieve a piece of jerky, holding one up to offer to David. "How'd you get it out of your mouth?"

"Yes, please," David said, nodding to the jerky. "I thought you were not hungry?"

"It's something to chew on," Adelyn said, taking a second strip and returning to the fireside.

"Fair enough," David said, drumming his fingers on the side of his leg and taking the meat in his right hand. "To answer your question, I had to wait until they were changing shifts again, then I coughed into my hand. From there, I just had to cut my palm with a fingernail and use the blood to mark a circular rune onto the cloth."

They both sat in silence for a few moments, gnawing on the meat. Once the water was hot, David pushed himself to his feet and crossed to his saddlebags, taking out a couple of rags. Returning to the fire, he sat down cross-legged, laid one rag on his leg, and dipped the other in the pot. Looking at her face in the firelight, then, he paused. "You have blood on your neck."

"What?" Adelyn put a hand to her neck, and her fingers came away with old, crusted blood. "Oh."

"I will clean that, too," David said, holding up the rag in his right hand, keeping his left to his side. "Hold still. This might sting a bit."

"It already stings," Adelyn said, scooting closer so that he could reach her face.

The makeup came off easily, but her skin was red and raw, and blisters had formed beneath where she'd painted the runes. David wiped at it with a light touch, but Adelyn still sucked in a breath and clenched her fists at the first contact.

Hesitating, David asked, "Are you all right?"

"Fine, just get it over with," She said through clenched teeth, shutting her eyes and taking deep breaths to block out the discomfort.

"I will be done soon," David said, resuming the work. "There was a lot of spirit in these runes, you are actually quite lucky that the burns are not any worse."

"I feel lucky," Adelyn said. "So are you going to teach me magic now?"

"You told me you were not a witch," David said. "Now you want me to teach you magic."

Adelyn bit her lip, and blushed underneath all the makeup and injury. "I...sorry. Will you teach me?"

"I said I was not going to keep teaching you to fight," David said. "I was not lying."

Sighing, Adelyn tried to think of a counter argument, tilting her head as she thought. "You—ow!"

"Hold still," David admonished.

"Sorry." Adelyn moved her head back, keeping her face as still as possible. "You don't have to be a liar to be wrong—you just made a mistake."

"My teaching skills have not improved, and I am still not confident that you would not hurt someone if given the opportunity. Look up," David said, wiping at the makeup on her chin.

Adelyn pointed her face up, eyes still clamped shut. "I

rescued you! And besides, if I can fight, then next time—"
She hissed in pain as David wiped at a bruised part of her
face where Duncan had hit her. "Next time we get in a brawl
like that, you won't have to exhaust yourself to—ow!"

"This cut is pretty bad," David said, his frown audible. "I
do not have anything to stitch it or give it a bandage."

Adelyn chewed her lip, tasting salt water and makeup.
"Can't you use a spell to heal it?"

"I am not particularly adept in healing," David
explained, cleaning the wound. "I have a few spells for
specific circumstances, but even in those instances I am not
able to do more than prevent shock and death so a physician
can fix the problems. I can heal the cut, but it will leave an
ugly scar. You can look down."

"Then I'll have a scar. It'll scar if you don't heal it
anyways," Adelyn said, facing forward again. "Are you going
to teach me or not?"

David was silent for a moment, wiping at her forehead,
then carefully cleaning away the makeup over her eyelids.
Only once all that was done did he say, "You are clean. I will
need my journal to prepare a spell for that cut. It was not in
my saddlebag, did you—"

"I read it," Adelyn said, opening her eyes. "Sorry."

"Here," David said, handing her the dry rag with his
right hand and getting to his feet. "To dry your face."

"You're not upset?" Adelyn asked, gingerly wiping away
the salt water from her face.

"The information in that journal was necessary for you
to rescue me, since you lacked your own books," David said,
walking to her saddlebags and looking through them. "It is
not fair of me to be upset with you."

"That's not a no," Adelyn pointed out. "You're mad."

"I am not mad," David said, finding his books and taking

out the pertinent ones, along with Adelyn's pencil. "How much did you read?"

"None of the journal entries, only three of the jokes," Adelyn said. "I have to ask, why—"

"You saw the portraits?"

Adelyn shook her head. "They...the charcoal was ruined when I fled through the river. Who were they?"

David's face fell and he quickly looked away, drumming the four fingers of his left hand against his leg. "Old friends, people I used to know. Memories."

"I'm sorry," Adelyn said.

They were both silent for a while, and when David spoke, he changed the topic. "Where is the book now?"

"Butler's other saddlebag," Adelyn said, pointing. David retrieved the book, walking back to where Adelyn was seated by the fire.

Pointing with his right hand, "Can you give me that rag?"

Looking at the dry rag in her hand, Adelyn nodded and handed it over. David accepted with his left hand, and her gaze lingered on the stump where his thumb was supposed to go. She hadn't noticed that before. He always had on gloves, and after they'd fled, he'd kept his left hand back, preferring his right.

Curiosity getting the better of her, she asked, "Can I ask what happened to your hand?" David visibly stiffened, and Adelyn regretted asking right away, adding quickly "Sorry! You don't have to answer that."

A few seconds went by, then David spread out the rag over his hand, carefully marking a few runes on it with the pencil. "It is fine," he said. "It was a childhood injury."

Adelyn chewed her lip for a moment, then asked, "How do you use that hand normally? I think I would have noticed, glove or no glove, if you couldn't use that thumb. Is it a spell?"

"Did you see a brass device with my possessions?" David asked. "It is a prosthetic, held in place with a couple straps. It is spirit powered, to either extend or grip in place. By no means a replacement, but it serves well enough." He made a few more marks, then held up the rag. "This will do the trick."

"What runes are those?" Adelyn asked, looking at David's handiwork with curiosity. It was a variety of marks, encircled by a nine-pointed star.

"Roughly, 'Heal the cheek wound,'" David explained, gesturing. "Syntax for runic markings is rather different from what you are used to, but that is the essence. The star denotes healing, if that is what you wanted to know."

Adelyn nodded. "And the word for healing is 'Heyl', right?"

"It is an easy one to remember," David confirmed. "Now, hold still a moment."

Adelyn turned her head so that her cheek was easily accessible, and David pressed the rag up against her wound. She felt a tingling sensation, then David muttered a few words, and then the tingling was replaced by a complete numbness which faded into pins and needles over half a minute.

Moving her cheek, Adelyn put a hand to where the shotgun pellets had ripped at her, feeling a scab and nothing more. "That's a bully spell," she commented.

"Get some sleep," David said. "We have a long day of riding tomorrow."

Adelyn hesitated. David had been pointedly not mentioning a certain topic, and she didn't want to sleep without discussing it first. "You said you knew where my parents are. Is that where we're headed?"

David paused. "They had a bag of Beor silver in that desk. Those coins were only minted at the Beor Keep, before the war. Old coinage is melted down and reforged into pins and daggers once any bank gets ahold of them. It only makes sense that the coins were recently recovered from the keep, which means…"

"Someone is at the keep," Adelyn finished. "Where is it?"

"Where is it?" David replied. "North. It is an ancient castle, built into a mountain's face. The Stone Warriors used it as a stronghold during the war. We are not going there."

"Then where?" Adelyn asked.

David grimaced. "I am taking you home."

CHAPTER 20

An alarm was raised in Triom one day, alerting the city guards that a thief had stolen from the king. One guard, watching the north gate, was alarmed to see a rider, mounted on a black horse and in a great hurry to leave the city.

Naturally, the guard called for the rider to stop. The rider protested, but halted and dismounted.

The guard took his time to search the rider, checking his bag, his pockets, looking for any stolen property. When he couldn't find anything, he apologized, and let the rider pass.

A little time later, a messenger ran up to the guard, panting and out of breath. "Has anyone come this way?" he demanded.

"Just one man," the guard explained. "I searched him, but he didn't have any stolen goods on him."

"Good," the messenger said. "The king has said he'll take the head of any man who lets the thief escape."

"Out of curiosity, what was stolen?" the guard asked.

"Why," said the messenger, "The king's horse!"

- Taken from a collection of jokes written in a private collection. It's worth noting that, prior to the president's conquest of the city, Triom's king rode a black stallion known as Wisdom

ADELYN SAT UP STRAIGHT, shocked. "What? We know where they are! We can rescue them."

"I was hired by you to locate your family," David said. "I have done that. My obligation is fulfilled. I will not kill myself in a suicide attack against an army."

Shaking her head, Adelyn said, "You fought twenty bounty hunters when you weren't ready for it, and without either of us being armed. You can fight them too!"

"I *was* armed, with magical tools, and they weren't ready for a fight with a wizard." David said. "And from what you have said, it was more than thirty people that attacked your township, among them a sorcerer. I can fight thirty men, but fighting a sorcerer is not a sure thing, and fighting both at once is not going to be feasible in the slightest."

"But you can bring heavier weapons and prepare a better spell to hit them," Adelyn pointed out. "And I will be ready to back you up with all the spells you can teach me."

David shook his head. "I never promised that. And you seem to be forgetting the 'Keep' part of 'Beor Keep'. How much do you know about it?"

Adelyn tried to remember, then shook her head. "Not much."

"It was a stronghold used by the Stone Warriors during the war. The place is a maze, dug into the side of a mountain. On level ground, a group of Stone Warriors could fight five to one and have good odds. In the keep, it was more like fifty to one fighting in the halls, where the larger force would get lost, and couldn't bring their number to bear. And all that's assuming that that any attacking force could get over the wall. It's nigh impenetrable, and the surrounding terrain is too inhospitable for a long siege."

"So how'd you get flushed out?" Adelyn asked.

"Three of the Thirteen hit them on the same day as the Rocksfield massacre," David said, his voice lowering. "No one made it out."

A half a minute of silence passed. Then, Adelyn said, "So you would know the layout, right?"

David looked sharply at Adelyn, then his expression softened. "Yes, I do."

Adelyn brightened, building momentum toward an idea. "So we won't get lost. And if we get in, we will be in those narrow halls, where they can't use a number's advantage."

David shook his head, sitting up. "Adelyn, I see what you are getting at, but—"

"And if I'm backing you up, it won't be a straight fight when we see their sorcerer, because I'll be able to back you up. Maybe I can't throw spells like you can, but all I have to do is slow him down so you can hit him."

"Adelyn, it is not that easy!" David said, but she wasn't about to stop yet.

"Plus, my father was a captain in the war, and I know many of the other townsfolk were soldiers as well, not to mention any other slaves that they have. If we can break them out, and get them weapons, then getting out will be a breeze, we'll outnumber then by a ton."

"Adelyn!" David exclaimed.

Adelyn finally stopped, looking at David. "What? It could work."

David shook his head, drumming his fingers against his leg, jaw clenched tight. "Even with your help," he said, slowly. "I cannot beat that many people in that context without killing them. It is simply too many."

Grasping for a straw, Adelyn asked, "What if you just held them down and I killed them?"

"Could you actually do that?" David asked, turning to look at her. Adelyn shook her head, and David nodded. "That is what I thought."

Adelyn slumped, sighing. "So it's hopeless?"

David stopped drumming his fingers and looked up at the sky. "Yes." After a pause, he repeated, "I promised to find your family, and I have done that. I am sorry I cannot help you further."

Defeated, Adelyn leaned back, mulling over what he was telling her. A thought occurring, she said, "You haven't found them, though."

"What?" David asked.

"You only think you know where they are," Adelyn said. "This is still guesswork. You can't know for sure until we rescue them."

"Until we rescue them..." David mused, glowering. "Adelyn, we would both die. I am not going to do that. It is pointless."

"Fine," Adelyn said, crossing her arms. "Break your promise to me, then."

David began drumming his fingers against his leg, staring up at the cloudy sky. "You are going to make me do this?"

Adelyn nodded. She felt only the tiniest hint of guilt for this—she needed his help, after all.

David groaned. "Then we are going to need help."

"Any hope of getting the peace officers to help us got thrown out when they tried to arrest us," Adelyn said. "They have our names, and they know what we look like, there's not a chance we're going to get their help."

"Not the peace officers," David said, shaking his head.

Adelyn followed his gaze upward, then rolled her eyes. "Are you getting religious? You want a watcher to come save the day?"

David looked down at her, frowning. "No."

"Sorry," Adelyn blushed. "Then who?"

"I have a friend," David said. "We fought in the war, they showed me how to use a sword."

"Your friend can help?" Adelyn asked.

"Yes," David said, getting to his feet. "Since you insist on dragging me along on this suicide mission, I will ask my friend for help. We should get some rest. You used a lot of energy on those spells, and we have a long day tomorrow."

He retrieved their sleeping bags, carrying one in each hand, and Adelyn asked, "How far are we going?"

"Arcere," David said. "It's a week's travel north, but the Beor Keep is northeast of here, so we are only adding a couple days to our travel."

"What's their name?" Adelyn took her sleeping bag, rolling it out by the fire.

"What?"

"Your friend," Adelyn said. "I want to know who they are."

"Oh," David said, tugging off his boots. "Mary Atkins. Now let us get some sleep, you will want to be well rested tomorrow."

Adelyn paused, a glimmer of hope in her chest as she asked, "And why is that?"

David smiled back, getting into his sleeping bag. "Because, if we are doing this, you are going to need to know magic, which means I have to teach you. *Good night*, Adelyn."

...

"Tell me what you know," David said, holding a biscuit

in one hand and his dueling hook in the other. He was back in his own clothes, gloves and necklace all returned to him.

"Do we have to do this while sparring?" Adelyn said, standing across from him with her father's cavalry saber raised. She was tired, having only gotten a little sleep before the sun rose, but excitement was pushing weariness to the back of her mind for the time being.

"If you cannot remember it in a fight, it is not going to be of any use to you," David said. "At least not what I can teach you. Besides, we need to conserve time while resting the horses, there is a lot of ground to cover. Just practice forms for now."

"A few words, then," Adelyn said, raising the sword through the defensive gestures that she remembered. "I can only remember a couple without checking in advance. 'Shtap' is 'Throw', 'Shane' is 'Light', 'Bren' is 'Fire', there's a few others. I only know a couple runes, but that's not as important since I can just look them up when I need them."

David nodded. "All right. Vocabulary is important, but you can learn that better from a book than I can teach you. Besides, a good understanding of words is important, but we are short on time, and good technique will do you better than variety for now." He took a bite of the biscuit, then attacked slowly with his hook, gesturing for her to continue.

Biting her lip, Adelyn thought for a moment, slowly but gracefully moving to parry his strike. Her injured arm was stiff and slowed her down, but moving at practice speed, it wasn't the handicap that it would be in a real fight. "Okay, technique...well, you need something to hold, like a wand or your necklace, you need something for power, and you need something to imagine, which is what you are thinking about. You put power into the thing you hold, think of the spell you want, then you say the right word to start the spell, and it does whatever you were thinking of."

David spat out the biscuit in his mouth, glaring at the remainder of stale bread in his hand. "Well, you are not entirely wrong," he said. "But that is a terrible way to describe the process."

"It's worked for me so far," Adelyn said, defensive of what she'd learned.

David chucked the rest of the biscuit at her head, crumbs of dry dough splattering against her cheek.

"Ow!" Adelyn yelped, lowering her sword and rubbing her cheek. The skin was still sore, but felt better than it had last night, save for where it had just been struck. "What was that for?"

"You have to be ready for any attack," David said. "And those biscuits are terrible. I cannot teach you if you argue with what I have to say."

"Okay," Adelyn said. "How would *you* describe it?"

"I..." David paused for a moment, lowering his hook and thinking. "Give me a moment to think of a good metaphor."

"All right," Adelyn said. She returned to her practice, moving through stances and forms with grace, but no speed.

A minute went past before David had something he was satisfied with. "All right, so...magic is like pouring water into a wide vessel. The water is power, and can be drawn from many sources—so long as the source is not contaminated, it is indistinguishable. The vessel is what you are using to cast the spell. Its shape is determined by the runes, its volume by the size of the object, and the ability to store water by the materials that the object is made from. Silver and gold are ideal choices, but iron is like pouring water into a pot made from a sponge. Are you understanding this?"

"Yeah," Adelyn said, thrusting forward at the air. "It's making sense."

"Good. Also, your elbows should be in closer to your body." David grinned, thinking for a moment before he continued. "When you think on what the spell is going to be, that is like pouring water into the vessel. You can pour it differently, to fill up different parts of the vessel, but you cannot pour the water into parts of the vessel that do not exist—in the same way, you can use a tool to cast many spells that relate to the runes you have carved into it, but you cannot use it to cast a spell without at least one relevant marking."

"That makes sense," Adelyn said, tucking in her elbows as she returned to a base stance. "So what is casting the spell like?"

David hesitated, drumming his fingers on his leg and frowning. "All right, maybe that is an incomplete metaphor."

"It's alright, I think I'm starting to get the point," Adelyn said. "It's more fluid than what I was describing, that's what you're saying, right?"

"The point is that you are not putting together a list of ingredients in an assembly line. When you cast a spell, you are mixing thoughts and ideas with spirit to create something tangible. Your thoughts and the runes do not simply exist alongside each other, they multiply each other, as do the words you speak when you cast the spell. If they are in perfect harmony, your spells will work more effectively than if they are simply done like steps in an instruction book." Looking over at Adelyn and pointing, he said with emphasis, "You are not merely some spirit machine working on rote tasks, you are much more than that—you are a witch."

"Hmm," Adelyn said, the corners of her mouth turning

down as she lowered the sword, resting for a moment.

David's expression shifted to confusion. "What?"

"I'm not a witch," Adelyn said. "You might not mind as much, since you learned your magic before the Thirteen came along, but—"

"Oh." David shook his head. "No, you are right, I misspoke, and I am sorry."

"It's all right," Adelyn said, thinking of how she could change the subject. "So, spirit comes from people, right? Our energy, blood, all that."

"That is correct," David said. "For all practical purposes, spirit comes from humans, pretty much exclusively. It is theoretically possible to draw spirit from a dragon or a thulcut, but the difficulty in doing so generally outweighs the value."

"How much energy does a person have?" Adelyn asked. "I don't know how you'd measure that."

"There is no specific metric," David said, "But a good rule of thumb is that everything multiplies by twenty—all the blood in a person will give you twenty times the spirit that their energy will, and a lifetime's worth of memories are worth twenty times that."

"Could I just take the energy from someone else and use it to cast spells?" Adelyn asked. "Or just take from them until they can't stay conscious."

"A good idea, but no." David considered for a moment, then said, "In theory, magic users really only have one talent that regular people do not—we can feel spirit, conduct it through our bodies, and channel it without the assistance of machines. People do not just have spirit in their bodies, at least not in quantities that can be used for any serious spells, the energy in their bodies has to be converted first. I believe that a few non-sorcerers managed to convert their energy into spirit using some kind of meditation, but it is not a viable source of power."

"Could I take the spirit from a power line on the street, then?" Adelyn asked, crossing to Butler to get a drink of water.

"You would probably break the surge protector," David said. "But if it did not have one, then yes. In many ways, our ability to move spirit is more important than the ability to actually cast spells. Sensing the spirit in objects—feeling it in the air, knowing how it moves—allows us to do things that no normal person could, even without casting a spell."

"Is that how you fight like you're the Pariah himself?" Adelyn asked.

David hesitated. "I do not know who that is."

"Never mind," Adelyn said. "But you know when people are going to attack, even if you can't see them."

"Oh," David said. "Yes. Spirit never really goes away when it dissipates from our spells, is simply fades into static. Weapons are made of iron or steel or bronze, which all have it in common that they react strongly to that static. As magic users, we can feel that. With practice, you can fight a room of people blindfolded, using only the spirit in the air to guide you."

"That's...wow," Adelyn said. "How long did it take you to learn?"

David thought about that for a moment. "Four years of constant training, give or take."

Adelyn's face fell, disappointed. "Oh. Not going to be useful in a week, then."

"No," David agreed. "We should get back to riding. Do you have any questions for me?"

"Why do you have a book of jokes with all your magic spells?" Adelyn asked, walking back to Butler.

Smiling at that, David holstered his hook and took a drink of water. "I believe you know, memory can be used as a source of spirit."

"I'd heard something about that," Adelyn said. "But what does that have to do...oh. Seriously?"

David grinned. "Even if you are careful, memories bleed into each other, and if you use important memories you can burn out things you did not intend to. Jokes are easy to segregate in your thoughts, though, they are individual concepts that are easy to memorize and it will not hurt your other memories to use them."

"That's why you are terrible with jokes?" Adelyn asked, smirking.

"Sort of," David said. "I did not like many jokes before, which is why I did not mind using them as my spirit fuel of choice."

"There's other choices?"

"Sure," David shrugged. "Eh, most sorcerers I know use poetry." He laughed, adding, "I met one who used to carry a dictionary around, and memorize all the words that were longer than ten letters. He told me, 'If I needed 'em for talkin', I wouldn't need the book to remember 'em!'"

Adelyn giggled. "So I should get a poetry book?"

"If you do not like poetry," David said, getting into the saddle. They were still riding through woods, avoiding real traveling routes, which had slowed them a little as they rode that morning.

"How soon before we can get back on the road?" Adelyn asked. "It's faster travel if we can follow one."

"Faster, but then we have to deal with the bounty hunters and peace officers following us. We stay off the road."

"We went off road last time and still had to deal with

bounty hunters and peace officers," Adelyn pointed out. "How do you know we won't be followed now?"

"I do not know, but by tomorrow afternoon we are going to be at the ruins of Eddwind, and most men will be too superstitious to follow us through." He started forward, and Adelyn followed behind a second later.

"Eddwind?" Adelyn said, feeling the hairs stand up on the back of her neck at the name. "Are you sure that's a good idea?"

"You are not superstitious, are you?" David asked.

She shook her head. "No, but I'm not certain it's a good idea to travel through a battlefield like that. Wouldn't it be dangerous?"

"Nobody is there," David said. "Ghosts are not going to attack you. Any magical traps have long since lost their potency, and even if they had not, I could sense and evade them easily enough."

"What about non-magical traps?" Adelyn asked.

"They set the city on fire before leaving," David said. "No physical traps are still going to be working."

"Of course they did," Adelyn muttered. "Have to set an example for any potential rebels, right?"

"It was the last stronghold for the Sovereignty," David said. "They had fifteen magic users and a quarter of a million men, plus two stolen war machines. When faced with either using overwhelming force, or a siege which would last years and give the Sovereignty time to regroup and prepare a counter-offensive, the president chose overwhelming force. Even with the Thirteen working in unison, it took twenty more witches and wizards to bring down the walls of the city."

"Why so many?" Adelyn asked.

"Stone walls are hard to destroy with magic, and they are

hard to destroy with anything else when there's magic reinforcing them," David said. "Stone does not shed magic like iron, but it takes a lot of spirit to move it. Add to that the protective magic by the Sovereignty's sorcerers and sorceresses, and it was a formidable defense. The Thirteen alone would still have been able to overcome the magical defenses, though, had the defenders not stooped to using human sacrifice to boost their spells with overwhelming power."

Adelyn sucked in a breath. "I hadn't heard that."

"It is not common knowledge," David said. "As part of the terms of their surrender, the defenders asked that it be kept secret."

"What surrender?" Adelyn said, holding back a sneer. "Nobody survived."

Shaking his head, David sighed. "No soldiers survived. They needed the Sovereignty leadership alive, though, to make their army's surrender official, so they could declare the war was over."

"How many?"

"Eighty people, I think. Maybe a hundred. Exact numbers are hard to come by."

Adelyn swallowed. "A quarter of a million dead women and men, and that's what you want us to ride through."

"That, or we risk being tracked down by peace officers and having to fight them. I am optimistic about our odds in that fight, but do not want to risk hurting anyone or being delayed." David sighed. "Also, it will take half a day to travel around if you do not want to go through."

"Then let's do it," Adelyn said. "But I want to be clear that I think this was a bad idea."

David shrugged. "Duly noted. I will be sure to mention that when we arrive on the other side of the city unscathed."

CHAPTER 21

Of course, the probability of surviving a journey to the islands is slim for several reasons, even besides the most obvious one. Few ships are capable of traveling without supplies from the mainland for more than a week, and even if they could make the eighteen-day round trip, the danger of a storm hitting during that time is great. On top of all of this, the islands are not particularly large, and without landmarks to navigate by it can be difficult to keep a precise course. A method has been developed to navigate using the position of the stars at night, but the reliability of this technique has not been extensively tested.

- Excerpt from research paper studying the Lost Islands

ADELYN COULD TELL they were getting close long before they could see Eddwind proper. They crossed no specific marker nor line, but as they got closer the trees grew thinner until there were none around, and the foliage gave way to scrub grass and eventually to barren dirt. Most signs of the battle-field had been cleared away, tents and barricades packed up and carried off, but there remained splintered wood and ashy piles where bonfires had been made years before.

At David's recommendation, Adelyn had continued wearing the cloak she'd bought, and today it was flapping heartily in the wind as they rode, at least until she pulled it down over herself to act as an extra shield against the cold.

"Your father was a captain, right?" David asked, navigating around a patch of rubbish that was half buried in the dirt. "Where did he serve?"

"Far south of here," Adelyn said. "In the plains around Garrison. By the time they put Eddwind to siege, he'd been off the battlefield for most of a year, though."

"Captured?"

Adelyn shook her head. "Surrendered. He and about twenty others had been harassing the president's soldiers and bringing in supplies to Garrison. They knew a siege was coming, but they wanted to hold it off as long as possible. This was back when the Stone Warriors were...eh, back when you were still fighting," she explained. "Sorry, do you care about this?"

"I am interested," David replied. "Go on."

Adelyn had to stop for a moment and pull Butler to the side to avoid riding over a broken sword stuck in the ground, then she continued. "Well, we knew that we didn't have the manpower to go on the offensive, but it was hoped that if we held on long enough then the attacking forces would get demoralized and go home. Dad had the idea that if they could lure a few companies closer to Garrison, they could surround them and capture scores of soldiers without any combat." Pausing, Adelyn looked at the sky for a moment and then corrected herself. "That's what he told me, anyways. They were preparing for a siege, and a thousand prisoners take a lot of food."

"You said this was about a year before the Eddwind siege, right?" David asked.

Nodding, Adelyn said, "You see where this is going?"

"I think so," David said, "But keep going. We will be able to see the city over the next ridge, by the way."

"Well, Dad was going to lead a raiding party, hit a nearby camp," Adelyn said, nodding. "They were going to start a fire and make a clamor. Ammo was scarce, so they didn't have a lot of guns to spare. About fifteen of them snuck into the camp with matchbooks and oil, ready to light everything up—he never told me how they got past anyone keeping watch—anyways, they got close enough to hear some soldiers talking around a dinner fire. They were talking about the reinforcements coming—they'd just got word that an army was approaching. There wasn't going to be a siege at all, they were just going to take Garrison by force and sweep through. Dad wasn't sure if they were all going to be able to sneak out without being caught, so he sent two of his people to ride back to Garrison as quickly as possible to deliver a warning, then surrendered with the rest of his people rather than starting a fight."

"Why not stick to the original plan? Army or no, a thousand casualties or more is no small thing," David said.

Adelyn shrugged. "The point wasn't the casualties, it was to slow down the advance and prevent a siege. He didn't want to kill folks for the sake of killing folks if it wouldn't help anything. The president's army was good to him and his men, relatively. A lot of people'd be dead today if he didn't surrender."

"So was your mom one of his riders?" David asked.

"No, they met well before... the... war..." Adelyn trailed off as she looked over the ridge, finally able to look across the terrain and see the ruins of the city.

Where there had once been a wall, there was now only a wide pile of stone and rubble that stretched from horizon to horizon. No space had more than two stone blocks stacked upon each other, and Adelyn couldn't see more than a dozen blocks that were even fully intact.

Grasping for something to say, Adelyn commented, "I guess the magic defending the walls wasn't strong enough."

"Strength is not everything," David said. "Brute force could never have taken down these walls without precision. Watch your footing, there are many pitfalls on the approach to the wall."

"Pitfalls?" Adelyn asked. "I thought you said there weren't traps?"

"Not traps," David said. "Craters and dugouts. Residual scars in the ground where explosives were detonated. Do not worry, all the mines were tripped."

Swallowing, Adelyn asked, "Mines?"

David paused, then explained. "Explosives, buried in the ground. They detonate when someone passes over them."

Adelyn pulled Butler to a stop, looking at the ground in front of them hesitantly. "And you're certain they were all cleared away?"

"They were," David said. "Or, at least, the mines at the entrances to the city were. So long as we do not tread away from the main path we will be fine."

"Pardon me if I don't find that particularly encouraging," Adelyn said. "You can ride in front."

It took half an hour to reach the edge of the crumbled wall, the duration less from the distance and more from the careful pace they had to keep, avoiding obstacles on the scarred ground that grew more and more dense as they approached the edge of the city. Old bits of tent canvas and abandoned firepits gave way to splintered wooden palisades as they neared the wall, and those eventually grew thin just as the deep holes and pockmarks in the ground grew common.

There was no sign of the gate that had once stood, but the place where it had once been was still easy to find, thanks to the large battering ram half buried in mud and overgrown with weeds. Even buried as it was, it still stuck almost ten feet in the air, with a massive length of wood and banded iron dangling limply on the ground from worn leather straps.

Staring as she dismounted Butler to lead him over the rubble of the wall, Adelyn asked, "So is this where they finally breached the walls, then?"

"What, here?" David asked, looking around. "No. At least, not first. Most of the heavy artillery hit the north gate, they were only able to breach here once the magical defenses had been taken down."

She continued staring at the ram. "This isn't the heavy artillery?"

David didn't answer, instead tilting his head to think. "We should make a detour while we travel through the city," he said, apparently satisfied with whatever conclusion he had drawn.

Adelyn pursed her lips. "What for?"

"I want to show you something," David said, taking his horse by the reins and leading the way around the meter-high stone blocks that were piled on the ground around them. "It will only take a few minutes to get there."

"Can't you just tell me about it?" Adelyn asked, following his path closely. "I want to get through the city as quick as we can."

"I will tell you a bit of history as we walk instead," David said. "And magical theory. It is two lessons in one, really."

Chewing on her lip, Adelyn consented. "Fine, if you think it's worth it."

"Great!" David beamed, circumnavigating a pile of rubble. "So, the magical defenses of the city were not just strong because they had a lot of power going into them. They were built with massive runes, spread all across the city in a network of defensive magic, and in order to get to the people powering those runes, the Thirteen—plus the other wizards and witches they had with them, and a guard of some of the best soldiers in the president's army—had to first take down the runes themselves."

"Why couldn't they just go kill the sorcerers and sorceresses?" Adelyn asked. "Drop the magic at its source."

"Because those defensive runes did not just protect the city, they also protected the people who had set them up," David explained. "The defenses were layered. Smaller shields cost less energy, so as you got closer into the city, the stronger the defensive magic grew. Even when the north gate fell, it was only a few minutes before there was a magical barrier to stem the tide of soldiers coming into the city. It is this way, by the way."

He pointed down a street, or what was left of it. The houses and buildings on either side had burned to the ground, marked only by the charred foundations where they had once stood, the street was cluttered with debris. Barricades, both formidable and makeshift, had been pushed out of the way but not fully cleared, so while they could ride through, it was by no means fast going.

Adelyn nodded, following along. "I get it, I think. They were disarming the defenders."

"Exactly."

"Why not just build the runes in the very center of the city?" Adelyn asked. "So that they can't be destroyed."

"Reach," David said. "Projecting a spell over a long distance consumes vast amounts of power. By putting down the runes everywhere that they wanted the magic to reach, they were able to conserve spirit, at least relative to how much it would have cost otherwise."

"So the Thirteen started taking down their runes," Adelyn said. "Are you taking me to see one of the runes, then?"

"No. We are heading over there," David added, gesturing to a ring of stone buildings a couple stories high. Their roofs were gone and windows shattered, but the stone structures had fared better than their wooden neighbors.

"Then what?"

"Well," David explained. "While they were pushing into the city, one of the Thirteen had an idea. They were hitting some pretty heavy opposition, and the magical wards and traps throughout the city were slowing the group down heavily since they had not yet destroyed any runes. The Blue Flame thought that if he snuck off on his own, he could slip through the wards and spells without any opposition and destroy some of the runes on his own, allowing the rest of the group to progress."

"He?" Adelyn asked. "How do you know the Blue Flame was a man? Or are you just guessing?"

David blinked, hesitating for a moment. "The Stone Warriors had...some intel, on the Thirteen."

"Sure," Adelyn said, furrowing her brow, trying to remember what she knew about the Thirteen. "Why not the send the Clear Cloak? They were the warding expert, right?"

"Oh, certainly," David said. "But the Thirteen needed the Clear Cloak with the group to dispel and confuse the spells coming at them. It is easier to block an attack if they cannot hit you, after all. Besides, the Blue Flame was known for taking on personal challenges, at risk to his own person."

"So the Flame slipped off on his own and destroyed some wards," Adelyn said. "I still don't get what we're going to see."

"He did not destroy any wards," David finished. "The defenders were preparing a counter-offensive, and he stumbled into it. Instead of taking down a ward, he took them on instead."

"So we're going to the site of a battle?" Adelyn asked.

"A battle, yes," David said, pausing for a second so that they could round a corner around one of the stone buildings. "But not just any battle. Did I mention that the defenders had stolen a war machine?"

Around the corner, they walked into a courtyard, and Adelyn sucked in a breath.

The machine that stood in the center of the courtyard towered over everything around it like a statue of some heretical god, more than a story tall despite being hunched over like a man twisted in agony.

Adelyn had seen humanoid spirit machines before, simple puppets that could wave or turn, put up in displays by merchants trying to sell toys or trinkets. The theory was the same here, but she could barely fathom that the monstrous machine in front of her operated on anything like the same rules as those novelties. It was built from cogs and tarnished brass, and though the pipes and gears on its frame no longer moved, Adelyn still felt her knees weaken in fear as she gazed upon it.

"He killed it?" Adelyn asked in a hushed tone.

"Nothing to kill, it was inanimate," David clarified, apparently unperturbed. "He killed the pilot and destroyed the machine, though. You see the armor around it?"

Adelyn glanced down, only then seeing the broken and fragmented suits of armor scattered on the ground, made from etched brass that resembled the hulking machine above them. Though none were fully together, a whole suit would have been seven feet tall at least, and much larger than any man.

"Yeah," she said.

"That is spirit plate. It is charged with blood, or by a sorcerer, and grants the wearer unparalleled defense and massive strength. These were acting as an honor guard to the war machine, alongside perhaps sixty soldiers wearing regular plate armor. The Blue Flame killed them all, and then shattered the spirit plate and used the rest of the residual spirit and the blood from the men to fuse the war machine into a single piece of metal."

Adelyn stared, whispering, "Lords abandon me…" as she surveyed the damage. "And that was just one of the Thirteen, without backup or support."

"Well, he had the element of surprise," David commented. They both stood in the courtyard for a minute, drinking in the remains of the battlefield, and then he leaned toward her a bit and added, "I could have done it better."

Raising an eyebrow, Adelyn looked over at David. "You think you could upstage this?"

"Sure," David said. "I am as good a sorcerer as any of the Thirteen, and the Blue Flame was reckless. To my understanding, he attacked straight away without a plan or any preparation, and almost lost a couple of limbs in the process."

"You're as good as the Thirteen?" Adelyn asked. "Don't get me wrong, you are amazing, but I think the Blue Flame could fight more than thirty men in the street if he could do this."

"This? It is easier to kill someone with magic than to restrain or disable them without causing any harm," David said, trying to hide the insult he felt at that. "With practice and precision, it barely takes a whisper of energy to kill someone if they are not wearing iron or steel."

"So you could take one of the Thirteen in a fight?" Adelyn asked, smirking as she realized. "You just brought me here so you could brag."

"Sure I could, with a bit of preparation." David considered his words for a moment, then said, "I almost killed the Blue Flame, once."

Adelyn straightened, facing David. "What? How?"

David paused. "When the Thirteen attacked the Stone Warriors, there was a plan to take him out. The Flame had a reputation for taking duels and challenging anyone that could potentially be seen as a rival. There was a plan to lure him off by offering a challenge—the notorious wizard of the Stone Warriors, offering challenge, was something he couldn't have refused."

"So what happened?"

"We should get moving," David said, turning his horse to head through the courtyard.

Adelyn frowned, pulling Butler up beside him. "What happened?"

David took a breath. "A general serving the president's army got wind of the plan, and sent him and a couple other members of the Thirteen off to infiltrate the Beor Keep, while the rest of them massacred the Stone Warriors."

"That's why you weren't at the battle," Adelyn realized, passively taking Butler around one of the fragmented suits of spirit armor, her gaze lingering back to the war machine in the center of the courtyard.

"The ambush was completely avoided," David confirmed. "The only surviving members of the Stone Warriors were those that were put in place to kill him."

Adelyn stared for a moment longer, then looked back at David. "Would it have made a difference if you killed him?"

"Maybe, maybe not," David said. "The Thirteen were not just a group of powerful witches and wizards, they were a trained team who fought together as a tightly cohesive unit. Take out one of the supporting columns, and the rest of the team would be weakened."

"But you said that the Blue Flame had a reputation for duels and challenges?" Adelyn asked.

"That was the flaw in the plan," David said. "The Blue Flame was, in a sense, the weakest of them, but also the strongest. He could take any of them in single combat, but offered the least to the group as a whole."

"And you think you could beat him?"

David considered his words carefully, then said, "Had I not sworn to never take another life, the Blue Flame would not have survived a month past the end of the war. If I cannot take a life, however, I do not know if I could match that level of skill and power."

"After the war?" Adelyn stopped Butler, staring at him for a moment. "How did you know where he was?"

David didn't answer for a moment, deciding how much he could tell her. "Like I said before, the Stone Warriors had some knowledge of his identity. Even after the war ended and the Thirteen were disbanded, I could have used my knowledge and found his location."

"Could you still find him?" Adelyn asked.

David shrugged. "If I really wanted to."

"Fair enough," Adelyn said. "So, if you could beat him, you should be able to beat the sorcerer who took my parents, no problem."

"Unless he is remarkably good at combat," David said, tilting his head to the side for a moment and focusing. "The Beor Keep was abandoned after many of the halls were intentionally caved in, but its location was not made common knowledge. The president's army has many sorcerers and sorceresses aside from the Thirteen, and many of them were of a very high rank. I am guessing— hoping, I suppose—that some middling sorcerer took up residence there is abusing his old authority to build a force of bandits."

Adelyn spat on the ground, grimacing. "That sounds like something one of the president's lackeys would do."

David glanced around a bit, then pointed his horse toward an alleyway. "Through here, this should take us in the right direction," he said.

"Shouldn't we stick to the main roads?" Adelyn asked.

"This leads to the main road, eventually" David explained. "And there is an ambush if we go back the way we came."

Adelyn almost responded, then fully comprehended what David had said. "What?"

"It seems I was wrong about the city being abandoned," David said, his voice as calm and level as always as he pulled his horse forward. "Three or four people. Do you think you are ready for a practical test of your skill?"

"I'm sorry, I'm not sure what you mean?" Adelyn asked, eyes widening, keeping Butler where he was. "We're going to be attacked?"

"I will handle all but one of them, and observe to make sure you are not badly hurt by whoever remains," David continued, ignoring her question. "I recommend you prepare to draw your weapon, I cannot say how soon they will attack. Also, you should continue moving, they will suspect a trap if they see us idly standing here for too long."

"You're serious," Adelyn said, looking around and seeing no one, but reluctantly leading Butler forward.

"Serious," David said. "Absolutely."

"How'd you notice them?" Adelyn asked. "I haven't seen a thing."

"I stay on my guard," David pointed out, the statement sounding like chastisement. "Though I did not see them, I could sense their energy. A source of spirit is not hard to detect in a place so devoid of life as here."

Adelyn took a deep breath, then reached for her sword, keeping her hand on the hilt. "And you'll make sure I don't get maimed?"

"I can guarantee it," David said. "Consider this a practical exam. If I need to intervene, you will have failed. Is that fair?"

"Fair enough," Adelyn agreed. "Should we dismount?"

"Dismount? No. They may not attack for some time, but I will tell you when they are about to attack us," David said. "Good luck, I expect you to do very well."

CHAPTER 22

... Once Eth'ram Beor was finished with his conquest of the central range, he turned his efforts toward establishing a lasting legacy. When he started the construction of the Beor Keep, it was planned to be the first of many citadels and strongholds within the mountains.

However, upon its first completion, he decided that rather than move construction to a new fortress, he would instead further reinforce the keep, adding a second layer of walls and digging deeper into the mountain.

His untimely death may have left his tentative kingdom in turmoil, but his daughter, Merriam, was able to keep order by extending the length of the project, adding more rooms and corridors, increasing the size of the keep even more, keeping much of the workforce busy while she established her political allies and cemented her rule.

After she died, many years later, her oldest child—a son by the name of Jacobi—took power. Worried of diminishing crops and long winters with new war brewing on the horizon, Jacobi ordered an expansion of the storerooms and lodging within the keep, so that in the event of a siege, all of his liege Lords and soldiers would be able to last through a full year before running out of provisions.

By this point, the tradition was firmly established, and since then, seventeen generations of the Beor line have each added some sort of addition or renovation to the facility. It became a rite of passage for anyone ascending to rule the central range would not have a legitimate rule until they had added at least a single room to the ever-growing maze of tunnels or chambers buried in the mountain. (During one notable dispute between twin siblings over who would get to rule after the passing of their father, Hannah Beor famously took a pick and shovel and dug out a closet in her bedroom, then declared that—as her brother had not yet added to the family legacy—hers was the more true claim.)

There are also common legends of people getting lost in the keep, making some wrong turn down a passage that had been abandoned for generations. Some of these legends end with the wayward soul stumbling upon riches or hidden stores of great value and then returning to fame and fortune, but most end with their mind being lost forever, unable to navigate out of the endless twisting hallways and rooms of the keep.

At the time of writing, there are seven 'official' map records available on record in the Presidential Library, and none of them take into account any recent tunnel collapses or other damage done. As you can see, then, your request for an up-to-date map of the Beor Keep are...untenable, at best.

- Taken from a letter penned by an assistant Presidential Archivist in response to a request for an accurate map of the Beor Keep, in preparation for a siege

THE ATTACK DIDN'T COME for most of an hour. They'd gone down the main road for a good portion of the way, only detouring when they came to a large gash in the earth forming a deep trench they couldn't cross on horseback.

Pulling to a side street, Adelyn glanced around, noting the relatively cramped conditions compared to the main road. The alleyway ran between two crumbled buildings, with perhaps ten feet of space between them. Only half the width was decent footing, the rest covered with heaped dirt and stone.

"This would be a great spot for an ambush," Adelyn commented, looking up at the top of the walls, where they disintegrated into loose, precarious blocks. "If—"

"Quiet," David said, holding up a hand. "They are coming."

Adelyn looked over her shoulder and saw two figures wearing tarnished, mismatched armor. Their size was difficult to gauge at a distance, but neither was of a height with Adelyn, and neither seemed to be all that bulky beneath their scavenged armor. One carried a rifle, but the others were armed with swords and spears. All their weapons were held at the ready, but none seemed about to attack.

"Behind us," Adelyn said.

"In front of us," David added, pointing forward. Adelyn checked and saw two more figures, wearing similarly incongruous armor sets.

"I thought you said there were three?" Adelyn asked, looking between the two sets of aggressors.

"I said there were three or four," David corrected. "These two are wearing a lot of iron, it is hard to pinpoint that."

"So how do we handle them?" Adelyn said. None of the figures had tried to approach from either end of the alley, content to keep their distance for the time being. "Can you take three, if one of them is on the wrong side?"

"I can shield one side of the alley," David replied,

turning his horse so that he was facing the two behind him and drawing his dueling hook. "We take two out together quickly, before they break through the shield, and then turn on the other two. That..." He frowned, tilting his head and looking to his right, Adelyn's left. Hesitation flickered across his expression, then surprise.

His arm shot up and he shouted, "Get back! *Ansyr! Gild ansyr!*"

The wall exploded. Shrapnel chunks of stone and mortar flew out like they were shot from a cannon, hitting David's impromptu shield less like it was an impenetrable wall and more a tentative barricade. David was thrown bodily from his horse, tumbling to the ground out of Adelyn's line of vision. She was able to remain in the saddle, barely, but Butler reared up in a panic at the sudden explosion and it was all she could do to cling to the reins.

From the debris ran a figure clad head to toe in a full set of iron plate armor, a small buckler on one arm and a sword in the other. Adelyn didn't try to attack, or even block the first swing of their big, iron sword, she just rocked back and jumped out of the saddle, falling to the ground heavily with Butler in between her and the iron warrior, her sword clattering a few feet away.

This defense provided no respite, however, as the two people from the closer end of the alley had already reached her, both armed with spears. She rolled to the side to avoid them for a moment, but this only gained her a fraction of a second before they were on top of her again.

"*Shtap!*" she called, in a desperate attempt at a defense, channeling power through the rune hanging around her neck. There was no effort to throw back the attackers, she just sent the energy upwards toward their spears, redirecting their attacks harmlessly into the air and leaving them both exposed.

There was no time to get her sword, so Adelyn just leaped up from the ground at the closest of them, getting underneath the spear and driving them both back to the ground, skidding on rubble both old and new.

If it came to infighting, she had the advantage of size, but was at a loss against their armor. The tackle did buy her time, though, getting her away from the assailants just as the one in iron armor made it around Butler, and just as the other two assailants from the far end of the alley made it to the melee.

Adelyn lost track of the other members of the melee as she and her attacker tumbled in the rubble. Their armor made them slow and heavy, but they were able to twist their weight and get on top, gravel scraping against the back of Adelyn's jacket as they held her down.

Not waiting for them to start hitting her, Adelyn took only a millisecond to consider what weapons she had at her disposal before settling on the most destructive thing she had. Channeling energy into the appropriate rune, she shouted, *"Bren!"*

A gout of fire shot out from just above her chest, spraying against her assailant with enough intensity to make them scream and recoil, falling backward and away. Butler whinnied in terror and the sounds of surprise and fear from the other assailants, but the light and heat were too intense for Adelyn to look and see clearly. The blisters on her cheeks flared up in pain, but the spell had served its purpose, buying her several precious seconds to consider how to escape before the torrent died away.

It all depended on what condition David was in. He'd taken a nasty fall, but Adelyn had no way of knowing how well he'd landed. If he could walk, she might be able to steal his idea and put up a shield behind them, at least to get them clear of the combat for a moment, but if he couldn't move under his own power then she would have to carry him, and doing that while also casting a heavy-duty spell and trying to flee from their assailants would be a losing prospect.

The spirit in her runes exhausted, and with no proper fuel for the flames, Adelyn's spell began to falter and sputter, fading almost as quickly as it had started. She had to blink a couple times as her eyes adjusted to the relative darkness, and once she could see again, she realized that she had sorely miscalculated. She wouldn't need to lift a finger.

David was to his feet, hands held up and to his side, fingers spread and palms out. His lips were moving in a silent chant, and the three assailants in mismatched armor were held against the crumbling walls around them, pinned in place as though their armor were glued to the stones. The only figure not held in place by a spell was the one clad all in iron, and he was on the ground, held in place not by magic, but by David's boot pressed against his head.

"Adelyn!" he said, breaking his chant when he saw her stand. "I cannot hold this for long. Gather their weapons."

It took Adelyn a second to get her thoughts back in line with the reality of the situation. Getting to her feet, she looked around on the ground, moving as quickly as she could to pick up the fallen swords, scorched rifle, and splintered, broken spears. David had returned his hook to its strap by his side, and she put her father's cavalry saber back in the scabbard on her own belt, tossing the other weapons in a pile several paces away.

Looking around, she started. "Where is Butler?"

David stopped chanting again, and this time the

assailants dropped to the ground like potato sacks, no longer held in place. Once he did so, he turned to his horse, opening a bag and retrieving his jacket, pulling it on.

"Your horse turned and fled at the fire," he said to Adelyn, panting for breath, once his jacket was on. "I saw where he went. We can track him down momentarily." Redirecting his attention to the figure under his boot, he added, "Are you conscious?"

There was a muffled response that Adelyn couldn't make out, the voice made distorted and tinny by their helmet. David started to kneel, then looked at one of the mismatched armor sets that had started to move.

"If you try and resume your attack, I will not be so merciful," he warned, before kneeling by the iron warrior and lifting the faceplate on their helmet.

"Yeth," the warrior said, talking over a lip that was swollen and bleeding. He looked to be perhaps fifty, with a scraggly graying beard that hadn't seen any care in some time and several pockmark scars on his face. "I'm conthious."

David nodded, standing up and clapping his hands together to clear any dust from his gloves. "Is there anyone else in the city that may attack us?"

"Don't think tho," the warrior replied, turning his head to spit out some blood. "Big thity, though."

Looking around at the other assailants, David frowned. "Where did you get the explosive?"

The warrior moved a bit on the ground, and it took Adelyn a moment to realize he had tried to shrug. "Found some old trapth. Took 'em apart, and back together."

Moving to the first of the mismatched assailants, David took off their helmet, checking to see if they were awake.

She was not, but David was apparently satisfied that she wasn't badly injured, and so moved to the next.

"I thought you said there were three or four," Adelyn said, as David checked on the assailants.

"I did not expect one of them to be wearing iron plate while the others were not," David said. "It was an error on my part."

"I guess," Adelyn said, looking to the woman—the girl, really, she couldn't have been more than seventeen—who had been using the rifle. "Why didn't you shoot us?"

"No ammo," she said. "Got some powder, but ran out of bullets a while back. Just had the rifle to keep you from runnin'. Had been hoping you might have some."

"We do," Adelyn commented. "But I'm going to hang onto them, sorry to disappoint."

"Get me some water," David said, to Adelyn. He was down on a knee by the burned spearman—without his helmet, she could see that the attacker was a he.

"Is he okay?" Adelyn asked.

"Is he okay? I will need to take off his armor," David said. "Get me some water."

Adelyn looked over her shoulder, then said, "My canteen was with Butler."

Gritting his teeth, David took a breath, drumming his fingers against the side of his leg. "Then go get Butler."

Adelyn blinked once, then turned and walked down the alley in the direction Butler had apparently run off to.

It took her a moment to spot the horse who had taken shelter a few blocks away beneath a mostly-intact awning, and several more moments to calm the spooked animal, speaking in soft tones and reassuring him that things were safe. By the time she returned to the alleyway, their assailants had all been roused and were sitting against the undamaged wall, and David had removed the spearman's armor and pulled up his shirt, examining the burns on his torso and face.

Leading Butler into the alley, Adelyn removed the canteen and passed it to David, trying to avoid looking directly at the spearman. She winced to see the injuries, burned flesh and peeling skin making her cringe away with both discomfort and guilt. "How is he?"

"How is he?" David asked, looking up and accepting the water. "He should live, as long as we clean out the burns. There is a problem, however."

"What's that?"

"No bandages," David said. "They do not even have any clean cloth or washed clothes. We have used some of what you bought, and what remains will not be enough. Your clothes and mine are both filthy from days of travel. There is no chance of keeping these burns clean without bandages."

Adelyn shrugged. "Magic, then?"

"I am played out for spirit," David said. "But I may be able to put together a decent spell and fuel it with blood, or your energy. Either way, we will need to get these wounds clean before I do anything else." Turning his gaze to the warrior in iron, he asked, "Arlo, do you have the supplies to build a fire?"

"Juth' have her do it," The warrior, Arlo, said, gesturing to Adelyn.

"Don't be churlish, he's trying to help," Adelyn chided, pursing her lips.

He moved in his armor again, more recognizable as a shrug now that he was sitting up, spitting out a bit of blood before he replied. "We have a bit of wood and scrub. It'll do."

"Take us to it," David said. "I will clean out the wounds, then work out a spell to heal these burns."

Arlo eyed him suspiciously, but before he could voice a concern, David said, "I am aware that most people would not heal their attackers, and that you have reason to be suspicious, but I give you my word that I will neither rob you nor attempt to harm you unless you are the aggressor. Besides, if I wanted to hurt or rob you, you would not be able to stop me."

"Fair 'nough," Arlo said, pushing himself to his feet and groaning a bit as he put a hand to his back. After a short stretch, he offered hands to the other attackers, then looked over to David. "How are we going to move Wilson? 'S not far, but I don't know about carrying him."

"Help me get him onto my horse," David said. "We can strap him into the saddle so he doesn't fall out. Which way is it?"

"Through 'ere," Arlo said, gesturing roughly toward the hole in the wall. "Got a campsite."

"A campsite," David repeated. "Is it far?"

Arlo glanced up as he considered it. "Five'r six minutes, on foot."

"On foot...how far is that?" David asked. "Fifteen-hundred feet?"

"I...no idea. Why?"

"Just a moment." Stepping to his horse's side, David dug in his bags for one of his books, retrieved it, and flipped to a page with a complicated rune sketched out on it in great detail. Crouching, he put a hand to the ground and concentrated for a moment, then whispered a few words that Adelyn didn't know. A barely noticeable tremor passed through the ground, and then David stood, satisfied.

"What was that?" Arlo asked, his fat lip causing less of a lisp now that it wasn't profusely bleeding.

David gave a small shrug of his shoulder. "What was that? Checking for traps. If you had any further armed explosives tucked away here, they would have just detonated."

"You could have jus' asked," Arlo commented.

"I do not trust you."

"Fair."

David gestured ahead. "You go first, in case this alley just leads to a covered pit full of spikes. My spell would not detect those, but a man of your size certainly would."

"Also fair."

They headed down through the open path, led by Arlo and the intact members of the group, followed by David and Adelyn, and then finally by the horses carrying supplies and their patient.

A few minutes passed, then David repeated his spell, checking for any further traps. Once he was satisfied, they continued, and another minute went by before a handful of ragged tents surrounding a firepit came into view, huddled together between a set of small tents built to provide shelter from the winds.

Once they were within a few paces, Arlo gestured to his eclectic group, issuing orders he expected to be followed without question. "Albert, Melissa, help me clear an area for Wilson to lay down. Chris, start a fire. Once you've got that done, take off your armor and be sure to clean it, we don't need it falling any more apart than it already is."

Adelyn looked around the campsite a bit. The tents were thin and ragged, and dirt and weeds had started to collect and grow over the edges, making them blend with the terrain as though they'd been abandoned. The fire pit itself was stacked with old wood stripped from the surrounding buildings, and was stacked over an ankle-deep pile of ash that looked as though it'd been rained on.

"Adelyn!" David called from by his mount. "Help me get Wilson down."

Reacting quickly, Adelyn crossed to where David stood and took Wilson by one shoulder, lowering him down from the horse and carrying him to the spot on the ground that had been cleared away. As they set him down, David looked over to Adelyn.

"Go get the cookpot from my saddlebag and put some water on to boil," He said, returning to Wilson and pulling away his shirt.

"I...yes, sure," Adelyn said, standing and returning to David's horse.

Adelyn had to look through his bag for several moments to find the pot, digging it out from his other possessions. Filling it with water from her canteen, she brought it back inside and set it over the fire.

Checking back in on them, she said, "Are you going to need your magic books?"

"Yes," David said, looking over at her from where he stood by the table. "And my pen."

Adelyn retrieved those as well, and then his knife as an afterthought. There was a brief pause while David planned out the runes he would need and drew them precisely down on the paper, and by then the water had started to simmer, so Adelyn brought that over as well before going and grabbing the rag from David's bag.

"Wilson, can you hear me?" David asked, looking down at the burned man on the table.

Wilson seemed to be pretty out of it, but he nodded once

and mumbled something unintelligible in response to David's question.

"I do not think you are ready to channel the energy for the spell yourself," David said, as he began washing all of the burn marks and charred flesh, where the searing hot metal of Wilson's armor had pressed against his skin. Wilson cringed away, groaning in pain where the cloth touched him, but David ignored the wordless protest and continued his work. "Channel the energy into one of the runes you keep around your neck, and then I will siphon it out and apportion it toward my own spell. This will take a very long, consistent supply of spirit. Understand?"

"Yes," Adelyn said, pulling one of the strings around her neck to retrieve the rune and holding it up. "Wouldn't one of your tools work better, though?"

"Would not one of my tools work better?" David stared at Adelyn for a moment, then nodded his head in agreement. "Yes, I am sorry, you are right, I am being foolish." He pulled the silver chain from about his neck, holding it out so that Adelyn could take the other end. "Just keep the silver full of spirit and do not distract me from my chant."

Glancing at Arlo, David added, "You will need to hold him down while I work. If any of your people attack me while I am doing this, Wilson will die, and the rest of you will fare little better."

"We weren't plannin' on another ambush," Arlo said, nodding to Wilson. "Just patch him up."

"I cannot heal him completely," David explained. "I am only going to heal the burns to the point where they are not at risk of infection. The burns will still leave bad scars, but it will not be debilitating to him."

"'Till he tries to get in good with the ladies," Arlo

quipped, kneeling to hold Wilson down. Adelyn smirked in spite of herself.

"Okay," David said, ignoring the quip. "Anyways, I just want you to be aware of what I can and cannot do for him. I am going to start now. Hold him down." A second passed, and he glanced at Adelyn. "Spirit?"

Adelyn blinked, then took the message and started leaking energy into the silver rune. The effort was akin to jogging down a mountain road, except that her muscles didn't tire and her breath didn't grow short. David began chanting, and Adelyn felt the familiar tingle of power as he siphoned away the spirit in the rune and channeled it into his own spellbook, starting the process of healing.

Wilson cried out, muscles tightening and body stiffening in discomfort as the first of his burns began to scab over and heal, flesh slowly growing to replace the scorched tissue. Arlo held him down by the shoulders and kept him from thrashing, but even so, any attempt at non-magical medicine would have been impossible with all his writhing. David initially winced at the shouts of pain, but braced himself and continued his chant with only a second of hesitation.

As the minutes slipped by and slowly turned into more than an hour, she found her strength beginning to flag. There were dozens of burns to heal where the armor had pressed against Wilson's skin, and Adelyn was running low on strength to heal them all. Keeping one hand on the chain, she pulled David's knife from her pocket, and moved to prick her finger to draw a spot of blood.

David didn't say a word; he couldn't without interrupting his chant, but one of his hands shot out and took her wrist before she could prick her finger. He shot her a look, and while Adelyn didn't understand why, she got the message and lowered the knife.

The last half an hour of the spellcraft, Adelyn felt her energy level continue to wane. She didn't realize that her hands were shaking until David shot her another look of annoyance, and she looked down to see the silver chain rattling. It took a concerted effort to reduce the tremor, and she could do nothing about the sweat dripping down her forehead.

Her feet were starting to fall asleep, but she couldn't walk away or stretch her legs to return a bit of feeling, so she braced her free hand against the table, continuing the flow of power into the silver. She started losing track of seconds, blinking to realize that David's chant had jumped to a different place.

Finally, he started upon the largest burn, magic slowly healing it from the edges inward. Adelyn was unsure if she could keep the power coming and thinking that David surely had enough energy to at least finish the spell, but she didn't give up even as darkness started to encroach into her vision, and her thoughts started to cloud, memories bleeding into her thoughts.

"Where are they?"

"I don't know. They left hours ago, it shouldn't have taken this long."

"Do you think the raiders—"

"No. They'll be okay. Why didn't you ride out with them?"

"I-I couldn't."

"Why not? Adelyn? Can you hear me?"

"Adelyn! Can you hear me?"

Adelyn blinked a couple times, looking around. "What?"

"The spell is done, you can stop." David said. Adelyn realized with a bit of surprise that his hand was on her shoulder. "I think you blacked out for a moment."

Adelyn nodded weakly, rubbing her eyes to try and bring them back into focus.

David looked over to Arlo, who was still kneeling by Wilson. "Wilson will mostly likely survive. I want you to start as large a bonfire as you can build, though, and keep it fed for at least a day. This will ensure that my time here was not wasted."

"I thought the spell healed 'em?" Arlo asked, brushing off his knees as he got to his feet.

"Most likely," David said. "But it would be best not to take chances. Trust that I know what I am doing and do not want Wilson to come to any further harm from his injuries."

"If you say so," Arlo agreed. Gesturing to the other bandits with him, he said, "Start gathering firewood."

"Thank you," David told him. "Adelyn, do you think you can get onto Butler without my help?"

"I'm not a child," Adelyn mumbled, nodding. "Of course I can." She started to take a step forward, but her foot was completely asleep, and her heel failed to keep straight. She tumbled forward, and David caught her before she could hit the dirt.

Steadying her, David said. "You are out of strength. Let me help you."

Adelyn felt her cheeks flush in embarrassment, feeling weak and stupid. She'd run out of spirit while David was counting on her. Nodding sheepishly, she felt David slip his arm under her shoulder, supporting her and turning them both to where Butler was standing. Adelyn shifted her feet listlessly beneath her, focused on staying upright.

After walking for a few leagues and crossing the distance to Butler's side, Adelyn turned to climb into the saddle, putting an arm around David's body for more support. Her fingers touched something wet and cold beneath his jacket, and she pulled them away, confused to see sticky, half-dried blood. "David?"

"A piece of shrapnel," David said, keeping his voice low. "From the explosion. I did not want them to know I was hurt, in case they saw the injury as an exploitable weakness they could use to defeat us. It did not go deep, so you need not be concerned."

"Doesn't it hurt?" Adelyn asked.

"Doesn't it hurt? Oh, like dragon fire," David agreed. "But that is no problem for me. What is worse was that it made my spell difficult, spirit from blood comes in fits and starts, and the static of it makes a precise spell a challenge."

"You need to heal yourself," Adelyn said.

David shook his head, pulling Adelyn up toward her saddle. "I will be fine."

Frowning, she went along, climbing into place. "I don't believe you."

"You are tired," David said. "Your judgment is clouded. Can you sleep in the saddle?"

"I dunno," Adelyn said. "It didn't work so well last time."

"If you need, I can tie you into the saddle so you don't fall out," David said. "I will lead us out of the city, but you need to rest."

"I don't know if I'll be able to."

"Try anyways, for your own good," David said, walking over to his own horse.

She was out before he was in his saddle.

CHAPTER 23

My thesis can be explained by this syllogism:

-Firstly, nothing which exists can cause something which does not exist to begin existing out of nothing.

-Given that, anything which begins to exist out of nothing, cannot have been caused by something which exists.

-According to the Divine, (those who pray to the Divinities,) the universe was created out of nothing.

-From 2 and 3, the universe was not caused to exist by anything that exists.

-The Divinities are defined as beings which caused the universe to be created out of nothing.

Following these statements, the Divine must either admit that the Divinities do not exist by definition, or that neither logic nor reason exist by necessity.

- Excerpt from an essay by Gib Danielson, explaining his rejection of the Divinities and resulting faith in the Lords.

For once, Adelyn felt rested when she woke early in the morning, stretching and yawning as the sun came over the horizon. The relief of being rested was quickly lost next to the aches and pains in her body, and as she sat to look around she had to wince and twist her neck to work out a kink. They were in a fairly open plain, their small camp set up next to a lone scrubby tree that the horses had been hitched to.

She'd fallen asleep in her riding clothes and jacket, and whenever they'd stopped, David had apparently lowered her onto her sleeping mat and left it at that. She felt sweaty and stiff, and had a bad headache that turned the brilliant sunrise into a blight on her morning.

"Good morning!" David said, his tone chipper. He was sitting by the tree, polishing his silver necklace with a small cloth. "We made a lot of progress yesterday, considering the circumstances, but we should get on the road as quickly as possible. How are you feeling?"

"I'd kill a man for a cup of coffee and some Dr. Gregories," Adelyn said, rubbing a finger against her temple.

"Doctor Gregory?" David asked sharply, sitting up. "Do you need medical attention?"

"It's a pain tonic," Adelyn said. "I feel like someone drove a tent stake through my head."

David paused for a moment, then nodded in comprehension. "I cannot offer any coffee," he said, "But if you have a headache, I may be able to assist with that."

"How's that, a spell?" Adelyn asked, pushing herself to her feet and shuffling toward Butler. "Also, s'water gonna be scarce the next few days?"

"It is not exactly magic," David said, "But it is related. As for water, I do not think so."

"Great," Adelyn said, slipping off her jacket and grabbing her canteen. She splashed water on her face and arms, then poured a little more over her head, doing her best to wash away a bit of the grime that clung to her skin. "So what's your fix, then?"

"Are you able to take the spirit from items, yet?" David asked.

"Haven't tried it," Adelyn replied.

"It is not very difficult," David said. "Just do what you normally do, but backward. Here, do you mind?" He raised a gloved hand.

"I...don't know what you're gonna do," Adelyn said, confused.

David blinked. "I am going to fill the glove with spirit and put it to your forehead. Try and take out the energy."

"Sure," Adelyn said. David took a step toward her and placed his hand on her head, as though she was being anointed. She could feel a strong tingle of energy in his glove, and tried to think thoughts of pulling that energy away.

It took a few seconds, and then the motion clicked into place, and she pulled the energy into herself like a pump taking up water. In an instant, her headache vanished, replaced by a mild feeling of pins and needles.

"Lords be damned, that's a neat trick," She muttered, blinking a few times.

"It is not a cure-all," David explained, "But a little burst generally does well for spirit hangovers."

"Spirit...what? I didn't know that was something that could happen."

"Sorry," David said. "That is not the technical term. When you overuse spirit and exhaust yourself, it gives you a blinder of a headache the next day. Your body thinks that it exhausted itself through work or sleep deprivation, and when it discovers nothing amiss it does not know how to respond."

"I'll have to remember that," Adelyn said, checking her pack for any provisions. "You didn't happen to hunt any game while I was out, did you?"

"No," David said. "What kind of game were you hoping for?"

"Some wild hotcakes and butter," Adelyn said, shrugging. "Anything besides what we've got. If I have to go another day on that jerky, I might choose to starve instead"

"There are always the biscuits," David pointed out.

"Right," Adelyn said. "I'm saving those, to pound in some tent stakes."

"Tent stakes..." David mulled it over for a moment, considering the problem as he began folding up Adelyn's sleeping roll. "It is two more days to Arcere, there will be good food there. Can you wait that long? It will be some time out of our way to stop elsewhere for provisions, but if we need to, then—"

"It's fine," Adelyn said, grabbing a strip of tough jerky from her bag. "I'll make it." A second went by as she gnawed on it and swallowed a bite, then she added, "David, I'm sorry."

David faltered, letting the sleeping roll go slack under his hands. "You're sorry. What for? You have done nothing wrong."

Adelyn shook her head, tossing the remainder of the jerky back in her bag. "I cost us a day. If I'd been able to fight like you, we wouldn't've had to come back here to heal him. I couldn't even keep up when I was just fueling your spell."

"Adelyn, those things were all my fault," David said, standing to face her, though his gaze avoided her eyes and landed somewhere on her scarred cheek. "I knew we were being followed, but still led us into an ambush. I knew it was a difficult spell, but never considered if you were strong enough for it. You do not need to blame yourself."

"I should have been better," Adelyn said.

"You were good enough," David said. "I could not expect more."

Turning away, Adelyn took another swig of water, changing the subject. "What was the fire for?"

"Hmm?"

"You had them start a big fire," Adelyn said. "You never specifically said it was for the magic, and I don't know what a bonfire'd do to help that spell anyways."

David nodded, understanding the question and grinning. "If any peace officers are following us, they will be almost certain to see the smoke and go to investigate. It should keep them busy, for a while."

Adelyn snickered. "Should we get back on the road?"

"We should," David said, tying her roll to Butler's side, then walking to his own mount. Hauling himself into the saddle, he winced, putting a hand to his side.

"Are you okay?" Adelyn asked.

"Fine," David said. "I will be fine. It is nothing."

"If you say so," Adelyn said, frowning.

...

As David had said, it took two days to reach Arcere, and Adelyn was pleasantly surprised when the town came into view.

There were no great walls, no sweeping vistas, and no massive swaths of buildings—for once, their destination was a small town, barely larger than Marstone. It was still a fair sight larger than her hometown, but she could see from one end to the other as soon as it came into view, and the largest building was the modest Church of the Divinities at the center of town, practically sparkling with paint that couldn't be more than a year old.

"Do you know which house she lives in?" Adelyn asked, as they rode toward the town.

"Which house she lives in?" David shook his head. "No."

Adelyn sighed. "Well, it won't take long to go from door-to-door if you don't. I'm sure someone will know her."

"Someone will know her? I don't think we will have to ask someone," David said. "We have been out of touch for some time now, but unless I am mistaken, I have a way to locate her."

"What's that?"

"After the war, she..." David started, drumming his fingers on his leg and pondering his words for a moment. "Never mind. It will be obvious soon enough, and she can explain herself better than I can."

"That's a little cryptic," Adelyn commented.

"Be patient. I would rather not do a bad job explaining things."

They continued riding, and within a few minutes were at the center of town. A trip that was refreshingly short, in Adelyn's opinion. Rather than turning toward any nearby row of houses, though, David dismounted in front of the church, moving to start hitching up his horse.

"Why are we stopping here?" Adelyn asked, raising an eyebrow.

"Because we are going inside," David said. "Come on, we are wasting time."

Adelyn raised an eyebrow but complied, dismounting and tying Butler to the hitch. "So she believes in the Divinities?"

"Why do you guess that?" David asked.

"Because we're going into a church," Adelyn said, flatly. "Does she?"

"Yes, she does," David said. He walked up the pair of old wooden steps to the front door of the church and pushed it open, walking inside and holding it open for Adelyn to follow.

The church was similar to the one in Marstone, the only other real church Adelyn had seen in detail. Low chairs were organized in rows facing the back, where a raised stage and lectern were set up. In front of the stage sat a metal vessel about two feet across for collecting blood offerings, though it was made of silver, and not brass like the one that she'd seen when she still lived at home.

Flanking the vessel were two upright bins for accepting other sacrifices, and if Adelyn had to guess, there was no doubt a larger pit behind the church for accepting the seasonal offerings that would be burned or destroyed to beseech their 'gods' for better weather or a good harvest. Everything in the church gleamed with shine and polish, and the floorboards lacked even the smallest of scuffs or splinters that she'd grown accustomed to from such a heavily used building.

Glancing around, Adelyn saw a woman sitting at a table near the back of the temple, wearing a plain blue tunic and a simple ribbon to tie back her hair. Adelyn knew that the woman was part of the clergy, though couldn't place what her role was. As the door shut with a thud and a movement of air, the woman looked up from where she sat, spotted the pair of them, and got up.

"Hello!" Adelyn called, as the woman—*a priestess, maybe?*—walked toward them. "We're looking for someone, and thought you might be able to help."

The priestess hurried her stride as she grew closer and,

with ten paces left, broke out into a full run toward them. Adelyn stepped back in surprise, briefly wondering if this was some kind of attack, and then the priestess threw her arms around David and pulled him into a hug. He stiffened and winced in pain, then relaxed and put his arms around her as well.

They shared the embrace for several seconds, until Adelyn awkwardly coughed into her hand. "You know each other?"

"Undertow. It's been a while," the priestess said, a broad smile on her face. Adelyn blinked, surprised to hear David addressed by his last name.

"Seven years," David said. "I try and write, but it is hard to see if you reply, I am rarely home."

"I appreciate the effort."

"Your hair is longer."

"I'm surprised you noticed."

A second went by, and Adelyn cleared her throat to get their attention. "I take it you're Mary?"

The priestess looked over at Adelyn, her smile flickering for a second. "Yes. And you are?"

"Adelyn Mayweather," Adelyn said, extending her good arm to shake. Mary accepted the gesture, and as she did Adelyn caught sight of the scarring from repeated cuts on the palm of her hand, as well as an abundance of track marks on the inside of her arm, telltale signs of Mary's faith.

"It's nice to meet you, Adelyn," Mary said. She must have seen the scar on Adelyn's cheek, but she didn't comment on it, instead asking, "Are you a peace officer as well?"

"I...not exactly, but I'm working with David," Adelyn explained.

"Some raiders kidnapped her family, and another fifty-odd people besides," David interjected. "She hired me to help her track them down and rescue her family."

Mary nodded. "And that brought you here? I must say, those aren't the happiest tidings for a visit, but it's still nice to see you."

Adelyn stepped in before David could continue. "They're in the Beor Keep," she said. "And since you were a Stone Warrior like David, well...we thought you could help."

Mary's brow furrowed for a moment, and then her eyes widened and she looked to David. "You told her that?"

"I—" David started. He began drumming his fingers against his leg, but at a look from Mary his hand stiffened, pressing flat against his pocket to keep from rattling.

"I inferred it," Adelyn interrupted. "He said that you had fought together, and I put two and two together. I'll admit, though, I didn't expect, eh..." She gestured vaguely at the chapel they were standing in.

Mary looked at David and frowned deeply, the expression looking foreign on her face. "You want me to fight with you?"

"Yes," David said.

Mary straightened, turning to Adelyn. "Would you please excuse us for a moment, Adelyn?"

"I...yes?" Adelyn said. "I'll check on the horses."

"We won't be long," Mary said, watching Adelyn pointedly as she turned back to the door, slipping through and letting it shut behind her.

She quickly walked down the stairs to the street level, letting the boards creak noisily beneath her feet, then turned back and carefully walked up the side of the staircase, placing her feet over support beams to avoid any unwanted noise. Once atop the stairs again, she leaned against the door, placing her ear against it and listening in.

"... does she know?"

"I told her I fought with the Stone Warriors,"

"Why would you do that?"

"It is the truth."

The sound of Mary's exasperated sigh came through clearly. "I won't argue with you on this, David. If that's what you told her, it's what you told her. But how much does she know about me?"

"About you? Only that you taught me to use a sword, and that we fought together in the war," David said. "Mary, none of this matters. People need our help."

"You know I gave up that life."

"I am only asking you to take up your weapons," David said. "You need not take up your old life as well. Your gods would not want you to stand idly by and let those people die, would they?"

"Don't patronize me. You don't believe in the gods, you don't get to appeal to them."

"I am not appealing to them, I am appealing to you."

"I'm not the only person you could have gone to. Why couldn't you have just let me be? I'm happy here. I'm helping people."

"I cannot go to any other peace officers, even if they could help, and nobody else I trust is within five hundred miles."

"What about Adelyn?"

"I like Adelyn, I want to help her."

"But you don't trust her?"

"I do not trust her in a fight. She is not strong enough."

"But do you trust her at all?"

"I promised her my help."

"David, speak plainly. I know you too well for you to bandy words around me."

"She has been dishonest with me in the past. I believe that I have the whole truth from her now, but I cannot say I fully trust her."

"But you're following her?"

"Fifty people or more are being held at the Beor Keep, Mary. A sorcerer is keeping them there. It does not matter if I trust Adelyn."

There was a lengthy pause before Mary said, "For all you talked about changing, you're doing the same thing you did in the war."

"No, I am not."

"You mean it is just coincidence that you are planning to assault a fortress and an army singlehandedly? Even if you have a good reason, you're still just seeking out the fights because you enjoy it."

"You are wrong. It is not the same"

"How so?"

"If this were the war, I would not be asking for your help."

"I always helped you in the war."

"But I was never smart enough to ask first."

A half a minute passed, and then Mary's laughter echoed through the door. "Do you remember that time...it must have been just after the war broke out, you challenged the whole guardhouse to a duel?"

"I would have won that!"

"Sure, and you'd have put them out of commission for a month while they recovered, too."

"Adelyn is probably wondering what's taking us so—"

Adelyn pulled away from the door, stepping gracefully down the steps and crossing to Butler's side. Ten seconds went by, and then the church doors opened, Mary holding it open and waving to her.

"Sorry about that, you can come on in," she said, smiling wearily at Adelyn. "Well, I've food in the parsonage, as well as running water and a guest room. The two of you must be tired, why don't you come on over and I'll give you a place to rest and something to eat. What do you like?"

"Do you have any jerky?" Adelyn asked, walking up the steps of the church for the third time in as many minutes. "Or flour biscuits?"

"I...no?" Mary said, tilting her head as she kept the door propped open.

"Then whatever you have will be excellent," Adelyn said, walking inside.

Mary blinked, then nodded with a smile. "You've been on traveling rations for a while, then?"

"A couple weeks now, off and on."

"Well, I promise to serve real food," Mary said, glancing over at David, who was leaning against the wall. "Undertow? I assume you have no objections?"

There was a moment of uncertainty, and then David stood up straight and nodded. "Of course not."

"Wait, let's wait a moment," Adelyn said, holding up a finger. "I don't want to distract from the issue at hand. Are you going to help us?"

Mary took in a breath and replied, "We'll talk about it over dinner."

Adelyn furrowed her brow, then shook her head slightly. "That sounds like a 'no'."

Mary slowly walked a couple steps closer, so that she was looking Adelyn in the eyes. "Child. Don't disrespect my hospitality, or you may find that I'll not be inclined to help you."

"I'm not a child, and I've no need for hospitality," Adelyn shot back, surprised by the harsh response but unwilling to back down. "And are you really so callous that you'd let innocent people die because of a little disrespect?"

"I need to think on it for a spell," Mary said. "And you'd be better to keep a polite tongue, we're in a place of the gods."

Balking, Adelyn started, "If the gods were real, they'd already think ill of me, a few impolite words won't change that. And—"

"*Adelyn,*" David said, with the same intonation he used when casting spells. His tone made her stop, back straightening in apprehension. "Stop."

"You're *agreeing* with her?" Adelyn demanded, whirling on him. "David! She's threatening not to help because I asked for a plain answer!"

David gritted his teeth, hands clenching and unclenching in frustration. "I do not care if she threatens to kill your horse, you will not raise your voice at Mary, or I will abandon you myself."

"You're taking her side?" Adelyn asked, almost shouting.

Throwing his hands in the air, David said, "I am taking her side? I am doing no such thing! But she is my friend, and I will not stand to have you two fight!"

"Thank you," Mary added appreciatively.

David wheeled back to her, saying, "But you should know better than to agitate her. The girl's parents were captured and may be dead, Mary. I know you have compassion, but you do an ill job of showing it sometimes."

Mary pursed her lips. "Compassion isn't in words, but in actions."

"Then act," Adelyn said, trying to keep the edge from her tone. "Help us. Please."

Mary sighed. "You should attend to your horses and get washed up. I'll prepare dinner. If that answer is unsatisfying to you, then you are free to leave." She turned, stalking out the door and leaving Adelyn and David alone.

"Well," Adelyn commented dryly. "I think that went swimmingly."

CHAPTER 24

Day 297. Food is running low. We began our trek home three days ago, but have been forced to take cover in a cave and wait for an ice storm to blow over before we can make any progress. Starting a fire would bring dragons, so we are huddled with our pelts and trying to stay warm with other means.

Morale is a rare resource. After making the decision to abandon our quest, dashing any hope of finding a land beyond the realm of dragons, much grumbling began, and some even talked of mutiny. Some of them believe that, if they push through, they'll find the realm of the gods.

To be honest, I envy their beliefs. They can imagine a place that is warm and comfortable, but I know that we are doomed to live in this cold forever. Even if we make it home, we can never shake the ice that has begun to cling to our bones and to our very thoughts.

- Journal entry, found with the bodies of five explorers near the western side of Hoban's Passage. The original research team was composed of six dozen people. Most deaths were recorded in the journal, but the cause of death and ultimate fate of the final five, including the author, is unknown

THEY ATE IN SILENCE, save for the noise of spoons scraping against the bottom of soup bowls. Mary had made stew with fresh cornbread, and Adelyn took to eating it with a fervor. Even if the tension in the air wasn't so palpable as to make the hairs on the back of her neck stand up, conversation would have waited until dinner was finished.

Finished her second helping of stew, she pushed away the bowl, feeling more full than was comfortable but not regretting her indulgence for a second.

"Would you care for a coffee, Adelyn?" Mary asked, standing to collect the bowls.

"Please," Adelyn said, standing as well, deciding it couldn't do any harm to finally be polite. "And allow me to help with the washing."

"Very well," Mary said. "Bring in the stewpot, if you will. Undertow, coffee?" David nodded his head, drumming his fingers on the table. "Three cups, then." Mary turned, walking stiffly to the kitchen.

Adelyn hefted the half-full stewpot, carrying it as she followed behind Mary. The house was not a large affair, consisting of a simple dining room, a small kitchen, and a pair of smaller bedrooms. The kitchen had indoor plumbing to provide water, a recent addition, judging by the pipes jutting in through holes bored haphazardly through the wall.

Mary filled a kettle with water and set it on her stove, a wood burning affair that was old but well-maintained. "Do you take it with cream?" She asked, accepting the stewpot from Adelyn.

"Sometimes, depends on how good it is," Adelyn said, watching as Mary tip the stewpot over a trash bin, scraping out several spoonfuls of stew onto the garbage.

"*Thank you, Amel, for providing us with this bounty of food,*" Mary said reverently, before righting the stewpot and covering it with a lid. Catching Adelyn's skeptical expression, she added, "If you're going to say something critical, save your words."

"I wasn't," Adelyn said.

"At least you sometimes know to hold your tongue," Mary said. "Rinse out those bowls, will you?"

"Papa kept faith well enough, and my brother once he was old enough," Adelyn said as she obeyed, washing out the soup bowls and silverware. "It's not as though I've never seen someone who believes in the Divinities before."

Mary paused before setting the stewpot over the stove. "If your family was faithful, how—"

"Did I end up a heretic?" Adelyn asked.

"I wouldn't have put it like that," Mary said.

Adelyn shrugged. "I was always skeptical. A Tarraganian disciple came through town, what he had to say made sense."

Mary made a 'Hmm' noise, and Adelyn decided to change the subject. "So you saw David fight in the war. What was he like?"

"Have you seen him fight?" Mary asked.

"A few times," Adelyn said.

Mary nodded. "Well there you go. I imagine it's quite the same now as it was then."

"But he holds back now," Adelyn said. "It's obvious he could do more if he wasn't trying so hard to keep from hurting anyone. I have no idea how he does everything he does, and that's without seeing him go into combat with no holds barred."

Raising an eyebrow, Mary thought for a moment. "He was terrifying. Even without magic, he could beat any soldier in single combat. With spells to back him up, I've never seen his equal, at least in a duel. It was heresy, of course, but it had a sort of beauty to it if you weren't the one facing him down."

Adelyn frowned. "Heresy?"

"The magic," Mary clarified. "I am not judging him, I have committed many sins of my own, but magic is not meant to be controlled by mortal hands."

"Then why do sorceresses exist?" Adelyn asked, genuinely curious, if insulted. This was new doctrine, not something that had been preached explicitly in her home-town. People hated witches, sure, but that was just general paranoia.

"It's a gift by the gods, to facilitate sacrifices and prayer," Mary explained. "Mankind had no way to speak to the gods directly, and so the gods gave us the ability to move the ener-gies of life so that we could be closer to them. It was corrup-tion that led to humanity taking this ability and using it to manipulate reality ourselves. We took a gift and turned it into a weapon."

Adelyn's brow furrowed. "What about magic users who don't believe in your gods?"

"There is no reason they cannot repent for their actions," Mary said, "But if they do not, they'll be purged upon their death, as will all nonbelievers."

"You do know that David's magic could have won the war for us, right?" Adelyn asked. "Were things a little differ-ent, the Stone Warriors might have held off the president's soldiers long enough for us to arrange a counter offensive."

"I was there, Adelyn," Mary pointed out. "I saw him fight. I'm well aware of what his magic can do."

"Do you think I'm wrong?" Adelyn said.

Sighing, Mary shook her head. "Magic didn't help the Sovereignty fight off the president, magic helped the president win. Many hundreds of thousands died because of the Thirteen's sins. Had they not turned the gods' gift into a weapon of destruction, the president would never have won."

"Look, none of this matters," Adelyn said. "You've fought with David before, right?"

"A couple times," Mary said. "Fought alongside him, too."

Adelyn frowned at the joke. "Just do that again. Our differences of faith don't have to matter. I'm fair sure that both your gods and mine will approve of our saving innocent people."

"That's not the issue, child," Mary said. "Rescuing innocents is noble and good, but if we defy the gods and soil that which is holy to do so, we may save their bodies but damn our own souls in the process."

"For what it's worth, most of the people who were taken follow the Divinities," Adelyn said. "I didn't take their religion into account when I decided *I* was going to help them."

Mary put a finger to her temple, taking a deep breath for a moment. "Go ask Undertow how he likes his coffee, please."

"Cream until it's white, sugar until you can't taste the coffee," Adelyn said from memory.

That made Mary smile a little. "Some things never change. Wait in the dining room anyways, if you please, I've got to think about things for a moment."

"Do those things involve working on a polite way to tell us 'no'?" Adelyn asked.

Giving her a level look, Mary said, "I don't bandy words with the intent to deceive. If I knew for certain that I meant to tell you no, I'd tell you know straight away."

"Sure," Adelyn said, shrugging one shoulder. "Take your time." Walking back through the house, she pulled out her chair next to David and sat down.

"Did you two fight?" David asked.

"Only a little," Adelyn said. "Are you sure we need her?"

"If you want to survive the rescue, yes," David said. "I have other allies, but nobody close, and nobody that I could call on quickly. I knew Mary could be called on at short notice because she is not doing anything of value."

"Don't tell her you think that."

David nodded. "All I am saying is that we need her."

"Why not hire some mercenaries?" Adelyn asked. "You have the gold, don't you?"

"I have the gold—well, no. I had the gold, and may have some more, but we would need to travel west to find a good bank that would take my credit," David said. "It has been almost three months already, yes? A few weeks more would not necessarily—"

"No," Adelyn said. "We're close. I don't want to wait any longer."

"Then Mary is our only choice," David said. "And—"

"And I've made up my mind," Mary finished, carrying in tray stacked with mugs and setting them around the table. "I'd like to help you, but if I do, we'll be doing it my way."

Adelyn noted that her coffee was black, but Mary supplied her with a small saucer of cream to accompany it if she so chose. "What's 'your way'? I'm not going to carry a holy sword."

"I don't want that, anyways," Mary said. "Last time David tried using a holy sword, it caught fire and melted."

David blushed, accepting his coffee with a nod. "It is not as though it just exploded on contact," he offered.

"No, you saw the runes on the side and tried to use it to cast a spell," Mary chided. She sat, holding her own coffee and musing for a moment. "Anyways. I can't expect you both to convert overnight, but I do expect you to respect my beliefs. That means no more quips or snide comments when you think I'm not listening, Adelyn."

Adelyn blushed. "Anything else?"

"I'm going to pray after every meal. I assume you're going to be getting more provisions for the road, so keep that in mind and bring extra," Mary said. "I'll also need a sword to break before we go into battle, or some other weapon."

"We don't have any spare weapons," Adelyn said. "Is there somewhere in town that sells them?"

"I have my knife, actually," David said, addressing Adelyn. "I will use my hook and a staff. You can take your father's sword." Looking at Mary, he said, "It is royal steel. Will that do?"

"I will settle for it," Mary said, nodding. "Finally, I want the two of you to speak to a priest and atone for your sins."

Adelyn looked over at her sharply, eyes narrowing. "You want me to abandon the Lords?"

"I want you to go into this with pure souls," Mary said, shaking her head. "You don't need to say a prayer or dedicate your belief. Just talk to the priest, tell him what you've done, and he'll absolve you in the eyes of the gods. If you don't believe in the gods, then you can pretend it's just an old man telling you a story."

"My Lords will not see it that way," Adelyn said. "Going

through the motions of apostasy is no different than abandoning them any other way."

"Those are my conditions," Mary said. "If you want my help, I won't accept no for an answer."

Adelyn considered it for a moment, then asked, "If I talk to him, will he repeat anything I say?"

"Once he absolves you, your sins are gone. Not worth repeating," Mary explained.

"But will he repeat anything? I need a promise that he'll not speak of what I tell him," Adelyn said. "Regardless of what I say, what I admit to, I need his promise that it won't ever leave that conversation."

Mary nodded, smiling. "I can understand your hesitation, and no, it won't."

"Then I agree," Adelyn said. "David? What do you say?"

"I am thinking about it," David said. "Two minutes."

Adelyn nodded, drinking her coffee. Idly curious, she started counting off seconds in her head, as close to accurate as she could.

When her count reached one hundred seventeen, David said, "The Watchers will not care so long as I keep my vows and help them preserve the world. I will do it."

"Thank you," Mary said. "I will arrange for you to talk to him tomorrow morning. Firstly, though, we need to discuss a plan. What resources are available to us, what we know they do have or might have, what our current plan is."

Adelyn paused, chewing on her lip. "They've got a sorcerer, we know," she said. "At least thirty people, that's how many attacked my home town. They're holed up in the Beor Keep, and have at least a few scores of people prisoner."

"Probably at least another fifty fighters, if not more,"

David said. "And we do not know how many slaves they have bought, but we can safely double the number of prisoners as well."

Mary nodded. "Any idea what they're doing?"

"Beor Keep used to have some pretty full vaults, before... well, before the Thirteen collapsed most of the tunnels." David said. "We know they have Beor silver. Could be they are trying to get everything buried in there."

Making another mental note, Mary said, "That's going to be a hard fight, even under ideal conditions."

"Have you kept up your training?" David asked.

"I haven't fought anyone since the war, no. If we can spar on the way, that will hopefully shake the rust out of me. But one great wizard and a couple good fighters is still no match for one wizard and a hundred decent soldiers." Eying Adelyn, she added, "Can you? Fight, that is."

"All right," Adelyn said. "David has been training me. But..." She glanced over at David, who avoided her eye contact. "Your numbers are wrong. We haven't just got one sorcerer."

Mary paused, frowning in confusion and then widening her eyes as she realized what Adelyn meant. "Girl, you're a witch?"

"A sorceress," Adelyn corrected. "But yes, I am."

Mary nodded, and a few things seemed to click into place as she considered it. "Gods be, I don't like this, but it may have to do."

...

The priest was a short man with a large mustache, a balding pate, and an overwhelming odor of perfume that did very little to cover up the further overwhelming odor of a man who had not washed in several days.

"You're not what I expected," Adelyn commented, looking down on him.

He grinned sheepishly, extending both hands in a gesture of greeting. "Archibald Smith. What were you expecting, my child?"

Adelyn looked at his hand, then took it after a moment of hesitation and shook. "I suppose I thought that your robes would be black, for one," she said.

Archibald looked down, inspecting his robes—a loose fitting cotton affair with a floral pattern. "Ah, yes, well. I keep my dress robes aside for service and special occasions. Much more comfortable in these." He tapped his bare feet on the floor of the church, wiggling his toes.

Smirking, Adelyn asked, "Two sinners coming into the fold is not enough of a special occasion to you?"

Blinking, Archibald spluttered for a response. "I—well, yes, but—what I meant, was—"

"She's just giving you grief," Mary interjected, stepping between them. "Are you ready, Adelyn?"

"I'd rather let David go first," Adelyn said.

"He's not here yet," Mary pointed out.

"He said he was right behind us. I'll wait." Adelyn leaned against the wall, looking over at the priest. "So, Archie, how long have you...worked here? Been a priest here? I'm not sure the terminology."

"Since the war," Archibald explained. "I was a chaplain posted nearby, and the old priest was killed in a raid."

"Why would they kill a priest?" Adelyn asked.

"I don't suppose they meant to, my child," Archibald said, shaking his head. "Magical firestorms don't exactly care much where they burn, though, and he was in the church when it went ablaze. Mary here helped us rebuild from the ground up, the divine grace that she is."

Mary shuffled her feet, shrugging. "It was only reasonable. I can't serve in the chapel if there's no chapel."

Adelyn looked around, nodding as she looked at the decadence. "Well, you did a good job."

"Thank you," Mary replied. "But I was only one of many who pitched in."

Footsteps creaked on the steps outside, and Adelyn glanced that way. "David's here."

The door swung open and David walked inside, holding a coffee and looking tentative. "Is this him?" he asked, glancing between Archibald and Mary.

"Archibald Smith," the priest said, extending his hands to David in the same gesture he'd offered.

David wrinkled his nose, stared at the priest's hand for a moment, then took a drink of his coffee. "So where do we do this?"

"There's a room in the back," the priest said, smiling with a vaguely cheerful expression. "I'd offer you something to drink, but it seems you came prepared."

"Prepared," David agreed. "We should get this done with."

"I...right, of course. This way, my child," he said.

"I am not a child," David said, pursing his lips.

The priest shook his head. "We're all children, in the eyes of the gods."

Frowning, David said, "I am still not *your* child."

Archie opened his mouth, then shut it, showing his teeth in something resembling a smile. "Let's head to the back room, then."

"Indeed."

They both walked down the walkway between pews, leaving Mary and Adelyn standing alone in the church.

"I'd give a gold piece to watch how this goes," Adelyn commented wryly.

"That interested in Undertow's sins?" Mary asked, arching an eyebrow.

Adelyn waved a hand. "More that I'm interested in watching Archie spiral into madness."

"He's easily startled," Mary said, moving to sit down in one of the pews. "But he's more tenacious than he appears."

"He mentioned magic fire," Adelyn mentioned. "And we're close to Eddwind. I know the Thirteen spent a lot of time around here near the end of the war, did they—"

"Yes," Mary said, cutting her off. "This was one of the many towns ravaged by them. It wasn't even a strongpoint, but there were soldiers quartered here, and the Thirteen were available while a plan was struck up to deal with Eddwind, so they burned half the place to the ground."

"I imagine it's no coincidence you decided to come here, then," Adelyn said.

Mary looked up at her sharply. "What do you mean by that?"

"The Thirteen destroyed your fellow soldiers, almost all the rest of the Stone Warriors," Adelyn clarified. "You wanted to try and fix something that they'd destroyed."

"Oh, I...yes, I suppose. The location was also convenient, I'll admit, and the countryside is beautiful." Mary looked around the chapel, eyes glazing over slightly. "Tell me, how is David doing?"

Adelyn blinked at the sudden topic change. "What?"

"He was...a live wire, if you will, before the war. On edge all the time, ready to fight at a heartbeat's notice. To be honest, it's probably why he was recruited, but...I just want to know how he's faring on his own." She looked across the church, eyes resting on nothing in particular. "I was always around to take care of him during the war. For all his strength, he's always needed guidance from someone with more acuity. I worry how he's doing by himself. Once a commanding officer, always a commanding officer, I suppose."

"David doesn't strike me as someone who needs a caretaker," Adelyn said.

"He doesn't?" Mary asked, looking at Adelyn critically. "You've noticed that he's different, right?"

Adelyn shrugged. "I don't see how that matters. He's plenty capable of caring for himself."

"The magic helps," Mary conceded.

"No," Adelyn said. "It's not that."

Mary pursed her lips. "I think I know David a little better than you do, Adelyn. You've barely known him a month."

Adelyn shrugged. "If you say so. He's doing fine. He's already recovered from the ambush, I think. At least, he doesn't seem to show any pain."

Mary frowned. "Ambush?"

"When we were crossing through Eddwind," Adelyn explained. "A piece of shrapnel hit him in the side."

Mary pursed her lips a bit. "Have you seen the wound?"

"No," Adelyn admitted. "But—"

"Gods be," Mary swore, but she changed the topic. "What was he doing before this all started?"

"When I met him, you mean?" Adelyn asked, receiving a nod in answer. "He was traveling with some merchants that had a warrant out."

Eyes widening, Mary asked, "He was working with criminals?"

"No, no," Adelyn clarified quickly. "He was traveling with

them until they reached a military outpost, where he was going to arrest them."

"Oh," Mary said, nodding.

"Do you think this plan is actually going to work?" Adelyn asked. "Not doubting your skills, but there's still only three of us."

"That'll depend on what they've got," Mary said. "At least half of our planning relies on speculation and guesswork."

"It's not all guesswork," Adelyn said. "We—well, you and David know how to navigate the keep, you know the likely spots where they might be keeping prisoners or slaves."

"The *likely* spots," Mary emphasized. "And we *knew* how to navigate it. It's been years since I've been there, and the keep is built like a maze."

Adelyn shrugged. "That's an advantage to us, though. We're outnumbered, but can beat just about anyone in an even fight, what with our magic and your training. If the whole place is a maze of halls, we can't be overwhelmed."

"We went over this last night," Mary said.

"We made plans last night," Adelyn replied. "I know the plans. I want to know what you think."

Mary gave in, tilting her head and considering the question for a moment. "I think... we have fair odds, if Undertow can handle their wizard. He's kept up his practice and I don't know of many people whose skills could match his during the war."

"Then we should be fine," Adelyn said, nodding.

Mary shook her head. "That's not what I said. Undertow's fighting at a disadvantage. He won't kill his opponents. They *will* kill him, at least if they get the opportunity."

"I can help him, back him up," Adelyn said.

"No, you're sticking with me, he's fighting his own

battles." Mary chided. "You can barely swing a sword, and I'm not going to be throwing around any magic. That's the plan, that's what we're going to do."

Frowning to one side, Adelyn said, "Well yes, but if the situation arises—"

"Then you will stay out of the way." Mary put up a hand to silence further argument. "David won't say it, but there's another reason why you're sticking with me. If you are there when he's fighting the wizard, you'll be a harm more than a help, since he'll have to protect you and fight the wizard both."

"I can handle myself," Adelyn said, biting her tongue from saying anything more aggressive. "I'm no liability."

Mary sighed. "Not against a regular soldier, but against a trained wizard who knows what he's doing? You're barely more of a nuisance than a stumbling drunk."

Knuckles popping as Adelyn clenched her fist, Adelyn asked, "So, even if we're just standing by, watching the spectacle, you don't want me to help?" Mary nodded, and Adelyn didn't have any retort ready. Neither of them said anything else, and as the silent seconds slipped into minutes, Adelyn's gaze returned to looking around the chapel.

"How long does this usually take?" Adelyn asked, trying to broach the silence.

"That depends on the individual," Mary said. "But knowing Undertow, it may be some time. He tends to be thorough."

Adelyn nodded, then paused mid-gesture as a thought struck her. "You and he," she said, letting the words hang for a moment.

Mary glanced at her. "Yes?"

"During the war, or before, did you ever..." Adelyn

trailed off. "You two seem awfully close, I was just wondering if you—"

"Were lovers?" Mary finished, chuckling softly. "No, child. Certainly not. I'm not sure he ever had so much as a thought of romance, at least not during the war, and he's not mentioned anyone in his letters. What makes you ask?"

Adelyn shrugged. "I was just curious. The topic never came up in conversation while we were on the trail. Not that he talks about much of anything in his history, now that I'm thinking on it."

"He keeps his cards close to the chest," Mary agreed. "I know most of his past, but I'm not sure anyone knows all of it."

Seeing the opportunity, Adelyn asked, "Do you know why he got his tattoos?"

Mary pursed her lips, shaking her head. "That's not for me to share. He'll tell you in his own time."

"But you know why he got them," Adelyn persisted.

"I do," Mary said.

Adelyn bobbed her head slightly in a nod. "Does it have to do with the war?"

Mary gave a heavy sigh, more for show than anything else.

"Sorry," Adelyn said.

Mary nodded to acknowledge the apology, but didn't pick the conversation back up.

David took another ten minutes to finish, returning from the experience with a tense expression on his face and a priest who looked considerably less genial.

"Undertow," Mary said, standing.

"I do not want to talk on it," David said, shaking his head and starting to walk past her. Mary caught his arm, making him flinch.

"David Undertow, are you injured?" Mary asked, her tone scolding.

He stiffened further, looking away. Mary didn't wait for a response, she simply seized his shirt and yanked up, revealing a fresh bandage flecked with spots of blood.

"David," Mary said, intoning the word like an oath.

Twisting, David shoved her away, hurrying to pull down his shirt. "I am *fine,"* he said.

Mary shook her head, exclaiming. "You're not!"

"It will be healed by the time we arrive," David said. "It is nothing."

Taking on a scolding tone, Mary said, "Were you even going to tell me? That sort of injury—"

"I am *fine,"* David insisted, turning to walk out the door, fingers clenching into a tight fist. "Leave me be!"

Mary started to follow, but Adelyn stepped in her way. "I need to talk to you."

"Not now," Mary said, looking past her. David had stormed out, slamming the large church doors behind him.

"Yes, now," Adelyn said. "It is about my talk with your 'minister'."

"If you've got concerns about Archibald, you don't have to speak with him, we can find someone else," Mary said, trying to dismiss her concerns. "I know he's a little eccentric, but we don't have a large clergy in town."

"That's not it," Adelyn said. "What I wanted to say is that, to put it simply, I'm not David."

"How do you mean?" Mary asked, finally facing Adelyn.

"David won't lie, for any reason," Adelyn said. "When he tells you that he talked to the priest and confessed all his sins, you can trust him."

"And I can't trust you?" Mary asked.

"When it comes to this? Not really," Adelyn said, shrugging. "I will still go through with what I promised, but you've got no reason to believe me, so from your perspective I may as well skip the whole thing."

Mary put a hand to her forehead, closing her eyes and breathing in deeply. "What is your point, child?"

Adelyn shrugged. "I don't want to do this, and if I do, I'm going to put in the minimum effort and then immediately repent to the Lords. Besides, I'm pretty sure you were more concerned with David's spiritual welfare than mine. I was hoping you'd allow me to skip the pageantry."

Mary opened her eyes, looking up at the sky. "And you waited until David was done so that he wouldn't object to my letting you off while he had to go through with it."

"He wouldn't have to know," Adelyn said. "Like I said before, I'm comfortable telling a lie if it makes him feel a bit better."

"I appreciate your candor," Mary said, her tone flat. "But the problem still exists that I won't fight alongside you if your spirit isn't pure."

"Well," Adelyn said. "I had another proposal, instead. I don't want to talk to your priest, but I will read your book while we're traveling to the keep."

Mary turned her head sharply, raising her eyebrows in surprise. "In good faith?"

"Talking to an old man in a bathrobe won't convert me," Adelyn said, shrugging. "Maybe your books will. I won't promise any results, but it's going to be your best shot at getting me to go along with your faith."

Mary paused, then nodded. "We've got six tomes in total," she said. "I'll pack them all. I'm not sure you'll have time to read them all, but just in case."

"Sure," Adelyn said, not mentioning that she'd read all

the books before, and hadn't been convinced then. "I'm going to go find David."

"I'll procure the provisions we'll need, we should be ready to depart by the end of the day." Mary said. "And Adelyn...I'm glad you're keeping an open mind."

Adelyn didn't bother to correct her.

CHAPTER 25

Pinning down the beliefs of the locals who call themselves 'Watched' (pronounced 'Watch-ed') is a bit of a pain, as few will speak to our census takers, and those that do mostly have told them to do anatomically impossible acts of self-reproduction. Many probably remember that their beliefs were outlawed only a few years past, and don't believe that the president's rule will be any kinder to them. On account of this, much of what I record below is hearsay and secondhand, and should be treated as such when entered into the Presidential Archives.

Comparing their faith to that of the much more loquacious Watched who live along the coast, there are many similar beliefs —the most primary one, of course, being their belief in the 'Watchers', a divine collection of beings who apparently care for the earth and grant sorcerous powers to whomever they deem worthy. Besides that, though, their faith seems to have diverged greatly. They apparently believe in a smaller number of Watchers, numbered in the dozens and who are all named, and that each watcher can grant powers to dozens or even hundreds of people should they so choose.

While this is mere speculation on my part, and probably

requires further study before it's admitted to any records, it seems to me that their beliefs have been cross contaminated with that of the Divinities—legends and mythology surrounding the Watchers includes various creation stories that closely resemble that of the Divinities. These myths are not told by any Watched on the coast, lending credence to my belief that their faith has been mixed and diluted with that of other local religion.

- Excerpt from a census report on religious beliefs of the Middle Western city of Greenfield, to be added to many such reports and admitted to the Presidential Library

MARY HELD out an apple for her pale horse, idly running a hand through the old mare's mane as she watched David and Adelyn train. "You're doing that wrong," she called.

Adelyn lowered her sword, sweating profusely despite the slight chill in the air. "What? My stance?"

"Not you," Mary said, nodding toward David. "Him. Undertow, you're teaching the girl wrong."

David wiped his brow and walked over to his horse, grabbing his canteen forcefully and popping off the top. After taking a long drink, he asked, "Wrong? What am I doing wrong? These are fundamentals. I am certain that I have not forgotten how to do this."

Mary shrugged, letting her horse finish off the apple before walking back to her saddlebag. "Sure, if you've got unlimited time and don't expect her opponents to have anything except a sword."

"Except a sword..." David said, rolling one shoulder. "Statistically speaking, the majority of people she will face will either be equipped with a sword or a gun. If it is a gun, magic or evasion will be necessary as defense, so I am showing her how to defend against a sword."

"Is she going to be an expert in eight days?" Mary asked. "Because that's how much time you've got to teach her before we arrive." She took a few steps closer. "Besides. *You* need to be resting. You've got that wound that needs to be healed before we arrive, remember."

David glowered, and he began drumming his fingers against his leg, then stopped, clenching his hand into a fist. "I told you, I am—"

"You're hurt!" Mary said, throwing up her arms in exasperation. "What's the harm in admitting it?"

"I can push through," David said, fingers clenching and unclenching in an idle motion, like they wanted to move but he was holding them back.

"You don't have to," Mary countered. "And you're wasting your time, anyways. She needs to know more than defense"

"What is wrong with defense?" David asked. "I am trying to keep her alive."

"You know what makes it really hard to attack someone?" Mary asked, before answering her own question. "A sword through your belly. Takes the fight out of most people I've met."

"Only if you can get the sword into the belly," David countered. "Adelyn is still not at the point of being able to get around any competent fighter's guard."

"She doesn't have to be," Mary said, walking back to her horse and digging through her saddlebags.

"Then how—" David started, before glancing to his side in thought. "Okay, fair, but her training will be incredibly lopsided. It is best to learn the fundamentals first, then start combining what you know."

"What'm I missing?" Adelyn asked, glancing between the two of them.

"How much magic do you know?" Mary asked. "I'm

assuming your training has been pretty segregated, only doing magic or swordplay, never both at the same time?"

"Oh," Adelyn said. "No, we haven't."

Mary pulled her hand from her bag, holding a long whip. "Undertow, I'm taking over Adelyn's training. Rest. Heal. I've got this."

David hesitated for a moment, then gave a long sigh and held out his hook to Mary, hilt-first. "You have got this," he agreed, sounding resigned.

"I need the refresher course, besides," Mary said. "And you'll still be needed, don't you worry. I can't exactly teach her magic, now, can I?"

"I suppose your religion would frown on that," David agreed.

Turning to face Adelyn, Mary asked, "How focused are your attacks with magic?"

Biting her lip, Adelyn considered for a moment and said, "I can usually hit my target? We've mostly been working to control spirit."

"That's important too, but you're going to need precision," Mary explained. "I'm going to hold out this sword in a standard defensive pose, I want you to try and focus the spell so that it begins between my arms and pushed outward, breaking my guard. That way, you'll be able to come in for an attack. David, can you show her how to do that?"

David nodded. "Give me a moment to consider the best words to use for that, to compensate for Adelyn's lack of focus."

"Hey!" Adelyn objected playfully.

"Once you've got this down," Mary commented, getting them back on track, "We can see about using some basic leg strikes that work with your spells. That may have to wait until our next break, though, the horses are almost rested."

"Okay," Adelyn said, nodding. "Let's get to work."

...

Mary's training, combining magic and swordplay at once, proved to be more tiring than either had been individually, and Adelyn was more than happy to get back on the road.

Unfortunately, the 'road' proved to grow rougher and less hospitable as they continued working their way forward. The rolling terrain grew steeper, and the path which had long since given way from gravel to dirt was now beginning to look less like a path and more like a deer trail.

On top of this, Mary's old mare was not as used to traveling as Butler or Ace. With the steep, rough terrain, they were stopping far more frequently to rest the horse. Consequently, Adelyn found herself subjected to more, harder training than she'd grown used to, and Mary seemed unconcerned with how taxing Adelyn found her training regimen to be.

David used his newfound free time to begin replacing the sketch of Mary that he'd once had in his journal, before Adelyn had dunked the book in the river. It took him a long time, with much careful thought behind every pencil stroke, but over time he managed to create a very close likeness of Mary's face, though in his sketch she had short cropped hair.

In between training sessions, Mary ensured that Adelyn kept her promise, leading the way so that Adelyn could read through the Books of the Divinities. It was only possible some of the time—Adelyn had to often take the reins so that they could navigate a difficult patch of terrain, but whenever she wasn't needed to steer, she was put to reading.

When they stopped for a meal break she ate voraciously, digging in to Mary's packed provisions. Neither jerky nor biscuits had made it into their bags—instead, they had bread that would still be fresh for a few days, late summer fruit, potatoes, cheese, and a food made of dried beef, rendered fat, and berries. Mary insisted the dish was good and filling, but Adelyn refused to try the mix while there were other options.

The food restored some of her strength, but even so she was growing weary by mid-afternoon. She'd balked at the idea of asking for a reprieve, but her strength was flagging, and she was beginning to think that her pride could take the hit if it got her some rest.

As they crested a rise in one of the many rolling hills, Mary pointed down toward the valley in front of them. "There's a shady spot down there where we can break," she said.

David nodded, and Adelyn decided it was time to voice her objection, when something caught her eye and she had to do a double take. "What's that?" she asked, pointing forward.

"Hmm?" Mary asked, eyes following Adelyn's finger.

"Way in the distance," Adelyn explained, trying to interpret what she was seeing into words that made sense. "It's really faint, but...Lords, are those mountains?"

Mary laughed, asking in an amused tone, "Child, have you never seen mountains before?"

"I've seen a picture, once," Adelyn said. "I knew they were big, but...those are *big*." She stared, trying to guess how tall the hulking formations were in front of her. They had to be a day's travel away, and yet they were plainly visible, sticking up above the light cloud cover. "Why're they white on top?"

"White on top?" David asked. "That's snow."

Adelyn furrowed her brow, confused. "What?"

"You do know what snow is, right?" Mary asked.

Adelyn rolled her eyes. "Yes, I know what snow is, but it's barely chilly out, and harvest season has a month yet. How's there any snow?"

"Temperature drops with altitude," David explained. "At the mountaintops, it is as chilly as any winter's day."

"Good thing I replaced my coat," Adelyn quipped.

Mary titled her head, then asked, "What happened to your old coat?"

"Which time?" Adelyn asked. "First time, David held me at knifepoint and the back got cut."

"And the second time?"

Adelyn shrugged, trying to convey casual flippance. "I got shot."

Mary blinked, then glanced over to David. "She's not joking, is she?"

"No, she did get shot in the arm," David confirmed.

Considering that for a moment, Mary asked, "What happened?"

"David was fighting some local color," Adelyn explained. "I had to rescue him. Someone didn't take kindly to that."

Mary put a finger to her head, sighing. "Why am I getting the impression that I should have asked more after the nature of your journey?"

Glancing over at David, Adelyn said, "I think I should start from the beginning. It's rather a long story."

She summarized the events of the past weeks, from hiring David to the present. The telling carried them to the bottom of the hill, through the entire rest, and another ten minutes past that as they got back on the road. Mary didn't seem to mind the lapse, too curious about what had happened to interrupt. The reprieve was enough for Adelyn to catch her breath, and when they stopped to rest again an hour later, she was ready to train once more.

When night fell, they set up camp, lit a fire, and ate a token meal. Once they'd eaten, Adelyn sprawled out on her sleeping mat and was out like a light before David or Mary had even laid down.

In the morning, Adelyn was the last to wake, smelling fresh coffee and morning dew, a combination of smells she wasn't expecting. Mary insisted on morning exercise before Adelyn ate, and once she'd downed some coffee and bread, it was back on the trail.

It was another hard day on the road, interspersing riding and training. David taught her magic while they were in the saddle, Mary taught her swordsmanship and combat when they stopped, Adelyn read holy books when she had the time. Adelyn managed to make it through the training, but she had to call for a short rest around mid-day, and once again she was completely exhausted by sundown.

On the third day, they were in true mountain terrain, and with that came rougher riding and harder ground. This led to longer breaks to rest the horses, and with the extra time Mary began adding stretches and plain physical exercise on top of the combat training. Adelyn wanted to protest fatigue, but Mary was going through the same exercise and training—minus the magic, at least—and she didn't want to give in when her tutor was handling her own burden without complaint.

That evening, they ran out of bread. Mary produced corn biscuits that she'd kept covered and wrapped in a cloth to help preserve them, but Adelyn refused them. Once the fire was lit, she again fell into a deep sleep.

Halfway through the fourth day, Adelyn gave in and

tried the beef dish that Mary had packed. The texture was not to her liking, but the taste was reasonable and felt more nourishing than snacking on fruit and cheese.

After inquiring after how much ammunition was available, Mary also recommended that they take some time to practice Adelyn's marksmanship.

On the fifth day their training took a reprieve as they had to cross a narrow mountain trail and had no room to spar. Adelyn found herself feeling sick and lightheaded for much of the day, and so the respite was perfectly fine with her.

They ran out of coffee on day six.

On the seventh day, it rained, which meant that Adelyn did not have to read the holy books for fear of getting them wet. Mary's training went on without hindrance, teaching Adelyn to fight amidst mud and rainwater.

On the morning of the eighth day, Mary had a changeup prepared.

"We're not going to practice today," she said, passing Adelyn the last apple.

"Why not? I think I'm getting pretty good," Adelyn said. Despite the exhaustion of the past week, she felt good. She felt *strong.* She could take on the world and win, as long as the world favored her right side—her left arm still wasn't up to full strength.

Mary nodded. "You could be doing much worse, that's for certain, but we've got to keep our strength for the fights to come. We're getting too close to the keep, and we don't know if they have scouts posted. Swords make a cacophony so loud that Azahim would hear them from the desert. That's out, along with any magic that makes considerable noise, and any rifle practice."

"That's most everything you've shown me," Adelyn said. "So will it just be exercise, then?"

"Unless you've got anything you want to learn that'll be quiet," Mary said.

Adelyn shrugged. "I can think of a few things. We can talk about it on the road."

Mary nodded. "It'd be nice to spar and warm up before we spring the rescue, but stretching and prayer will have to suffice. For what it's worth, you've been a good student."

David laughed, and Adelyn looked over at him. "I'm missing something funny?"

"'You have been a good student'. I am fairly certain that Mary has never spoken those words in that order before," David explained, grinning. "If nothing else proves it, that does—she has grown sentimental."

"Or maybe," Mary said, "It's just the first time I've had good enough reason to say it. I had to put in extra effort to get you up to scratch, training Adelyn was practically easy."

"Tell me that when Adelyn works for a week straight with no rest," David said, adding as an aside, "No offense, Adelyn, you really have been doing very well."

Mary laughed. "You had to train for a week straight because you'd not have learned quickly enough otherwise!"

"Wait, wait," Adelyn said, injecting herself into the banter. "I *did* just train for a week straight. Learning spells and practicing my aim in the saddle is not rest, by my estimate."

David paused to consider for a moment, then said, "Well...not exactly."

"He's being literal," Mary added, turning to pack up their sleeping rolls. "A week *straight.*"

Adelyn nodded. "He's always literal, but...wait, what?" Spinning to look David in the eye, she asked, "How?"

David avoided her gaze, shrugging. "It is not efficient in the slightest, but spirit can be extracted from blood and used to energize another individual so that they do not need sleep. Because of my magical ability, training me to prepare for the war was seen as a priority, so excess blood was diverted to maximize my training. I trained for around one hundred and seventy consecutive hours before the infusions of magic couldn't sustain me any longer."

Adelyn nearly staggered at that. "That's...wow."

Mary stepped up behind David and put a hand on his shoulder, making him flinch away. "I was only joking a moment ago, Undertow. You were a good student."

"I am aware," David said, frowning for a second before reconsidering his words. "I mean, I am aware that you were joking. But thank you."

Mary smiled. "And you're right, I've grown sentimental."

David's expression flickered for a moment, then settled on a smile. "We should get on the road. We want to reach the keep before nightfall."

At mid-morning, they ran out of trail, striking out up the wooded mountainside on a course that David had plotted. It was slow going, made slower by the regular stops to reroute or move around impassable terrain.

As they approached, they discussed their plan in low tones, going over details and making sure that everyone was in agreement and had not forgotten anything. Many of their decisions would depend on details that they couldn't know —location and number of enemies, for the most part. Fighting every single bandit head-on would be a losing proposition, but with luck that wouldn't be necessary.

As the sun started to lower back down, their low conversation drifted off into silent contemplation, David leading the way along the quietest path that he could find. Adelyn was starting to feel a tingling excitement in her fingertips, adrenaline and anxiety fighting for control over her body. This was going to be it, one way or another, unless David had horribly miscalculated and the keep was empty.

Finally, David held up an arm, turning back toward them and whispering. "We are almost there. It is about the time that we should dismount and go on foot, in case someone hears—"

"Hey!" The voice was not one that Adelyn recognized, and it came from not far away. "Who on the gods' earth are you?"

CHAPTER 26

Third day of planting season, 5A

I was out tending my garden today when a woman approached from the mountains. I'd been expecting an envoy with mail, but she came from the wrong direction, and she carried neither bag nor pack, and her clothes were torn all to shreds and hanging on her body in a bundle. I don't know how the poor thing handled the cold, never mind how she evaded the dragons.

After inviting her to my home and dressing her in Gabrielle's old things, she finally began to speak to me a little. She says she was part of an expedition north, to determine the extent of the mountains. They'd gone under cover of snow tents and carried little meat, to avoid dragons.

I believe her to this point, but her story of a great forest full of trees big as striders, of creatures bright and shiny like candied apples who would kill a man at a touch, of insects large as a man's head...they ring untrue in my ears. If the gods saw fit to create such monsters, surely they would save them for the deepest pits of the purged.

- Diary entry, written after conversations with the last surviving member of the North Forest Expeditionary Team

ADELYN SPUN BUTLER AROUND, looking for the source of the voice, leaning down toward where the rifle was strapped to her saddlebags.

"No," Mary said quietly, putting up a hand to stop Adelyn, then raising her voice, "Thank the gods, someone's found us!"

"Found us? What?" David asked, looking over at her.

Pulling her old horse alongside David, Mary gave him a light slap on the shoulder. "We're *lost*, dear, whether or not you'll admit it." Glancing up, she shouted, "Hello! Who's out there? Can you point us to the road?"

A second passed, before the voice echoed back from the woods. "If you'll pardon us, I'm going to stay right up here where you can't see me. Lotsa suspicious characters out here in this bit of noplace, can't hurt to be cautious."

"That's all right!" Mary shouted back, glancing over her shoulder at Adelyn and making and giving a significant glance. "Could you be a saint and point us back toward the road? It seems someone can't navigate quite so well as he *thinks* he can."

"What're you doing out here?" The voice was easy to hear, but echoed through the trees, and as much as Adelyn tried she couldn't pinpoint the source of the voice.

"My husband and daughter were traveling west. We heard there's work in the capital, and we wanted to get through the mountains before the harvest season ended and they became impassable."

"You armed?"

"Abandon this," David muttered, quietly glancing from

side to side. "They are too far away, I cannot sense them. Adelyn, draw your—"

"Hush, I've got this," Mary said, shaking her head. "Yes, of course we're armed! Like you said, it's dangerous out here."

There was another pause, and then the voice called down. "Y'all mind raising your hands up real high, so I can see you don't have any of those weapons ready to use on me."

"Can I trust you to treat us fairly?" Mary called out.

The response came flat and without menace. "Ma'am, all respect to your concerns, but if I wanted a corpse of you, I'd just have to pull my trigger."

"Ah," Mary said. "I appreciate you haven't done that yet."

"*We need to run,*" David hissed, eyes darting through the tree line.

"Put up your hands, *husband dear*," Mary said, putting emphasis to ensure David didn't miss anything. "I'm sure we can trust this man."

The voice echoed down. "Your husband seems a mite twitchy! Something we need to be concerned about?"

David sighed, his shoulders slumping as he raised his hands into the air. "I was against this venture from the start." Glancing at Mary, he asked, "*Now* do you believe that this was a dangerous idea?"

"Yes, dear," Mary said. "Daughter, do as the man says and put your hands up."

Adelyn obeyed, still trying to figure out where the man was, right up until he walked out of the trees toward them.

His outfit wasn't exactly camouflage, but it was a long jacket of dark canvas died with browns and greens of a similar shade to the surrounding terrain, and a matching cap pulled down over his pale face. He held the rifle one-handed, between his elbow and side so that he could wave it around while holding a similarly polished six-shooter in his other hand.

"How's the hunting?" Mary asked.

"Not great," he said. "And—"

"You are hunting alone?" David asked. Mary gave him an annoyed glance, but didn't interrupt.

"Yessir," he said, eying David. "Not enough game to really get a hunting party together up here, anyways. You folks've lost your way, then?"

Mary nodded, turning her annoyed glance into a mild glare in David's direction. "*Someone* recommended we take a shortcut, we've been wandering the area for two days now."

"Gotcha," the hunter thought for a moment, then gestured up at the sun with his revolver. "Well, you gotta follow—"

"*Bynd,*" David intoned, twisting his right hand in a complicated gesture as soon as the revolver was pointed away.

The hunter went rigid, hand tightening on his pistol and sending a shot into the air, echoing through the trees like a thunderclap. David was off his horse and wresting away both guns before the echo had time to fade, and had the hunter disarmed before Adelyn had time to pick up her rifle.

"Gods be, Undertow, I had that handled," Mary said with a sigh, gracefully climbing down from her horse.

"He is clearly with the bandits," David said, glancing over his shoulder at her. "We can question him and get more information."

"He just fired a shot. There's sure to be more of them coming," Mary said.

"Will they?" Adelyn asked. "He's supposed to be hunting, right?"

"He said he is," Mary agreed. "But who says we can trust a sinner in the woods?"

David shrugged. "Well, we should ask." Waving a hand through the air, he dismissed the spell holding the hunter in place. David caught the man before he fell to the ground, then pushed him against a tree and pointed his own revolver at his face. "I am going to ask you some questions and make some statements. Nod yes, shake your head no. Do not call out. Do you understand?"

The hunter nodded.

David showed his teeth. "Great. You are with a group of people living in the Beor Keep, yes?" The hunter nodded again. "And—"

"You can't kill me!" the hunter blurted, quickly, before David pressed the revolver barrel into his cheek.

"Why not?" Adelyn asked.

David sighed. "I am asking the questions, Adelyn. Let me handle this, please?"

"I want to know," Adelyn replied. "Why can't we kill him?"

David slumped a bit, then made a 'move along' gesture with the barrel of the gun. "Why can we not kill you? Answer her."

"If you kill me, the wizard," The hunter paused, clarifying, "Er, *our* wizard, that is, will know. He always knows when someone dies. He'll come out here to kill you."

"Come out here to kill me? Maybe that is what I want," David said. "I am not afraid of some other wizard."

"Well, you should be," the hunter said, shaking his head. "He's not just any wizard, he's one of the Thirteen."

David faltered for a moment, almost lowering the pistol

before he caught himself, reasserting the gun. He looked over at Mary for a moment, and Adelyn looked over as well to see that she was wearing a tight, worried expression.

"Which one?" Mary asked, her voice more calm than her expression would have implied.

The hunter glanced up at her, then said, "The Blue Flame."

"Bullshit," David said, twisting his hand and hissing words more rapidly than Adelyn could hear.

"Undertow, wait—" Mary started, but before she could object, the hunter slumped to the ground, unconscious. "You couldn't let me get *one* question in?"

"He was a liar," David said. He began drumming his fingers against his leg in fits and starts, unable to settle into a rhythm. "We could not trust anything he says. We should just get on the road and find out the truth for ourselves."

"Wait, how do you know?" Adelyn asked, interjecting herself. "What if he was being honest?"

"He is not," David said. "Why would the Blue Flame be out here?"

"You're dodging my question," Adelyn said. "Why—"

Mary cut in. "Drop it, Adelyn. Now. We aren't learning anything from him now."

Adelyn bit her tongue, sighing and slumping her shoulders. "We've got to be close. How soon do you think we'll—"

Thunder roared from the revolver as David fired it into the air, five shots in rapid succession. Once the gun clicked empty, he tossed it to the ground and started shrugging off his jacket. "Mary, take the horses and back off a ways, take the liar with you. Adelyn, climb a tree with your rifle, get out of sight, but make sure you can see me. I am going to put on his coat and wait to ambush anyone who comes to his rescue."

Mary clenched her jaw, then relaxed it. "Undertow, any reason you didn't consult me *first*?"

"I want this to be over," David replied, folding his jacket and stuffing it into a saddlebag. "And I did not want any argument. The course is set now. Adelyn, you should start climbing."

Adelyn started to move to grab her rifle, then stopped. "No. You climb the tree, I'll put on the coat."

"The coat..." David frowned, taking a step toward her. "No, that is not my plan. I—"

"If they shoot you from ambush, we are dead in the water," Adelyn said, holding her ground. "I'm the weakest link of the three of us."

"I can—"

"Furthermore, you two look nothing alike," Adelyn pointed out. "If they catch one glimpse of your skin, it'll be obvious that you're not the same man. I at least match his complexion. You're the one who didn't give us any time to argue. Either climb the tree, or we both sit down here and wait for them."

Inhaling deeply, David shook his head, snatched a few weapons from where they were strapped to his saddle, donned his jacket once again, and walked over to the sturdiest looking tree in the area. He scrambled up the trunk, climbing like he was born to it.

"We're dead in the water if you get shot too, Adelyn," Mary commented, quietly. "Three people. That's the plan. You're at least as valuable as Undertow."

"Abandon that," Adelyn said. "I'm a boon, not a requirement. But you should get moving, we haven't got much time."

Mary looked like she wanted to argue, but instead knelt

to the hunter and pulled off his long jacket, passing it to Adelyn. "Help me lift him onto Butler."

Adelyn assisted in that, looking around the woods at every twitch and noise, sure that it was other hunters coming to investigate the gunshots. Grabbing the hunter's cap before Mary left, Adelyn stuffed her hair into the hat, doing her best to look as close as possible to the hunter.

With that done, she drew her pocket knife, inhaled sharply, and then drew it across the palm of her hand, making a thin cut that immediately began bleeding profusely. Once a small pool had collected in her hand, she smeared the blood on her face and on the canvas jacket, hoping to disguise herself and confuse anyone who saw her.

Sitting down against a tree, she stuffed the knife into a pocket, let her arms and hands go slack, and waited.

And continued to wait.

Ten minutes passed, and Adelyn started to wonder if anyone was ever going to come looking. Every time she thought about giving up the charade and asking David if they should continue, though, she heard a twitch or a rustle in the trees and felt some uncertainty return.

Finally, she decided that she was definitely, certainly going to give up—just as soon as she was certain that last noise was from some ambient source, and not a bandit set on ambushing her. Before she could make the decision, though, a scream echoed through the trees, loud and pained enough to make Adelyn's blood curdle.

Scrambling up to her feet, she looked around, trying to decide which direction the noise was coming from. David dropped from the tree, landing next to her with something akin to grace, looking around with equal confusion.

The scream stopped, and Adelyn asked, "What was that?"

"What was that? Abandon me if I know," David said. "It was not the sound of a man in combat, for sure, or even some kind of hunting accident. If anything..." His eyes widened, and then his face fell.

Adelyn glanced around. "What is it?"

"Which direction did Mary go?" David asked. His hand began tapping against his leg unfettered as he looked around, trying to discern the direction she'd gone in.

"That was Mary?" Adelyn asked, spinning around to try and point out where she'd gone. "Is she ok? We—"

"It was the hunter," David said.

Their conversation was interrupted by another scream, louder than before, barely recognizable as human. "What do we do?" Adelyn asked.

David sighed heavily. "We wait. We will not be able to find her quick enough to intervene." He pressed the palm of his hand into his forehead, shutting his eyes in frustration. "Dammit, I should have known she would do this."

Biting her lip, Adelyn hesitated before asking. "It's not all bad, right? She's trying to get information?"

"Unreliable information," David said. "He was already willing to lie when there was no torture. Now, he will convert to the Divinities if it means it will end the pain— nothing he says can be trusted, even more so than before."

"So why's she bothering?" Adelyn asked.

"I suppose Mary is more trusting than I am." David said, spitting out the words with apparent spite. "We should stay alert for other hunters, but I do not think anyone is coming."

Adelyn cringed as a third cry of pain echoed through the woods. "Isn't there something we can do about it?"

"You could use a spell to block out the sound," David suggested, drumming his fingers against his leg. "Beyond that, no."

Adelyn bit her lip, then pulled the wooden ring out from where she wore it around her neck—she'd taken the time to sand and polish it to a smooth, perfect ring and then whittle small shield runes into its surface, though it was the same tool she'd been using since their travels started.

Tapping her finger on the magical implement, Adelyn asked, "It'd be... *ansyr*, for shield and... sound would be *hash*?"

"*Ansyr* and *hash*?" David asked, blinking once before considering the words. "Oh, yes, that would work."

"Great," Adelyn said, slipping a hint of spirit into the wooden ring and whispering, "*Ansyr hash,*" letting the spell fill the air around her. The air snapped and crackled for a moment, then the sounds of the forest vanished.

She could hear her own breathing, the noise acutely apparent in the absence of all other sound. It had seemed quiet before, aside from screams and conversation, but the quiet whistle of wind and rustle of trees were conspicuous in their absence, like losing a tooth and feeling the gap where it used to be.

An inaudible hum was present in the air around her, the energy from her spirit made manifest—Adelyn couldn't see or hear it, but its presence was nonetheless obvious, crackling a couple inches from her skin and dissipating slowly, like smoke being blown away in comically slow motion.

"I guess it worked," Adelyn said, her voice echoing in her ears. David's lips moved, but made no noise. Curious, Adelyn asked, "Can you hear me? Nod your head if you can, I can't hear you."

David spoke again, then frowned and waved his hand forward, breaking apart Adelyn's spell.

The sounds of life came crashing back suddenly and violently, loud and vying to be heard, almost as if it was angry about being forced away. "What was that for?" Adelyn asked, rubbing her finger in her ear.

"I should have considered," David said, though he seemed distracted "But you should not deafen yourself while we are watching for an ambush." His words were punctuated by a hoarse shout, though it lacked the vigor of the last few screams.

"Right, of course," Adelyn said sheepishly. "Sorry."

"Good work with that spell, though." David added. "You have grown a lot more flexible with what you can do. I could not hear a word that you said."

"Thanks."

They waited in silence for a few moments, then a few more.

"The screaming stopped," David commented.

"Or his voice is gone," Adelyn pointed out.

"Mary would not let his voice go out," David said. "Otherwise he could not answer questions. She must have gotten what she wanted."

Adelyn shrugged, leaning against a tree. The screams were still echoing in her ears, and it was bothering her. She wasn't exactly sympathetic for anyone who'd been a part of her family's kidnapping, but even still, the sound had been unsettling.

"So Mary knows how to torture people," Adelyn commented, after a long silence. "I imagine she picked that up in the war?"

"The Stone Warriors needed information and were not scrupulous in how they got it," David said. "Mary knows human anatomy as well as any physician."

Adelyn frowned. "David, you're talking as though you're hiding something."

"I am hiding something?" David asked, drumming his fingers against his leg once again. "How do you mean?"

"When you're not being honest," Adelyn explained. "You do this thing where you answer questions with accurate but unrelated statements. Just now—you didn't say that Mary tortured people in the war, you said that the Stone Warriors needed information, and some stuff about Mary, but you never answered what I said."

David took a breath, glancing around. "Mary will be back soon, we should get ready to—"

"David."

"Mary tortured people in the war," David snapped, drumming his fingers more rapidly. "I think you should ask her about this, though. It is not my place to tell you."

"You tell me all kinds of other things about Mary," Adelyn said, "Why—"

"My ears are burning!" Mary called, approaching with the horses, no longer hauling a prisoner. "Are you talking about me?"

David's hand stiffened, freezing in place as he responded. "Mary, you should have told me what you were planning."

"If I'd told you, Undertow," Mary said, "You would have objected. *I did not want any argument.* I only had a couple minutes until he woke, and I wanted to get him tied up and restrained before that happened."

Adelyn cocked her head. "How'd you know it was a few minutes?"

"Because Undertow still uses the same spell to knock people out," Mary said. "A pinch to some blood vessel or another, I think. Quick, painless, fairly safe, but it only lasts a couple minutes."

"The carotid artery," David clarified, sighing. "I would

have argued because the exercise is pointless. What did you learn?"

"He says their wizard is just someone who fought for the president," Mary said. "He invented the Blue Flame to scare us off, Undertow, you can abandon your worries. The keep's due north from here, and there's an entrance to the right of it. He says it shouldn't be locked, but if it is, you can take it apart. We won't need to scale the wall after all."

Adelyn jumped in before she could continue. "Did he say where the prisoners were kept?"

"I'm getting to that, child," Mary said. "They use a spirit generator, and they keep that by the slaves. We can trace any spirit cable back to the generator, and then to the prisoners."

"And if he is lying?" Adelyn asked, skeptical.

"He's not."

"How do you know?"

"Because it all makes sense," Mary said. "They'd want blood from the prisoners, so they'd want the generator near, and tracing the cables back is just common sense."

David grimaced, but bobbed his head in a nod. "The logic is sound."

"How many bandits are there?" Adelyn asked.

"He says fifty," Mary said. "That's something I can't confirm, though. For what it's worth, the number is lower than we guessed."

Swallowing, Adelyn nodded, putting on the bravest grin that she could manage. "Let's go be heroes?"

CHAPTER 27

Month of Harvest

27th Day

1700. Evening shift at the eastern entrance. I drew the short straw again. Hopefully someone brings me some food while it's still hot this time.

1820. No events of note.

1820 - 2. No food to speak of, either.

1830. Bill returned from hunting, with a couple rabbits. Promised to ask about dinner being brought up to me once he gets down.

1900. Pretty sure they forgot I was up here.

1903. Heard a gunshot. Probably nothing, but it sounded like several shots in succession. Timothy is the only one still out hunting. If I don't hear from him in twenty minutes, I'll see about getting someone to go look for him.

1912. I think I just heard screaming. A wild animal may have attacked Timothy. I called for help, we're going to head out once we have a search party together.

1924. Got four people up here, plus myself. According to the wizard, nobody has died, so we've got good hopes of finding him. Heading out momentarily.

1925. Thought we heard motion outside. Called out to Timothy, but no response. May be Peace Officers. Holding tight for a moment.

1925 - 2. Think someone just tried the handle. No knock or message. Someone is trying to get in, and if

- Excerpt from log book, found in the Beor Keep. Last entry

"IS THAT IT?" Adelyn asked in a low voice, looking up at the stone wall in front of them.

"There are no other castles in the area," David replied with equally hushed tones.

Mary scowled. "Keep your voices low."

The three of them stared up at the wall from where they were crouched in the undergrowth, and Adelyn told herself that what she was feeling was awe, not fear. It was twenty feet high, stone and mortar, with eroded rocky spikes at the top to deter anyone trying to climb over. It was set into the mountain in a way that resembled a natural outcropping, except that its design was acutely hostile to outsiders instead of being merely implicitly hostile.

Once they'd come into sight of the wall, Mary had taken David's knife and broken it at the handle. The royal steel made it prohibitively difficult to snap the blade itself, but once the wooden handle had broken, Mary threw the blade into the woods and made her prayers to the god of combat.

"There's the door," Mary whispered, pointing to the right. It looked like a recent addition, a wooden feature set in a matching frame set that looked as though it had been built over a hole in the wall. "You know the plan. Adelyn, gather any weapons that we can use. I take point with your magic to keep me safe. Once we get to the slaves, we arm them and fight our way out."

"Let's go, then," Adelyn said, standing up and taking a couple steps forward.

David grabbed her arm, stopping her. "If someone is in there, they will hear you coming and shoot you from the other side of the door before you can stop it."

"Fine," Adelyn whispered back. "What, then?"

Before she could get an answer, a voice called out from the other side of the door. "Timothy? Is that you?"

As the voice called out, David took off to cross the distance between him and the wall, soft footsteps barely touching the ground. He only had a couple paces between him and the wall by the time the shouting stopped.

Mary looked at Adelyn and pointed to the door, whispering, "As soon as he takes down the door, we go in like we practiced. Understand?"

Adelyn nodded, gripping the sword in her hand, adjusting the bag slung over her shoulder, and taking in a long, deep breath. She was loaded for bird and beast, carrying every weapon that they might need and that would slow down the others, but even with all that she felt unprepared.

David was edging toward the door, inching with careful, meticulous steps. Watching, Adelyn unconsciously held her breath, as though exhaling would give away their position and lose them the element surprise.

It took days—or perhaps twenty seconds—for David to get all the way to the door. It took a heartbeat after that for the door to fly inward, swinging as though David had kicked it, rocking so hard in its frame that the hinges nearly buckled. Gunfire erupted briefly, but it flew through the open doorway, striking only air. David stayed perched behind the wall, and the hail of bullets quickly paused.

"Go! Go now!" Mary shouted, and Adelyn followed behind her, shouting out the spell she'd been preparing.

"Gild Ansyr!" she screamed, forming a shield in front of them. It had taken practice for her to make one that could move around, but that practice paid off, and the two of them ran toward the door under the cover of the magic barricade.

Someone saw them immediately and a shouted warning turned the gunfire in their direction, but either the shield did its work or their aim failed. Adelyn could feel the energy crackle and fade in the shield as it diverted bullets away from her and Mary, and knew that it wouldn't hold up long, but it just needed to last long enough for...

The volley of gunfire ended, and David spun into the room, hook in one hand, staff in the other. Sounds of combat were briefly all that Adelyn could perceive, and by the time she made it through the door, three of the bandits were disarmed and a fourth was out cold on the floor.

Adelyn raised her sword to the fifth bandit, but before she could attack, Mary's whip cracked with a sound that made her ears pop, and the bandit's rifle fell to the ground.

"Stand down!" Mary shouted. The bandits hesitated, and when Mary cracked her whip in the air, the unarmed men and women decided it wasn't worth it to keep fighting. The four bandits who were still conscious raised their arms in the air, holding still.

"Stay perfectly still," David snapped at them, closing his eyes and focusing for a moment before flicking out his wrist. In the course of a second, each bandit slumped to the ground, unconscious.

Without a word, Adelyn removed the bag from over her shoulder, hastily taking pistols and knives from the bandits.

"This one's empty," Mary commented, checking a rifle and tossing it to David.

David nodded, crouching by one of the bandits drawing a knife. He sliced open their palm, set down the knife, drew a wand from the bandolier around his chest, smeared it liberally with the blood, then finally pointed the bloody wand at the gun and hissed a spell. There was a flash, and he dropped the rifle. "Any more?"

"These two," Adelyn said, holding up a second rifle and a revolver. David repeated the process for both, rendering both guns useless to anyone who might reload them. They stuffed the remaining weapons into Adelyn's bag, then she slung it back over her shoulder and stood.

"Get as much spirit as you can from the blood, then we'll move," Mary said, doing one last check around the room. "We can't have long."

"Can you feel anyone coming?" Adelyn asked David. "Sense their spirit, that is."

David drummed his finger on his leg, concentrating for a moment before shaking his head. "Too much stone. I will need to be in the same room with no obstructions."

"Well, at least the wiring is all in place," Mary said, pointing to a spirit light bolted into the wall. Copper wiring was strung away from it, running toward a doorway. A hole had been bored through the top of the doorframe to let the wiring pass through it, and cool night air was wafting in from the small gap in the frame. "If our guesses are right, only ninety five bandits or so to go."

"Easy as spitting," Adelyn commented.

Nodding slight, Mary said, "Undertow, stay to the back, I'm going to take point. You've got to save your strength to fight their wizard. Adelyn, a shield, if you please."

Adelyn crouched by the fallen bandit, wiped some blood

onto the runes of her shield necklace, and assented. "Ready." Mary nodded, grabbed the handle of the door, and threw it open.

Her eyes widened a fraction as she looked out, and almost as soon as the door was open, she barked, "Shield!"

Startled, it took Adelyn a half second to gather her wits and shout the spell, and a few bullets made it past her before she got out the Sacrosanct words, raising the magic over the doorway.

"How many?" David asked.

"Seven," Mary said, breathing heavily, body pressed against the wall. "Behind barricades. I think all of them have guns, not sure. A few had armor on. There's stables to the left, but nobody was shooting from them, I think they're empty. An open courtyard otherwise. They're the only thing between us and the entrance to the keep proper."

The gunshots ceased as they realized it was having no effect, and instead someone shouted out at them. "You all peace officers?"

"Yes!" Adelyn shouted back. "And there's a hundred more on the way! Surrender, or we'll riddle your bodies so full of holes that the pastor won't be able to identify what's left of you."

"Abandon that!" came the shouted reply. "You're full of it."

"How far is the space between us and them?" Adelyn asked, quietly, before more loudly adding, "You really care to test that theory?"

"Ten yards, maybe," Mary said. "Can you shield me for that distance?"

"Should be able to," Adelyn said, reaching over her shoulder and passing David her rifle. "Here. I'm going out with Mary."

David accepted the rifle, nodding. He wouldn't shoot anyone, of course, but the bandits didn't know that. With luck, they'd have enough sense to duck behind cover when David started taking potshots at the air above their heads.

"Here's the deal, girl!" the bandit shouted, as Mary held out three fingers from the hand gripping her sword. "You and anyone with you are gonna throw all your weapons out that door and surrender." Mary closed one finger, so only two remained. "Then you'll walk out, hands pointed up toward the sky." Another finger closed, with only one remaining. "And then, if you didn't hurt my friends too bad, we'll—" Mary closed her fist around the hilt. It was time to go.

Gathering spirit from blood, Adelyn recharged the barrier that had started to fade. Mary leaped out the door with Adelyn on her heels, David leaning out to spray bullets as fast as he could chamber rounds in the rifle.

The courtyard was mostly sparse, providing little cover for them to duck behind. Not that it mattered, since Adelyn could provide her own cover. The keep entrance, built into the side of the mountain, looked crumbled and old, and a large set of double doors twice the height of a person were blocked by a few wooden barricades and just over half a dozen men and women looking to bar their entry.

The bandits returned fire from their position, lead rounds hitting the barrier of energy and bouncing off. Each impact made the invisible wall of spirit fray and dissipate a little more, but Adelyn kept her focus on keeping the shield in between them and the bandits.

They ran parallel to the barricades, getting around to the left side of their line before Mary charged forward. The bandits swore, collectively realizing that they couldn't draw a bead without risk of hitting their own.

Adelyn finally gave up holding the shield when they were within striking distance and, seemingly aware the instant that the barrier was gone, Mary leaped at the closest bandit with a vicious strike.

The bandit tried to fire at her at point blank, but was holding a rifle and couldn't aim properly at such close quarters. Mary, having no reservations about inflicting serious injury, batted his arm out of the way and ran him through with her sword, letting go of the blade rather than trying to pull it out.

Adelyn had planned on assisting with the fight, but she could barely react quickly enough to hit a target before Mary had dealt with them. The woman fought like David, able to dodge attacks before Adelyn even saw them coming. Mary's whip cracked out with terrifying speed, harassing and delaying anyone who tried to draw a bead on her with a revolver or rifle, giving her a chance to run them through with whatever weapon she had on hand.

Producing a knife from seemingly nowhere, Mary lodged it firmly into the chest of the next bandit, holding them up as a shield against gunfire for just long enough to wrestle away their revolver and fire three rounds from it into the next three, each shot landing. When the revolver clicked empty, Mary dropped it, turning to face the last two.

Rather than stand there dumbstruck, Adelyn turned herself toward something useful by moving to the downed bandits, kicking away their weapons. One of them, bleeding but aware, tried to stand. Adelyn scrambled to kick him in the head before he could rise, knocking him back down, a few teeth absent from where they'd been a moment before. She moved to kick him again, and then a tempest of spirit snapped up around her, rattling her senses like a clap of thunder.

She staggered, blinking a couple times, startled by the burst of power that had ripped into being. It wasn't a spell, it was too raw and unfocused, but she couldn't think of what else had released such power.

David was a few seconds behind them, abandoning his empty rifle rather than reloading it as he crossed the distance to the wooden barricades. "They know we are here," he commented. "This was probably just a token defense. We need to get inside before anyone else shows up, so we cannot be surrounded."

"What was that?" She asked, looking to David for answers, since Mary wouldn't have any idea what they were talking about.

Looking grim, David said, "When someone dies, all the spirit in them gets released at once."

Adelyn swallowed. She had known that they were going to see the face of death tonight, but the confrontation with it still rattled her.

"Focus," Mary said, pointing to where the copper wire was strung from wooden poles leading to the double doors. "David, tell us what's behind those doors."

"A large entry hall," David said. "Hallways split off in all directions from there. I should lead on this, in case they are planning another ambush for us."

"Let's hurry, then," Adelyn agreed, bobbing her head in a nod, shaking off her worries. "Suppose any of these guns are worth gathering up?" She added, looking around at the bandits on the ground, incapacitated by pain or completely unconscious.

"No time to check," Mary said, planting a foot on the first bandit she'd attacked and pulling out her sword.

Walking to the doors, David gave them a gentle push to see if they would open. They did, smoothly, barely resisting his push. The oiled hinges moved without a squeak of protest, a stark contrast to the deterioration of the keep's exterior.

The interior gleamed. The polished marble floor had cracks, but they'd been smoothed over and patched, clean flags displaying an unfamiliar coat of arms hung from large pillars. No furniture was around and no people were there save for the three of them, but that only served to make the chamber feel larger and more imposing in the absence of anyone for scale. Spirit lights cast the whole room in pale blue light, giving the entire place a cold, unreal atmosphere as though it were simultaneously cared for and abandoned, maintained and untouched.

Hanging underneath the spirit lights, large copper orbs decorated with gold filigree were placed, with copper wire running between them in the same way as the lights. "What're those?" Adelyn asked, pointing.

"I'm not sure," Mary said. "I wouldn't touch them, to be safe."

David walked cautiously through the hall, looking around. "We are alone, for the moment," he said. "They must all be deeper into the facility." Looking up at the banners, his fists tightened, and Adelyn could have sworn she felt spirit start to crackle around him.

"Undertow, do you know what those are?" Mary asked.

David glanced over at her, fists loosening into a light grip. "What those are?"

"The copper orbs," Mary clarified, pointing at one.

David frowned, approaching one. "I do not know. These are runes, but..." He trailed off, frowning. "Adelyn, do those seem familiar to you?"

Adelyn looked again, thinking for a moment. "Dobson's factory. He had a stack of those being made."

David nodded, considering for a moment. After a second, he placed his hand on the orb, shutting his eyes in concentration.

"Didn't you say not to touch it?" Adelyn asked.

"Yes, I did," Mary replied, clicking her tongue in disapproval.

David opened his eyes, taking a couple steps back, mouth agape. "Watchers abandon me, that is clever."

"What is it?" Mary asked.

"What is it?" David had to search for the right words for a moment. "A...a seismometer."

"Oh," Mary said. "*Gods.* Do you think it works?"

Adelyn frowned. "What's a seismometer?"

Mary hesitated. "A device that detects earthquakes."

"It uses a pendulum," David clarified. "It is carefully weighted, so that even the slightest tremor in the ground causes the pendulum to move, so that the presence, direction, and intensity of the earthquake can be measured."

"I don't get it," Adelyn said. "I mean, that'd be smart to have inside a mountain, I guess, but what's the big deal?"

"It's not measuring earthquakes, child," Mary said. "Right, Undertow?" David nodded, and Adelyn finally realized what they were talking about.

"It's measuring spirit?"

"I cannot say how precise it is," David said. "He can definitely tell when spells are cast, and if anyone dies near one of these it would send up a warning like a claxon. It might even be able to detect fresh blood, or simple movement and activity, in which case..." Looking around the entry hall, he said, "They will know wherever we go unless we knock this system out or I stop their wizard."

Adelyn nodded, raising her sword and approaching the

nearest of the copper orbs, raising the blade to cut the wire running from it. "Then we destroy th—"

David stopped her. "That is a live cable, Adelyn. Cut through it, you will get a nasty shock."

"So what do we do?" Adelyn asked, lowering her sword.

"We keep moving," Mary said. "Same plan, just with more caution."

"You keep moving," David said, looking up at the cables running from column to column. "I am going to deal with their wizard now. No point waiting for him to come to us."

"Is that wise?" Mary asked, frowning.

"Did you look at the banners?" David asked in reply.

"Not closely," Mary said, glancing up. "Why does—oh."

Adelyn, increasingly tired of being the odd one out, asked, "What's the issue? Is that coat of arms for a powerful family or something?"

Mary answered first. "It's the symbol for—"

"The Blue Flame," David finished.

Adelyn's eyes widened. "The hunter wasn't lying."

"Maybe not," David said. "Either way, I am going to find this wizard, and I am going to hurt him. The cable for these seismometers should lead me to him."

"What if you run into more bandits?" Mary asked. "This is a bad idea. We should stick together."

"If I run into more bandits, I will handle them," David said, his voice low. "You need to rescue Adelyn's family. I need to do this."

Mary stepped forward, putting a hand on his shoulder. "Undertow—"

David jerked away, wheeling to face her. "*Mary.* I am going."

Mary staggered back a step, not expecting the force of his response. "Fine. Go. We're wasting too much time here."

David turned and walked away, staff gripped so tight that
Adelyn expected it to shatter in his grip.

Adelyn furrowed her brow, looking between him and
Mary. "Wait a moment, what—"

Mary snapped at her before she could finish the question. "We're moving, Adelyn. You're going to have to be on
point with the magic."

Adelyn swallowed, pushing back trepidation. She took a
deep breath, cleared her thoughts, and nodded.

CHAPTER 28

Annie Nichols came in here today, swearing up a storm and raving about something she'd seen in the woods. I calmed her down over a hot cup of coffee, let her tire herself out ranting, then got out my notepad. She said there was something in the woods, that it had attacked her cattle, that she didn't feel safe in her own home.

I naturally assumed it was a wolf, or maybe a bear—we don't get much of either in these parts, but occasionally one will get starved enough to come all the way. When I asked her about it, though, Annie swore it wasn't. She said it walked on two legs, that it looked like a man, except its eyes glowed bright like torchlights. It hadn't eaten the cattle, she claimed, only slit them through the belly and left them to rot.

At this point, I figured she'd gotten to drinking some bad moonshine, so I made a note of it and put the matter to rest. I'll go out in a day or three, see about the cattle, maybe see about finding this 'man with the glowing eyes' she was raving about. It's nothing, but if I show up with a gun it'll put her fears to rest, and if there's really a wolf on the prowl I can deal with it while I'm out there.

- Widely copied and distributed report written by a peace officer, allegedly made one day before Annie Nichols was found murdered in her home, killed by a single slit through her belly

"So are we going to talk about that?" Adelyn asked, following Mary as they traced a wire out of the hall, down one of the many passageways it branched into.

"No," Mary said. "Ask Undertow once we're out of here."

"What happened to needing him?" Adelyn asked. "If this is a suicide mission without him, what are we—"

"If we leave now, we'll never make it back in, and Undertow will die." Mary said. "He can't defeat their wizard and fight his way out as well. Do you want to leave?"

Adelyn's answer came automatically.

"Then we keep going, and..." Mary stopped, looking around. "Gods leave me for a fool."

Adelyn looked around. "What?"

"Shield," Mary said. "Now. Strong as you can—"

Adelyn stopped listening at 'Shield', already prepared. Throwing all the spirit she could into the runes around her neck, she put up a barrier all around them, blocking both the hallway in front of them and the opening behind them.

Looking back and forth, Adelyn couldn't see anyone— the passage was well lit by spirit lamps, and she could see a good hundred feet down before it forked. A gentle breeze came from vents placed beneath the floor, making her shiver. "What's wrong?"

"I'm a fool. Their wizard's got to have a line run so he can talk to his people," Mary said.

"Okay," Adelyn said. "That's sensible, but—"

"These devices detect spirit," Mary continued. "And if

Undertow goes storming in like a madman, throwing magic around..."

"Their sorcerer will send everything he's got after David," Adelyn finished.

"He wouldn't stand a chance," Mary agreed.

Adelyn hesitated for a moment. "Wait...so why were you concerned for our safety? Why the shield?"

Mary frowned with one side of her mouth, almost imperceptibly shaking her head, and Adelyn realized after a second what she was getting at.

"You..." Adelyn started, feeling a knot form in her belly. She was getting tired of playing catch up with the two Stone Warriors. "The shield wasn't for defense."

"I would've said something, but there was no time," Mary said, the closest thing to an apology that Adelyn was going to get. "We needed to throw up a flare as quick as possible."

"You'll have to take the bulk of them," Adelyn said. "If they come from both sides. We don't have David watching our backs, it'll just be you and me."

"Keep the shield up as long as possible," Mary said, looking up and down the passage. "If this turns into a shooting range, we're fish in a barrel."

"This takes a lot of spirit," Adelyn said, trying to gauge how well the shield was doing. "There's a lot of rock everywhere, it's not helping. I'm not sure we can do this on our own."

Mary took in a long breath, held it for a couple seconds, then sheathed her sword and extended an open hand. "Give me one of the guns," she said. "Oh, and drop the bag. It'll slow you down." Adelyn nodded, sliding the bag over her shoulder and dropping it to the ground, fishing out a revolver.

"Will this do?"

"That's fine," Mary said, moving her whip to her off hand before accepting the gun and sticking it into her belt. "Take my hand," she said, extending an open palm.

Adelyn complied, gripping Mary's hand loosely in her own. "What are you doing?"

"Making sure that we don't do this alone," Mary said. Clamping down hard on Adelyn's hand, she took her whip and quickly wound it around both their wrists, pulling it tight.

"Hey!" Adelyn said, trying to tug her hand away. "What the—"

In one fluid motion, Mary produced her knife and drew it in a quick cut over the whip, slicing clean through digging into the flesh beneath. "*Garesh, Ansire, accept our sacrifice,*" she intoned, releasing her grip.

"Ow!" Adelyn yelped, jerking her hand away and letting half the whip fall away from her wrist. The cut to the side of her thumb wasn't deep, but blood pooled from it and the injury stung enough to be annoying. To her added frustration, the spirit in the blood seemed to have dried up as soon as Mary gave her prayer, ensuring it couldn't even be used for magic. "Mary!"

"There's no time to get mad at me," Mary said, drawing her sword and the new gun. "Listen."

Adelyn had to force herself not to take Mary to task, relenting and following Mary's instruction. Footsteps, coming down the hall with the varied clatter of a poorly organized horde, some thirty-strong.

"Get that shield back up," Mary said. "They're almost here."

Raising her hands, Adelyn assented, channeling power into the shield. It had started to fray, slightly, and if she wanted to keep it up for much longer it would need to be rebuilt from scratch. For now, though, it would hold.

A voice echoed down the hall, faint but audible above the approaching footsteps. "Watch out! One of 'em's a witch!"

"Sorceress," Adelyn muttered as, a hundred feet down the hall, figures rounded a corner and came into view.

"Nobody's behind us," Mary said, checking over her shoulder. "We should—

Gunfire burst out, putting holes in Adelyn's invisible shield, but the advancing throng of bandits didn't slow down—they apparently had no interest in stopping and setting up lines of fire.

"Do we stay here?" Adelyn asked. "Or do we meet them?"

Mary hesitated for a quarter of a second, a flicker of a smile crossing over her lips. "Let's put the fear of the gods in them."

Adelyn nodded, concentrating enough to shove her shield forward down the hall, raise her sword, and charge. Mary raised both sword and revolver, roared a battle cry that nearly made Adelyn lose her footing in surprise, and together they ran.

Bullets flew toward them in a disorganized peppering of lead, but the distance between them shrank with alarming speed, and soon it became impossible for anyone to draw a direct line of fire save for the people in front. What bullets did get fired all bounced harmlessly off of Adelyn's shield. Then, they met.

The shield that Adelyn used was designed to stand up to bullets and projectiles, but she'd put a lot of spirit into it, and she was moving it forward as fast as she could run. The bandits either lacked iron-based armor or hadn't had time to put it on, and so nothing absorbed the shock of the impact for them—the invisible barrier shattered as the front line of raiders crashed into it, but it was enough to stagger a half dozen of the bandits and send them backward, tumbling into each other.

Mary's gun cracked out with six little popping noises as she met them. The hallway was so wide that three people could stand abreast if they kept their arms at their sides, but in combat, only one or two people could cross swords with Mary, and only a couple more would be able to draw a gun on her.

Or, rather, they *would* have been able to draw a gun, had Adelyn not been there to intervene. Someone with a scar over her eye managed to aim a revolver at Mary, but a barked spell and a jolt of spirit sent that pistol into the air before the trigger could be pulled. Another spell hit the same bandit at the ankles, knocking her sideways like she'd been tackled, and then she was lost in a sea of bodies trying alternately to move forward and attack, or to flee against the vicious blows that Mary was delivering with her sword.

Adelyn continued her harassment, rarely delivering a blow solid enough to take out any target, but disrupting and breaking apart any pocket of resistance that might have otherwise been able to stand up to Mary's onslaught. Their practice had paid off—Mary was able to move smoothly around Adelyn's spells and evade attacks like she'd choreographed the fight.

The violent release of spirit came again, as strong as it had been in the courtyard, but Adelyn was less startled this time and only skipped a couple beats before honing her focus back on the fight. She couldn't feel bad, not for these raiders who'd taken her family, not when mercy would mean her own death. The next time she felt the tempest of energy, she pushed past it without hesitation.

This initial combat didn't last for long, before the bandits realized that they were going up in a way that wasn't going to last long, but their forward momentum now worked against them—those fighting at the front couldn't retreat without running into their own ranks, and as dense and tight as they were packed, it took them a long time before they were able to regroup and back up, abandoning five or six of their number in the process. By the time their retreat was done, no less than half the pack was bleeding on the floor.

Taking down the last of the forward group, Mary turned to face the rest of the block, who'd managed to get a cluster of rifles to the front of their ranks and had them pointed in a forwardly direction from twenty paces away.

"Adelyn?" Mary asked, noting this with mild concern.

"A shield's already up," Adelyn said, holding out both her hands, quietly adding, "Can't hold it forever, though."

Mary nodded, facing the group, keeping her eyes on the rifle while crouching slightly so she could fish a loaded revolver from off the ground. "I will keep fighting until I've cut through every last one of you! How many more of you want to die tonight?"

"There's two of you and a lot more of us!" someone called back, though the caller was hard to distinguish in the crowd. They sounded uncertain, but tried to keep up the bravado and added, "We're not scared!"

Mary took a step forward, and one of the bandits holding a rifle flinched, squeezing the trigger. The bullet hid Adelyn's shield and stopped, harmlessly. "Oh?" Mary asked. "Not scared?"

"Hurry it along," Adelyn whispered, putting more spirit into the shield.

"You're not the only one getting worn out," Mary whispered back. "I need to catch my breath."

One of the forward bandits raised their voice, shouting, "How about you surrender, and we let you leave!"

"If we want to leave," Mary pointed out, "You can't stop us. We could just turn and walk away!"

"Could you?"

A hollow boom echoed from behind them, and Adelyn felt a creeping dread come over her. Turning to look over her shoulder, she noticed the figure blocking their exit. Their silhouette reached nearly to the ceiling of the passageway, and as they slammed a fist into the stone wall, another loud booming noise reverberated in Adelyn's ears.

"Mary, we've got a problem," Adelyn said. "I'm pretty sure that's spirit armor."

Mary briefly looked over her shoulder and saw the figure that was approaching lethargically. "Can you handle it?"

"I don't know," Adelyn said. "I don't think so. Not alone."

"Then we're dead," Mary said.

"No," Adelyn said, looking back at the throng of enemies, somewhat worse for wear after their first assault. She had been hoping to save her ace in the hole, but it seemed as though she wasn't going to get a better chance.

She'd agreed to read Mary's books, but Adelyn never had the slightest intention of respecting the teachings she'd found there. The "holy books" were nothing but tripe and stories. She couldn't care less about the text found within.

David had said that she should learn something she didn't care about if she planned on using her memories to fuel magic. Converting memory to spirit was something she'd never done before, but she knew the theory, and she had few choices except to try.

With the words of a verse rested firmly in her head—a bit about a couple gods in a land dispute—she focused those thoughts, converting it into spirit and channeling that energy into the rune around her neck. The spirit flowed in fits and starts at first, then something clicked into place and the magic began raging inside her, torrents of force. Adelyn could feel it buzz with more energy than she'd ever tried to use, and even then it kept coming. The wood began to heat against her skin, the spirit flowing out, more and more, energy beyond what she knew what to do with.

Struggling to cut it off, Adelyn shouted, *"BREN!"* at the top of her voice, converting all that energy into fire.

The spell ripped out of the rune with a fervor, flames licking at the walls and ceiling, hungrily searching for air to burn. Men screamed, diving to the floor to try and escape the heat and pressure that filled the hall, but their attempts to escape did little to prevent the rolling fire that moved through them without concern for who it touched. If spirit burst into existence with the passing of any of the bandits beneath her firestorm, Adelyn couldn't feel it, too taken with controlling her own spell to sense what other spirit was in the air.

Even Mary shrank back, looking at Adelyn with shock as the fire continued to plume into being. She managed to regain her wits as the spell flickered and finally died, and she took Adelyn's arm.

"What in all the gods' names was that?" She demanded.

Adelyn blinked, dizzy from the exertion, trying to parse Mary's words. "The...you mean the Lords?"

Mary blinked, then shook her head. "Come on, we've got

to go. Don't look." She drug at Adelyn's arm, pulling her through the hall.

Despite her warning, Adelyn couldn't help but peek at the carnage. The flame had melted the rubber coating that protected the copper spirit wires on the wall, and several lights had exploded in the heat.

Looking down, Adelyn had to put a hand over her mouth to keep from gagging. People—It was difficult to distinguish between men and women—lay on the ground, some writhing in pain, others simply laying still. Those who had dropped the ground seemed to be better off, but none had escaped unscathed.

The smell of burning flesh caught up with her a second later, and had it not been for Mary's firm grasp dragging her past the burned people, Adelyn might have stopped in place to gape.

They kept up their pace, passing those who Adelyn had burned, returning to the open hall. "This way," Mary urged, pointing down a side path, where two cables converged.

"The armor," Adelyn said, looking over her shoulder. It had slowed, whoever wore it seemed to be surveying the carnage.

"We'll deal with it later," Mary said. "This way." She continued holding Adelyn's arm at the wrist, pulling her down the hall. Adelyn could see blood on her arm now that they were out of the melee, a long gash that she hadn't noticed before, and she remembered something.

"The weapons. I left them—"

"Doesn't matter," Mary said. "In here."

They stopped in front of a door, a new one made of heavy wood and set into a much older stone frame. It was locked, so Adelyn stepped in, blasting it down with a burst of force.

Men yelped in surprise and fear as the door flew inward, hinges splintering and falling back. Adelyn looked in and saw rows upon rows of cells, iron bars set in front of stone rooms just deep and wide enough to set two beds and leave walking space between them. Men were huddled in those cells, pressed against the back walls as though trying to hide.

"We're here to help you," Mary said, strolling in confidently and taking stock of the cells. Her feet clicked on metal as she walked in, stepping over grates that would provide fresh, breathable air in the tunnels. "This is a rescue. Where do they keep the keys?" There was a moment of stunned silence, without response, and Mary barked her question again. "Keys! Where?"

"A guard wears them," One of the prisoners finally responded. "They used to keep them on a hook, but after we tried to escape, there..."

"Sis?" The question wasn't loud, and didn't interrupt the conversation between Mary and the other prisoners, but as far as Adelyn was concerned it cut through every other voice in the cell block.

She froze, then turned. The figure who'd spoken was tall, broad, with a scruffy beard. He looked...not weaker than she remembered, exactly, he was still strong as an ox, but the muscle was leaner, no extra fat or tissue. He hadn't been fed well enough, and that made Adelyn want to punch someone.

"John," she said. Tears had started welling in her eyes at the sight of her brother, and she wiped at them, trying to keep her composure. "I... Mom and Dad. How are they?"

"Good, I think," John said. He looked almost as shocked as she felt, holding the bars of his cell to stay upright. "They're in a different cell block. We send messages when we can, but... Sis... what are you *doing* here?"

"Rescuing you," Adelyn said, smiling behind blurry vision. "Dullard. What's it look like?"

"They have a wizard!" John said. "He's going to kill you, or—"

"We have one too," Adelyn said back. "Two, actually. And he's a Stone Warrior."

John blinked, but before he could say anything else, Mary cut in. "Adelyn, these bars are iron. Can you break them down?"

Adelyn had to shift gears in her head before she could respond. "Not easily," She said. "Or quickly."

"Then we have to move on and find another way to get them out," Mary said. "We haven't got long."

Adelyn paused, then drew her father's sword, passing it between the bars. Her brother accepted the weapon, staring at it for a moment.

Imploring, Adelyn said, "Take it. I have magic. We'll be back for you."

Her brother looked at her, and it was apparent that he wanted to break down the bars of the cell and pull her into a hug, but even as strong as he was, that wasn't going to happen. "Be safe. I love you."

"Thanks, you sap," Adelyn said. "I love—"

A roar came from the hall. The armor had caught up to them.

"Adelyn, it's time to go!" Mary said.

Nodding, Adelyn gave her brother one last look, then walked back into the hall, raising a shield with a word.

A few stray shots fired their way, but the shield blocked them, spirit absorbing the lead rounds. She surveyed the opposition, feeling overwhelmed.

To one side, the spirit armor stood, waiting for the right time to attack. To their left, a dozen more bandits had gotten organized, and several of them had taken the time to don armor.

Mary stepped out and looked around, and came to the same conclusion Adelyn had. "Do you have the strength to repeat that fire?"

Adelyn knew she couldn't, but tried to summon the power anyways, thinking she could cast a weaker rendition of the same performance. The rune around her neck lost spirit as fast as she tried to fill them, burned and broken beyond repair.

"I can't," Adelyn said. "Fire is off the table."

Mary nodded. "Then, gods be willing, you'll have to defeat the armor alone. I will handle these ruffians. Throw the shield forward for me?"

Adelyn was puzzled by her oath, but there were more pressing questions for the time being. "What if—"

"Do it!" Mary ordered.

Adelyn nodded, focused for a second, and pushed her shield forward. The rifles all fired in unison as the bandits sensed an attack, nearly breaking the shield before it hit them, but that bought enough time for Mary to charge forward once again.

Turning away, Adelyn faced the figure in spirit plate, who had started walking forward. Adelyn did the same, her walk turning into a jog and then to a run as she got closer, building momentum so that she wouldn't give herself the opportunity to chicken out or back away. The spirit lights mounted on one side of the wall cast massive shifting shadows as the armor approached, blocking out light that would have gone over the head of any person of normal.

When only a few paces away, Adelyn readied a spell,

throwing a blast of energy forward with as much force as she could muster. It hit square on the breastplate, energy slamming into the bronze armor with the force of a battering ram.

In response, the armor slid back a few inches, steadied itself, and charged forward, fists swinging.

The armor didn't even have any weapons built onto it, other than thick, reinforced plates of armor layered in front of the wearer's hands. A club or mace would have been redundant, not to mention awkward to wield in such a cramped space. One of those giant fists came down toward Adelyn, and she only narrowly managed to duck underneath the blow.

Standing in a defensive posture, Adelyn faced down the hulking suit of armor, trying to spot a weak point that she could cut through. There were small areas of weaker plating around joints and flexible areas, but striking any of them would require precision that Adelyn didn't have, especially not while she was trying to avoid being crushed by that massive fist.

"Surrender," she offered weakly, holding out her hands, ready to dodge any attacks.

The armor hesitated for a moment, as though considering, and then swung an arm out, smashing a fist into the wall and sending out chips of stone flying toward Adelyn.

Yelping, she jumped backward, pouring energy into her runes and barking out *"Bren!"* in the hopes that it might work better, forgetting that her runes were broken. A gout of fire burst into existence in front of her, but it sputtered immediately, doing little except lighting the hall for a moment.

The armor hesitated for barely a second, then dug its heels into the ground and leaped forward with instant momentum, charging through the dwindling sparks and swinging at Adelyn.

Ducking backward again, Adelyn threw a weak blast of energy at the armor's legs, forcing it to stop and catch its footing, buying her enough time to duck backward and avoid having her head taken off by the attack.

Stumbling away, Adelyn threw up a hand, channeled some power into a shield, and repeated the spell to actualize it, backpedaling hard in an attempt to get out of striking distance.

As with the charging bandits before, there was no chance that Adelyn could put up a shield that would stop the armor in its tracks. On the other hand, if it were more focused and precise, it could potentially stay together long enough to have some effect. In response to Adelyn fleeing away, the armor pursued, charging forward, raising a fist to strike, an unstoppable force coming down a narrow corridor.

It was caught completely off guard by the trip line. The shield was low and as strong as Adelyn could make it, while the armor was top heavy and with a considerable head of momentum. It flew forward and crashed into the ground, kicking up clouds of dust and sprawling out with sounds of metal scraping against stone.

Taking a half second to catch her breath, Adelyn readied herself to continue the fight. She'd given away her sword to her brother, but she was hardly unarmed. Before the armor could get up, she leaped over it, careful to keep away from any armored hands that might try and crush her legs.

Sprinting away, the shadows on the wall flickered and shifted as the crossed the sixty feet to her destination, skidding around a corner, past the burned and injured bodies of the bandits who couldn't drag themselves to safety, running up the sloping hallway to a stop over the bag full of guns. She drew out two revolvers and jammed them under her belt, then pulled out a repeating rifle, and turned to face her opponent.

The armor had gotten back to its feet and turned to face her, approaching with considerably more caution than before. Adelyn aimed and fired, to little effect, ejected the cartridge, fired again, then threw the gun forward and stumbled back to avoid a swinging blow from the armor.

Breathing heavily, Adelyn walked backward as quick as she could without losing her balance, drawing one of the revolvers and pointing it. Six gunshots echoed in the hall, six rounds bounced off the armor with a clang, and then a seventh clang rang out as the gun itself bounced off the armor's breastplate.

"Dammit!" Adelyn shouted, pulling out the second revolver, pointing it at the armor without examining it, and pulling the trigger.

To her surprise, the bullet punched through the breastplate near the shoulder, and a voice cried out in pain from beneath the armor's ludicrously thick helmet. Unfortunately, the kick from the pistol was also about four times what she'd been expecting, and the gun flew from her unprepared grip. The armored warrior's cries were muted and distorted by their helmet, but rage and pain were plenty clear despite the distortion, and the fist that swung forward recklessly told the story just fine on its own.

Adelyn dodged again, trying to avoid being clipped by the attack. The armor was heavy and slow, certainly, but she was getting tired and each dodge was narrower than the last. Still, the shot had gone through, and judging by the size of the hole, it wasn't a mosquito bite that'd hit the armor's wearer. If it came down to attrition, Adelyn might even be able to hang on, she'd just—

"Adelyn!" Mary's voice echoed down the hall, calling her attention away from the armor. This nearly cost Adelyn her head, as an armored fist swung at her to exploit the moment of distraction.

She ducked the attack, seeing no opportunity to get around the armor and run to Mary's aid without throwing a monster of a spell, and she was quickly growing too tired to throw out anything of that much force. There was only one option she saw, and it was a stupid one.

Damning herself for a fool, Adelyn threw herself at the armor in a reckless charge. It hadn't expected that, and that bought her half a second to aim her hand, grabbing at the hole in the armor where the revolver had punched through.

Sharp edges of metal cut at her fingers as she stuck them into the hole, and as she jammed a finger into the padded clothes beneath the bronze plate, she felt blood. More than enough to cast any spell she desired.

The armor's wearer roared, turning a fist backward so it could smash at her while she grappled, and Adelyn reacted with panicked speed, pulling out all the spirit she could and desperately yelling out, "*Shtap!*"

The resulting boom was deafening, as the spell caught the armor up and flung it backward like a leaf in a windstorm. Adelyn's fingers were shredded as the armor was ripped away from her hand, gouging away bloody strips of flesh that made her cry out in pain, but it was nothing next to what the armor suffered.

There was no time to hesitate, but Adelyn still took a second to clear her head before getting up and shuffling forward, out of breath and unsure how much help she'd be in any more fighting. The passage had scrapes and gashes dug into the stone where the armor had bashed into it at high speeds.

She could also see the armor, lying on the ground fifty feet away from where it'd been when it had been hit with the spell, dented and scraped, not looking nearly so intimidating as a heap of brass on the ground. It had been thrown so far that it passed the intersection Mary was fighting in, and...

It was moving.

Adelyn's eyes widened as the armor began to stand, still moving despite the last attack. "Are you *kidding* me?" She muttered, picking up the pace and forcing herself to jog so that she could get back to Mary before the armor caught up to her.

Rounding the corner, she came into view of Mary, who was bleeding from a second cut on her arm, just below the first. She had been forced backward, taking on the role of defense, and her breath was coming in pants. Adelyn tried to summon some energy so that she could throw a bolt of force, but when she put it into the rune around her neck, it vanished, diffusing into the air. Trying her last good rune, Adelyn was able to get together a shield and throw it up, buying Mary a few seconds to retreat while the remaining bandits pushed through the mild resistance.

"How many left?" Adelyn asked, panting for breath as she stopped by Mary's side, looking over her shoulder to see that the armor was slowly rising.

"Half a dozen?" Mary responded, raising her sword and pushing back the first to get through the shield. "Three more showed up while you were gone."

"I don't have long!" Adelyn said. "I—*Ansyr!*" She reacted just in time to block a bullet meant to hit her between the eyes.

"Blood! Use it!" Mary shouted back, turning so that her injured arm was propped up toward Adelyn.

Wiping her hand on Mary's arm, Adelyn pulled the spirit from the blood, focusing it and using the spirit to reinforce the shield.

"All I can do right now!" Adelyn said, turning back to the armor and praying to the Lords that Mary would be able to handle the remaining bandits.

The armored warrior had a pronounced limp as it staggered forward, but when it pounded its fist against the wall, it was made clear that the armor had plenty of strength left to crush the life out of Adelyn.

The shadows on the wall shifted slowly and irregularly, huge silhouettes lurching forward in pantomime with the armor. Adelyn looked around the ground for a weapon but saw only a small knife. Throwing out spells was a losing proposition, she had lost all her runes save for shields, and Adelyn didn't have the spirit to pull out another doozy anyways.

Spotting something she could use, Adelyn felt herself smile in spite of the situation. Taking a couple steps forward to get out of Mary's way, she planted her feet on the floor and rested one arm against the wall, letting the armor approach.

As it edged towards her, Adelyn clenched her fists and shouted, "Last chance to give up!"

The armor's wearer roared back, anger and pain alongside bravado as it leaped forward over the last few feet, grabbing at Adelyn.

Instead of dodging out of the way, Adelyn just cast the strongest shield she could in a tight circle around herself, letting the armor grab her. Its grip was crushing, but had to get through a layer of magic first, giving Adelyn time to strike.

Adelyn yanked with the knife as hard as she could, cutting away at a cable from where it was strung through the light. As the knife cut through the protective coat on the cable, it made contact with the copper line beneath and the spirit gave up running into the lights and began running into Adelyn.

It was more force than she knew what to do with and Adelyn didn't manage to harness a single bit of it. She had been planning to use the spirit to cast a spell, but it overwhelmed her with pain, making muscles spasm and clench as power coursed through her body.

Still, as good a conductor as she was, the spirit found itself a better home—the massive assembly of copper and bronze that was the spirit armor. The power of the spirit passed through Adelyn and into the armor, arcs of energy so tangible that they could be seen by the naked eye. Shouts and a scream echoed behind her, but could barely register it over the pain and sensation of the spirit coursing around her.

The lights went dark, and then Adelyn's vision did the same.

CHAPTER 29

It was decided to abandon the northern deserts almost before the war was even declared. While the stated goal of 'Complete unification of the human race' can never technically be met so long as the nomads stay free, there was effectively no point in the attack.

The nomads—Holburns, they call themselves—have no cities, no exportable resources, no great works to speak of. They are known to create delightful songs and music, but such a creation is not economically viable. Subjugating them would be very difficult, for they thrive in conditions that none of the president's soldiers could survive in for longer than a week.

Until such a time that the nomads begin building houses and exporting resources of value, we will leave them be.

- Historical report on the decision to spare the Holburns, found on the second floor of the Presidential Archives in Triom

"... Keep looking! Abandon us, she's got to be around here somewhere."

"How are we supposed to look, by the gods, we can't see anything!"

"Someone's coming with lamps and torches, but if that damned witch can see in the dark, we don't have time to wait."

Adelyn opened her eyes, but for a moment wasn't sure if it had worked. She could feel the slight touch of cool air on her eyes, but the passage was completely black. She could hear shouts and stumbling feet around her, but eyes provided no useful information.

Shutting them again, Adelyn focused, trying to wish away the pain growing at the back of her head or the sharp stings of pain in her arm. Things weren't hopeless, but she needed a plan.

Her muscles ached and responded stiffly and slowly, protesting the shock she'd suffered. Her hand in particular was completely rigid and lacking almost entirely in sensation; and even with great effort she could only get her fingertips to twitch in response. This numbness was probably a boon, though, as it kept her from feeling the burns and damage that'd otherwise leave her writhing in agony. On her chest, she could feel angry burns where her force rune was hung around her neck, irritated skin that stung at any agitation.

She determined that it would be possible to walk, and probably to run, but fighting would be a fool's errand unless her opponent was asleep or a child. Magic was still a possibility, but if she'd been unconscious for long, it wasn't enough to overcome her fatigue.

"Adelyn," a voice whispered, almost startling her enough to elicit a yelp. She held back the cry of surprise, focusing on the word.

"Mary?" Adelyn whispered, her voice as low as she could manage without being completely inaudible. "How—"

"That doesn't matter," Mary responded quickly. "Just listen. You need to find David and get him back here."

"Bu—"

"No buts. We need him now. Don't take no for an answer. Drag him here if you have to."

"I can't," Adelyn said, putting her good hand over her mouth as she heard footsteps run past, only a couple feet to her side. "They'll hear me, and if they catch me..."

"Gods abandon me, girl, move!" Mary's voice left no room for argument.

Adelyn scooted away, wincing as she heard her own feet scraping on the stone. There were footsteps echoing throughout the blackness everywhere, the direction of the noise entirely impossible to determine. With luck, they wouldn't be able to tell her footsteps from that of others, and—

"I think I hear something!" one of them shouted, their voice close by. "Over here!"

Adelyn swallowed, pressing herself against the wall and trying to think of an escape. She could feel the dead spirit cable brush against the back of her neck as she flattened her body against the wall. Following that, she knew she could determine the direction of the passage, but getting there was another problem—bandits were all around, a seeming swarm of them based on how their footsteps echoed, and she didn't dare make a noise for fear of being found out.

Blinking once, she shut her eyes in focus, concentrated as much as she could, given the distractions, and invoked a brief spell. *"Ansyr hash."*

The sound of footsteps died instantly, silenced completely as the magic surrounded her, stopping all sound from coming in or out. Her own breathing echoed loud and overbearing, the rush of pumping blood and the little pops of aching joints standing out in ways she'd never notice otherwise.

Clenching and unclenching her good hand, Adelyn turned to her left and started walking.

It was strange and unbalancing to move without sight or sound keeping her in check. The slight upward incline of the passageway turned into a steep mountain she had to climb, and without the patter of her feet on stone or the visual confirmation of forward momentum, she stumbled to the ground within a few steps, sucking in a breath as she scraped the skin of her palm when she caught herself.

Righting herself, Adelyn crept forward more carefully, step by step. She could picture the other bandits moving around her, inches away, perhaps readying a weapon to strike before Adelyn could see and react.

Shaky step after shaky step, she shambled forward, going slow to keep her balance. A thought occurred, nagging and making the rush of her blood pound faster in her ears as it echoed around in her head without any noise or sight to distract her from it.

'I could not hear a word that you said'. That had been what David said. He'd not mentioned footsteps. It was entirely possible that Adelyn had already doomed herself—her footsteps could be echoing through the hallway like a beacon, and she would never know without dropping the spell to check and see. That would spell her capture as certainly as shooting a flare, though, and Adelyn was flagging in strength and couldn't just reassemble the spell infinitely. Unless—

A shoulder brushed against her, and Adelyn panicked. Shoving away at whoever had touched her, Adelyn took off in a sprint down the corridor. She tripped and fell within a few steps but scrambled back up, briefly running on all fours before planting a hand on the wall, using it to guide her steps and keep her balance as she ran, occasionally stumbling but managing to keep her pace. She couldn't look back and she couldn't stop.

The stone scraped lightly against her fingertips as she ran, acting as a compass and a map right up until the wall disappeared without warning. She sprawled out on the ground for the third time in a minute, realizing only as she stood and felt around that she'd made it back to the entry hall.

Her breath echoed in her ears, hoarse and ragged from the sprint, but she allowed herself a moment to rest before continuing her movement. She could already feel her spell fraying and falling apart—the energy didn't like being constantly slammed against stone floors, and was responding by fading into air. Rather than a shield around her body, it was turning into a vague haze, but that was fine. She'd gotten out of the thick of it, silence was no longer half so critical.

The light throughout the whole keep had seemingly gone out, and with the heavy doors shut, only the faintest cracks of light shone through from the moonlight outside. It was enough to make out what room she was in, but even if she'd remembered which hallway David had gone down, she'd not have been able to identify it in such darkness.

Pawing forward, Adelyn searched for the thing she needed to navigate in such an environment. She managed to reach one of the big columns, and slowly shuffled around it, feeling to try and find—

"Aha!" she exclaimed, then winced as her shout reverberated right back at her from off her spell, like shouting into her own ear. Still, it was worth celebrating—she'd found one of the seismographs, and with that, she had her map.

Hand on the cable, Adelyn pointed her back to the thin beams of light coming from the door and began walking. She soon came to a Y-split in the wires and had to feel it for a moment before guessing at the right way to go.

As muted sound slowly worked its way through the spell, Adelyn felt her balance improving, and the cable helped a great deal as well. She made a good pace, at least as far a she could tell, walking down the same way David had gone. What tiny beams of light had been visible soon vanished out of sight behind her, and Adelyn was again walking blindly through an unfamiliar passage.

As she walked, she felt the floor beneath her feet change from tile to marble, cold and hard under her boots. A few steps later, she felt a sudden jolt of pain burst from her toes as she kicked something hard and metallic—it shifted slightly in response to her kick, but not in any significant way.

Hesitating, Adelyn tried to decide if it was safe to draw a light. She couldn't hear anyone, even with the spell most deteriorated. A light would help her move faster, too, but if someone saw her...

Putting a tiny hint of spirit into the rune on her neck, she whispered, *"Brenshane,"* all in one word. The fire rune couldn't hold a charge of spirit for a second anymore, but she only needed it for an instant to get such a simple spell going. A point of flickering light appeared, giving off heat and illumination.

Gasping, Adelyn stumbled back a few steps. On the ground around her was a half dozen men and women all in ostentatious plate armor, decorated with runes and embossed silver filigree. It wasn't true spirit armor, but the gilded armor—when charged—would still provide a major advantage in any combat situation.

Each armored figure was out cold, or worse. Adelyn assumed they weren't dead, based on who she figured had disabled them all, but that was only a guess.

One of them gave out a groan, and Adelyn slapped a hand over her mouth to keep from yelping in surprise. She stepped backward, certain that the nearest figure was about to lash out at her. Her heart was beating fast enough that she felt certain it would crack a rib if it pounded any harder in her chest.

It took a moment to realize that she'd channeled more spirit into her shield rune, a reflexive response that accomplished little more than to waste energy. She released the spirit, telling herself that she was playing the fool—there was no threat to be warded off. She was safe, for the moment.

Carefully moving forward, Adelyn skirted around the nearest of the figures, stepping over bodies and trying not to bump into anyone, as though that might wake them from slumber. Tired as she was, she stumbled after a few steps, foot catching on an outcropping of armor. She caught herself without falling flat again, but the sound of armor clattering as she tripped over it was a claxon in the narrow hallways.

Adrenaline spiking, Adelyn jumped up and continued forward, faster and less careful. One of the people on the ground started to move, a slow, sluggish effort to sit up, but Adelyn wasn't going to wait for that to turn into an attack— as soon as she'd cleared the six figures on the ground, she broke into a full sprint, only remembering to follow the path of the cable on the wall after she'd made it twenty paces away.

Her dim firelight—still hovering by the downed figures where she'd left it—only gave the faintest hints of the passage walls from so far away, and so she was back to traveling by feel in lieu of drawing a new light.

She encountered no other obstacles. The floor transitioned again, from marble to—oddly—what felt to be carpet. The wall, still stone, had added texture to it where presumably some decoration or architectural difference marked it. After half a minute and two turns, a faint blue light came into view at the end of the tunnel, not flickering, and from too far away for her to make out a distinct source. Picking up her pace now that she could see, Adelyn hurried down the passage, the light growing stronger as she grew closer.

She could now see that the walls were decorated with faded murals and tarnished silver ornamentation. All were cast in a sickly pallor from the blue light, but she guessed they'd be glorious in the light of bright torches, depicting scenes of great battles and heroic figures in the heat of combat. She had no time to take in any specific details, but the mere length of and number of murals told a story of its own; a massive, seemingly endless history, embellished by old silver and clouded gemstones that would sparkle and shine if polished.

A thought occurred, and Adelyn stumbled as the decision to hesitate reached her feet before it reached the rest of her. The light was probably magical, which meant that one of two people was at the end of the corridor—possibly both.

Slowly walking forward, Adelyn approached down the hallway with more caution, taking careful steps that were as close to noiseless as she could manage. The carpet helped with this, muting her footsteps further, letting her approach the light enough to make out where the hallway opened into a larger chamber, and to make out indistinct voices—shouting, arguing, she couldn't tell about what.

Staying close to the wall as she edged closer, Adelyn crouched down and got onto her belly once she was a few paces away from the door. She could see now that the chamber was massive, and filled with displays of once-opulent wealth. From the end of the hall, a stairway led down into what had to be a throne room, which was fifty feet tall at least. Pillars were set up with anachronistic silver torch sconces set up between modern, cheaply assembled spirit lights, copper wires running through the room and showing no concern for aesthetic sensibilities.

Four statues as tall as the room itself were set up in each corner of the great hall, all depicting enormous heroes of some sort. Armored or not, all were armed and stood like guardians, though their size implied that they'd guard against something greater than any human army; They were large enough to overpower dragons if they came to life.

At the end of the throne room was, of course, the object which gave the room its name; a great chair, sat atop a raised platform. As fitting with the design all around, the chair appeared to be of pure silver, and unlike the silver around it, this had been polished to a mirror shine.

Adelyn took all of this in within the space of a second, glancing around the room before settling on what she truly cared about. Atop the raised throne sat a figure, and below that figure, a man stood on the ground looking like he was ready to kill.

The figure in the chair was a tall man—over six feet, if Adelyn were to guess. He wore a ringlet of silver over silky brown hair that flowed past his shoulders, crown and hair both decorated with gaudy blue gemstones. His robes went down to his ankles, flowing blue fabric decorated with white trim. He sat slouched to one side, holding an ebony-black staff, silver-blue light emanating from smoking runes around one end. He appeared as a demigod, standing over an empty, decayed court, and Adelyn knew without even thinking about it that this was what the Thirteen must have looked like in the battlefield—a range of colors, but each exuding deadly power by their mere existence.

In contrast, David stood below in cotton shirt and pants, face stubbly from a week without shaving, white-knuckled fists holding his hook and staff, stance guarded and ready to attack at any second.

Close enough now, Adelyn tried to focus so she could hear what they were saying.

David's voice was clear and clipped, as precise as ever. "Your guards could not so much as slow my attack. I have tracked you here, across the length of the realm, to hold you responsible for your crimes."

The man in the throne laughed, a practiced laugh that echoed with faux casual arrogance. "I do not have a care as to how you found me, that is not important. Any ruffian with a lick of magical inclination could fight past my guards, the fools. You do not scare me, and some tin badge does not incline me to give in to your authority. Surrender, and I may show mercy!"

"You are a liar, and a coward, and *weak*." David spoke plainly, but spat out the last word like an oath, or perhaps even a spell. The words reinforced the challenge already implicit in his defiance.

The statement had its desired reaction. The man in blue slammed his staff into the ground and threw himself onto his feet, roaring. "*I AM THE BLUE FLAME.* I have killed thousands of men, crushing their lives like insects! If you do not surrender, you will be no different!"

David nodded. "Eight thousand, three hundred and fifty-one."

This caught the Blue Flame off guard, and he raised his eyebrows in confusion, snapping, "What?"

"The Blue Flame was directly responsible for killing eight thousand, three hundred and twenty-three people in battle, or as part of combat operations, twenty-seven of whom were sorcerers and sorceresses." David said. "He also killed twenty three kings, queens, or monarchy. Finally, he murdered five people."

Trying to regain the heat in his voice, the Blue Flame continued his rant. "Then you're—you are aware! I will crush you like an insect!"

"You already said that," David said, lowering himself to one knee. He placed his hook on the ground in front of him, and his staff, then pulled the gloves away from his fingertips and laid them both down on the ground before standing again and taking a few steps back. He took the silver chain from around his neck, letting it dangle from his fingertips.

"What are you doing?" The Blue Flame demanded, rage and confusion coloring his face.

David took a breath, and then began to speak softly, as though he were repeating something he knew by heart, yet still cared enough about to take extra care in the recitation. "You are a powerful figure, but the time of your ignoble reign has come to an end. You did not surrender before we attacked, nor when your people were dying to our assault. You have given up your right to surrender now."

The Flame froze, confusion flashing across his face, and then realization, and then...fear. He recovered quickly, but Adelyn knew that she had seen it there, just for a split second. "I do not need to surrender! I can kill you without—"

"I would not see fit to attack you with any low or base trickery," David continued, ignoring the ranting. "Or in any way where you could not defend yourself. When a person such as you falls, they should fall knowing it was due to their own weakness, not due to some deception or treachery. As such, I will allow you to choose the terms of this fight." He paused, then added in a less scripted tone, "Do you understand what I am talking about?"

The end of the Flame's staff began to glow brighter. "No!" he shouted, trying to take a step back, his heels bumping into the silver throne behind him. "You are just some cheap magician! You will not—"

"We may fight with blade, or with magic, or with fists, but know that whatever you choose, I will ki..." David's speech hit a hitch, and he had to stop himself. "I will defeat you."

The Blue Flame straightened. "If that is the case, I *Bren*." His words shifted into the spell like water, and Adelyn wouldn't have realized he'd done anything had a torrent of cobalt fire not leaped from the end of his staff, lighting up the room like a star. David was completely consumed by the blaze, and Adelyn had to wince back from the heat and cover her eyes at the light.

When it died, scorch marks marred the floor and pillars, the red carpet leading to the throne was completely incinerated into char, and the metal spirit lights nearby were melted slag, dripping from their sconces.

David, his weapons, and the small patch of carpet that they stood atop were completely unscathed.

"Magic, then," David said, kneeling to pick up his gloves and staff as the Blue Flame spluttered for a response.

Quickly jerking on his gloves, David stiffly rose, pointed his staff at the mass murderer above him, and said, "You may pray to the gods of your choice, if you so will it."

The Blue Flame chose not to, instead roaring in anger and leaping forward, off the raised platform, shouting something that had to be a spell or an oath. David raised his own short staff, shouted in response, and as the Blue Flame's charging leap came to its end, the two wizards began to fight.

CHAPTER 30

Available for purchase:

Mossweed Oil - Cures toothache, fever. Two daggers per bottle.

Dr. Gregories Cure All - Heals small cuts, cures Headaches, Flu, Cough, mends broken bones. One sword per bottle, contains six doses.

Sleeping Potion - For insomnia, sleeplessness, lethargy. Eight pins per bottle.

Magician's Lotion - Used by sorcerers. When applied, grants a hint of magical power to anyone. Three swords per bottle.

Also on offer:

Bloodletting treatments, administered by a physician trained in sorcerous arts. Will balance your moods, level your spirit, and bring you in tune with the gods.

- Advertisement, painted on the side of a traveling physician's cart

THEY MET with thundering shouts as spells erupted on both sides. A razor thin blade of blue fire cut outward toward

David, but he jumped back and threw out his hands, and a gale of wind blew downward, prematurely ending the attacking wizard's leap and sending the fire splashing into the ground where it cut into the tile floor.

A second ball of fire erupted in the air, billowing outward like an explosion that'd been slowed down and controlled, manipulated into shape rather than being allowed to expand freely. David moved his hands in a flowing gesture, spinning the silver necklace around like a pendulum and chanting loudly with a string of words that Adelyn neither recognized nor understood. Across him, the wizard held out his staff, standing in a powerful stance and speaking words of his own.

Sorcerer and wizard stared off like that for a moment, their magic words forming a sort of harmony as the ball of fire rippled and moved, first shifting toward David, then toward the Blue Flame, twisting and extending and contracting back as they vied for control.

David broke the stare down first, hopping to one side and then charging forward, hands out and chant still echoing. The ball of fire suddenly slammed forward, but it moved to a space David was no longer at, and so the Blue Flame turned his focus away. As soon as neither of them were minding it, the ball of fire spread out and consumed itself until it was just a puff of smoke—there was no fuel for the flame, only oxygen and spirit to burn.

Neither spellcaster acknowledged this. The Blue Flame swung his staff like a club, little needles of fire shooting out and diving toward David. Each needle struck his spinning necklace but seemed to have no effect on the metal, then David was within striking distance and swung out the staff in his right hand.

The Blue Flame blocked this attack with his own

massive staff, but David hadn't just been attacking with the staff—the three foot length of wood hit the Blue Flame's staff with a boom, launching the wizard backward. He tumbled onto the stairs leading to the throne, rolling to the side in time to dodge David's follow-up attack—a bolt of fire that splashed against the marble stairs.

The Flame rolled so far as to go over the edge of the stairs, falling to the ground and catching himself, using the stairs as a barricade to protect against attacks for a second while he stood upright before charging back into combat.

Glancing away from the fight for a moment, Adelyn tried to think of any way to help. Even if she had the spirit for it, throwing spells into that fray seemed like a bad idea, as likely to hurt David as it was to kill the target she was intending to hit. She didn't have a gun—all their weapons were in a bag, back in the dark hall, too far away to be remotely useful. Rushing into the fight with fists raised wasn't even a serious option, which left nothing that Adelyn could think of.

She cursed herself for not grabbing a weapon on her way. Even if she couldn't have retrieved a gun, she could have taken a sword from one of the people in the plate armor.

A shout and a flicker of multicolored lights distracted her attention. Looking down, she saw David twirling his staff in his hand and shuffling backward in a dance, across from the Flame, who was standing in a more stable stance, staff held out like he was bearing a spear against a charging horde of invaders. Blood was visible on David's shirt, a sticky red blotch on the fabric, but that may have been intentional, to get some spirit—without seeing the cut, Adelyn couldn't be sure.

Small needles of fire were darting at the Blue Flame like

a swarm of bees, each one a slightly different hue. These needles splashed against an invisible barrier harmlessly, but each seemed to have a slightly different effect—one splashed out like hot oil spreading on the surface of a lake, another nearly pierced through the shield and then stuck in it, staying together in a hardened point.

Adelyn realized after a moment that David was keeping up his attack just to harass the Flame, so that there'd be no chance of striking back. The Blue Flame's shield was having to constantly shift and change in order to stand up to the broad spectrum of attacks, so he couldn't leave it be and prepare a counter attack of his own.

Or, at least, that was the theory. The Blue Flame, apparently fed up with this, roared a few words of his chant at greater volume, then raised and swung his staff outward. As far away as she was, Adelyn could still feel the crackling sense of spirit as his shield redoubled in power, forming a nigh impenetrable barrier. David continued his attacks against it for a half second longer then, abandoned trying to get through that shield with brute force, backed off.

For a second, at least, both sorcerer and wizard ceased their chanting and spellcasting, catching their breath. Neither exchanged words. Words were an opportunity to get caught off guard. Instead, they watched for opportunities, slowly circling like dogs ready to pounce. The shield would only provide protection for a little longer, and any second—

David barked out a spell and the Blue Flame responded as though he could see it coming—if he felt the spirit in David's spell, he probably *did* see it coming. The arc of energy that erupted from David's hand was diverted into the ground, splashing harmlessly.

Shouting something in response, the Blue Flame directed his staff upwards, and Adelyn felt the force even from across the room. The effect wasn't immediately obvious, but a deafening 'crack!' echoed through the throne room, and a moment later one of the massive statues began to tip, building speed as it toppled forward, an unstoppable tide of stone falling straight toward David.

He swung his staff and dodged backward in the opposite direction of the pillar, and though David couldn't dodge the spray of smaller gravel that flew up when the boulders smashed into the polished marble floor, he blocked that with a spell. The head of the monument flew free of the statue, rolling a few paces away from its body, altering the terrain of the fight.

There was a half second's reprieve as sorcerer and wizard were separated by the statue, before the Blue Flame came flying over the torso in an impossibly high arc, staff smeared with blood and swinging down as he gave up magic for combat—both of them were still chanting spells in tandem, but those spells were now accompanied by strikes and physical attacks—the Blue Flame wielding his staff like a spear, David responding in kind with grappling and more stocky blows from his shorter weapon.

They fought like dancers, each blow countered and parried away in time for the next, moving in lockstep—David slowly advancing to try and get into his opponent's guard, the Flame retreating to stay at arm's length where his staff would have a greater advantage.

It was only when an arcing back fist from David went wide that Adelyn realized their attacks had more than what was plainly visible—his fist struck the massive stone head to his side, but instead of breaking his fist like would be expected, he broke off a chunk of the head, shattering a polished nose into pebbles.

The Flame's staff came up to meet David's chin, and he

only narrowly dodged back from it, but as his balance was off, the Blue Flame shouted something and the head of the statue suddenly shifted, lurching toward David.

The boulderous head slammed into David's side, sending him into a tailspin that landed him on the ground. The Flame's staff, which now had spectral wisps of fire dancing around its tip, swung down at David in a motion resembling a pickaxe into hard dirt. David managed to roll out of the way, and the staff threw up chunks of stone the size of apples where it hit.

David managed to get back to his feet, but something had shifted in the battle—he was holding his left arm close to his side, which meant that his staff was unavailable to be used as a weapon. If the arm wasn't broken, it was at least too injured to be used.

Adelyn felt a sudden chill wash over her, a cold spot that formed at the small of her back and filled her with dread, the looming specter of failure washing over her as she realized things were hopeless.

David staggered back against the next series of attacks— he still had his silver chain with the spinning pendulum ring, letting him ward away attacks, but he'd gone from being on the offensive to playing defense, backing away despite having the shorter reach.

Lying stock still, Adelyn could feel the bursts of spirit as the Blue Flame threw himself forward, pressing his advantage, spells lancing out and just barely being deflected away by David's shield. They were brute force attacks, presumably meant to wear down defenses and whatever reserve of spirit David had left from the blood on his arm and the energy keeping him on his feet.

David backed away in circles, going around the statue's head, careful not to get too close in case of another attack from the side. Blasts of pure spirit came at him with such force that it made the air ripple and gave off bursts of sound, the deep boom of cannon fire accompanying each shouted spell.

Adelyn bit down on her tongue. She wanted to cry out, but it would be a distraction to David and potentially spell out her own death—a desperate act that would serve nobody except the Blue Flame.

As the Flame lunged forward again, leading with his staff, David only barely managed to get to the side of the attack. It burst through whatever shield he had and came within a half-inch of touching David, making his shirt billow as the spell pushed air in a gale. David had to jump backward to avoid the Flame's next attack, a swing sideways meant to catch David in the belly.

Pumping his good hand forward, David shouted out a few words, only one of which Adelyn recognized—a thin wall of fire came into being between him and the Blue Flame, but even Adelyn could see it was a piddling defense. It made the Flame hesitate for a second, but that was all.

The Blue Flame leaped through the thin wall of fire, ready to hit David with another attack that would surely put him down for good. He made no attempt at subterfuge— David's shields had grown weaker against every attack, and his most recent counter offensive was the desperate attempt of someone who was out of options.

The spell lancing out from the Blue Flame's staff formed in slow motion with sparking energy, making the runes on the black wood glow. As he rushed through the thin, almost harmless fire, the energy coalesced into a ball of flame, resembling a baton if not for the fact that one end was molten hot and growing. He stabbed this forward at David, releasing the fire and letting it explode out in all directions, spreading with enough heat to char flesh from bones in an instant.

As quickly as it was released, though, the magic fire died.

It didn't simply get blocked or have no effect—it seemed to wink out of existence, shut down harmlessly without even singeing what bits of carpet remained around them. David, letting the silver chain hang from his wrist, grabbed the wizard's staff in his own hand, then lashed out with the staff his broken arm, catching the Blue Flame in the throat.

There was no spell backing up the attack, but three feet of hard wood hit the Flame just above the collarbone, stopping his momentum cold. The Flame made a choking noise, letting go of his staff and grabbing at his throat.

David, now holding the black staff in his right hand, tossed it to the ground and let it clatter against the stone in the now-quiet room. He held his own staff in his left arm, raising the weapon in emphasis. The arm had never been broken, David's feigning weakness had all been a trick.

He stepped forward, driving his foot up squarely between the Blue Flame's legs.

Gasping for air and retching from the pain, the Flame's legs buckled and he fell to the ground, rolling on his side. David didn't relent, but neither did he bother using magic— he just kicked the Flame in the belly, once, twice, and a third time for good measure.

"I should kill you right now," David said, and though his voice was low, Adelyn could hear it plain as day. He bent and ripped off a chunk of the cowering wizard's robes, stuffing the scrap of cloth into the Flame's mouth as a cheap emulation of a gag. "You certainly deserve it, you...coward. You liar. You are trash." He stood, drove another angry kick into the Flame's chest, and then walked a slow circle around him.

"You are lucky that I made a promise," David continued. "To take no life, by accident or by design. Had I not made that promise, you would be a little red splotch on the floor."

The Blue Flame, trembling, looked like he was going to spit out the gag and respond. David pointed his short staff at the wizard's face and simply shook his head. "Letting you live does not mean I need to leave you whole. Spit that out, and I will shatter your teeth.

"You think you can rule by fear," he continued, once it was apparent that the wizard was going to offer no further resistance or complication. "That the name of the Blue Flame will command respect, because your own cheap, pathetic talent wasn't enough to draw men on its own."

Crouching, David punched the wizard square in the nose, affecting a sick 'cracking' sound. Then, he placed the tip of his staff under the wizard's chin, jamming it hard against the bone. "But *I'm* the Blue Flame, and I have done enough evil in this world without some cheap magician using my name for wickedness."

Adelyn gasped in spite of herself, the sound muffled by the hand over her mouth.

Taking in a breath, he started to shout, *"RAH—"*

"Stop!" the voice called out from just above Adelyn. It was a feminine voice, echoing slightly from within a helmet and shouting with unquestioned authority.

The speaker held Adelyn at the point of a knife. She'd snuck up on Adelyn midway through the fight, just about when David had been hit by the boulder. Based on her weight, she was wearing a full set of armor, though whether it was steel or brass, Adelyn couldn't tell.

David did stop, looking over his shoulder. He had to

squint, and could only just make out the two figures in the dark passageway. "Who are you?"

"Stop, or I'll kill this girl!" the soldier called out, digging the knife further into Adelyn's back and releasing the hand so that Adelyn could cry out in pain without obstruction.

Adelyn obliged her, screaming as she felt the knife cut deep into the meat of her back. The knife stopped an inch into the flesh, held in place by a deft hand.

"Adelyn?" David called, standing and facing them.

"I don't know who this girl is, only that she's with you," The soldier called. Directing her voice down, she said, "Girl, is your name Adelyn?"

"Yes!" Adelyn shouted, trying to keep the shout from becoming another scream.

"There you go!" the soldier shouted, her voice confidently casual. "Now step away from my wizard, or you'll need to get a new daughter!"

"She is not my daughter," David said, almost reflexively.

"I'll still kill her!" The soldier shouted. "Won't I, girl?"

Adelyn nodded, again shouting, "Yes!"

The soldier's smile was almost audible. "All I have to do is push down this knife another inch and it'll go through her spine! Do you want that?"

"No!" David shouted back. "Do not hurt her!"

"Then drop your weapons! You have until I can count to five. One!"

David hesitated, hands briefly tightening around his staff.

"Four!" the soldier shouted. "I can't count so good. Better hurry up!"

David hesitated a fraction of a second longer, then released his hands and let both his staff and chain fall to the ground.

"Okay, now strip down to your skivvies! I don't want you pulling a knife or a gun out of someplace! Once you've done that, step a few paces away, get on your knees, and put your hands on your head like you can't find your hat."

Adelyn could feel blood pooling at her back, and tried to think if she could use that spirit for something.

"Don't even think on it, girl," the soldier whispered. "I felt you tense up there. Don't know what you're planning, but I guarantee, nothing you do will be faster than me pushing this knife straight out the other side. Understand?"

Swallowing, Adelyn nodded her head a couple times.

"Good."

David was tugging at a boot, halfway through the job of stripping down. "Adelyn is just here to rescue her family. Take me captive, but let her go!"

"Keep working!" the soldier called back, ignoring the request.

Once down to a pair of cotton boxers, David removed the mechanical thumb strapped around the palm of his hand, setting it on the pile of clothes and backing away. Lacing his fingers over his head, he dropped to his knees, calling, "Okay. You can let her up now!"

"You heard him," The soldier said, shifting her weight so that Adelyn was no longer pinned to the ground. "Get up, Adelyn. Slowly."

Adelyn complied, feeling the cold steel follow her up, the blade a reminder not to do anything too quickly.

"We're going to walk down the stairs now," the soldier said. "Careful now. I would hate for my hand to slip and accidentally run you through." Then, after a deliberate pause she added, "Hate to lose collateral."

Adelyn slowly shuffled forward, taking the stairs as carefully as she could manage, not wanting to appear as though she were trying to get away from the knife.

Across the throne room, the wizard was starting to rise to shaky legs. There was a breath throughout the room as all eyes paused to watch him stand, before the soldier urged Adelyn forward with the slightest jiggle of the knife.

Limping, the wizard crossed to his staff and bent awkwardly to pick it up, wincing and clutching at his midsection as he did so. With the weapon in hand, he walked behind David, holding the staff in a manner that made his magical tool resemble a club.

"So I'm a coward, eh?" He asked, his tone nasally and pitched higher than it had been before. He swung the staff. It struck the back of David's head with a solid THUD, and David slumped forward, hitting the ground without any attempt to catch himself.

"David!" Adelyn yelled. When she realized that the knifepoint was gone from her back, she pushed away from the soldier and ran forward, flying down the last couple steps and across the throne room.

Crouching by his side, she rolled him over, shaking his shoulders. David didn't respond, eyes shut and body limp. "Come on!" Adelyn yelled, "Wake up!"

"He's not dead, merely unconscious," The wizard pitched, spitting out blood. "He'll live, at least until I decide otherwise."

Standing, Adelyn turned to glare, pointing a finger at the wizard. "You coward! He was unarmed, he wasn't any threat, he—"

The wizard slapped her across the face, open handed but without any restraint. It hurt, leaving a large red mark across her face where his palm struck her cheek.

"Speak to me in such a tone again, I'll keep a closed fist," the wizard said. "And remember, girl. He continued to strike me many times after I was down. I only struck him the once."

By the time he said that, the soldier had crossed the length of the throne room. Removing her helmet, she knelt in front of the wizard, short hair sticking up in odd directions. "My lord."

"Anna," the wizard said. "The rest of the guard?"

"Alive, my lord," Anna confirmed. "Some were terribly injured, but they'll live."

The wizard nodded. "It seems I am in your debt. Thank you."

"My lord, I'm supposed to guard you," Anna said, head down. "You don't owe me a thing, I was only doing the job you hired me to do."

The wizard shook his head. "Nevertheless...how much of his lies did you hear before you interrupted his speech?"

Head still low, Anna said, "A fair piece. I didn't want to cut into your dance early, in case my threat came up on a hitch or he didn't go for it."

"Then you heard his false claim," the wizard said, nodding. "Of course you know I am truly the Blue Flame, not he. I would appreciate your keeping such rumors to yourself. It would not become you to spread lies such as those."

Adelyn clenched a fist, objecting. "He doesn't lie! If..." Hesitating, she added, "If he says he's the Blue Flame..." She frowned, trying to puzzle out the contradiction. As far as she saw, there was no way for it to be true—he couldn't be of the Thirteen *and* be a Stone Warrior. He was lying about something, no matter what. Glancing at David, she tried to reevaluate what he'd told her, whether anything was true.

"My lord," Anna said. "Can I speak my mind?"

"Yes, Anna," the wizard said.

"You know I fought in the president's vanguard," Anna said. "We had more than one occasion to fight with the Thirteen. They wore those robes, masks, sure, but when we were routing some border baron down south, the Blue Flame's robes got all tore up."

"Was that robe over my face?" The wizard asked, eyebrow raising.

"No, my lord," Anna said, breaking her prostrate gaze to look between David, half-naked on the ground, his dark skin completely exposed. Then, the wizard, whose complexion was pale as driven snow. "But...well, I can't say who it was under those robes, but they weren't you. I've always known. I ain't following you 'cause I think you're some hotshot wizard, I'm following you because you deserve it. You belong on that throne."

The wizard hesitated, then gave a stiff nod. "Very well. Still, I would appreciate if you do not speak of this."

"I can hold my tongue." Anna confirmed. Looking at David, she asked, "What should we do with these two?"

"Pick a cell, lock them up. Make sure he can't use his hands and can't move. Keep the girl out of his reach." He paused, then added, "Girl, are you armed?"

"No," Adelyn said, instantly.

Anna rolled her eyes. "Hand it over, Adelyn. What've you got, a knife?"

"I don't have a weapon," Adelyn repeated.

"Girl, you are not fooling anyone," The wizard said, stepping forward. "If you don't hand over the weapon, we'll search you and find it."

Swallowing, Adelyn said, "I don't have a knife, or a gun, or anything. I had one, but I lost it a while ago." If she didn't mention the runes around her neck, maybe she could get the jump on Anna, once the wizard wasn't around, and—

"Anna?" The wizard asked. The soldier stepped forward and knelt, patting down Adelyn's trousers, checking her boots, and then standing up and checking around Adelyn's shirt.

Anna came away with Adelyn's knife, and the bag of silver daggers and other coins. Adelyn bit down on her tongue and had to restrain herself to keep from trying to fight back at that—her family's savings, gone in a heartbeat, the last resource she'd had left.

"No real weapons, just this," Anna said.

Sighing, the wizard stepped forward, and put a hand on Adelyn's shoulder. She felt the subtle buzz of spirit as it passed over her body. It was hazy around her belt buckle, but focused with razor-sharp clarity and filled into the shield rune around her neck.

Eyes snapping to the string holding up the three runes, the wizard grabbed it and jerked the necklace off of Adelyn, holding up the magical conduits. "She's a witch," he said.

"I'm a sorceress," Adelyn corrected.

Eyes sparkling, the wizard said, "Make sure *she* can't use her hands, either. This whole debacle may prove to be profitable after all."

CHAPTER 31

I have restrained the animal, and am about to begin testing. My assistant is taking notes, and I will be dictating. Don't worry, lad, just ensure you mark down the important things I say, you don't need to get every word. It's easy, as I promised. No, don't write this part, wha

Note One: Anesthetics have been applied, and the pig has stopped squealing. I am making the first incision. Blood flow seems usual.

Note Two: I have obtained samples of blood from the rear flank, side, jowl, and near the heart. I am running each through the extractor, to see if any amount of spirit can be extracted, and where it is most intense.

Note Three: No results. If there is any spirit in this beast, it's so little as to not show up on the machine. It seems my theory will have to wait until they give me a live human to test on. The board seems hesitant, but the value of my work will surely sway them.

Note Four: The butchers have offered me two tacks, rather than the usual one tack and three swords, if I break down this animal for them before delivering the carcass. I'll therefore be working on this animal a moment longer than normal.

- Dictated lab notes, made during research on spirit extraction

"Gaah!" Adelyn choked, spitting and shivering as cold salt-water was dumped over her head and back, drenching through her jacket and into her clothes and hair, running down her pants and dripping into her boots. "Abandon you, you Lords-damned piece of—" She shut her mouth and eyes as Anna splashed a bit more water right into her face, cutting off her rant.

The restraints were built with old wood and new steel hinges, bolted into the floor to prevent unruly prisoners from toppling it over. It was a simple design—a wooden board, cut in half lengthwise, holes bored into it for the neck and hands, then closed over Adelyn with hinges and latches. Her hands were a foot from her face but held completely impotent, unable to do more than point or make rude gestures.

The wooden holes for her wrists and neck had steel rings that dug into her skin, and no matter how much Adelyn jerked and pulled against them, she couldn't get herself free.

Twisting her hands and trying to resist anyways, Adelyn screamed profanity and bloody murder to Anna, who was casually setting down the now-empty bucket in the corner of the room. She'd been left guarding the two of them while the wizard took care of some other affairs and waited for David to wake up, with a half dozen buckets to ensure Adelyn didn't dry out.

"Lords damn you, let me out of this or I'll kill you!" she shouted, face red and knuckles white.

Her feet were the only thing not held tightly in place,

merely held down by some loose iron shackles, and the restraints proved not only impossible to free from, but intensely uncomfortable to boot.

Across from her, David's head was turned to the side so he wouldn't choke himself and suffocate while unconscious, and in order to restrain his thumbless left hand that would just slip out of the normal cuff, his arm had been wrapped tightly with a cord and tied into place in the steel cuff. He hadn't been soaked with saltwater, at least, probably under the assumption that his briefs would pose no significant threat.

Uncrossing her arms—which were still clad in the heavy bronze armor—Anna crossed the small cell room to where Adelyn was bound, leaning down in front of her. "Listen, Adelyn. You can shout and scream and yell until your voice goes out, or you can shut up and give me a little peace and quiet. Either way, I'm not going anywhere until the wizard tells me one way or another what to do, but if you stop making such a racket, I might be inclined to be a little nicer to you when you find yourself needing some water. Got it?"

Adelyn briefly considered the question, then spat in Anna's face. "Let me go, or I'll set you on fire with a word."

Anna wiped her face and rolled her eyes, stepping just out of spitting distance. "You're not too bright, are you, kid? I spend just about every day guarding a wizard, I know how all your tricks work. Maybe if you were free you'd be a bit of a threat, with your magic powers and what-not, but right now you're all locked up and soaked with salt. It don't matter if you threaten to peel the skin from my bones and rub broken glass on the exposed flesh, it ain't gonna be scary."

"Until I get out," Adelyn said.

Anna shrugged her shoulders, crossing her arms once

again and leaning against the wall. "If. And that's a helluva if."

Adelyn glowered, tugging once again at her arms in an attempt to get them free.

"So you're here for your family then, huh," Anna commented. When Adelyn continued to glare, she threw up her hands. "What do you want, kid? You're stuck here, I'm not gonna leave just because you're throwing a tantrum. We may as well talk."

Adelyn heaved her chest in and out in a breath, readied a tirade, and then dropped it. Anna was right, even if she was also easily described by a long stream of profanity. "My parents and brother were captured by your wizard, along with some-odd fifty people. You attacked my hometown, burned half our buildings and more of our crops, then left with most anyone able to fight you off."

Anna scratched her chin thoughtfully. "This'd have been what, three months ago? Something like that?"

"Something like," Adelyn confirmed.

"Don't recall any parent-son pairings in that group," Anna commented. "Who's your brother?"

Adelyn shut her mouth and resumed her glower.

"Come now," Anna complained. "It's not as though I'm going to go put splinters under his fingernails just 'cause his sister is a troublemaker."

"John," Adelyn said. "He's tall. Kinda quiet."

Anna's eyes lit up and she smiled—not a reaction that Adelyn had expected. "Big John? The guards all love him. Follows orders, works without a word till you say 'quit', never complains about nothin'."

"Sounds like him," Adelyn said.

"He said he's not related to nobody, though," Anna continued. "Said he was just in the town working odd jobs."

Adelyn bit off a curse. If he'd lied to keep his relation-
ships secret, she had just blown their deception. "Eh, there
were two Johns. You must be thinking of—"

"Ah, save it," Anna said. "Still, whatever. Brother, not
your brother. Either way. Takes a lot of sand to come out
here and take us all on like that, even with the Kingslayer
in tow."

"I didn't know he was the Blue Flame," Adelyn said.
"Lords abandon me, I didn't even know he was a sorcerer
when I hired him."

"Helluva coincidence," Anna commented.

"I'd been trying to find a bounty hunter for two months,"
Adelyn pointed out. "He's the first one to accept what I had
in payment. Barely even tried to negotiate, accepted all my
conditions."

"Still," Anna said, looking at David. "Never seen nobody
put one over on my wizard like that."

"Who is he?" Adelyn asked. "Your wizard."

Anna shrugged. "Dunno. Figure he knows this keep well
enough, probably been here before, might've actually been
a Stone Warrior before the war. Never asked."

David coughed, then inhaled sharply as he came into
consciousness, immediately surging against his restraints
and finding them just as inescapable as Adelyn had.
"Watchers be—where am I?"

Looking around with panic in his eyes, David bucked
against the cuffs around his wrists and neck, and for half a
second Adelyn even believed he could get out. The restraints
held, though, and after ten seconds of struggling, David gave
up, though he continued to open and close his right hand in
a motion that reminded Adelyn of a gasping fish.

"David," Adelyn said, trying to pretend that she wasn't

feeling the exact same panic that he was. "We've been captured. I don't know where Mary is, but I don't think she was killed. You're okay, for now. If they were going to kill us, they would have done it already."

"Done it already..." David said, but instead of following that up with a statement, he just repeated it again. "Done it already."

Anna frowned, apparently deciding on something. Quickly checking that both Adelyn and David's restraints were tight and not going to come loose, she said, "I'll be right back. If you so much as think about trying to get out while I'm gone, I'll bust your lip."

Barely noticing this, Adelyn kept her attention on David. "David. I need you here. Talk to me. Are you okay?"

"They would have done it already," David repeated, eyes clamped firmly shut.

Anna looked at him skeptically, then shut the door, locking it behind her with the solid 'shunk' of a deadbolt being forced into place.

"David," Adelyn said, concerned by his repetition. "I need you to snap out of this."

David repeated the words 'Done it already' a couple more times, hand opening and closing. Adelyn could hear a consistent rattle, but whether his leg was shaking or he was tapping his foot, she couldn't tell.

After half a minute, David fell silent.

Adelyn waited another thirty seconds, then asked, "David? I... I need you to—"

David began screaming, a ragged desperate cry, fighting once more to be free of the restraints with all the fury of a man fighting for his very survival. Pulling and jerking until his wrists were bleeding and his voice was raw, David only gave up and sagged in his restraints when he physically couldn't fight anymore.

"Okay," Adelyn said. "You're not okay. You can't talk right now. That's fine, I just need you to listen. Can you do that?"

David didn't respond, but his low breathing didn't seem to show any resistance either.

"If you have any tricks to get out of here, we need them right away. Mary is hurt. She might have been able to crawl away and hide, but we can't rely on her. If she's armed at all, it's with something she scavenged, her whip was cut before we started fighting. I..." A realization struck her, derailing her sentence.

"She fights with a whip. She trained you, she fought with you in the war, and she fights with a whip." Thoughts swirled around in her head, until she spoke her deduction aloud. "Mary is the White Death."

David didn't confirm this, but he didn't deny it either, still panting.

"Sorry, that doesn't matter," Adelyn said. "Look, David, I'm sorry. This was my fault. If I'd been watching my back, I wouldn't have been caught, and we could have gotten out of here. I'm sorry." If David heard this, he made no response. "I don't care that you lied about who you were. I understand completely, I would probably lie about it too had I done—"

"Not a lie," David said, weakly.

Briefly just happy that David was talking, that moment was quickly overcome by confusion. "What?"

"I said I fought *with* the Stone Warriors," David said, the words coming slow but steady. "That can mean either alongside or against. Not my fault if you misunderstood."

Adelyn blinked once, then twice, then found herself laughing. Light chuckles at first, and then a full belly laugh that built until tears were running down her face. "L-Lords abandon me," she spluttered between choking laughs. She couldn't help it. The world around her had just grown too absurd.

"Why are you laughing?" David asked, which only triggered another fit of hysterics.

Tears made rivulets down her face, making streaks in the half-dried salt on her skin. "I-I'm sorry," she giggled. "It's just too much."

"Too much?" David asked. "What is too much?"

"You. Me. Everything," Adelyn said, wishing she could gesture broadly and settling for a slight wave with her hands. "I'm a *farmer.* We're being held prisoner in this ridiculous fortress by a wizard who wears minstrel robes to scare his followers, and my best friend in the world is a war criminal whose double-talk is so ludicrous that the world's best lawyer would still call it a bit much, and I'm a *farmer.*" David was silent at this, and Adelyn pulled back a bit. "I'm sorry, I shouldn't have called you a war criminal. That was unfair."

"Unfair..." David mumbled, lost in thought. "You consider me your best friend?"

Adelyn glanced over at him, surprised. "You've saved my life some-odd three or four times now. You crossed the length of the plains to help rescue my family. Of *course* I do, maybe discounting my brother. It's not really fair to compare family."

"Comparing family," David mused. "If you say so. I have no particular love for mine, but that may be the exception."

A thought striking her, Adelyn glanced up at the ceiling as she did a bit of calculation. "You would have joined the army when you were...what, thirteen? Fourteen? Did you run away, or did they just not care?"

"Not care?" David asked. "I have no idea. I have never met either of them. They may be dead."

"Oh," Adelyn said, chewing her lip for a moment. "I... would love to talk about this later, but we're in a bit of a tight spot right now. I don't know how much time we have before Anna and that wizard return, but it can't be long. Do you have the spirit to fight?"

David was quiet for a moment, shutting his eyes, then snapping them open. "Adelyn, I believe someone is standing at the door."

Adelyn swore, then asked, "How do you know?"

"How do I know? I can feel the spirit in the air, just barely. It seems like there's something brass and the size of a tall person standing there. If I had plans to escape, or the energy to fight, sharing them would be a fool's errand." He paused, then added, "Would you like to hear a joke?"

"What?" Looking at David skeptically, Adelyn shook her head. "No. And besides, you're terrible at—"

Oh. Right. Spirit.

Nodding, Adelyn asked, "How many jokes do you know?"

"Do I know? Half a dozen, none of them that lengthy," David said. "But still, they are good to pass the time."

"Perhaps a bit later," Adelyn said, nodding. "Any other thoughts?"

"Thoughts, thoughts...none that are helpful and pertinent," David said. "But keep talking. Please. I want something to focus on."

Turning her head awkwardly in the stockade, Adelyn asked, "What happened to your thumb?"

"Something else," David said immediately.

"Okay," Adelyn said. "How did you join the Thirteen?"

David shut his eyes, furrowing his brow in annoyance. "I

do not wish to discuss that question either, Adelyn. Something else."

"I...okay." She thought for a moment, trying to think of a more innocuous question. "You never knew your parents. How'd you get your last name?"

"My last name?" David asked, eyes darting to the floor as he thought about the answer. "Just because I did not know my parents does not mean I did not keep their name."

"That's not an answer," Adelyn said. "Tell me straight. Did you get your parents name?"

David hesitated, and for a moment, Adelyn could have sworn he was blushing. "No."

"How did you get your last name, then?" Adelyn asked again.

"When I was a small child, I stayed at a children's home," David said. "It was not a home. It was really little more than a building with cots and thin soup in the evening, but it was better than naught. They did not care one mite what we got off to in the day, so I would wander the coasts and try to find pins that had fallen from the pockets of sailors."

"So the sailors gave you the name?" Adelyn asked.

"Not the sailors, exactly," David said. "Most of the sailors were not in port long enough to recognize me. But a few of the dockworkers did, so they made a joke of it. As they explained it, we were by the coast, and I was always managing to end up right where they were about to step."

For once, Adelyn found herself as the one raising an eyebrow, confused by what the joke was. "I don't get it."

"Undertow," David said, spacing it out. "Under toe."

Adelyn snorted, getting it after a second's confusion. "Why didn't you change it?"

"First, because everyone knew me and it would have done no good," David said. "By the time I could have changed it, I had a different name for all but a select few anyways, and after that, changing my name would have been a form of deception."

"So changing your name is a lie, but saying you 'fought with' the Stone Warriors is okay?" Adelyn asked, smirking.

"I was taken as a prisoner," David said, changing the subject on a pin.

"What?" Adelyn asked, caught off guard by the sudden change in conversation topic.

"I was taken prisoner as a child, when I got my power," David repeated. "They kept me shackled in a windowless basement. I broke my own thumb so that I could slip my wrist free, but did not get it set properly, and it had to be amputated. When the local government caught wind of my escape and what had happened, I was covertly recruited into training. I was young and very stupid, and their offer of a home and of money and of a purpose was enough to tempt me."

Nodding, Adelyn reflected on that for a moment, before the timeline struck her. "Wait, how old—"

The door swung open, and Anna waltzed inside, taking a stance of attention. Adelyn could see at least two more guards in the brass armor outside, also standing stock straight and with a hand to their foreheads.

Footsteps came through the doorway, slightly off-tempo, like a badly weighted metronome. Step-step. Step-step. Step-step.

"Adelyn, I need you to remember this," David said, the words tripping over each other as he explained. "If I die, go to the central bank in Triom. I have sent them a letter with a description of you and my consent form—the number to access my accounts is 'Eight three four six five'."

"What?" Adelyn asked.

"Repeat that number back to me," David said. "I need you to remember it. Eight three four six five."

"Eight three four six five," Adelyn said.

"Good," David said, repeating, "Good. Do not forget it."

The wizard came in. He still wore his blue regalia, but it was now accompanied by a large white bandage covering the center of his face, and he had two matching black eyes giving him the appearance of a raccoon. If his expression hadn't been one of such rage, Adelyn might have giggled.

"Anna, close the door," the wizard said, his voice less nasal than it had been, but still clearly spoken by a man with a broken nose. She obeyed, shutting it soundly and moving the latch into place. It was a purely symbolic act, of course, since neither David nor Adelyn could have gotten to the door whether it was shut, latched, or wide open, but the 'shick' of the lock being slid into place still made Adelyn feel a bit more trapped than before. She shivered, but told herself that it was only because of the cold breeze coming from the air vents.

"How come they don't get to come in?" Adelyn asked, gesturing with a finger to the other guards standing outside the door.

"They didn't save my life," the wizard said. "Anna is the only one to have earned my trust. You should keep a civil tongue in your head, girl, I am not inclined to show mercy to you after your little fireworks display against my men."

"Are you sure you can trust her?" Adelyn shot, ignoring the warning. "She did take a long time to decide she wasn't going to abandon you. A few more seconds, you might have been killed, but she just kept watching."

Glancing over at Anna, the wizard raised an eyebrow, but not one of suspicion. She nodded, producing two lengths of cloth and crossing over to where Adelyn was restrained.

"Open your mouth, Adelyn, or I'll break y'er face," Anna said. Adelyn hesitantly complied, and Anna stuffed one cloth into her mouth, tying it into place with the second. It tasted dusty, and upon experimentation, she found that any words were too distorted behind the gag to be intelligible.

"That'll be a little more peaceful," the wizard said, walking to David and crouching in front of him, so that he was looking in David's eyes, and David had to struggle to avoid meeting his gaze. "Do you like my stocks? I had them specially built to hold wizards. They worked so well on the regular folks that I had a few more made up, but just know that these were made with you in mind."

"Pillory," David said.

The wizard paused. "What?"

David cleared his throat, staring down at the floor. "Stocks are for the feet. These hold my hands and head, so it is a pillory. How many people were burned? I would like to help heal them, if you will so permit me."

The wizard blinked, "You want me to let you go, so you can...heal my men? You know that I could kill you any second I desired, yes?"

David nodded. "If you are going to kill me, I ask that you do it now."

"Oh, I'm not actually gonna kill you," the wizard replied, after catching up to the conversation. "You're too valuable to kill. I'm just going to ask you some questions, and every time you lie, you're going to lose a finger. Answer all of my questions truthfully and fully, and I will let you go. Know that I will detect any falsehood."

David nodded, and Adelyn bit her lip, watching anxiously.

"How many are in your party?" The wizard asked.

"Three," David said. "Including myself and Adelyn."

"Are all of you wizards?" The wizard asked.

"No," David said. It almost looked like he was going to leave it at that, when he said, "Mary is a witch. Adelyn is a sorceress."

The wizard furrowed his brow, thinking for a moment. "I know you're lying, because I know what happened in that hallway, but your face is honest." Standing, he turned to Anna. "We need to talk to the crew, see if they missed anything."

"I never lie," David said.

"Even that's a lie," The wizard said. "Everyone lies."

"Not me," David said.

The wizard smirked, sure that he had the upper hand. "Okay then, Mr. Never Lies, explain to me this: How come only one person was casting spells when my army was being torn apart by your lackeys?"

"Mary believes in the Divinities," David said. "She has given up magic. If she had not, she could have defeated your army without her heart beating a tick out of time."

The wizard frowned. "Who is she?"

"Her name is Mary Atkins," David said. "But you would know her better as the White Death."

Straightening, the wizard glanced over at Anna. There was a brief nonverbal conversation, and Anna nodded, walking out the door. Low discussion could be heard, and then Anna returned.

"Workin' on it," Anna said.

"Good," the wizard said. Turning back to David, he asked, "Who else knows of what we are doing here?"

"The peace officers in Petra have some understanding, but no inclination to do anything about it," David said.

"Other than that, some may have an inkling, but to my knowledge none know your location."

"That's good," the wizard mused in his nasal pitch, short breaths whistling through his nose. "What was your plan, anyways?"

"Attack while you were unprepared," David said. "Gather any weapons and guns we can on the way, then pass them out to your prisoners so that we can fight our way out. What was yours?"

The wizard opened his mouth, then closed it. "Huh?"

"Why all the prisoners and slaves? David asked. "What are you putting them to work at?"

"Ah, yes." He nodded, standing up and stepping back. "My fortress was in disrepair, with many a collapsed tunnel or clogged airway that needed fixing. When I and the other Thirteen—"

"You mean when *I* and the other Thirteen," David said, unable to stop himself from correcting their captor.

The wizard whispered something, and David coughed in sudden pain. "I am the Blue Flame," the wizard said. "You are an imposter. Say it."

"I do not lie," David said. The wizard twisted his hand, and David's face started to turn red.

"Mmmm!" Adelyn called out, trying to speak over the gag in her mouth.

"*Say it,*" the wizard repeated, leaning in to whisper. *"Loud enough that everyone can hear."*

David clenched his jaw, shaking his head in resistance. Finally, the wizard lowered his hand, and David gasped in a huge breath.

"I want you to know, I was going to do this anyways," the wizard said, holding out his hand in the direction of Anna. "A loose wizard is too much of a threat to me. Useful, yes, but a threat nonetheless. I can't take away your power, but I can make sure you can't use it."

Anna hesitated for the briefest second, something that only Adelyn noticed. The wizard kept his gaze locked with David's as she took a knife from her belt, passing it to the wizard.

David's eyes widened in tandem with Adelyn's. "You said you would not kill me. You said you would let me go."

"I'm a liar," The wizard said, shrugging one shoulder. "But I'm not going to kill you. *Bren.*"

A tiny fire erupted just beneath the knife, long and narrow and hot enough that Adelyn wished she could shield her face.

Pupils shrinking to dots, David tried to pull away, once again bucking at the stockade that kept him bound. It was just as futile as it had been, but his attempts to escape were even more frantic and forceful, reopening scrapes on his wrist that had only just started to scab over, bruising the back of his head as it slammed into the metal brace that kept his neck held down.

"Hold his head in place," The wizard said. "I don't want to slip and kill him."

Anna paused for a bare fraction of a second, then stepped forward. David managed to grab the hem of her shirt with the tips of his fingers, pulling tight and holding on with a death grip.

Stopping, Anna looked down at David, who returned the gaze, looking her right in the eye with an expression of pleading terror. For a moment, Adelyn was certain that Anna was going to give in and back away, then she grabbed David's head in two armored hands, holding his mouth open.

The screams were almost deafening in the tiny cell, but the wizard paid them no heed.

Once the knife was glowing white, hot enough to sear flesh at a touch, the wizard let the spell dissipate. With motions that were surreally casual, he grasped David's tongue between two fingers, pulled, and then raised the knife.

Adelyn surged at her own restraints, trying to shout, 'No!', and producing a sound more like, 'Nnnnnph!"

David tried to turn his head, but Anna clamped down harder, holding him in place. His screams were more and more ragged as he lost his voice to fear, and then the wizard moved in.

The cut was short and quick. Pulling in one smooth motion, the wizard tossed David's tongue to the floor, stepped back, and lowered the knife. "You can let him go, Anna," he said, and she obeyed, releasing David and letting him sag in the restraints. His scream was still audible, but it had lost its force, fading to a thin, reedy cry of anguish.

"That was simple enough," the wizard said, turning to look Adelyn right in the eye. "Your turn."

CHAPTER 32

We made a breakthrough today! Most of the team doesn't seem to realize how big this is, but it is huge.

While exploring the caves, we found a large decorative area carved into the wall, with marks scratched in a complicated pattern. At first we just thought it was some kind of incomplete piece, but then someone mentioned that it looked a bit like stars, and...I think he's right. They don't match any star charts we've got, but that makes sense, because some of these caves are millennia old, and haven't had a human walk them since before recorded history.

We've got people working to date the cave. Once we know that, we can start piecing together which marks corresponds with which stars, and then we will be able to calculate how fast those stars are moving, and even what they'll look like in the future.

I've opened the Tenish White, the one I was saving. Tonight, we're going to celebrate.

- Journal entry written by an anthropologist while working to excavate caves in the central mountains

. . .

DAVID'S MOANS of pain lingered in the background as the wizard paced over to Adelyn, repeating his fire spell with a flourish to get the knife back up to searing temperatures.

Adelyn squinted and turned her head as the fire grew closer to her face, making her eyes water and giving a phantom reminder of the now-healed burns she'd inflicted on her cheeks. She tried to plead, but of course the gag was still in her mouth, and so it all came out as mumbles.

"Let's get that off of you," the wizard said, reaching toward the knot holding the gag in place.

"Wait," Anna said, taking a step forward.

The wizard paused, raising an eyebrow in Anna's direction, and Adelyn noticed how bloodshot his eyes were beneath the bruises. "Anna," he asked, his tone polite. "Are you questioning my judgment?"

"Only offering a suggestion, my lord," Anna said, quickly. "I didn't get the chance to mention, but we have her family someplace. And from what the crew said, she's a country mile from being a match for you, the lass with the sword did a helluva lot more damage. We—you can use her, my lord."

The wizard considered it, then lowered the knife. "Who's in her family?"

"Big John," Anna said. "I think he was lying about not knowing anyone. Don't know who her parents are, yet, but that'll be easy enough to seek out."

The wizard nodded, raising the knife once again in a menacing gesture. "I'll have to find out, then."

A pounding fist came at the door. "Sir! There's been an escape!"

Stiffening, the wizard turned and called. "Who?"

"The men's block!" the voice called back. "One of them got his hands on a sword, and—"

The wizard swore, foisting off the knife in Anna's direction. "*You* find out who her parents are. I'm going to go put this trouble to bed, once and for all."

Anna accepted the blade, looking pointedly at Adelyn. "She'll talk, my lord. You can take the rest of the guard with you on the search, I'll keep things under control here."

The wizard turned slightly so that he was facing Anna directly, trying to sound imposing in spite of his nasal pitch. "Mind your words, Anna. You don't give me instructions."

"Sorry, my lord," Anna stiffened. "I only meant that I will not need any help."

"Then say what you mean," the wizard said.

"Yes, my lord."

The wizard stalked out of the room, his limp less pronounced now than it had been. Anna latched the door behind him, turned to face Adelyn, and tossed the knife on the ground.

She crossed the short room and made two short tugs to undo the knot holding her gag in place. Spitting a few times, Adelyn forced out the wad of fabric and cleared her mouth of the dusty taste.

"Lords abandon you," she muttered.

"Come off it, Adelyn," Anna said. "I saved your tongue just there. And I'm not gonna torture you, neither, so long as you tell me what my lord wants to know."

Adelyn gave her as level a look as she could manage from her low position. "And why should I?"

"'Cause if you don't, I'll walk down to where we keep the slaves, find your brother, and shoot him in the leg," Anna said flippantly.

Adelyn considered it for half a second, then said, "Dad's name is Lyman, Mom's name is Marci."

Anna beamed, drawling, "Now weren't that easy? If there

were still anybody around I'd ask you to scream, make sure things sounds plenty violent, but we're all alone."

"Your 'lord' is a monster," Adelyn said.

Anna rolled her eyes. "Like he's any worse than your friend? This keep belongs to my lord, it's his right to defend it." There was a lengthy pause, where Adelyn didn't respond, then Anna said, "He's not all bad. You're only seeing him at his worst."

"When's he at his best? When he's kidnapping innocent people for slave labor? When he's burning our crops just for the sport of it?"

Anna leaned against the wall, crossing her arms. "You'd best learn to keep a civil tongue around him. I stopped him the once, but he won't hesitate to cut it out if you keep giving lip."

Twisting her hands, Adelyn said, "Fine, you win. I'll stop giving lip. Can I get something to drink?"

"Coffee service's closed," Anna quipped. "Try again in the mornin'."

"I just want some water," Adelyn said, quickly adding. "*Not* saltwater. I'm thirsty."

Anna threw up her hands. "Anything else?"

"Yeah," Adelyn said. "The key to these restraints and a big sword."

"Don't push it." Anna started to walk toward the door, then her step hitched and she turned back. "You're not thinking to do nothin' foolish now, are you, Adelyn?"

"Like what?" Adelyn asked. "Get myself captured by an evil wizard?"

Anna rolled her eyes again, unlatching the door and slipping out, locking it audibly behind her.

Adelyn waited to a count of five, listening to footsteps dwindle in the difference, then said, "Okay, David. I'm going to get us out of here." Looking over at him, she asked, "Are you with me?"

David shook his head, which was at least a response. Adelyn took that as positive confirmation, pressing on.

"You said you broke your thumb to get out of your restraints, once. I can do that too," Adelyn said.

David shook his head again.

"Are you saying I shouldn't do that, or that I can't? Or something else?"

David shook his head a third time, and Adelyn gave up trying to get helpful answers.

"Okay," She continued. "Just hang in there. I'll get you out. I just…need to figure out how."

As soon as she looked over the problem, she quickly realized that breaking her thumb wasn't going to be possible. There was no way to actually hit her thumb against anything while she was held in place by the pillory, or to apply any other similar force.

"All right," Adelyn said, thinking aloud. She wasn't sure if the action was to try and calm down David or herself, but regardless of which, it didn't seem to be working. "So that won't work. But I can still—"

The door handle rattle and Adelyn swallowed nervously. Anna had barely been gone a minute.

Did she hear anything?

The door handle jiggled again, and the door caught on its deadbolt. Adelyn barely heard an exasperated plea to the gods, and then a voice, low but recognizable. "Undertow? You in there?"

"Mary!" Adelyn exclaimed, before realizing she could keep her volume down. "David can't—just talk to me."

"The door's locked," Mary whispered. "I can't break it down without considerable noise, and I'm in no state to fight. Everyone should be distracted for a while if the escapees do what I told them, but I don't want to risk causing a ruckus. Do you know where I can get the key?"

"Anna—eh, one of the guards has it," Adelyn said. "She's in brass armor, I think she can handle herself. She went to get water."

"I saw her go by," Mary said. "That's when I moved to come this way. She doesn't have a helmet."

"Don't kill her," Adelyn urged.

"Why not?"

"She has information," Adelyn said, chewing her lip in thought. "And if you do kill her, the wizard will know."

"Is he the Blue Flame?" Mary asked. "Do we know that for sure now?"

Adelyn bit down, drawing a drop of blood from her lip. The confrontation could wait for another time. "Yes. The wizard is the Blue Flame."

"Shh," Mary said. "I need to go. Gods willing, I'll be back with the key in a moment."

"Hear that, David?" Adelyn asked. "We're getting out of here. Mary will save us."

David didn't answer. He didn't even shake his head. Adelyn added that to her mental list of things to worry about, along with trying to plan what she would do once free of her bonds.

A few moments passed, each one taking a bit longer than the last. Mary couldn't be hiding that far away, and Anna would be back any moment. If it broke out into a straight fight, would she hear it?

As seconds grew into a minute, and then two, Adelyn grew more certain that something had gone wrong. Anna had fought off the ambush, or heard something and grown suspicious, or maybe Mary's injury was worse than they realized and she'd passed out from blood loss. About when Adelyn was convinced Mary wouldn't be returning, and had started making new plans to escape, the door latch slid and swung open.

Anna walked in, eyes furious, a hand over her mouth. Mary was directly behind her, a knife held over Anna's throat, forcing her into the little cell.

Mary walked with a pronounced limp, and blood stained her pant leg from the thigh down, but it looked as though she was able to carry herself, and had two swords and a pistol stuck through her belt should it come to a fight.

"Is this Anna?" Mary asked. Adelyn nodded.

"Nice to see someone else being held at knifepoint for once," Adelyn commented. "Get David out first, then me."

"Anna, the key," Mary said, pulling her hand away from Anna's mouth. "Where is it?"

"Gods be—" Anna started, but she stopped as the knife pressed deeper into her neck. "Hold on, witch. It's around my neck."

"She's not a witch," Adelyn said, at almost the same time Mary said the same. Mary gave Adelyn a quick glance of confusion, then brushed it off and tightened her grip on Anna.

"Aargh," Anna replied, eloquently. "Can I getcha the key, or will you cut my throat if I move my arms?"

"Slowly," Mary instructed.

Anna raised one arm, taking a string of keys from around her neck and holding it up. "'Is the little one. Kinda sticks in the lock, gotta turn it gentle."

Mary nodded, though Anna couldn't see the motion. "You do it. Undertow, I'm getting you out of that thing, just hold on." When David didn't even nod, Mary looked at Adelyn. "How long has he been silent?" She didn't seem to notice the tongue on the ground only a few inches from her feet.

Adelyn shook her head. "Just get him out."

Mary raised an eyebrow, but pushed Anna forward. "Get that open, now."

Anna raised the key to the small bolt on the side of the stockade, jiggling it a bit to fit into the lock. It turned, clicked, and the lock popped open. With that done, Mary was able to flip open the top of the stockade, freeing David from his bondage.

David pushed himself back, staggering against the wall and slumping to the floor, pressing his palms into his forehead. He took deep breaths, fingers on his right hand drumming rapidly against his scalp.

Mary nearly walked to his side, then caught herself, straightening the knife a bit and pointing Anna toward Adelyn. "Get her free."

"This's all pointless, y'know," Anna said, but she complied. "Once the wizard finds you, he'll just kill you, or lock you up just like these two."

"You're assuming he'll be able to stop us," Mary said. "Even if he beat Undertow in a duel, if Adelyn and I are backing him up, we'll give him a run for his money."

Anna snorted, unlocking the stockade. Adelyn threw off the restraints and pulled away, rubbing at her wrists stretching her back.

Watching, Anna replied, "You're barely walkin', she's clearly spent her shot, and he's not winning any duels unless they invent a cure for elinguation." She pronounced each syllable of the last word separately and badly, 'ee-lin-guh-way-shun'.

There was a pause as Mary furrowed her brow, translating that last word in her head, then her eyes widened and the knife tumbled from her hands. Letting go of her captive, Mary turned to David, mouth agape, running to his side in a heartbeat.

"Undertow, gods, I'm so sorry," she said, crouching, the words tumbling out almost automatically among half a dozen other small comforts. Mary tried putting a hand on David's shoulder, and he pulled away. When she tried again to embrace him, David shoved her away with one hand, sending Mary tumbling into a sitting position. Tears glimmered on his face, but the cries were silent save for an occasional choked breath.

Anna watched this, bemusement plain in her expression. Even with Mary distracted, she hadn't bothered trying to fight back or escape. "Fight's sure gone out of—"

A fist crashed into her jaw, driven by Adelyn with all the force her tired arms could muster. Unprepared for the attack, Anna staggered, and Adelyn hit her again, driving a knee into her stomach—that attack wasn't as effective as Adelyn had hoped, and in fact bruised her knee when the attack hit polished bronze armor.

Anna coughed, then threw up her arm to block the next incoming attack, shoving Adelyn away and backing up toward the door. "Gods, Adelyn," she said. "I'm not gonna try and stop you. Don't have to."

"This is your fault," Adelyn said, shrugging off her sodden coat. "I should kill you. I *would*, except—"

She stopped.

A few seconds passed, and the sound of David mumbling something incomprehensible filled the room, punctuated by Mary's attempts to comfort him.

Anna cocked her head and asked, "'Cept what?"

Eying the warrior, Adelyn said, "Don't run," then crossed over to where David was sitting, sat down by his side, put the coat down on the ground by her side and waited. Mary started to ask a question, but Adelyn put up a hand to silence her, and Mary took the hint.

Twenty seconds passed, and Mary said, "We don't have time—"

"We do," Adelyn said simply, not letting it become an argument. "Shh."

Anna watched this from the door, arms folded over her chest. She looked like she meant on commenting, but ultimately held her tongue, and Adelyn was begrudgingly grateful for that.

As David's voiceless muttering slowed, Adelyn finally spoke, using clear, direct tones. "David, I know that you are hurting, and that you feel tired and that you have no strength right now. You can recover for two minutes longer, but then I will need you to listen to me, because I will need your help. Is that all right?"

David's hand stopped drumming against his head and pressed flat for a moment, then he nodded.

"Okay," Adelyn said, releasing a breath.

David's chest heaved as he made a visible effort to calm himself, and Adelyn quietly counted the seconds to herself. She wasn't going to strictly enforce the two minute time limit if David wasn't ready, but she had the feeling that she wouldn't have to.

At fifty four seconds, David reached out and took Adelyn, pulling her into a tight hug. She started, surprised by the embrace, then reciprocated, holding the sorcerer as he gently shook in her arms.

A minute passed. David nodded his head again, straightening his back.

"Better?" Adelyn asked.

David nodded, and Mary cut in. "Undertow, I'm so sorry. I should have been there, should have helped—"

"It wouldn't have mattered," Adelyn said. "David won the fight. But that doesn't matter now, we need to move forward, and I've got a plan for that. David, nod if you agree, shake your head if you disagree, put up a hand if you don't understand. Okay?"

David nodded, sniffing and wiping snot and tears from his face with a bare arm.

"Here, just a second," Adelyn said, turning to her coat and searching through the pockets. She thought she might find a cloth so David could wipe his face, but instead felt a small lump in an inside pocket and felt her odds of success improve dramatically. Pausing on that, she ripped out a patch of fabric from the lining and passed it to David.

He smiled gratefully, wiping his face down with the damp material.

"We don't have a vast amount of time," Adelyn said. "I don't know how soon the wizard will return, but it's not going to be long. I have a plan, but it hinges on you. Even without magic, you're the strongest warrior I know. Can you still fight?"

David nodded his head.

"Okay," Adelyn said. "If I cast a spell, can you add spirit to it and keep it going without me? You remember those jokes, so you should have spirit reserves aplenty."

David nodded again.

"Okay. I'll need you to show me the runes and Mary to tell me the right words," Adelyn said. Mary looked at her sharply, and Adelyn returned the look.

"I don't know magic words," Mary said.

"Abandon me if you don't," Adelyn said simply. "We

don't have time to argue this. You *will* tell me the right words. I'm going to cast a spell to make you two invisible and silent, or as close to it as possible. David, you'll keep the power barely alive while the two of you hide down a side hallway. Meanwhile, I'm going to smear fresh blood on every one of those size graph things I see, leading in a path away from you, making a big arrow for the wizard to go after. I want you to wait fifteen minutes, or until you're certain he's well past you, and then pour spirit into the spell. All right?"

David started to nod, then put up a hand.

"Can you not manage the spell like that?" Adelyn asked.

He shook his head.

"Does it have to do with you?"

Another shake.

"Me?"

A nod.

"You're wondering how I'm going to get away from the wizard," Adelyn said.

Another nod.

Adelyn sighed deeply, resigning herself to the plan finally. "I'm not."

"Adelyn—" Mary started.

"Once I run out of size graphs—" Adelyn said, pausing when she saw David's expression. "What is it?"

David glanced at Mary, who corrected, "It's 'seismographs'."

David nodded his head a few times, and Adelyn bit her tongue before continuing. "Once there are no more *seismographs,* I'm going to wait until I can see or hear the wizard, then I'm going to run as fast and far as I can until I hit a dead end or he catches me. I can't beat the wizard, but with the blows David hit him with, I can at least outrun him for a while. You are going to run under the camouflage spell, get to the prisoners, and get everyone out."

David shook his head, then jerked his thumb at himself.

"No," Adelyn said. "I have to be the bait. Even without magic, you're better in a fight than me, and once you have everyone free, you're going to have to fight your way out. Mary can't do it either, because she can't outrun the wizard."

Mary's brow furrowed. "What if the wizard doesn't take the bait? He's going to be busy putting down the escape attempts, and it's an obvious trap."

"I'm not so sure it's obvious," Adelyn said. "David's already challenged him into direct combat once. With luck, he'll think it's another challenge."

"How are you going to cast spells? You'll want some way to throw around magic, and you've got nothing to do it with."

Showing her teeth, Adelyn said, "Actually, I do." Digging in the pocket of her coat, she pulled out the little book of magic she'd learned her first spells from. The cover was damp, but it wasn't soaked through, and when Adelyn flipped to the pages with the printed runes, they proved to be completely dry.

Anna blinked. "How—"

"When it's closed, it's just a book," Adelyn said. "Open it up, it's got the runes available, perfectly serviceable."

"Adelyn," Mary said, putting a hand on her shoulder. "Even with the book. This is suicide."

Adelyn put a hand on Mary's, squeezing it. "If I don't do this, we'll all be prisoners for the rest of our lives, assuming he doesn't kill us outright for trying to escape."

Anna cleared her throat. "Beggin' a moment of your time, Adelyn," she said. "This plan doesn't involve killin' me, does it? Because I'm not seein' what's to stop me from giving away your plan if you don't stick a knife through my skull, and I'm really not gonna go along with that."

Giving a toothy grin, Adelyn asked, "Well where did you think I was going to get all the blood?" Anna blinked, and Adelyn shook her head. "If you don't fight back, we'll knock you out and leave you in the same place they hide. By the time you wake up, it'll be too late for you to do anything."

"And if I do fight back?" Anna asked.

Mary pulled the revolver from her belt, pointing it at Anna. "Then I kill you after all," she said, finishing the thought so that Adelyn didn't have to. "Your death would be a wonderful torchlight for the wizard to follow, besides."

Adelyn nodded at Mary, then glanced back at David. "Are you okay with this plan?"

David shook his head.

Pursing her lips, Adelyn rephrased the question. "Do you understand everything, and will you do what I'm asking?"

David heaved in a huge sigh, squeezed his hands into tight fists, and nodded.

CHAPTER 33

Do not chase the Strider, son, for he is wise and great,
  And if you try to catch one then you'll surely seal your fate,
  But he said, don't you worry now, for my plan is first rate,
  To start I'll catch a dragon, see, and it'll be my bait.
  - "To Catch a Strider", Gregorian's Rhymes for Children

"So how does this work?" Adelyn asked, as Mary adjusted the straps on her armor. Anna's armor wasn't a perfect fit, but it was close enough to work with a bit of loosening and tightening in various places.

"Just fill it with spirit," Mary explained, struggling with a tight buckle. "The armor will do the rest. It's got wires and runes everywhere, it'll spread out the power where it's needed."

Adelyn nodded. "And those runes will do what, exactly?"

"Looks like defense," Mary said. "This armor is pretty light, wouldn't stand up to punishment over a lengthy fight. Keep it charged, though, it'll take a pounding better than any steel plate."

"Against magical attacks too?" Adelyn confirmed, exhaling sharply as the breastplate was tightened over her chest. The padded jacket beneath it kept any of the brass pieces from pinching or bruising, but it still caught her off guard.

"Sorry," Mary said. "But yes, it should. As long as you keep it charged, anyways. Don't let the wizard touch you, or—"

"Or he'll just sap the power and use it to hit me with a spell," Adelyn finished. "I'm aware. If he's close enough to touch me, I've already lost."

"Armor looks as good as I can get it," Mary said. "Don't be a fool. You're not going to win a fight with him. No armor on your head or hands, either, so don't think you're close to invulnerable. Good luck, Adelyn, and may Maridon grant you speed."

Adelyn frowned skeptically for a moment. "And may the Lords keep you safe."

Mary pursed her lips, but dropped the subject, glancing over to where David was completing his own task—marking runes onto a round stretch of fabric that had been cut from Anna's undershirt. "Give us two minutes to get hidden, okay?"

"You look ridiculous," Anna commented. She was leaning against the wall, wearing Adelyn's sodden coat and a pair of shorts. David was keeping the pistol trained on her, much to her chagrin. "Never worn armor before, eh, Adelyn?"

"Always time to learn," Adelyn said. "I don't hear you offering any advice."

"Get a set that fits you proper," Anna suggested. "An' don't bend your legs too much. The plate pinches in the back of the knee."

"Thanks," Adelyn said. "Where do you want to get cut? I'm gonna need blood, but I'll let you pick where we get it from."

Anna paused for a moment, then said, "Palm, I guess. S'traditional."

"You sure? Hurts to get cut there," Adelyn commented. "Doesn't heal great, either."

"Sure," Anna said, nodding.

Not pressing the issue, Adelyn took the knife from Mary and rattled over to Anna, hearing the armor clink as she moved. "Pick a hand," she said, raising the blade.

Anna moved with practiced speed, one hand striking Adelyn's wrist, the other one fluidly catching the knife backward as it flew out of Adelyn's grasp.

Stabbing viciously, Anna drove the knife through Adelyn's hand, eliciting a cry of pain. With Adelyn in the way, David didn't have a clear shot with the gun, and Adelyn's only weapon had just been taken from her.

Anna didn't bother trying to get away with the knife to make a second attack, she just punched Adelyn in her unarmored face, inducing a crunchy noise from her nose.

Feeling the tingle of spirit on her hand, adding the sensation of pins and needles atop the injury, Adelyn sucked out the energy and poured it into the armor she wore. She didn't have a particular plan, it just seemed like the only thing she could do without more time to react. The steel blade still sticking out of her hand impeded this somewhat, and she lost energy in the transfer, but it was enough to fill the bronze plates, surrounding her with the buzz of spirit and, as well, seeming to fill her limbs with fresh strength that had been lacking just a second ago.

Throwing a clumsy punch with her uninjured hand, Adelyn was both happily and unhappily surprised. Happily, because the blow struck with enough force to double Anna over and throw her to the ground. Unhappily, because her fist wasn't fully closed, and the punch twisted her pinkie finger to an oblique angle. David approached with the gun and Mary stepped in with a sword then, ensuring Anna couldn't keep up the fight.

"Ow, ow," Adelyn said, stepping back and looking at her hands. One was still bleeding, and the little finger on the other was already starting to swell.

"Are you okay?" Mary asked.

"Yeah, I think," Adelyn said, still staring at her hands. "Help—help me get out this knife."

Sticking the sword back in her belt, Mary put one hand on Adelyn's wrist and the other on her hand. "Close your eyes," she said, then jerked out the blade in one smooth motion.

Adelyn whimpered in pain but didn't cry out again, proffering her other hand. "The little one?" She asked. Mary took it and twisted the finger back into place, eliciting a second whimper.

"I'd say don't move that finger too much, but..." She trailed off, shrugging. "Not like you have a choice."

"Got it," Adelyn said. "Can I get that knife? I still need some blood from Anna, and..."

David shook his head and pointed at the door emphatically and shoving the circle of fabric that he'd marked with runes into Adelyn's hand.

"What?" Adelyn asked. "There's no hurry, I...oh." Looking down at the armor, feeling the spirit buzz in the air, she realized that the timetable had been moved up considerably. She was practically glowing with spirit, and that was going to give away the game. "I have to go. Get hid, stick to the plan, get everyone out."

Mary, apparently coming to the realization at the same time, paused long enough to give Adelyn a sword and then grabbing David's hand so that they were in contact with each other. "Gods be with you."

"The spell," Adelyn pointed out, quickly channeling energy through the runes and reciting the long string of words that Mary had told her.

She didn't have a lot of experience with complicated spells such as these, and the effect was rather less dramatic than she'd hoped. David and Mary both faded into grayness, their pallor and shade matching that of the stone wall behind them. It was less 'invisibility' and more a form of light camouflage, but hopefully it would do.

"Good luck," Adelyn said, before turning to run out the door.

It wasn't clear if the extra strength she felt was an effect of the armor, or simply the buzz of adrenaline that had come from combat, but once Adelyn was into the hall she shot down it like a bullet. If the armor slowed her at all, it was only just so, and once she had built momentum down the hall she was running as fast as she ever had.

The seismographs were paced perhaps twenty paces apart, and Adelyn tagged each as she went past, staining them with her blood. She went down intersections at random, taking whatever path was lit, trying to guess which way would be the longer route.

Her path took her through a large training room, stacks of decrepit targets and broken arrows stuck in the corner. She briefly considered stopping there and using it as the venue for her confrontation, but ultimately decided it wasn't far enough and kept going out the other side, into another of the seemingly interminable hallways and rooms that snaked into the earth.

She was able to tag less than two dozen of the brass orbs before they stopped, along with the lights. There were more lights in a box, along with spools of copper wire to run, but nobody had finished the task yet. The hallway continued, but without the spirit lights, it was as black as the hallway had been after she'd beaten the warrior in spirit plate.

Chewing her lip for a moment, Adelyn thought things through. She hadn't run far enough, if that was the whole diversion it would never last long enough for David and Mary to spring their escape. She needed a new plan, to buy more time.

Next to the last light, in big block letters, she wrote, '*Come and fight, coward,*' with an arrow pointed into the blackness, all inked with her blood. It was a simple enough message, and hopefully one that would enrage the wizard enough for him to follow.

She couldn't backtrack, the wizard would be too likely to sense her and realize the trap. Instead, she did exactly what the note implied, walking into the darkness. She lacked her initial speed, having to move more carefully in the black hallway, and as she moved she passed rows of doors, spaced every dozen steps or so on each side.

Peering into one of the doors, Adelyn looked into the blackness inside and considered that she'd need a light. Flipping through her little book, Adelyn found a useful rune and whispered, '*Shane*', lighting up the room with gentle white light. It was some kind of bunk area—a square room, roughly hewn out of the stone, with a pair of bunk beds on the right and left walls—eight beds in total, though one had collapsed into itself.

In the center of the room was a table ringed by chairs, and on the far wall was a pair of dressers. Adelyn walked over to check inside, stepping over the metal air vent on the floor and feeling a slight breeze under her feet.

She hesitated, staying over the air vent for a moment before moving on to the dresser. It was full of clothes— uniforms, it appeared to be, dark green clothes that had become brittle and stiff with age.

Walking out and pulling the light with her, Adelyn checked the door across from that and checked that room as well—another bunk room. Down another twelve steps, two more bunk rooms. Twelve steps more, one bunk, and a collapsed room across from it.

She kept a clipped pace until she reached the end of that particular hallway and found another closed set of double doors. Pushing one of them open to the sound of protesting hinges, half expecting to find an old broom closet or some other strange cu-de-sac, it instead opened into a wide room with two long oak tables and sets of benches flanking the table. Another doorway was beyond that, but the doors had fallen inward to show off a kitchen.

Peering around the room as she skirted the long tables, Adelyn tried to find something that would offer a hint of advantage. She didn't just have to get the wizard there, she had to keep him tied up for as long as possible. If she could injure him, it would be all the better. Anything to buy time or advantage to get the prisoners out.

She knew it would be lucky for her to last five seconds once the proper fighting began. She could barely keep up with all the spells being thrown around just watching his fight with David. If she had to respond to those attacks, she'd go down in a heartbeat.

Leaning into the kitchen, praying she'd find a suit of spirit armor and a war-machine to boot, Adelyn only found rows of wood burning ovens on rollers, a large hearth in the center, and stacks of dry firewood against the wall. There was indoor plumbing—no surprise, since nobody would want to carry buckets of water all this way into the facility—but when Adelyn tried turning the crank to allow water into a basin, nothing came out.

The air vents were still functioning properly, though, and the room was practically floored with vent gratings, to allow in enough air for the fires to burn without choking the cooks. On the ceiling in turn were more vents, all open.

More helpfully, there were rows of rusted copper cookware sat on shelves—copper that she could scratch runes into, given the time, and given a proper use for that many magical tools.

Unsure of how much time she had and whether it would even matter, Adelyn made her plans and got to work.

...

It took the wizard longer to arrive than she'd expected. Maybe he'd been delayed, maybe he just hadn't sensed her over the seismographs right away, maybe he simply was having trouble running to get her. Whatever the cause, Adelyn was able to prepare things more thoroughly than she'd expected.

She was panting and her throat was burning for a drink of water from all the running back and forth, but she reinvigorated the light one final time and sat down at one of the long tables, the kitchen to her back.

Adelyn saw the wizard before he saw her, coming to the last of his seismographs and looking around furiously. He read the message on the wall, turned to look in that direction, and finally caught sight of Adelyn's magical light floating in the air.

"This way!" be shouted, and Adelyn's heart sank. She'd been hoping to keep this a one-on-one confrontation. If he'd brought his whole honor guard—barring Anna—that would tilt the odds further against a lengthy confrontation.

Five people in gilded armor matching Adelyn's own came around the corner, and another dozen or so in light leather armor, all toting rifles, came behind. Adelyn swore, then glanced up in a hopeful prayer for assistance.

Wanting to get some kind of edge, she called out at the top of her lungs, "Coward! Come and face me alone!" Her voice cracked halfway through the shout, though, and it lacked the menacing presence she'd desired.

With only two points of light, the spirit light at the far end of the hall and the mage light behind Adelyn's head, it was difficult to make out distinct figures as the wizard marched up toward her. His glittering blue robes shimmered distinctly, but behind him was a mass of bodies, occasional bits of bronze and silver trim shining out to add texture to the throng of shadowy people.

The wizard led with his staff, thudding it against the stone floor with every step. Adelyn was pleased to note that he seemed to be genuinely using it for support, not just as a tool of intimidation.

She drummed her fingers on the table like she'd seen David do, trying to appear bored and disinterested as he walked up. It might be at odds with her shout a moment before, but the shout clearly hadn't worked, so she was changing tactics.

When the wizard was a few seconds out from the dining hall, she called out, "Sit down! I want to talk before I kill you."

He growled like a wounded beast, and for a second Adelyn worried he was just going to try and cook her in one spell before the fight could even get going. She had her book of spells ready with a page of shield runes open, but as far as

Adelyn could tell, she'd be just as well off holding the book between her and the fire.

"Where are your allies, girl?" The wizard asked in his nasal tones, striding into the dining hall. His five guards strode in behind him, their armor including helmets and gloves that made them distinct from Adelyn's own armor.

"I had them stand aside and block your escape," Adelyn said. "They'll let your people pass unopposed, but you are only leaving here if you best me."

The wizard scoffed, throwing up one hand. "You think you scare me? I'm—"

"You're *the Blue Flame*," Adelyn finished, putting special emphasis on those words. "And goodness knows, nobody can best *the Blue Flame* in combat. Sit. I want to talk first."

The wizard tightened his fists, but before he could respond, one of his crew in leather armor raised a question. "What's this wire?"

Adelyn bit off a swear before it could pass her tongue as the wizard looked down sharply, seeing the copper wire running across the floor. "Is this a trick?" He demanded.

Adelyn sighed, putting her cards on the table to avoid a premature fight. "I'd prepared some mood lighting for our fight. It's no weapon." She had filled the pots and pans with firewood, and run wires between them with the rune for 'fire' scratched in as many places as she could manage. She gestured to the four pots she'd set up in the dining hall, one at each corner, a bronze vessel with a chunk of firewood sitting in each.

"Hmm," The wizard said, putting one foot over the copper wire on the floor. He seemed to concentrate for a moment, then whispered, *"Bren cultt."* Ripples of spirit coursed through the wire, and the logs burst alight with...

blue flame. It burned like fire, but gave off neither heat nor smoke.

"Showing off?" Adelyn asked.

"You weren't?" The wizard turned slightly to address his leather-clad fighters. "Check the rooms. Make sure there aren't any other tricks." The dozen or so men and women turned and filed out to obey, leaving only the wizard and his guard. He turned back to address Adelyn, leaning on his staff. "Girl, I'm not stupid. You didn't cut off our escape. You took us on this wild goose chase to buy your imposter friends a chance to escape."

Adelyn frowned, which only gave away the truth. "Fine, yes. I thought David and Mary could slip out the entrance while you were occupied."

"Which is why I posted every remaining able-bodied person in my company guarding the door," The wizard said, grinning, his pallor sickly in the blue firelight. "If this is a stalling tactic, it won't help."

"Nobody else here!" one of the fighters shouted from the hallway.

"I'm not going to surrender," Adelyn said.

"I wouldn't accept it," the wizard said. "Anything else?"

"Yeah, two things. What's your name?"

"I've already explained that stalling is pointless," The wizard said. "You know who I am."

"Your name, though," Adelyn said. "All your lackeys just call you 'The Wizard' or 'my lord' or what have you."

"Your other question?" The wizard asked, moving on without answering.

Adelyn chewed her lip, then asked, "Why Marstone? Why my home? Why did you burn our crops?"

The wizard, still standing, said, "I needed workers, and there were no members of the royal army posted there."

Adelyn shook her head. "It took me almost month to get here. Even riding hard and straight, it's two weeks travel to get to Marstone from here, and you could've just bought more slaves and kept everything legal."

"Fine, fine," the wizard said. "You're right. In truth, I could have gotten the bodies anywhere. I could even pay for wage laborers, if I really wanted to, there's much silver still buried in this keep. I came to your town for the same reason I burned your crops."

"And why's that?" Adelyn asked.

The wizard shrugged. "To draw out a response. To trigger you into fighting back. My mistake was in not realizing you were a coward."

Adelyn blinked, confused. Was he talking about the town, or talking about her specifically? "Coward?" She asked.

"Of course," The wizard said. "Why else would a witch not fight back when her home is attacked?"

She went slackjawed. "You came for...me. But—"

"How did I know?" The wizard asked, grinning, his teeth shiny in the light. Then, the magic flowing as smooth and conversational as anything, he said, *"Gildshtap."*

Adelyn was ready for the trick, after he'd already tried to use it on David. She'd been caught off guard by what the wizard had said, but the moment it seemed like he was going to throw a spell, she dumped spirit into her armor, more into her book, and screamed, *"Ansyr!"* in response.

The shield didn't hold. It took the edge off the attack, but the spell still hit her like a charging bull, throwing her off the bench and backward, tumbling into the kitchen behind her. Had she not charged the armor, the attack would almost certainly have broken bones, but as it was, she was only left with a bad scrape on her cheek as she hit the floor.

Kicking one of the kitchen doors shut, she scrabbled on all fours, grabbing a strand of copper wire on the floor and feeling out the spell that the wizard had cast. Her first goal was to keep the soldiers at bay, to keep the fight at a one-on-one instead of a twenty-on-one. If she had a chance to scare them away, she would try.

Whatever was keeping the wood burning without giving off heat, it was a complicated, powerful spell that Adelyn would need months of practice to cast herself. However, it was a simple task to put it out, siphoning off what spirit she could and calling out, *"Bren!"*

The blue fire flickered a moment, then started coughing out smoke and heat, burning with real, natural orange and yellow flames. The kitchen was especially susceptible to the spell, since almost all of the cords of firewood were still stacked against one wall, and flammable wooden shelves were built against the other. They erupted with heat, and Adelyn had to shy away, shielding her face with her arm.

The shut door exploded into splinters. It didn't get thrown off its rusted hinges, exactly, it just disintegrated into shards of wooden shrapnel that sprayed Adelyn, bouncing off her armor with little 'ping' noises.

She recharged the armor as much as she could, backing away behind the hearth—ironically, she noted, the hearth was one of the few things not actually burning. At a loss for what else to do, Adelyn passed the book to her off hand and drew her sword.

The wizard came in shouting orders, his staff raised by his side. "Block the exit! Don't let her leave!" Then, turning to Adelyn, he raised his staff, shouting a chant that she wouldn't have recognized even had she been able to hear all the words.

Going for a general defense, Adelyn used the blood from

her cheek to raise another hasty shield around her in a bubble. This was barely done in time, as some of the burning firewood flew at her from the side, embers splashing against her shield. One chunk of wood made it through and clipped her arm, sending her into a spin, but she managed to stay upright long enough to flip the page of her book forward.

As tired as Adelyn was, a sustained fight was going to be hopeless. However, that didn't mean she couldn't do anything else to slow down the wizard. Filling the book with spirit until it felt as though it might catch flame in her hand, she shouted, *"Shtap!"* and unleashed the strongest spell she could manage in the vague direction of the wizard.

The spell was wide and broad, and only a bit of the energy hit him, the rest of it crashing into the appliances. One of the heavy bronze ovens lurched in place, rollers shifting from where they'd settled into place over decades of disuse.

The wizard laughed, approaching Adelyn. The room was getting hotter by the moment, but he didn't seem to mind the heat—he wasn't even sweating. Adelyn would have been sweating, had she not been so dehydrated that she had no moisture to spare.

"Is that the best you can do?" The wizard asked, as Adelyn stayed on the opposite side of the oven from him. He was enjoying things, taking his time, letting Adelyn play the mouse to his mountain lion. "You can't even *aim,* girl. *Shtap.*" As he barked out that spell, Adelyn felt the sword fly from her hand as though swatted away, tumbling to the ground.

Adelyn almost made a snide comment in response, then thought better of it. *Eh, he'll figure it out in a second,* she thought, repeating the same spell she'd just cast.

This time, the book did catch fire, burning her fingertips

as she shouted out the spell. She managed to focus the energy more this time, too. As such, none of the magic even touched the wizard—instead, every ounce of energy slammed into the oven, and it went tumbling across the floor like a rough stone skimming over an icy lake.

She bared her teeth in a grin as the oven struck home, slamming into the wizard and throwing him against the wall. The oven came to a stop in the doorway, splintering the remaining door into pieces and barricading the entrance against reinforcements. Hurting him was just a bonus, she'd wanted to block the doorway first and foremost.

The wizard stumbled away from the stone wall, holding his arm, face contorted in anger and pain. Adelyn realized only then that her plan had one small flaw; if before he had been toying with her, now he wanted to kill her in earnest. Worse, she had no book to put together another shield.

Diving out of the way as he roared out a spell, Adelyn hit the ground by the back wall, only taking the very edge of a powerful attack of force. As she tried to leap to her feet, though, a wave of dizziness hit her, and instead of jumping upright, she simply rolled onto her back, ceiling spinning as billows of smoke poured from the wood.

Grabbing a shelf a couple feet away, she heaved, pulling herself to her feet. The Blue Flame was visibly walking toward her, still apparently unaffected by the heat, though he was starting to pant.

He coughed as he flicked his staff upward in a wide swing, and she had just enough wherewithal to force what energy she had into the armor before she was raised into the air off her feet and then slung across the room like a ragdoll.

She had no way to course correct in midair, so she ducked her head and wrapped her good arm over it, shielding what she could before she struck the blazing fire-wood like a ball in a game of skittles.

Wind driven from her lungs, Adelyn gasped for breath and got a lungful of smoke in the exchange. The armor she wore was getting hot, and the tingle of spirit that filled it was nearly gone, but she found herself struggling to crawl away from the fire and to somewhere safer. Her vision was going black, and when she tried to summon more energy to renew the defenses in her armor, she only felt a wave of increased dizziness and the tiniest spark of energy, which flitted away before she could use it for anything substantial.

Something seized her leg, and she found herself hoisted into the air, upside down, coughing and desperately trying to suck in oxygen. In the blurry edges of her vision, she saw the wizard make a 'come hither' gesture with his hand, and she floated toward him, dangling from one leg.

Grabbing the breastplate, the wizard siphoned away the last dregs of spirit floating around in the armor, then roared a word and jerked hard, snapping the straps that held the breastplate in place and pulling it off.

Coughing, he said, "I should let you live, so that I can make this last longer."

Barely able to see, Adelyn tried to spit in his face and found that she had no saliva with which to convey the insult. She wanted to say something witty and clever, but all she could manage was, "Y-yer' stupid."

This time, when the wizard flung her across the room, the armor did nothing except rattle as she smashed into the oven blocking the doorway. Something inside Adelyn broke. Possibly multiple somethings.

On the ground, she gasped again for air, still drawing in no oxygen even without any smoke. That seemed good, but she couldn't remember why. Air. There wasn't any air, and she needed air.

Barely remembering that the wizard existed, Adelyn looked around desperately and saw an air vent on the floor, one of many. It was only a few steps away, and she reached for it, dragging herself forward, one weak pull at a time. Her lungs burned in tandem with her dry throat and blistering skin, the smoke and fire obscuring thoughts and vision alike.

Two feet from the vent, magic seized her once more and she went flying up into the ceiling, cracking the back of her head against the stone. Her scalp felt wet and hot, and she felt like that could be good for something, but she couldn't remember what.

When she fell back to the ground, she landed directly over one of the vents, another rib cracking somewhere in her chest. Thankful to the Lords, she put her nose right up to the metal grate of the vent and sucked in in a long breath, and...

Nothing. No air. Just the smell of old fabric.

Why... She thought, trying to remember. She'd...

She'd blocked the vents. Right. Heaving with all her strength, she ripped the grate up from the ground, managing to move it only a few inches. That was enough. She stuck her hand into the space, pulling out old green uniforms she'd crammed into the air vent.

Sweet, beautifully clean air wafted from the vent, and Adelyn took in a deep breath.

A nasal roar bellowed out from the wizard behind her, possibly a call for help, maybe an attempt at a spell, but if a response came Adelyn couldn't hear it over the roar of the fire. The wizard had ceased his attacks against her, apparently realizing that the kitchen was no longer a safe place to be, but if help came for him Adelyn didn't hear it.

Adelyn tried to laugh, but her lungs were weak and she was only able to wheeze. Face pressed into the vent, she blacked out.

CHAPTER 34

O god, o master, o Ansire, please let me beg of you now,
   O god, o lord, please answer, speak to me truly and plain,
   It seems, that now, you see, I may have broken a vow,
   I left my true love to the sea, and I fear that he's left your domain
      - Verse 2 of "O gods," a traditional folk song

"I'M SORRY, David, I can't. You know my vows. I'll offer her what medicine I know and every prayer I can make, but that's all."

A pencil scratched against paper with quick, jerky sounds.

"That's low. I can't break my vows for her."

More scratchy notes, cut off this time.

"Hold it—gods, she's awake."

Adelyn opened stiff, stinging eyes, squinting and trying to see. She could feel cool air on parts of her face, but most of her body was wrapped in bandage or cast, and when she tried to sit up she felt gentle hands push down on her chest.

It wasn't more pressure than you'd use to straighten a creased tablecloth, but it was still more force than Adelyn could overcome.

"Don't get up, Adelyn," the voice said. It was male, not Mary's voice, and it was familiar.

"D-dav..." She croaked, but her throat felt like sandpaper and she couldn't speak.

The figure over her spoke, and as her vision started to focus, she saw it wasn't David. He was too tall, too broad, with a face Adelyn had known since he was a boy. "Someone get her some water, gods. And get my parents, too."

A few seconds passed, and then she felt the trickle of water past her cracked lips and down her throat. It tasted clear, cool, and sweeter than honey to her tongue. Her vision cleared a bit more, and she managed to speak. "John?"

"Adelyn," her brother responded, smiling. "I'd hug you, but I'd probably break something." He didn't have on a shirt, only wearing a large bandage over his chest that had little red dots soaking through.

"You're hurt," Adelyn said, wiggling a few fingers in an attempt to point at the bandage. "Gon'need a doctor."

John laughed, though the humor made him wince and put a hand to his wide chest. "Sis," He said. "You recover enough that you can sit up, then I'll let you worry about me. Deal?"

Adelyn shook her head—only an inch in either direction, it hurt too much to turn it more. "Gonna worry now," she mumbled. "Water?"

John held up the waterskin, letting her get another drink, swallowing on his own dry throat with concern. "You're hurt real bad, sis. Burns all over, half your ribs broke, your arm, your face is a mess, your hands, your leg, your—"

"Shh," Adelyn said. John was building himself into a panic over her injuries. She ached all over, her entire body throbbing dully, some parts throbbing acutely. She still put on a brave face for her big brother. "S'fine. I'll heal good. Where'm I?"

"We set up a triage in the courtyard for everyone hurt in the escape," John explained, stepping back. "We outnumbered the guards two to one—three to one, after you dealt with them—so once we all had weapons, and their wizard was busy getting beaten up by you, they didn't want to fight too much. Plus your friends there cut through 'em like ribbons, those that did try and stand up to us. A few people still got hurt, though, and Davey—eh, Dave? David? He insisted on helping everyone we could. Some of us are a little mad he's helping those bastards who kept us locked up, but he wouldn't back down on that either."

Adelyn could now see that they were under a canvas cover, a largish tent set up as an impromptu surgical theater. "How'm I alive?" She asked, as the details of her fight started to come back to her.

"Once most of us were out, Mary told us to scatter, but that she was going back in to try and rescue someone. David was going too, and a few of us figured we weren't about to let them go back in on their lonesome when they just got our behinds out of the fire," John continued, leaning against a table with little surgical implements. "I didn't know it was you 'till after we volunteered. Had an inkling, since I knew you were busy somewhere, but she didn't say your name till we were heading back in.

"About ten of us went in total, armed for bear with whatever we could carry. Davey used those brass balls to figure out where you'd run off to, we found a bunch of the guards all confused and hacking up a storm of smoke, taught them a lesson or two. I—"

"Adelyn?" The speaker's voice cracked as they entered the tent, but now that she was fully awake, Adelyn recognized it immediately.

"Dad!" she exclaimed. Trying to look without turning her head, she saw that her mom was only a step behind. They hurried over, and Adelyn saw her whole family together for the first time in three months.

"Sweetie, thank goodness you're alive," her mom said, a relieved smile on her face.

"I'd hug you," Adelyn said, winking at her brother as she stole his joke. "But I'd probably break something."

They talked for twenty minutes, all of them catching up, Adelyn telling the basic notes of her story, her brother telling what had happened while they were kept as prisoners, her parents adding little details that only they knew. They'd have talked until sunrise, too, had Mary not stepped in.

"Adelyn needs to sleep," Mary said. "She has a lot of recovery ahead of her."

John looked hesitant, but nodded, glancing between their parents. "Of course."

"Let us know when she wakes," Adelyn's father added.

Mary nodded. "I will."

"Thank you."

The three of them walked away, leaving Mary standing over Adelyn.

"I've seen a lot of fights in my life, and a lot of upsets," Mary said, looking down at her. "That just may be the most surprising."

"I didn't expect to win," Adelyn said. "'S a nice bonus, though. What happened?"

"The wizard's people were trying to rescue their leader, but couldn't get close on account of the smoke," Mary said. "We took them by surprise and routed them."

"Sure," Adelyn said. "After that, though?"

"We found you in that kitchen. Fire was out, and some air had come back in from the hallway I guess, but the smoke was so dense I could barely see. David found you passed out, face up against a grate. You blocked up all the air vents?"

"Yeah," Adelyn said. "And I closed the ones in the ceiling too. I guess I thought he couldn't throw around fire spells if all the oxygen was used up."

"Well it worked," Mary said. "I found the wizard. He's dead."

Adelyn sucked in a breath, then nodded. "I guess I got luckier than he did, if I made it out."

"He wasn't dead when I found him," Mary said.

"Oh."

Mary nodded solemnly.

"He said he attacked my home specifically to capture me," Adelyn said, remembering the wizard's words.

Mary furrowed her brow. "How did he know of your power?"

"I don't know," Adelyn said. "But it has me worried. If someone found out about my power without my knowing..."

"Put it out of your mind, child," Mary said. "He was trying to distract you with a lie."

Adelyn wasn't certain, but she nodded anyways. "Speaking of lies."

Mary raised a sharp eyebrow. "What?"

"I know about you," Adelyn said. "Who you really are. Once I found out about David, the rest wasn't hard to piece together."

Mary froze, looking around to see if anyone could hear their conversation before responding. "And?"

"I'm angry that you didn't tell me," Adelyn said. "And furious that you didn't use your magic when it could have helped prevent much of this. But...you helped save me, you helped save my family, and if you want me to drop the subject and never speak of it again, I'll do that."

Mary stood silent for a few moments, then nodded. "Thank you."

"How's David?"

"You'll have to ask David," Mary said, words carrying a hint of bitterness. "Since he got a pen and a book to write in, all he's done was ask after you."

"I want to see him," Adelyn said. "Can you get him for me?"

Mary hesitated. "You do need rest. Maybe later."

"I want to talk to him now," Adelyn said.

Mary pursed her lips. "Only for a few minutes. Then, *sleep.*"

Adelyn nodded slightly, unable to move her head more than that for the pain in her neck.

A minute passed after Mary left, and she briefly started to wonder if she was going to come back at all, or if Mary was just going to wait for Adelyn to slip back into unconsciousness. Then, the tent flap opened, and David walked in.

"Hey," Adelyn said. "Thank you. So much."

David nodded, standing over her, not looking her in the eye. Without having anything to say or any way to say it, he seemed at a loss for what to do.

"We can learn signs," Adelyn offered. "Won't do good for spells, but it's better than naught."

David shrugged, taking a pencil and a small notebook from the bedside table next to Adelyn's head. He made a few notes, then held it up. 'I already thought of that.'

"Oh," Adelyn said. "Well, still."

Making a few notes to follow up, he added, 'There are schools of magic by the coast. I am going to ride down and see if any of them can restore my voice.'

"Is that possible?" Adelyn asked.

David shrugged, making another note. 'Will you come with me? The schools have much you could learn.'

Adelyn started to chew her lip, but the lip was split badly and the action hurt more than she'd wanted. "I...I'll think about it. They need me on the farm, it'll fall apart without my help."

They were silent for a few moments more, and then David wrote again. 'What happened to me was not your fault. Given a choice, I would do it again.'

Smiling weakly, Adelyn said, "Thank you. For everything." A thought struck her, and she added, "And I have to apologize. I know I promised you, but...I don't think I can pay you right away, unless we found where they took my money. You may have to stop by town in a few years once we've saved up a bit."

David shook his head, making a note. 'There were several hundred pounds of silver coinage stored inside the keep.'

"Oh," Adelyn said. "Well...then can I hire you to escort us back home? Lords know I'll be a terrible guard."

David nodded, and then put his hand on Adelyn's— gently, so not to agitate her broken finger, but in a small embrace nonetheless. He set down the book, its pages loosely open on the table next to Adelyn's head, and she was able to glance to the side and quickly read some of the older notes before it closed itself.

'Mary, I need you to heal her. I can't. I don't know if she's going to make it. She can't die.'

'Your vows would allow a child to die?'

'Don't do it for her. Do it for me. She's my friend.'

Looking away from the notes and up at David, Adelyn squeezed his hand with two fingers. "You'll be here when I wake up?"

David nodded his head, not making a motion to pull away his hand as Adelyn visibly began drifting back into unconsciousness.

"I'll see you then," Adelyn said, and then she fell asleep.

ACKNOWLEDGMENTS

Cover art by Christopher Kallini
Edited by An Avid Reader Editing

Made in the USA
Columbia, SC
17 October 2020